T. Jackson

C0-CEU-286

"Yes, I Want You," I answered softly.

Bates slid an arm under my shoulders and raised himself to lean over me, his other arm still circling my body. His mouth was tantalizingly gentle and at first he barely brushed his lips against mine. But the kiss deepened until I was aflame with sensations I'd never known before.

My hands locked at the back of his neck while his mouth moved to my lips with his tongue touching mine.

The past and the future no longer existed. There was only the *now* with Bates and me alone in the star-studded universe. I dug my fingers into his back, my body rising and falling with his.

Maud B. Johnson

TOMORROW AND FOREVER

PUBLISHED BY POCKET BOOKS NEW YORK

A POCKET BOOKS/RICHARD GALLEN *Original* publication

POCKET BOOKS, a Simon & Schuster division of
GULF & WESTERN CORPORATION
1230 Avenue of the Americas, New York, N.Y. 10020

Copyright © 1980 by Maud B. Johnson

All rights reserved, including the right to reproduce
this book or portions thereof in any form whatsoever.
For information address Pocket Books, 1230 Avenue
of the Americas, New York, N.Y. 10020

ISBN: 0-671-83636-6

First Pocket Books printing June, 1980

10 9 8 7 6 5 4 3 2 1

POCKET and colophon are trademarks of Simon & Schuster.

Printed in the U.S.A.

Part One

Chapter 1

THE RAIN CAME down harder as twilight set in, great sheets of water splattering the ground, drenching my gray woolen cloak, slapping the wet fabric against my ankles. Under the hood my hair was soaked, mashed tightly to my skull. Mud squished from my shoes. I walked gingerly, searching out the worst wagon ruts and sidestepping them. There was no stopping place, and I knew better than to seek shelter under the trees during a storm. When I was a little girl, I'd seen a child killed instantly beneath an elm tree that was split by a thunderbolt.

The road had to lead *somewhere*, I thought desperately. Surely there was a house further along. Or a town. I had walked since dawn, but I could not walk all night.

Lightning slashed the murky sky, illuminating the land in crystal whiteness. In the distance I saw a peaked roof with a cross on top. A church! It stood out like a beacon during that flash of light.

I hurried toward it, sloshing through puddles, slipping and catching myself to keep balanced. The build-

3

ing was a small rectangle set close to the road. Another fiery zigzag in the sky showed steps leading to a stoop, with the church entrance recessed about two feet. I stumbled to the door, grabbed the knob and twisted it.

The door did not move. It was locked.

Rattling the knob again and again, I pushed my shoulder against the heavy wooden slab, trying to force the door and knowing it must be a dreadful sin to break into a church. I had to get out of the storm. The lock remained firm.

All at once my courage vanished and so did my endurance. My knees buckled. I slipped down . . . down . . . down, huddling in the recess against the door, my wet cloak wrapped round my benumbed body to shut out the cold.

The light roused me, a lantern held close to my face. I had not realized I'd dozed.

"Wake up!" a man's gruff voice ordered. A big hand clutched my shoulder, shaking me until the flame in the lantern danced before my eyes.

"I—I meant n-no harm st-stopping here," I stammered. "All I wanted was rest."

In the orange glow I could see him squatting beside me. I shrank against the church door. He was a huge man in rough clothing. His face was coarse, jowled; a short growth of beard darkened his cheeks and chin. Black eyes squinted under thick black brows, and when he opened his mouth, some of the widely spaced yellow teeth were broken at the gums.

"Who are you?" he demanded. "How did you get here?" His tone and manner were frightening. His eyes stared through me.

"I walked," I said in a quivery voice.

"Walked from where?" He shook me again, his fingers biting into the flesh of my shoulder.

"From the Colony of Massachusetts."

"Damn it, lass! You're in Massachusetts now! Where do you live?"

The panic intensified in me. I didn't know who he was, but by sheer size and strength he could force me to go back. I had nothing to return to. Trying to collect my wits, I kept silent. He leaned nearer, hovering over me.

"I was passing and when the lightning flashed I saw you on the church property," he growled. "You tell me what I need to know. Who are you and what are you doing here? Running away from your husband?"

I flung my chin up. "I'm not married."

"How old are you?"

"Eighteen." It was a small fib. I would be eighteen in a month.

The man flicked his tongue across his lips. "Are you indentured?" he asked in the same menacing tone. "You're a servant escaping from your master and your dutiful obligations! Don't you realize there's a penalty for that?"

"No!" I blurted out. "I'm not indentured! I've done nothing wrong! That's God's truth!"

"Then answer my questions. Be quick about it. Do you have a family?"

He might shake answers out of me if I didn't give them voluntarily. I told him my mother was dead and that since her burial I'd lived with her friend in New Bedford.

"What about your father?"

"I don't have a father."

"Everybody has a father, lass. Do you mean he's dead, too? Or you don't know where he is? Or," his lip curled, "you don't know who he is? You're a bastard?"

I did not answer him. The word *bastard* made me cringe despite having heard it all my life. I was fearful what this burly stranger would say or do next, but to my amazement he rocked back and forth on his haunches, exploding into rough laughter. Perhaps he read the reply to his question in my face.

"Well, lass, we have something in common because I never knew my father's name either," he commented as the laughter died. "This friend of your mother, is it a man or a woman?"

"A woman. Susan James."

"She pushed you off her premises?"

I hesitated, wondering how much to tell him, deciding to be honest to a point. "Susan was barmaid in a tavern near the New Bedford docks, but she's getting married soon and going off to Rhode Island with her husband," I said. "I couldn't stay there by myself so I left. Susan said I would find work and a place to live further south."

"You intended *walking* south?" He laughed again. "How far south, lass? All the way to Carolina? If you've come from New Bedford today, you've scarcely covered seventeen miles and at that rate you might reach Charles Town next year—if the Indians don't scalp you first."

The picture he was painting made me shiver. Suddenly, I felt very small and forlorn. When he spoke again a bit of his gruffness had disappeared, and a silky note crept into his voice.

"How would you like a sea voyage South?" he asked.

"I don't have any money for that."

"It won't cost you a shilling and it'll help you on your journey. I work for a fine gentleman who owns ships. He's getting together a group of ladies like yourself to go to Charles Town. We need one more to round out our number. It's good fortune for both you and me that our paths crossed tonight. You'll have food and a place to sleep on board the ship, and when you reach

Carolina there'll be a welcome waiting such as you've never dreamed of. Your friend Susan was smart. There's a better life for everybody in Carolina. Sunshine aplenty, freedom to worship any way you want. A husband, too, if that's what you're after. How about it, lass? Agree and I'll take you to my master this very minute. I—"

He broke the sentence off, jumping up to listen to something in the distance, his head cocked to one side. The hard downpour had changed into a misty drizzle, the lightning and thunder had ceased. I also heard the sound, a clop-clopping on the muddy road, coming closer and closer.

As the horse reached the church, the man who had awakened me swung the lantern in a shallow arc. A rider reined his mount. The horse snorted. "Whoa, Caesar. Whoa, boy," reached my ears, followed by a stunned question. "McGregor?" The newcomer leaned forward in the saddle.

"Oh, it's you, Captain," the man with the light answered. "Hardly a fit night to be taking a ride, I should think."

"I just left Irving and I'm on my way to the ship."

The voice was deep and extremely pleasant. From where I sat by the door recess I could not make out his features, seeing merely the silhouette of a tall man on a horse.

"I was about to ask if you'd tag along with me and bring Caesar back to Irving's barn," the horseman continued. "But it seems your outdoors activities are too engrossing to warrant an interruption." He jerked his head toward me. "Don't you know a better spot for whoring than the church steps? And in the rain, no less! The devil will get your soul for misusing hallowed ground."

There was a lightness in his tone, teasing rather than criticizing, but I cringed at what he must be thinking about me.

"Not whoring, Captain," the reply rang out. "Although I'll admit it's a likely idea."

"Don't add lying to your other sins, McGregor," the horseman chuckled. "Why else would you be here at night with a woman?"

"I'll tell you why. Your crew is too damn superstitious to sail with thirteen—uh—passengers, so Irving dispatched me to find number fourteen in a hurry. A right pretty lass she is, too. Or she will be once she dries out." He twisted around, holding the lantern to my face. "Care to have a look for yourself, Captain?"

Pulling my hood snugly around my head, I deliberately averted my face. I did not intend to be inspected as if I were a slave for the auction block.

But I needn't have worried. The rider declined the invitation.

"That's your department—and Irving's," the man said, laughing under his breath. "Mind you, we sail with the tide an hour after midnight and if number fourteen isn't aboard, it makes no difference to me. We'll sail without her."

"You'll weigh anchor tonight in this storm, Captain?"

"The foul weather will be ending soon. The rain has almost stopped and the wind is springing up, so I expect most of the clouds will blow away quickly. By midnight we should have some stars showing and a good breeze to let us leave port." He snapped his reins and the horse took off at a gallop, mud and water spraying in every direction.

The man with the lantern turned to me again. Now I knew his name was McGregor.

"You heard the Captain," he said. "A fine fellow he is and you should be proud to sail on his ship. Midnight is four or five hours away and that should allow you plenty of time to scrape the mud from yourself and have some warm food at Irving's house."

I hesitated, not sure what to do. "Who is Irving?" I asked.

"I told you about him. He's my employer. He owns six ships and he lives just beyond the rise of the hill. That's where I'll take you. Come on, lass. Time's a-wasting."

With the lantern in his left hand, he used his right to grip me by the arm, pulling me to my feet and out of the door recess so that I was on the stoop. I shivered as the wind struck, my damp clothing almost worse than none at all. McGregor was swinging his light impatiently without letting go of my arm. I would have to make an instant decision that might govern the remainder of my life.

The promise of warm food swayed me. My stomach heaved in aching hunger. At daybreak I'd eaten a piece of bread and slipped another piece into the pocket of my cloak, sure that long before dark I would find a hospitable family or temporary work which included bed and board. Nothing of the sort had happened. Once New Bedford was out of sight, the road became an uneven trail, sometimes wide enough for a wagon and at other times no more than a footpath through the woods. I had not seen a human being. I'd tasted nothing except water from a creek. When I had felt in my pocket for the bread, it was gone, fallen from its hiding place without my noticing. The hunger grew worse as the hours passed. Panic mounted when the sky turned dark and the storm set in. I wondered if I was lost, if somehow I'd taken the wrong path. It might be late April, but there was iciness in the air. As the rain began, I was too cold and wet and miserable to do more than plod on.

Watching the wavering flame in McGregor's lantern, I reminded myself that I had intended all along to go South, not actually knowing how far away that vague place was or where my specific destination would be. I had to walk because I lacked money to pay for a ship's passage. Even though I knew nothing about McGregor and the man named Irving, sailing was easier than walking. At sea there would be protection from the Indians. The tribes living near New Bedford were friendly for the most part, but I had heard fearful stories about savages in other locations.

If I said no to McGregor, how could I manage alone indefinitely? One day on the trail had been a near disaster. Even if I'd reached a town, I had no money to buy a night's lodging or food.

Food. . . . My tongue slid to the roof of my mouth, the empty ache in my stomach intensifying. McGregor had promised a warm meal.

"Well?" he raised the lantern to the level of my eyes, squinting at me while he shifted his weight from one foot to the other.

"I will accept your offer of a *free* voyage south," I answered in a steadier voice than I'd have believed possible considering the way my pulse was throbbing. Lest he had forgotten, I emphasized the word *free*.

Chapter 2

I WRAPPED MY arms around McGregor's waist, clutching him tightly for fear I would slide off the rump of the wet horse and land in the mud. McGregor in the saddle braced his feet firmly in the stirrups; my legs dangled. My only support came from clinging to him, which brought my nose against his back, filling my nostrils with the sour smell of his body. The rain did not wash away that putrid odor. I wondered how long it had been since the man washed himself or his clothes. How could anyone endure such personal filth? My mother had taught me to keep myself clean; bathing came as naturally as breathing.

Earlier I hadn't been aware that McGregor reached the church on horseback, an indication of how soundly I must have been sleeping when he shook me to consciousness. He had tied the animal to a tree at the rear of the building, he said, adding as he stretched out an arm and hoisted me up on the horse behind him that he wasn't a coward but neither was he a bloody fool. Since he didn't know how many people were waiting in the darkness, he considered it wise to investigate first; he had inched around the side of the church on foot before making his presence known.

I might have smiled if I hadn't been so chilled and so miserably hungry. The thought of this huge, rough man being leery of anything or anybody was ridiculous. The space by the church door was too tiny to give adequate shelter to one individual, much less to several.

"That lightning came and went in such a hurry I couldn't tell if it was a scoundrel or a duchess on the steps," he said, tossing the words over his shoulder.

Hardly a duchess, I thought wryly. But I did not know what a duchess looked like; I had never been face to face with a lady of rank. If I had been a duchess, I certainly would not have been sleeping outside that church in the storm. I'd have been safe and cozy in a beautiful drawing room with a rich carpet on the floor and satin cushions banking the settee. I'd be wearing a pale pink silk brocade gown, which swished easily as I walked. I would pour fragrant tea from a silver pot.

For the moment I was a little girl once more, playing a private game. There was no other way I could know that rich life as I wanted to, but my mother had experienced it. Growing up in London, she lived in a fine house with servants and a tutor. The daughters were taught to read and write and cipher just as the sons were. She drove her own miniature pony and cart, and had a special footman in crimson livery to attend it. Two seamstresses employed year round fashioned exquisite dresses and petticoats trimmed with lace and embroidery for her mother, her sisters and herself.

Thinking of my mother put a mistiness in my eyes. It's the rain water dripping from the tree branches—not tears, I told myself, but I knew better. I missed my mother dreadfully. Closing my eyes for a second, I could almost see her.

My mother and I had lived in a small room at the back of the inn near the New Bedford docks. The room and our food were her pay for cooking there. She brought me up as best she could, with no husband and precious little money but what the seamen slipped her after she visited them at night. She taught me and looked out for me and made me promise I would never sign an indenture paper as she had done. That indenture contract was how she arrived in the Colonies. And it had taken seven long years of her work to pay off the debt! She seldom talked about her girlhood, unless I asked. As a child, I accepted her explanation that my father was dead.

But I persisted asking questions as I grew older. Where was my father buried? How did he die? Why don't we have contact with his kin or yours? She would suddenly become very busy with a chore that needed all of her attention. Or she'd send me off on an errand, cutting my questions short.

I must have been seven or eight the first time a neighbor boy pointed his finger at me and sneered, "You're a bastard, Marley Lancaster. Everybody knows that. You'll go to Hell when you die and so will your mother!"

My face burned with shame and anger. Fear, too. Hell was a place of raging fires and everlasting torment, described endlessly and in detail each Sunday by the preacher. I ran home, praying silently my mother would deny the boy's accusation.

I found her on her hands and knees scrubbing the plank floor of the inn kitchen, a bucket of water and a dish of sand beside her. Without looking up at me, she said in a tired voice, "Don't track in until it's dry, Marley." The question I wanted to ask hardened in my throat. I remained outside, finding it easier not to know the truth.

Over the years I heard the word "bastard" many times, but I was sixteen before learning the facts of my birth. Even then the story had to be pulled and wheedled from my mother. She had been ill. I did not realize it but she would never be well again. That morning she and I were alone in the inn kitchen. I said impulsively that I was tired of being whispered about and told I was illegitimate.

"Is it true?" I blurted out to her.

Her skin went gray. The log fire on the hearth crackled, the soup in an iron pot suspended over the flame bubbled. Those were the only sounds in the still room until she sucked in her breath with a rasping noise.

"I won't deny it now that you're old enough to understand," she sighed. "But you mustn't feel guilty. The sin was mine, not yours, Marley. Your father and I loved each other very much but there were—were reasons why we couldn't marry."

"What reasons? Please tell me."

Her voice broke as she continued. It seemed my father already had a wife, a woman twelve years older than he. A shrew, my mother called her. The loveless match was arranged by the two sets of parents, and he was bound to this wife until one of them died. He and my mother met secretly as often as they could.

"I had just discovered I was to bear his child, but I hadn't told him—or told anyone," she went on. "He and I were in the attic of the carriage house of my home one night and we were—were lying together as husband and wife. My father found us and he was furious. I have never seen anyone so furious. He threatened the man I loved. Threatened to have him arrested and sent to jail or hanged if I ever so much as spoke to him again. It could have been done because my father was a judge. He had friends who owed him favors." Her mouth hardened, her beauty disappearing momentarily, making her face a study in bitterness. "My father disowned me and threw me out that night with nothing but the clothes I was wearing. He demanded to know if I was with child. I said yes, hoping he might relent, only it just made him more angry. He didn't even allow me to speak to my mother."

She had wandered around the streets of London until daybreak, unwilling to see friends or relatives for fear that somehow her father would use this as an excuse to carry out the threat to hang her sweetheart. In the morning she learned of a ship about to sail with a load of indentured people. No questions were asked of those who signed on, so she went aboard. The ship was bound for the Colony of Massachusetts across the Atlantic.

As she fell silent I'd asked a question I had to ask. "Do I have my father's surname?"

"Lancaster was my family name and I've kept it," she said. "As for Marley, I don't know if I heard the word or read it or what, but it seemed so pretty and soft, like water in a clear brook trickling over smooth stones. You were a beautiful baby, Marley, and I loved you from the start and wanted you. Even if I didn't have a husband, I couldn't abandon you or murder you before birth the way some women do with a child born out of wedlock."

She paused, waiting a long minute. "Maybe . . . maybe I shouldn't have stayed in New Bedford after you were born," she murmured. "I know what the townspeople think of me. I never dreamed they would heap my sins on your head. There was work for me here, though, and a place to sleep. I couldn't be sure I'd have those elsewhere, so I've stayed. But it could be better for you if you left once you're a little older. That might be the only way you'll have a decent life."

"Who is my father?" I persisted. "Don't I have the right to know?"

Defiance glimmered in her eyes, disclosing pinpoints of fire. "I won't tell you that—not you or anyone!"

"Wouldn't he want to know he has a daughter?"

"The result of a romance which nearly cost him his life more than sixteen years in the past? I doubt it."

She had spoken harshly, but then a wistfulness crept into her voice. "I know he loved me then . . . but I hope he doesn't think of me now because it will be less painful for him if he's forgotten. What I've told you today is private to us, Marley. I trust you to keep all of this to yourself. And I pray you will never sign an indenture paper. Seven years of working with no pay, and such hard, hard work—" She paused, shuddering. "Be smarter than I was, girl. Keep your virginity until you're legally wed in the sight of the Law and the Church no matter how much you love a man."

I did not betray her trust, not even after her death. She soon became too ill to continue working. The innkeeper demanded our room for his new cook. I don't know what we would have done if Susan James had not taken us into her tiny log house.

Susan, just twenty, had been widowed after a brief marriage. She was a saucy girl with reddish gold hair and enormous blue eyes that charmed any man she turned them on. She said bluntly that she intended remarrying just as soon as her year of mourning was over. Meanwhile, she worked at the inn where she and my mother developed a friendship. Occasionally I helped Susan in the taproom, always over my mother's objection. She feared I would take up with a rowdy sailor fresh from months at sea and eager for any woman in sight. I assured her it would not happen, although I had plenty of chances. I remained a virgin. There was no other work available for me except at the inn, though, and we needed the few coins I earned serving ale and rum.

My mother was growing sicker each day, fever draining her body and food not kept down long enough to give any nourishment. When she died a pain-wracked death, I could not wish her back to such suffering. But I needed her and missed her. Without her I was completely alone in the world—a frightening, desolate realization.

She died in January. The rest of the winter I thought about my future, especially the suggestion of having a better life away from New Bedford. It was easy to put off definite plans; the icy weather made travel impossible until spring. In late April the decision was made for me, a decision prompted by events beyond my control.

Susan's year of mourning had ended. She was considering a proposal of marriage from a well-to-do Rhode Island merchant, old enough to be her father, a man who came to New Bedford often on business and stayed at the inn. She was trying to make up her mind to settle for money and security rather than wait for love, having promised the merchant an answer on his next trip to Massachusetts. Tragedy unexpectedly struck. Her house caught fire and burned to the ground. Nothing was saved, not any of her belongings nor mine.

Susan and I were at work in the taproom when the fire was discovered. A bucket brigade was formed, the water coming too late to stop the blaze, and we reached home to find the chimney standing amid a few red coals and charred, smouldering timbers, smoke still rising from the ashes. Both of us broke down and wept. We took long sticks and poked into the ruins, hoping to save some little object or garment. It was a useless effort.

Our employer, the innkeeper, gave us an empty

room for the night, and we attempted to comfort each other. Susan said she would stay on at the inn until her husband-to-be returned within the month to pay her lodging bill and marry her.

"What about you, Marley?" she asked.

"I don't know . . ."

"You're much too beautiful to waste yourself here," she went on. "Massachusetts has nothing but sinners who make no bones about their evil ways and strict churchgoers who act holy and claim to be angels when all the while they're hiding their sins in the depths of righteous smirks. Why don't you go South? I've heard the seamen in the taproom talking about the coast of Carolina and Virginia. It must be wonderful to live in those Colonies. No snow and not even much frost in winter. Everything is lush and green the year round. The people there are different from the ones here. They don't pray all the time or live as if the Devil is looking over their shoulders."

"Maybe I will," I murmured. "I think I will for sure."

In new surroundings nobody need know my parents were never married. I wouldn't be tormented with the accident of my birth, a deed not of my doing. Maybe, I mused drowsily, in another location I would become rich and find happiness. Love, also, although I wasn't positive I knew what love was.

Money—love—happiness. The three words blended into one in my thoughts. Having money would mean living well, owning beautiful objects and lavish, shimmering gowns, keeping my own house. Most of all, having money meant security, something I had never known.

The next morning Susan was still sleeping when I opened my eyes. Dawn would come soon. I slipped out of bed, shivering in my muslin petticoat. I pulled on the brown homespun dress I'd worn the day before, the black stockings knitted by my mother, and my shoes. I wrapped my long gray wool cloak about myself. The garments I was wearing made up all my worldly possessions.

Rousing Susan, I hugged her and said goodby. She sat up in bed with the quilts clutched to her chin.

"Where are you heading?" she asked.

"South. I don't know exactly where, but when I find a spot I like it will be home."

"I wish I had the courage to come with you, Marley. But it's too—too unknown for me. In Rhode Island at least I'll understand what to expect. God bless you forever."

We were holding hands and I freed my fingers from hers, not daring to look at her again for fear my courage would falter.

A loose roof shingle flapping occasionally was the only sound in the inn, save the customary creaking of the building, as I tiptoed down the back stairs to the empty kitchen. The cook was not yet at her chores, and I was thankful because I didn't want to answer questions. Yesterday's coals had been banked with ashes so a fresh fire wouldn't have to be started in the morning; a bit of warmth seeped from the hearth. On the table a pewter plate held last night's cornbread. I lifted the napkin covering it, and broke off a piece of the crusty pone to eat. I put another piece into the pocket of my cloak.

Outside a pearly haze covered the landscape. The air was cold and biting for late April. A few patches of snow clung stubbornly beneath the trees and in shaded places. But the sky was streaked orange and pink, a sign of fair weather and sunshine later on. My spirits soared. As I walked through New Bedford and took the road south, the rosy dawn promised only good things ahead for me.

It was a fool's dream. If I could have known the future, I wonder if I would not have whirled around to retrace my steps.

Chapter 3

BOUNCING BEHIND MCGREGOR, clutching his smelly, wet back, I thought about the strange events of the last twenty-four hours. The fire, the exhausting walk, the horrible storm. I was stunned hearing myself tell a stranger I would board a ship owned by another stranger, sailing to an unknown destination identified only as "South."

I was not particularly shy by nature but neither was I bold. So many upheavals in an otherwise humdrum life left my head spinning. One thing was for sure: I made excuses to forget the cold and the hunger. I was better off than my mother had been the day she sailed from England. Like her, I had only the clothes on my back. But I would not be signing an indenture paper, and no child was growing inside my body.

Soon McGregor yanked the rein and the horse swerved in command, trotting down a cleared path between rows of water-laden trees. I made out the shape of a building ahead, set on a knoll, dark in front but with a pale glow from a second-story window.

"Irving's house," McGregor commented as we cir-

cled and stopped by a door in the rear. "I'll take you in
and then get the horse to the stable."

An ell extended from the main section of the house
into the back yard. Its shuttered windows allowed only
thin rims of light to escape yet hid any view of the
interior. We entered a dark corridor and then the ell
room. It was a kitchen—warmth pouring from the
mammoth stone fireplace, the air heavy with wood-
smoke, the delicious aroma of food cooking.

A woman in a plain black dress, a small black cap
tied under her chin, sat at a wheel spinning flax into
thread for linen cloth. Two striped kittens snoozed in a
basket beside her chair. She was less than middle-aged.
She glanced up, her hands continuing to twist thread
while she looked first at McGregor and then at me, her
eyes moving from my face down to the floor where
water dripped from my cloak into a puddle.

"Another one, McGregor?" she asked in a surprised
way. "I thought the ship was loaded. I don't know how
you're still finding anybody to sail at this time of night
in the rain unless you're digging up the cemetery."

"This lass looks plenty alive to me," he grinned,
jerking his head in my direction. "I swear this is the last
for tonight, Peg. Put some food in her belly and see if
you can make her presentable enough to suit Irving."

"I suppose you plan to eat, too—again?" Her mouth
curved with the barest hint of amusement.

He slapped his ample stomach. "Oh, I'll be back.
Don't throw the leavings out." Grinning once more, he
left the room, wet bootprints marking his path across
the floor.

The woman got to her feet and ordered me to
remove my soaked clothing before I caught chills and
fever. She was taller than I realized, cheekbones
prominent under pale skin. She didn't bother to

introduce herself or ask my name, although she addressed me in a kind voice, inquiring if my luggage was
in the hall. I told her I had no belongings and explained
about the fire.

"So that's why you're willing to sail . . ." she mumbled under her breath as if she was speaking more to
herself than to me.

"You're Mrs. Irving?" I asked.

"No. I'm in Mr. Irving's employment. His housekeeper." She poured warm water from the hearth
kettle into a shallow basin and brought a towel and a
bar of yellow soap from one of the wall cabinets.
"While you wash I'll see what I can find for you to
wear," she said. "Even with the hot blaze it's doubtful
if your garments will be dry by the time McGregor
returns. You can roll them up damp and let them finish
drying on the ship."

I'd already taken off my cloak and dress. Stepping
out of my petticoat, I stood naked before the fire,
turning this way and that to let the heat soak into my
skin before bathing myself thoroughly to remove every
trace of the day's grime. I shook out my hair, rubbing it
with the towel until it was dry. It fell below my
shoulders, thick and black, the ends curling slightly. I
had inherited my mother's hair and features—oval
face, violet-blue eyes, tilting nose, slender body, small
waist, and high, rounded breasts.

The housekeeper returned. She handed me a ruffled
petticoat and a pale mauve gown, the material soft and
finely woven. There was also a fine velvet cloak in a
deeper shade of mauve.

"Put them on," she said.

I did. Everything fit as if the garments were made for
me, but I removed the cloak and began to pull the dress
over my head.

"I don't have money to pay for such elegant clothes," I told her reluctantly, attempting to ignore the smooth fabric against my shoulders.

"Accept them as a gift," she came back indifferently.

"You're giving me your personal clothes?"

When she murmured, "No," I dropped my arms, letting the dress fall back into place.

"These things belonged to a French woman who was coming to the Colonies on one of Mr. Irving's vessels," the housekeeper said. "I don't know who she was or why she was fleeing Paris. She was fleeing, I'm sure, not because she wanted to settle here. A crewman let slip that she'd paid her fare with ruby jewels. Be that as it may, there weren't any valuables on her when she reached here. When her *remains* reached here— because it seems she was sick the entire voyage and she died as the ship was dropping anchor—Mr. Irving had her buried on his property and he went through her boxes. I was with him. I refolded each garment after he shook it out. He put her things in the attic where they've sat ever since. That was six—no, seven—years ago."

I touched the velvet cloak again. "Will he object to my wearing her clothes?"

"He won't recognize them. He'll probably think the outfit was yours all along. Oh, he has an eye for a pretty lass the same as any man, but mostly he's interested in having the women he sends South look attractive so there'll be no problems collecting his—"

She caught her breath, not finishing the sentence. Two bright spots of crimson suddenly appeared on her cheeks and vanished.

"Are you ready to eat?" she asked abruptly.

I was more than ready. There was cornbread in a tin warming box on the hearth. She took a ladle, filling a bowl from the iron pot hanging over the fire. The stew was delicious, chunks of meat in a rich brown gravy. I ate every drop and offered no objection when she refilled my bowl, savoring every spoonful.

Her unfinished sentence puzzled me. "What did you mean about Mr. Irving wanting the women he sends South to look attractive so he won't have a problem collecting something?" I asked. "Collecting *what?*"

She flushed again, shrugging. But she didn't have to reply, as McGregor opened the door and joined us. He raked his eyes over me and pursed his lips.

"This couldn't be the soaked baggage I just brought in, could it?" he asked with mock seriousness. "Peg, you've created a queen."

Under his frank gaze I moved one hand self-consciously to my throat. The mauve dress was cut low in a deep square neckline exposing a great deal of flesh. Glancing down, I could see the curve of both breasts as well as the little hollow between them. All my life I had worn high-necked garments of plain cloth, not only because my mother couldn't afford finery but because the Puritans disapproved of elegance in any form. My mother and I weren't Puritans and not everybody in New Bedford was, but enough people were to rule the community.

I was no longer in New Bedford, I reminded myself, but that did not ease the feeling that I was more naked than I should have been. The moment passed. McGregor apparently was more interested in food than in me. He dipped bread into the stewpot, slurping gravy and wiping his mouth on the side of his sleeve. "Come along," he said to me. "I just left Irving's room and he's waiting for you."

I followed McGregor into the cold hall, up a flight of steps, unable to glimpse the first floor of the house. The only light came from a candle in a brass holder on the stair landing. Once upstairs, he knocked on a door, turning the knob when a voice called out for us to enter.

We were in a square room with whitewashed walls. Its only furnishings were a desk, two chairs and a table holding several ledgers. The red coals in the fireplace glowed dimly; two candle flames on the desk projected dark and shadow. A man was seated at the desk, back toward us, scratching a quill against parchment.

We waited. Soon the man slid off the chair and stood up, a gnome handsomely dressed in black breeches, black coat, white shirt and a russet waistcoat. The fine clothes accentuated his pinched face and dwarfed body. "I am Seneca Irving," he announced. "So you're the newest passenger for my ship, the *Solace?*"

"Yes, sir." I watched his button eyes dart across my body.

"It will be a pleasure to have you travel aboard my ship if your affairs are in order—and McGregor tells me they are," the little man went on. "He said you're not indentured or leaving a husband and that you have not been judged guilty of a crime. Is this correct?"

"Yes, sir."

"You are going from this Colony because you are an orphan without a home? McGregor says this is so."

"Yes, sir." My voice came from the bottom of a well. I was instantly terrified that Mr. Irving would change his mind and refuse to let me sail. As shipowner he had the power to say no, and if he did, what would become of me?

"Very well." He turned to the desk and picked up the parchment. "Put your mark on this paper of agreement and McGregor will take you to the *Solace.*"

My throat went dry. "What paper?" I gasped. "I

won't sign an indenture! I didn't think I would have to do—"

"Hush, lass! Don't you raise your voice to me! This is an agreement that you have my permission to be a passenger. I take it you haven't traveled and don't know documents."

"No, sir. I haven't traveled." My tone was meeker, but I drew a long breath and forced myself to look squarely at him. "I know how to read and write, Mr. Irving, so I can sign my name instead of using a mark. I would like to read what I'm to sign."

His eyes narrowed. "Where did you learn schooling?"

"My mother taught me." To forestall more questions, I added, "She learned in England."

His annoyance was obvious. He tapped his fingers on the edge of the desk and pulled his lower lip. I must have pushed him too far! I was torn between remorse for fearing and courage for daring. Just as I was giving up hope, he handed the parchment to me.

I held the sheet near a candle, finding his script thin but the looped letters heavily shaded. It was hard to make out, but I managed:

I do solemnly swear that I am boarding the ship *Solace,* owned by Seneca Irving of the Colony of Massachusetts, of my own free will; that as of this day, the 22nd of April in the year of Our Lord 1717, I am of sound mind and body; that I will not hold the aforementioned Seneca Irving responsible for any dangers or mishaps which may befall me now or while I am his passenger from this day or afterwards; and that upon disembarking from his ship at a port of destination I will obey all instructions from the agents of the aforementioned

Seneca Irving until I am released from their jurisdiction.

I went through it twice, telling Mr. Irving I would sign. I could discover nothing objectionable, and there was no reference to being indentured or being in his debt for the cost of the journey. That was what I cared about.

Dipping the quill into a silver inkwell, he passed it to me, watching as I wrote "Marley Lancaster" in the spot he designated by pointing his bony forefinger.

"All right, McGregor." He waved one hand as if to indicate that I was dismissed. "In this weather you'd best use the tunnel rather than the path through the woods. And don't dawdle. The *Solace* will be leaving with the tide."

There was no goodby. The little man rolled up the parchment and placed it in a pigeonhole of his desk beside similar parchment rolls. I followed McGregor down the shadowy stairs and into the kitchen. The fire was banked. My damp clothing was folded and tied in a bundle.

As I wrapped the mauve cloak about myself, McGregor pushed the kitchen woodbox to one side, revealing a trap door behind the chimney. When he opened it, clammy air struck me full in the face and I stared down into a black hole.

"I'll go first and give you a hand down," he said. "Mind you, it's a ladder, not steps. But you may as well get used to ladders because you'll have plenty of them on the ship."

Shuddering, I hung back. "I—I believe I'd rather walk through the woods even if it's wet," I mumbled.

"No time for that. The tunnel is much quicker, only a five-minute trip to the water this way, and we'd have thirty minutes if we took the trail."

He lowered himself into the opening, carrying the lantern with him. "Easy now," he said, clutching my arm as I started down.

The ladder was shorter than I anticipated. My feet touched bottom quickly, putting me on hard-packed earth. The walls and ceiling of the tunnel were shored up with logs. Had those logs been placed tightly in a vertical position to keep the dirt from caving in? I tried not to think about the grim possibility. McGregor swung himself up the ladder again, reaching into the kitchen to close the trap door over our heads and leave us in darkness beyond the lantern flame. It was a total darkness, and it gave me an eerie feeling.

"I don't want this," I said, shivering involuntarily. "It's like—like a tomb."

"Scared of what you see or what you can't see?" He tried to be funny. I didn't reply.

The passage was narrow. We walked single file, with me dog trotting to keep up. The fear of being left alone and in darkness sent prickles up my spine. The light swung from his left hand, flickering and wavering as he moved his arm. Behind us and before us there was only black nothingness. Stale air and occasional drops of water oozed through the ceiling.

"Why does Mr. Irving have this tunnel?" I asked.

"His father made it when the house was built. It gave the family a way to escape from the Indians, should that be necessary. Convenient for getting to where the ships are anchored, too."

We continued to walk. Surely we're near the end, I thought, but didn't say it aloud. Suddenly, McGregor stopped, twisting around to face me without warning. I bumped into him, my nose grazing the buttons of his jacket and my hands flying up against his chest. The bundle of clothes fell from my grasp.

"So you just have to touch me, eh, lass?" he said,

winking. "Touch as much as you please. Any spot you please."

Stunned, I took a step backward—or tried to do it. One of his arms shot forward to circle my waist, pinning me between his body and the tunnel wall.

"What about it, Marley Lancaster?" he whispered with his face bent toward me. "You and me . . . right here and now. . . . There's time if we hurry and I suspect you're as ripe as I am."

The full implication of what he meant put the sour taste of vomit on my tongue. I tried to jerk away from him but it was impossible.

"No!" I exploded. *"No!* Let me loose!"

Swiftly he set the lantern on the ground. Keeping one arm around my waist, another slipped inside my neckline, his fingers probing and squeezing my breasts. I writhed in his grasp, trying desperately to get away. My efforts seemed to egg him on. He was laughing, obviously enjoying the tussle. A scream began in the pit of my stomach, burning a path upward as it rose into my throat.

"Yell your head off, lass," he laughed again. "Who can hear you from where we are?"

I managed to get my fingers to his face, clawing him, gouging at his eyes, digging my nails into his cheeks until I drew blood. With a furious howl he hurled me against the wall and flung his arm back to slap the side of my jaw with his open hand, the blow hard enough to send my chin crunching into my shoulder.

I could not see or breathe. The pain in my temples was a mallet beating against my skull. He would kill me if I continued to fight him. I was positive of that. Maybe he would kill me anyway . . .

My knees sagged. I sank to the ground. He was instantly on top of me, throwing my skirt up and straddling my body while he opened his trousers. The throbbing in my neck and jaw was so intense I could barely protest what was happening to the lower part of my body. He pried my legs apart with his hands and lay prone on top of me. The violent thrusts began, going on and on and on.

Finally, he was still. When he stood up I opened my eyes, one lid so swollen from the slap that I had little vision from that side. McGregor was standing beside me, the lantern still on the floor as he buttoned his trousers.

"On your feet," he barked to me. "We don't want the *Solace* to sail without us."

"I'm not going," I answered with a choked sob.

"Oh, yes, you are! You signed Irving's paper, didn't you? He'll have my skin if you don't go! So you're sailing on that ship if I have to beat you unconscious and sling you over my shoulder!"

"After what you just did to me, I don't want any part of you or Mr. Irving or the *Solace!*"

"You enjoyed it, Marley Lancaster. You may claim you didn't, but a wench always does." His mouth twisted, baring the broken yellow teeth. "Don't you try to tell me I was the first man for you. A lass with your body and your looks starts young, and she keeps at it for a long time. So hush and come along."

He gripped my arm, yanking me roughly to my feet. I tried to pull away from him but it only made him tighten his hold.

"I said I'm not going and I won't!" I came back hotly. "Mr. Irving has no claim on me. You don't either!"

"That paper you signed is legal! If you doubt what I'm saying, just you try to prove otherwise to a judge. Irving can have you punished for going back on your word in a signed document. You'd be flogged or put in the stocks or strapped to a ducking chair and held under water until you're blue—or dead. You put your name on the paper of your own free will—remember? That paper says so. And it says you're to obey what Irving's agents order you to do. That's me—one of Irving's agents."

He strode forward, half dragging, half pushing me as he hurried along the tunnel, his fingers so tight on my wrist that my arm was growing numb. It must have been a full minute before I remembered my bundle of clothing. I tried to get him to return for it, but he refused.

"No time," he snapped, pulling me on.

But you had time for rape, I thought grimly. Pain and rage were all tangled up inside of me. My body ached. At the same time, I boiled with anger. The virginity I'd safeguarded was gone. This man who made me believe on the church steps that he was doing me a favor guiding me to a wonderful future had turned into an ogre. No matter what I did, I was trapped. If I rebelled and Mr. Irving brought me before a judge, I not only would be dealt with in the ways McGregor mentioned, but I could be ordered out of the Colony of Massachusetts forever. Banished! The word made me tremble. If that happened, I would be forced to leave at once! It seemed better to board the ship now, as this offered the quickest route to a new area. Whatever befell me in the future, I was sure nothing could be worse than this animal man who had abused me in the tunnel. Nothing!

The tunnel was sloping upward, the ceiling gradually becoming lower. I could smell salty air. We must be nearing the end of the passage.

"No ladder here," McGregor said. "You'll have to bend over unless you want to bash your brains."

We crawled the last section on our hands and knees, emerging into woods. A short distance away a two-masted sloop riding at anchor in the choppy sea was visible. A gusty wind rattled branches over us, and the sky had cleared partially. Pale clouds billowed across a misty moon.

It was a relief to straighten up. I drew a deep breath, my lungs swelling with the clean, ocean air. Without letting go of my wrist, McGregor walked me out of the woods onto a narrow beach. A lone figure waited beside a dinghy at the water's edge, the man and the tiny boat silhouetted against the white sand and foaming gray waves.

"McGregor?" The man's voice was low, urgent. "Damn! Where have you been?"

"We were delayed," McGregor answered. "But we're here now."

"The Captain has already given a warning signal. My orders are to return to the *Solace* when he signals again whether you're with me or not. Look—" he pointed toward a pinpoint of light. "That's the signal. Put out your lantern. I don't want to set the dinghy on fire in this gale."

I barely glimpsed the man before McGregor doused the flame in the lantern. The sailor, had a pock-marked face and red hair. He was barefooted and wore a blue jacket over loose-fitting trousers. He looked just like the merchant seamen who came ashore in New Bedford after a long voyage.

The three of us got into the dinghy, the men taking the oars while I sat alone on the middle seat and tried to dodge the spray from both sides. Once again I became chilled and wet. The boat pitched violently, riding the crest of a wave and sinking down, rising again. My stomach pitched just as wildly. I gagged.

McGregor muttered a curse. "If you're going to puke, hold your head over the side," he growled.

"Don't watch the water, Miss," the sailor said. "That'll make you seasick for sure. Look up—at the

sky or the ship or whatever you can find to fix your gaze
on. Just don't watch the waves."

I stared at the ship close by. A row of men stood
perilously on the mizzenmast yard unfurling a sail. Tiny
specks in the air, like birds perched on a rooftop. I
could not imagine how the sailors held on in the wind
and managed the sail at the same time.

Clouds drifted over the moon as we reached the
Solace. Voices floated out of the dark and I glanced up,
startled at how high the deck was from the water. A
rope ladder dropped, and the seaman beside me
reached up from the tossing dinghy to catch it. "You
first," he said to me. "Get a firm grip and mind you
don't look down."

He held the bottom of the ladder. I put my feet on
the lower rung, moving up two steps and giving an
involuntary cry as he let go and the ladder swished in
the wind. I was sure I'd be thrown against the side of
the ship or into the water. Clutching the rope sides, I
pulled myself up slowly, rung by rung, my cloak
blowing out behind me, the salt spray filling my nose
and eyes. One foot slipped. With a terrified cry I found
the rung again and braced my feet on it as I mustered
strength to climb once more.

"You're almost here, lass," a voice came from the
deck. "Just a little further."

The voice was familiar, but vague. I had to force
myself to move my hands, one hand at a time, then one
foot at a time. The rope cut into my palms and the wind
caught the ladder once more, swinging it and me in an
arc over the ocean. With my eyes squeezed shut, I felt
for the next rung and then the next. Two pairs of hands
reached down to grab me under my arms and pull me
over the railing to the deck.

"Well, if it isn't the pretty lass who was on the church
steps," the familiar voice said. It belonged to the

Captain. He lifted a lantern, shining it on me. "What happened to your face?" he asked. "You didn't have those bruises four hours ago."

My teeth chattered from cold and I was trembling after the terrible climb up the ladder. A *thump!* sounded on the deck behind me. McGregor had just leapt over the railing and was near enough to touch me. Somehow I'd taken for granted *I* would board the ship and *he* would return to Massachusetts, but now I knew that was a foolish mistake on my part. Only God could guess what the man's revenge would be if I told the Captain the truth about my face. Or maybe the other seamen would figure I was fair game and want their turns, since McGregor had taken his.

"I—I f-fell," I mumbled.

To my relief the Captain ended his questions. He began giving orders, telling somebody named Browning to get the anchor hoisted and sending another sailor to notify the helmsman that the *Solace* was ready to move.

"McGregor, take this passenger below with the others," he added.

"Captain," a voice I hadn't heard before came from the shadows, "those wenches below have just gotten quiet and settled themselves down. If a new one goes in now and riles them up, we'll hear the bloody bawling all night. Couldn't this latest one sleep on deck tonight?"

"Jarvis has a point, Captain," McGregor said. "I've never heard such a noisy bunch as they were when I brought them aboard this afternoon while you were ashore."

The lantern was lifted once again. I gnawed my lower lip and deliberately closed my eyes, conscious of the ogling leers from all the unknown eyes in the darkness.

"She's already shivering and there's a lot of gale on deck for someone not used to it," the Captain's voice was deep and ringing. "Roark, take her to my quarters for now. I won't sleep until we're well underway and she can have my hammock for the next two watches. Use the light so she can see where she's going."

"I'll lead her there, Captain," McGregor said.

"The hell you will! The last time you were in my quarters without me to keep my eye on you, McGregor, two bottles of good whiskey found their path down your gullet!"

Loud guffaws came from the crew. "Roark, don't you stay below with the wench or she might get something in her belly besides the food she ate last," a sailor bellowed.

My face burned at the suggestiveness of the crack. A man, apparently the sailor named Roark, picked up the lantern and said, "This way, Miss."

I did not get a good look at him as he moved in front of me, his bare feet soundless. We went through a door into the deckhouse, down a short corridor and past another door which put us in a narrow, chilly room paneled with amber-colored wood. The one porthole stood open, a bright circle in the darkness.

I turned slowly, taking in the surroundings as much as possible in the faint light from the sailor's lantern. Three wooden chests were lashed to iron hooks extending from one wall. A table bolted to the opposite wall was covered with maps and charts. A straight chair braced against the table was anchored to another hook. A rope hammock latticed to form a pattern of squares was suspended diagonally between two corners. My gaze returned to Roark, who seemed scarcely older than I.

"If the Captain is letting you sleep here I don't suppose he minds if you use his blanket," Roark said, handing me a coarsely woven cover.

I glanced apprehensively at the swinging hammock.

"It's so high, I'm not sure I can get into it," I murmured.

"Aye, the Captain is quite a bit taller than you. Spread the blanket out first and lie on the center of the hammock and bring the sides up. I'll give you a boost."

He hung the lantern on a peg over the table before putting both of his hands on my waist and hoisting me into the hammock. Then quickly he grabbed the lantern and moved toward the corridor.

"Goodnight, Miss," he said.

"Wait—leave the light, Mr. Roark. Please!"

"I can't do that, Miss. I was surprised when Captain Hagen told me to bring a lantern below because he doesn't usually allow that. It's a light falling over that causes most fires at sea."

The ship lurched with a groaning sound. I tried to sit up and nearly toppled out of the hammock. "What was that?" I gasped.

"Just the pumps starting. We man them steadily when we're sailing. You'll get used to the racket."

"You mean the *Solace* is already leaking?"

"A little water comes past the seams of any ship, but you don't have to worry. The *Solace* has ample caulking." Roark eased out of view.

I hoped he was telling the truth, not merely attempting to reassure me. Pulling the two edges of the blanket together across my stomach, I tried to ignore my damp clothing and relax. My jaw still ached and the lower part of my body felt raw, but the intense jabbing pains were gone. It was a relief to stretch out instead of standing or walking or crawling—or fighting a threatening creature like McGregor.

The room didn't seem quite as black as it was at first when Roark closed the door. Moonlight filtered through the porthole, a misty, shimmering shaft of light which deepened and paled as the ship rolled in the sea.

The first hard pulsating of the pumps settled into a steady muffled sound. I was growing accustomed to the movement of the hammock, no longer afraid the swaying would spill me to the floor. Fatigue was catching up with me. I thought about Susan James and the inn at New Bedford, then about my mother. That phase of my life was over, I reminded myself drowsily, yawning and snuggling under the blanket. At last, I was warm enough to sleep.

Chapter 4

MY MOTHER AND I were walking through the woods near New Bedford when we came upon several carpenters building a house. She placed a smooth plank across a sawhorse, telling me to sit at one end while she stood beside the other end and moved me up and down. I was a child and she was beautiful the way she looked before she became ill, her eyes glowing with amethyst fire, her hair black and glossy. I squealed with delight and she laughed, giving me warm, loving glances. Then she was gone and I was still teetering on the plank, only now I was grown and strapped into a ducking seat nailed to the board with Mr. Irving and McGregor on either side, pushing me down to the edge of the surging, angry water. In another moment I would be under the gray sea. Gasping. Choking. Turning blue, as McGregor threatened. Or being held under for so long that I did not breathe at all, not ever again. I tried to scream, to make them stop, to protest what they were doing to me, but the scream wouldn't come.

"Wake up!"

A voice cut into the sleep fog and a hand rested on my arm, the touch gentle rather than the hurting grip of McGregor. "You must be having a nightmare," the voice said.

I opened my eyes to stare up at the handsomest man I'd ever seen. He was young, certainly no older than the late twenties, broad-shouldered, muscular. His light brown hair was streaked gold by sunshine. His smoky gray eyes set deep under blond eyebrows gazed out over his straight nose and curving mouth. I noticed his white shirt with long, full sleeves gathered at the wrists, the collar open at his throat, the blue coat slung over a shoulder. He had to be tall; he was towering over me.

The dream was so vivid I did not know if he was part of it or not. Nothing about the man or my surroundings seemed familiar. Yet I realized I must be in bed. I was lying down, wrapped in a blanket.

"Who are you?" I asked. "What are you doing in my room?"

A devilish grin pulled at the corners of his mouth. "I should be the person to phrase that question to you as it so happens you're in *my* room," he said, laughing softly at my consternation. "My name is Bates Hagen. I'm captain of the *Solace*."

"Oh—" It was a cry of embarrassment as my mind cleared. Everything came back to me. But the night was gone and now it was day, the sun beaming through the open porthole, the tangy smell of the sea saturating the chilled air. I sat up too quickly, forgetting that I was in a hammock, the sudden movement causing the ropes to twist so that I would have been thrown to the floor if the man hadn't reached out to catch me by the arms, carefully setting me on my feet.

"I take it you're not really at home on the sea," he smiled roguishly.

"It's my first voyage."

As I spoke I was attempting to straighten my clothes. The mauve dress and cloak were a mass of wrinkles, mute evidence that I'd slept in them. My hair had come loose from the pins during the night and now it fell in a dark mass about my shoulders.

"Do you have nightmares that bad very often, Miss Lancaster?" he asked.

"No. I—How do you know my name?"

His gray eyes were on my face. I had never been scrutinized so intently before.

"Who are you?" he asked without replying to my question. "How did you get involved with Irving? You don't look like one of his women."

"One of his women?" I gave him a questioning stare. "What do you mean by that?"

"One of the women Irving sends South. I've taken groups to Carolina for him twice before when there was space aboard for passengers after the cargo was stored. Most of those women were older than you. Different from you. A few were spinsters who seem to have abandoned hope of ever finding husbands at home. And no wonder, as plain as they are. The others," he paused, shrugging, "the others are the sort to take on any chap who'll buy them a meal or a mug of rum punch."

My cheeks felt hot at his veiled insinuation and I flung my head up. I knew about those women who would "take on any chap." I'd seen plenty of them hanging around the New Bedford docks when the ships sailed in.

"You're insulting, Captain Hagen!" I snapped. "I'm not like that!"

"I know you're not, Miss Lancaster. You don't fit into either of those groups and that's the reason I'm inquiring about your background."

His mouth softened slightly and I didn't fail to catch the note of sincerity in his tone. He tossed his coat to the desk chair, and at that instant the ship must have hit a huge wave because the vessel rolled sharply. I swayed and reached for the side of the hammock, clinging to it for balance. The tall man didn't have that problem, for he stood on the slanting floor, feet wide apart, thumbs tucked into his belt and four fingers of each hand spread against the dark cloth of his trousers. They were large hands, the skin golden brown from the sun, the fingers long and slender with blunt nails.

"I don't have a family," I said. "My belongings were destroyed in a fire. I was walking South last night when McGregor found me asleep on the church steps. He said I could have free passage on this ship."

Last night. It seemed a year since last night, a century since I'd told Susan goodby.

"That was all McGregor promised?" A grittiness came into the Captain's voice. "Irving told you no more than that?"

"What more was there to tell? I signed Mr. Irving's paper giving me permission to come aboard."

In the silence that followed I had the feeling Captain Hagen was on the verge of saying something else about the shipowner, but he did not. Instead, he asked about the bruises on my face, adding, "I had a good glimpse of you when I rode by the church last night, Miss Lancaster, and I'll swear you weren't bruised then."

I couldn't meet those clear gray eyes while I was mouthing a deliberate lie. Ducking my head, I stared at the floor planking. "I—I fell. In the tunnel," I mumbled.

There was no way of knowing if he believed me.

Telling me to come with him, he said he would show me to the women's quarters. We went down the same dim passageway where Roark had led me at midnight, leaving the deckhouse and stepping out into the morning sunshine.

The *Solace* moved rhythmically through the Atlantic under a vivid blue sky, the white sails taut in the wind. Glancing up, I saw men in the rigging overhead, and two sailors nearby were mopping the deck. Another group of seamen were coiling heavy rope near the bowsprit, McGregor in their midst. Captain Hagen called to him to take me below.

The bruises on my cheek and jaw must have been more obvious than I was aware because McGregor glanced at them, a scowl darkening his face. His greeting was a curt nod and a muttered, "'Morning," with the Captain in hearing. Once we were at the far end of the ship he made no effort at conversation, which suited me fine.

The area to which he led me was nearly as dark and dank as the tunnel had been and far less desirable than the Captain's cabin. McGregor hit a door with his palm and yelled, "Coming in," entering as he spoke. Several women screamed and one called, "Wait—" but the door was open wide by then and he pushed me into the room.

"While you're here you might as well empty the piss bucket, McGregor," a woman's voice said. "Bring it back in a hurry, too."

My first impression of this room, which would be my home so long as I was aboard the *Solace,* made me shudder. The odor was nauseating, the sickening stench of urine and human waste in stale air. McGregor strode to the middle of the room for the common bucket, sloshing its contents onto the already damp floor as he carried it out.

Later I was to learn that the floor was always wet. Spray blew in from the one porthole near the ceiling, and moisture seeped through the walls. There was never sufficient light or warmth to get rid of the dampness or the smell.

It was a narrow cabin with fourteen hammocks, seven on each side attached to the wall and to a beam which ran down the center of the ceiling. All of the hammocks were placed so close together their rope sides touched. The center aisle where the bucket sat was so small, two people could barely pass. There was no furniture nor room for any, although a few trunks and boxes were put in the corners, obviously the possessions of the thirteen women who were watching me.

I said my name and some of them gave theirs. A few lay in their hammocks, the retching and moaning a sure sign of seasickness.

"That's your spot," a woman who said her name was Prudence Hall pointed to the hammock closest to the porthole, which meant it was the least desirable. I realized she wasn't intentionally giving me the place where I could expect to be wet constantly. It was simply that all the other hammocks had been taken. While she was speaking, McGregor returned with the empty bucket; he dropped it in the center of the room with a lewd remark and a suggestive leer.

Before night I knew the first names of most of the women passengers, and I'd struck up a good relationship with Nellie Matthews who had the hammock next to mine. She was a woman of indeterminate age, neither ugly nor pretty, one of those the Captain probably would have termed "plain." She had a flat, open face, expressionless except when she gave one of her rare smiles. There wasn't a curve in her angular body.

It was Nellie who explained the routine to be followed on shipboard. In good weather the women would be allowed on deck from midmorning until late afternoon and we would receive our two daily meals then. If the sea was calm enough for a blaze in the firebox on deck, the morning meal would be hot. Otherwise, it would be cold like supper. When we were not on deck we were to remain in that foul-smelling cabin where we slept, and we had to obey any orders from McGregor.

Our meal that first morning was a slice of cheese and a warm, mushy concoction of dried beans which the sailors called "pease porridge." I didn't realize the cheese was a treat, that forty-eight hours later the supply would be gone and we'd eat only the tasteless porridge for breakfast.

Supper never varied: a ship's biscuit, hard as a rock and apt to have weevils, along with a bit of dried salt meat. The men were given a daily portion of rum, and smaller portions were provided for the women. I might have left the rum alone if the water ration had been adequate, but three skimpy cups of water a day were doled out from the wooden casks lashed to the aft part of the deck. Only if it rained, Nellie said, could we have anything but sea water to wash ourselves and our clothes.

Around noon that first day Nellie and I were standing together by the deck rail in the sunshine when Captain Hagen came up beside us.

"I believe you left these in my quarters, Miss Lancaster," he said, stretching out his hand to me with something hidden in his clenched fist. I opened my palm and received my hairpins. Turning on his heel, he strode off without another word.

"You spent the night with him?" Nellie's eyes widened. "I wondered where you'd been because you didn't board the ship with the rest of us."

"I didn't spend the night *with him*—just in his room and he wasn't there," I said quickly. I twisted my hair into a thick coil and pinned it just above the nape of my neck.

"I wouldn't blame you if he'd been in the hammock with you," she giggled. "He's a handsome man, that captain. I wish I thought the fellow waiting for me in Charles Town would be half that good looking."

"You're going South to be married?" I inquired.

"Of course." She gave me a puzzled glance. "Aren't you?"

"Maybe I'll find a husband eventually, but I'm not rushing. Not unless I come across a very rich man." I laughed softly. "I could fall in love with a rich man without any effort, but I'm not optimistic enough to believe it'll happen in a hurry. Once we dock in Charles Town I'm going to look for work and a place to live."

"You can't, Marley. You have to marry within three days after we're on land."

"Who says that? You're not making sense!" A new thought struck me and I spun around. "That isn't the law in the Carolina Colony, is it?"

"Didn't you sign Mr. Irving's paper?"

"Yes. But—"

I caught my breath. When I wrote my name on that sheet of parchment I'd thought it amazing that I could sail South without paying for my journey. I'd taken for granted McGregor spoke the truth when he said the ship's crew was too superstitious to want thirteen passengers.

Now a prickle of fear inched up my spine. If I had been misled. . . . Or simply tricked . . .

"We're to have husbands within three days of docking in Charles Town," Nellie said. "The three days are to allow the men who paid Mr. Irving to provide them with wives to have enough time to get word that the *Solace* has come into port, and until then, we have to do what McGregor says."

She clutched the railing so tightly the skin was stretched thinly over her knuckles. "I'm a little scared about marrying a stranger," she added. "It'll have to be better than the way I've been living in Boston, though. At least I'll have a man of my own in Carolina. In Boston I was with my brother. His wife died in childbirth last year and he has five children and needed somebody to see after them, and I was willing. A month ago he remarried, and his new wife and I don't care much for each other." She gave a small sigh. "I'm not young enough or pretty enough to attract a husband in Boston, but I understand women are scarce in the other Colonies. So maybe things will be better for me in Carolina. I think I can learn to love the man I marry if he's decent."

"I didn't promise to get married!" The words rattled in my throat. "Nobody can force me to do it!"

"Didn't that paper you signed claim you were to do what Mr. Irving and his agents commanded?"

My heart was thudding against my ribs as I remembered the last sentence on the sheet of parchment. ". . . I will obey all instructions from the agents of the aforementioned Seneca Irving until I am released from their jurisdiction . . ."

"I won't!" I repeated hotly. "Nobody can make me marry a man I've never even seen!"

"McGregor can make you, Marley." She gave a forced, unnatural laugh. "He's Irving's agent. Anyway, if you don't get married, what's left for you?"

"I don't know, but I'm going to find out."

"McGregor is over there." She gestured to a group of sailors engaged in a game of dice.

I had no intention of putting any questions to the man who had raped me. Going in the opposite direction, I didn't offer an explanation to Nellie because I was in too much of a hurry to get to Captain Hagen, and I knew the way to his quarters.

He was seated at the desk with a map spread out before him, the door open so that I didn't have to knock. As I approached, he glanced up, his face showing surprise, and he got to his feet.

"Something wrong, Miss Lancaster?" he asked. "Didn't I return enough hairpins? Those I gave you were all I found in here."

"Is it true that the women on this ship are to be married when we reach Charles Town?" I blurted out.

My urgency must have been apparent because the slightly mocking smile left his mouth and his eyes became serious. "That's the reason you ladies are going South, isn't it?" he replied.

"The others, perhaps. But not me! Mr. Irving never told me that. And I won't do it! I won't!"

"Wait a minute, Miss Lancaster. That's between you and Irving—or between you and McGregor. My job is to get the *Solace* safely to Charles Town and see that the cargo is unloaded and the passengers put ashore, not to take care of any promises you made to Irving."

"Don't you understand?" I pleaded frantically. "I didn't promise to marry! He never told me that was expected!"

"If you want to back out of the agreement, you'll need to speak to McGregor about it. That's the reason the man is aboard, to be in charge of the women."

"No! *No!*" My fists shot out and I pounded them against the Captain's chest as if that would force him to believe me. He caught my arms and held them, making me motionless. All of a sudden the fight went out of me.

"No . . . no," I said again, and this time the words were a moan. Helpless fear made my eyes mist with tears. I'd already had a taste of McGregor's brutal temper and his determination. Crying wouldn't help my situation and I didn't want to break down before Captain Hagen, but the tears continued in spite of my efforts to blink them away.

He released his grip on me and I moved from him, trembling, trying to get myself under control. To my amazement, I felt his hands on my shoulders and he turned me around gently so that I was facing him once more.

"You honestly didn't know that men in Carolina pay Irving to find wives for them?" he asked.

"I didn't. I swear it."

His jaw hardened, his lips thinning out. "Good God," he muttered. "I believe you, Marley Lancaster. This morning when I asked about your background I told you that you're not like the women Irving sends South." He sucked his breath in deeply. "You had better speak to McGregor and tell him what you've told me about your agreement with Irving."

"It—It won't help. McGregor was there when I signed, but he would claim I'm lying now even though marriage was never mentioned. In the tunnel when he and I were coming to the ship he said Mr. Irving would have me before a judge and punished if I didn't do as I was told."

"Irving probably could. He has the money to pay for what he wants." Captain Hagen looked right into my eyes. "Exactly what did you sign?"

I repeated the words as best I could remember, my voice cracking on the final sentence. Frown lines appeared in the Captain's forehead.

"Please help me," I begged.

"I don't know what I'll be able to do, but I'll try. I wouldn't want anyone choosing a wife for me so I can understand how you must regard this."

We were standing so near one another that the warmth of his breath fanned my face. His hands remained on my shoulders, his eyes focusing on my mouth, and I had the strangest feeling that he was about to kiss me.

It did not happen. He dropped his hands, tucking the thumbs into his belt in the stance I recalled. He didn't say I was dismissed, but his silence conveyed the impression that he was waiting for me to leave so he could resume his work on the map. With a murmured, "Thank you," I started for the door.

My lips quivered. An inner tingling I'd never before experienced made me weak and strong at the same moment as I walked to the deck. That wide curving mouth of Bates Hagen's would have been wonderful to kiss, and for some odd reason I was disappointed he seemed anxious to send me away. Nellie's remark about hoping a man like the Captain would be waiting for her on the dock in Charles Town made sense. I knew what she meant.

Chapter 5

ONE DAY BLENDED into another as my first week aboard the *Solace* came to a close. I found myself living for the hours in the fresh air, away from the smelly cabin and the quarrelsome women whose tempers flared over the slightest cause. I also lived for the moments with Bates Hagen, although he and I were never completely alone. He sought me out when I was on deck and I realized he must find me attractive. He didn't do that with anybody else, not even with Prudence Hall, a saucy red-head who flirted openly with all the crew. His conversation with the other women consisted merely of, "Good morning."

If Nellie and I were together when he approached, she promptly left. Later she'd tease me, making no bones of her envy.

"I like him," I admitted to her, unwilling to confess that the man was in my thoughts more and more.

"So do all the women on this ship, Marley. That's why they don't take up any time with you, especially Prudence. She'd never own up to it, but I believe she's jealous of you." Her hands fluttered to her mouth. "Does Captain Hagen ever ask you to go to bed with him?"

She laughed at my blush and my forceful denial. But in the next breath she commented that I shouldn't be too straight-laced. She knew what she was talking about, as she'd foregone a lot of pleasure in the past by clinging to her Puritan values.

Several of the women had found lovers among the crew, and it wasn't unusual to hear giggles and soft gasps coming from behind a coil of rope or from one of the dinghies lashed under the deck railing. I'd had that sort of invitation, turning each one down with a curt no, cringing at the thought of a man repeating McGregor's hurting assault when he took my body so painfully in the tunnel. As much as I might have enjoyed a kiss from Captain Hagen, I didn't think beyond that.

If McGregor knew of the sexy frolicking of his charges—and I was positive he did—he could scarcely afford to make an issue of it. He and Prudence Hall had their share of love trysts, which she boasted about when we were in our hammocks at night. Maybe that was the real reason I cared very little for her. I found McGregor so repulsive it was hard for me to see how Prudence could put up with him. Despite her solemn name, she was brash by nature, a trait I didn't much like. She and I had little to do with each other.

One morning on deck I asked the Captain where his home was.

"I was born in England," came the answer. "But the sea is my home."

I dared not inquire if he had a wife, although the question burned my tongue. As if he could read my thoughts, he added, "I've been in England so seldom I wouldn't recognize my own brothers and sisters, and

I've never stayed on land long enough to put down roots."

Another day, on a glorious sunny afternoon, he told me something about navigation, explaining that he used not only maps and charts but also the stars and tides and currents to get the ship to her destination.

"Where are we now?" I wanted to know, seeing the endless blue ocean meeting the horizon on all sides.

"Nearing the Virginia Capes. If this good wind holds and we can slip past Hatteras without a storm, we should reach Charles Town in a week to ten days."

I knew very little geography. "What's Hatteras?" I asked.

"A point of land on the upper coast of Carolina. It juts out into the Atlantic and the shoals and currents in the area can be damn treacherous if—"

He paused at the sight of my troubled face. I had a horror of being shipwrecked, something I'd mentioned to him earlier.

"Don't worry about it, Marley," he went on in a soothing tone. "The bad storms come in autumn, not in May."

"How did you learn all of this? I should think a man of your age wouldn't have had time to acquire so much knowledge along with enough practical experience to be put in command of a ship."

"Now, you're flattering me," he grinned. "My age happens to be twenty-eight. What's yours?"

"Eighteen. Almost."

He stiffened, tightening his lips. "Seventeen . . . scarcely grown," he said as if he was irritated by the fact. "I've been at sea longer than you've been alive. Nineteen years a seaman."

"You couldn't have been at sea nineteen years, Captain. Not unless you were just a child when you began."

"Aye, I was nine. In my opinion that's too young for a boy to be snatched out of his home, but my father didn't think so. He apprenticed me to a ship's captain on my ninth birthday. That's the very reason I won't have a lad sailing on my ship until he's at least thirteen."

"What sort of work can a nine-year-old do on a ship? I can scarcely lift one of those big ropes and a child wouldn't have as much strength as I have. Surely you wouldn't order a little boy to go high in the rigging and adjust the ropes."

"We call them 'lines' on a ship, Marley. Not ropes." His eyes twinkled as he corrected me, but in the next minute he was serious. "No, I wouldn't send a lad that age aloft—unless he wanted to go. And plenty of them do. A boy can fetch and carry or keep up with the time. When I was on my first voyage my main chore was to turn the hour glass and sound the bells for the change of watch. I wasn't used to sitting in one spot so long at a spell, and I detested staring at that glass of sand, trying to keep awake and trying not to think how homesick I was. If I dozed off or the captain thought I'd upended the glass too soon or that I'd forgotten and waited too long to do it and the bell wasn't on schedule, I could brace myself for a flogging."

He waited briefly before saying, "The man my father chose as my master distrusted all children. He never believed a word I said merely because I was only nine years old. Many's the time I've crawled into my hammock with my back bleeding from the cat-o'-nine tails, although I'd done nothing wrong."

The hardness in his voice matched the hardness in his eyes, an expression which passed so swiftly I would not have seen it if I hadn't been looking at him while he spoke. I had the impression that he did not disclose such personal memories and feelings very often.

Chapter 6

As WE MOVED further South the May temperature soared, but the Captain's "good wind" did not hold. We were becalmed for two nights and two days, the air misty and humid, the sails hanging limp at the masts and the sea smoother than a lake.

Inactivity and the sticky unseasonable heat made the sailors as grouchy and ill tempered as the women. Only the weevils inhabiting our dry biscuits thrived. Those weevils were so abundant I could not have swallowed a mouthful of the hard tasteless bread if there had been any alternative but hunger. Once Nellie found a biscuit without any bugs. When she exclaimed over it and held it up for everybody to see, a sailor snatched it from her hand and tossed it overboard with the comment that it must be poison for sure if the varmints wouldn't take a taste.

The crew cheered the morning the wind finally sprang up, but the gray fog still clung to the surface of the Atlantic. It was impossible to make out the tops of the masts or to look the full distance from one end of the *Solace* to the other, much less find the horizon.

I was on deck that morning, standing alone by the rail in the murky haze, thinking about the future, which made me tense with fear. I did not know how to help my situation. If only I had some money, I mused. Money would mean I could bribe McGregor. It would mean I'd be sure of taking care of myself on land. The delay caused by the weather had allowed me to put off a little longer the showdown when we docked. An ugly scene was inevitable and I dreaded it. Captain Hagen must have forgotten about helping me get out of the marriage contract. Or maybe he'd decided not to get involved. He hadn't mentioned it again. Reminding myself that Mr. Irving and his parchment were hundreds of miles away in Massachusetts gave me no comfort.

Out of the corner of my eye I saw McGregor approaching and I expected him to pass without stopping to speak, hoping it would happen. But as he brushed by he grabbed my left wrist in a hurting viselike grasp, ignoring my startled protest as he yanked me to the rear of the ship where the heavy wooden barrels of drinking water were stored. I thought he was about to rape me again and that location was secluded enough for him to do it, especially in the fog, but he had something else on his mind. In a hissing undertone he snarled that he would be forced to take a whip to me if I went trotting to Captain Hagen with any more lies.

"I don't know what you're talking about," I retorted, attempting to get free from his hold and finding it impossible. His fingers sliced into my wrist, sending a spasm of fire up my left arm.

"Don't play dumb with me, wench," he sneered. "You damn well know."

"Let me loose or I'll scream for help and this time

we're not in that tunnel, McGregor! Plenty of people will hear me!"

"You and your bloody threats!" But he opened his fingers. "You know what I'm referring to, Marley. Hagen tells me that you claim you don't have to take a husband in Charles Town and that's a damn lie. You'll accept the man I give you, the same as the other women accept their husbands."

So Captain Hagen hadn't forgotten after all! I would have been thrilled if I'd had time to think about it.

"Mr. Irving did not say a thing about marriage when I was with him and neither did you," I came back hotly. "I would never have signed anything if I'd known."

"He told you to obey me and I'm saying what you're to do. Can you get that through your skull? How else do you think you could have boarded this ship without a penny to your name?" He brought his face very close to mine, his lip curling into a sneer. "You'll marry, all right, though God have mercy on the poor bloke who gets you! I've seen your kind before. They think pretty features and a body to make a man drool let them do as they please, and they go back on their lawful promises and won't obey their masters. Not an ounce of loving in their hearts, either. You're as brittle as an icicle, Marley Lancaster. Just as cold, too."

"Cold to filthy bullies!"

"Don't you call me names, wench!"

We glared at each other, his black eyes almost lost under the bristling brows. I massaged my left wrist with my right hand, opening my mouth to remind him once more that I was under no obligation to be part of his and Mr. Irving's scheme.

But I clammed up without speaking. Anything I said would only make McGregor more vehement. I was anxious to be away from him before he hurt me again.

By sheer strength he could knock me to the deck floor or push me hard against one of the barrels and leave my back full of long, needlelike splinters. I'd seen a sailor do that to another after a quarrel. It was smarter for me to keep silent until Charles Town was in sight and to pray that Captain Hagen would be able to help me then. That was my one hope.

McGregor had said his piece and he stalked off. The gray fog swirled around me. I sat down on a coil of rope until my breathing returned to normal, desperation akin to panic making my throat dry and sending blood thundering in my ears.

If only I were on land I could run away from McGregor, I thought frantically. I could hide. . . . If I were on land I could have a decent meal . . . and a bath. . . .

A bath! I closed my eyes, trying to remember the sensation of being clean and wearing newly laundered clothes, of having my hair soft and fluffy. Now that the nights were warmer sometimes I removed the well worn mauve dress before going to sleep, but my petticoat had not been off my back during the entire voyage, and the two garments were stiff with perspiration and grime and salt. My skin felt like leather and my hair was a disaster, matted to my head by the ocean spray which showered through the porthole near my hammock.

The three scant cups of fresh water given us daily were hardly enough to keep down thirst. My efforts to bathe in a bucket of sea water had left me stickier and itchier than before, the salt caking on my body and remaining so that I always felt gritty. I wasn't alone in the filth, but the crew and the other women must not have been as accustomed to personal cleanliness as I was and it didn't seem to bother them.

If I could just rinse my face and hands with fresh water, I thought. If I could do it just once . . .

Staring longingly at the brown wooden barrels, I decided we had to be within a few days of Charles Town. Although it had not rained since the ship sailed from Massachusetts, surely there was ample drinking water for the remainder of the voyage. How could it be very wrong for me to take an extra portion of fresh water . . . merely one or two cups . . . barely enough to put three inches in the small wooden basin resting on the lid of the closest barrel . . .

As the thought crystalized I acted quickly. Getting the lid off the barrel was difficult, but I managed to slide the heavy slab of wood halfway to one side and I gazed into the depths of water. Drinking wasn't nearly as important to me at that instant as washing. I reached for the dipper, filled it and poured water into the basin. The liquid was a pale brown color and probably it was sour and brackish to taste, but at least it had no salt.

I leaned forward to scoop up a second dipperful when two rough hands closed around my throat from behind and a man cursed. Choking, I fought for air, letting go of the basin and dipper, the precious water spilling over his feet and mine as my fingers clawed at the hands squeezing my neck. I could not breathe. My tongue was swelling in my mouth and my eyes bulged and burned as if they were being ripped from their sockets.

"Don't you know stealing water is a flogging offense?" the man growled.

He dropped his hands at last and spun me around. I coughed and panted, gasping for air.

When my vision cleared enough to see, I recognized Hutchins, the quartermaster, a short, sinewy man with an uneven red scar running the length of one cheek, down his chin and across his chest. His eyes smouldered with hatred, all of it directed at me, and finding me into the water supply wasn't the sole reason.

On the fourth evening at sea Hutchins had asked if I'd like to join him behind a stack of spare sails in the stern. He would, he had whispered with a suggestive leer, show me how good it felt to have a real man boring between my legs. I said no and he must have believed I was teasing to lead him on, for he tugged at my skirt, getting one hand under it and past my petticoat until he rubbed his fingers on my bare thigh, inching them up toward my hip, and he would not stop. I'd twisted and squirmed until finally I managed to jerk my knee up, slamming it into his groin. He had bent over with a groan of pain and rage, clutching himself, and I had not lingered to see how badly he was hurt. I ran to the women's quarters and promised myself never to be on deck after twilight, no matter how disagreeable the other women were or how putrid the air in the cabin seemed. Since that night, I had purposely avoided the man.

Now it was just Hutchins and me in an isolated section of the ship. The fog was so dense it was doubtful if the lookout in the crow's nest could see us. Hutchins stood in front of me, pinning me against the water barrel with his thick arms outstretched on either side to form a cage so I could not dart away.

"McGregor will give you what you deserve," he said fiercely. "And it'll be my pleasure to watch. A man stealing water could get twenty or thirty lashes with the whip. Maybe a woman can learn her lesson with a few extra lashes—or maybe not."

"I was only going to use a tiny bit of water to wash my face and—"

"To wash?" he cut in. "Did you say *wash?*" He broke into coarse laughter. "You're a crazier wench than I thought. A crazy wench with the body of an angel." He raked his eyes from my face to my feet, his gaze lingering on my breasts.

I pretended not to notice and I was trying desperately to think of some remark I could make which would calm him. I was determined not to beg. I would not grovel no matter what he and McGregor did to me.

"Well, Miss Water Thief, I'll strike a bargain with you," Hutchins said. "You're a pretty piece of flesh all right, and if you'll lie down behind the barrels and spread your legs, and if what we do gives me pleasure, I'll pretend I didn't come upon you while you were pilfering water."

"I'll do nothing of the sort!" I blurted out.

"The lash hurts. You don't know how much. You'd carry scars on that soft back of yours as long as you live." He flicked his tongue over his lips. "Maybe that wouldn't be too long after the flogging. A whipping could end your life. Think about it. Maggots in your wounds. Pus forming in the lash marks. It's not a pretty way to die. You'd come down with a fever from the infection and it might take you days of screaming with pain before you breathed your last."

"And you think that would be a worse fate than my having you paw me?" I hooted with a bravado I didn't feel.

He laughed again. "You're a she-devil for sure. I like a wench with a bit of a temper, though. Makes the passion all the sweeter to subdue her."

I was quivering inside, terrified of what he would do next. But I made myself look at him.

"You touch me, Hutchins," I measured each word out, "and you'll get another pain like the last one I gave you. Only this time I'll fix you so you'll never have another woman!"

Anger contorted his mouth. Quick as a flash he

picked me up and slung me across his shoulder as if I'd been a sack of grain, one of his arms around my ankles so I could not kick and his other hand holding my two hands in an iron grip behind my waist. My face dangled against his buttocks, blood rushing to my head and beating against my temples. I tried to scream, but the cry was a thin wail which could not have been heard a yard away.

Hutchins walked rapidly toward the far end of the ship and the sailors snickered as we passed, shouting bold cracks under the apparent assumption that he was about to take me to bed. When we reached McGregor, the explanation Hutchins gave was brief. He had caught me stealing drinking water, he said.

"Put me down!" I demanded. "Put me down right now!"

"Hold her, Hutchins! That wench has been fairly begging for the cat-o'-nine tails and she'll get them now." McGregor spoke in such an exhilarated voice I realized he must be eager to have a legitimate excuse for punishing me.

I was still head-down on Hutchins' shoulder and I tried again to scream. McGregor tore a strip of cloth from the bottom of one of his trouser legs, then grabbed my nose, pinching it between his thumb and forefinger to cut off my air. As I opened my lips to breathe he stuffed the filthy rag into my throat.

"Now you can't screech," he said. "Hutchins, once we get her against the mainmast, you go spread the word that everybody who wants to see the show had better come running."

He actually was going to flog me. Until that moment I had not let myself believe he would do it. My eyes widened in horror and a wave of wretchedness engulfed me, leaving my body clammy with cold perspiration.

The two men stood me against the mast with my face

pushed to it as they lifted my arms over my head, binding my wrists to the mast with a rope. I gagged, but I couldn't spit with the sickening cloth in my mouth and my stomach heaved. Hutchins' description of the aftermath of a flogging echoed in my ears. Open wounds from the lash marks . . . maggots . . . pus forming and then a fever . . .

I will not cry no matter how much it hurts, I vowed to myself. God knew I couldn't scream, not with that gag in my throat. But I might strangle on my own vomit.

Looking back over my shoulder, I saw several crewmen and some women watching, the women's eyes filled with dismay although Prudence Hall was giggling. McGregor stood near me untangling the thongs of the whip, nine long cords of brown leather with the ends twisted to form a handle and some of the free ends knotted. I shuddered again. Those knots would gouge flesh from my back. They would slash my skin to shreds.

I squeezed my eyes shut and ducked my head as much as possible to protect my face, steeling myself for the first blow. There was a *swish!* followed by a faint gust of air. He must be lifting his arm, whirling the nine leather cords round and round his head to gain momentum—

"What the hell is happening here?" Captain Hagen's voice boomed out. "Drop that whip, McGregor! God damn it, man! Drop it!"

A thump sounded amid the scuffling noises. Trembling, I looked over my shoulder once more. The cat-o'-nine tails lay on the deck. Bates Hagen, his face as dark as a thundercloud, clutched one of McGregor's arms in a twisting grasp, which told me the whip had not been surrendered willingly.

"She was stealing drinking water, Captain," McGregor said. "Claimed she wanted to have a wash.

You ask Hutchins if you doubt me. He saw her with his own eyes. She'd taken the lid off the barrel and—"

"I am in command of this ship, McGregor," the Captain interrupted him. "You've sailed with me before and you know my rule about flogging. It is done on my orders and only on my orders."

"You might be in command of this ship, but I'm in charge of the women. That's Irving's decree. This particular wench has caused me a pile of trouble saying what she will do and what she won't. She deserves a whipping."

"When there is disciplining to be done on the *Solace* I will take care of it no matter whether the culprit is a passenger or one of the crew—or one of Irving's agents. Is that clear?"

Captain Hagen's voice was clipped and frosty. McGregor muttered something under his breath.

"I intend to deal with her," the Captain added. "Jarvis—" he jerked his head toward a sailor leaning against the rail, "cut her down and take her to my quarters. As for the rest of you, if you men don't have enough duties to keep you busy you'll be assigned extra watches. You women go below and remain in your cabin until you're given permission by me to come topside again."

The people vanished in silence, everyone except McGregor, Captain Hagen and Jarvis. And me, of course. Jarvis leapt nimbly to the mast where I stood. He was older than most of the crew, his hair peppered with gray above a grizzled face. He pulled a knife with a long, thin blade from his belt and sliced through the rope binding my wrists.

As the last strands popped and I was freed, my knees gave way. I would have fallen if I hadn't caught the mast and held tightly to it. Three pairs of eyes focused on me. I drew a determined breath and pulled the gag from my mouth, standing as tall as I could and summoning all my strength to follow Jarvis down the dim passageway to the Captain's cabin. The sailor did not speak, but he glanced at me curiously as he went out, leaving me alone.

Perhaps Captain Hagen intended to do the flogging himself. Maybe he thought it would spare my feelings if I was punished in privacy rather than in front of the crew and the women. Fear formed a knot in my throat, choking me almost as much as the gag had done. I swayed on my feet, needing to sit down, but I dared not get into the Captain's desk chair or his hammock. Flexing my fingers did little to restore the circulation to my numb hands. When I could stand no longer, I staggered across the cabin and collapsed on one of the wooden chests tied to the wall.

It was impossible to know how long I waited. Perhaps it was ten or fifteen minutes, perhaps longer. The terror ebbed away to be replaced by a humiliating shame. I'd brought this crisis on my own head. McGregor had deliberately tricked me in the past, but I had nobody to blame except myself for what I now faced.

Pale yellow sunshine filled the room, dispelling the shadows. The wan light wavered and disappeared, returning and going again. I moved my head in the direction of the porthole, realizing the bad weather must be near an end as this was the first glimpse of the sun in three days.

I stiffened as Captain Hagen strode into the cabin and slammed the door shut, stopping in front of me. His body was tense with controlled anger, his feet in the black boots wide apart, his shirt open nearly to his waist exposing a mat of tiny golden hairs. I made myself look up at him and cringed at the coldness in his gray eyes and the hard set of his tightly clenched jaws.

He didn't speak at first. He just stood there, glaring.

"Were you stealing water?" he asked finally, chipping each syllable out.

"I—I thought—Just a little. A couple of dippers . . ." My voice faltered. Lifting my head, I met his gaze. "Yes, I was taking water. I'm sorry, Captain, I—I never dreamed it would be so—so important."

"Good God, lass, don't you realize what a serious deed you've done? 'Deed' is hardly the term—stealing water is a crime! If everybody on this ship took one extra ration of water, how long do you think the supply would hold out?"

I didn't reply because I didn't know what to say.

"Are you so stupid you can't understand that those barrels of water—what's left in them—are between us and eternity?" he stormed on. "We've been becalmed for two days and two nights, and it damn well may slow us twice that long in getting to land for supplies if we don't keep a steady gale from now on. If the water is used up and there's no rain, how would you enjoy going without any water at all?"

I gnawed my lower lip, wishing I were any place else in the world as long as it was away from his angry eyes. "I'm sorry," I said again. "I—I guess I wasn't thinking about the danger. Just about myself."

"Is it true that you were planning to have a bath?"

The way his mouth twisted over the word "bath" made it seem evil. Nodding, I wondered if I could have suffered any more under McGregor's whip than under this man's disgusted expression.

"You think you're the only person on the *Solace* to want a bath? I'd like one. I detest shaving in sea water. But I do it and don't make a fuss about it—and neither do I dip into the barrels."

He began to pace, going the length of the cabin, walking briskly to the opposite wall and repeating the pattern several times until he stopped before me again. "What in the hell am I going to do about you, Marley?" he growled. "I'd punish anyone else. Flog a man—and that might be needless because the crew probably would toss him overboard and tell him to get all the water he wanted. But I can't see you whipped. If it was one of the other women, I'm not sure what I'd give her. Probably confine her to quarters until we reach port." He made a fist out of his right hand and ground it into his left palm. "Damn it all, don't stare at me like that with those big eyes of yours as if you were a wounded animal! It's hard enough for me to be this near you and not—" He broke the sentence off, his face flushing.

I had the feeling he'd said more than he intended, but it didn't help my state of mind to know he was concerned. I sat there in silence, trembling, drowning in my own humiliation.

With an odd suddenness his mood changed and the iciness left his features, his mouth instantly gentle. He picked my hands up from my lap, turning them in his as he examined the rope burns on my aching wrists. He had never touched me before and there was a strange comfort in the warmth of his fingers.

"I'll bet that hurts like the devil," he said softly.

"Yes," I admitted.

"You must have been scared, Marley."

"I was—terrified." I made an attempt to smile, but it came out wrong and my lips quivered. "I—I still am . . . a little . . ."

"You don't have to be afraid of me. I wish I had some salve for those rope marks. Maybe a taste of rum will stop you from shaking."

He opened a cabinet in the side of the desk and removed a flask along with two small white cups of ivory, each cup intricately carved on the outer surface. One carving was a fish which circled the entire bowl, the tiny gills and scales etched in minute detail. The other cup bore a seascape, a three-masted schooner with her sails rigged.

Filling the cups, he passed one to me. I took a small sip and then gulped the rest of the fiery liquid. It scorched a trail to my stomach and sent a surge of heat through my veins.

When I could speak, I said, "I've never seen cups like these. They're beautiful."

"They're made from whale's teeth. I did them several years ago. The mate on the ship I served on at the time was an expert carver and he taught me, but I'll confess to mutilating a few whale's teeth before I got the hang of it." The corners of his mouth turned up in a boyish smile. "That cup you're holding lacks a lot of being perfect. See where the eye of the fish is? It's too high in his head. And here," he pointed to a spot near the fish tail, "I cut deep and tried to smooth it out. I notice that every time the cup is used."

"Nobody else would see it. You have a great deal of talent."

"I doubt that. It helped pass the time. I did better with the schooner on the other cup and—"

"Captain!" Roark's voice rang out and he darted into the room, his eyes wide. "The lookout has sighted a ship flying Spain's colors! The fog lifted and there she was to starboard, almost on top of us!"

The two men dashed out. I didn't know if I should leave the Captain's cabin or remain where I was. Seeing another ship after such a long time without a glimpse of anything except water and sky would be exciting, but I had not been dismissed. Apparently my reprimand was finished, but I didn't want to make a move which would bring the return of Captain Hagen's anger.

I went to the porthole. Only the blue gray ocean and the rapidly clearing sky were within my range of vision.

In a few minutes the Captain returned, his face so grim that the questions I wanted to ask died on my lips. Without looking at me, he unlocked one of the wooden chests, took out a tan leather sling holding four pistols and put it across his shoulders. A knife lay beside his logbook on the desk. He inserted the blade in a metal sheathe and slid it in the top of his right boot.

"Marley, that ship has struck the Spanish colors and now she's flying a black flag," he said in a deadly cold voice. "Do you know what that means?"

"Pirates?" I swallowed hard, my mouth as dry as paper.

"Yes, pirates. I want you to remain below. Stay here in my quarters. I've sent McGregor and Jarvis to protect the other women, but you'd be seen if you went across the deck to join them and I don't want those barbarians to know we have women aboard. You are *not* to venture on deck unless the *Solace* lists badly or takes on enough water for you to know we're sinking. That means water past your knees. Do you understand?"

My yes was barely a word. I nodded.

"I'll come back in here for you when I can. Keep away from the porthole and above all, don't scream or make a noise to let your presence be known if we're boarded."

The full realization of what might happen was getting to me. "Are you trying to say there may be a fight?" I asked.

"One hell of a fight." His mouth stretched into a grim line. "They haven't fired on us, which means they must know what our cargo is. I hope to God they'll settle for taking it and leave the passengers alone."

"Why don't we fire on them? Wouldn't that scare them off?" The *Solace* had two guns mounted on either side of the bow. Until that moment I hadn't wondered about any cargo on the ship, as the vessel was loaded before I came aboard. But now the way he mentioned it was puzzling. "What are we carrying?" I asked.

Captain Hagen was hurrying toward the door. Either he had not heard my questions or he was choosing to ignore them. But he stopped, then came back to where I stood. Swiftly putting both his arms around me, he pulled me hard against him.

I gasped in surprise. The pistols of his shoulder sling cut into my breasts as his body curved against mine, but I didn't try to pull away. I held him as tightly as he was holding me, my heart pounding. There was nothing in the world for a wild, surging minute but this man with his tawny hair and smoky eyes—and me.

"Our cargo is gunpowder," he said in a hoarse whisper. "I may never have another chance to hold you and kiss you, Marley."

His mouth came down on mine, his lips firm and sweet. Very, very sweet. I opened my eyes and saw tenderness in his face, a longing, a desperate passion. His grip tightened until I was barely able to breathe.

The embrace ended too soon. He forced my arms from around his neck and thrust me aside, leaving the cabin without looking back, his shoulders rigid.

A tight dry sob rose into my throat, choking me. If the gunpowder exploded I might never see him again, might never kiss him. . . . If we were boarded and he was killed in the fighting. . . . God forbid, I thought starkly, pushing my fingers against my lips, which still throbbed and burned from his kiss. Until that instant I'd wondered if I was falling in love with Captain Hagen. Now I knew for sure.

Chapter 7

STANDING WHERE CAPTAIN Hagen left me, I was unable to move at first. No man had ever kissed me like that. His abrupt embrace and his lone searching kiss aroused such a violent longing I never wanted to be out of his arms. Now it might be too late for us to be together. Too late for anything!

The commotion on deck jarred me to my senses. Heavy objects were being dragged around. Men shouted and cursed, some speaking languages I didn't understand. Footsteps sounded in every direction.

Despite the Captain's order, I ran to the porthole—and drew away immediately, stunned. The pirate ship was in view, her name printed on the side, *Queen Anne's Revenge*, and a long row of guns was mounted on her deck. I had never seen such a large vessel before nor one so heavily armed. I counted twenty guns, aware that my view was only of one side. An equal number of cannon probably would be on her other side.

It was impossible to dwell on those guns because the men on her deck were more frightening in appearance

71

than the artillery. Some of her crew held grappling hooks. Others stood in the rigging clutching long ropes attached to the masts, which they could use to swing over to the *Solace*. They were a scroungy, evil-looking lot, their eyes aglitter with the lust for battle, all of them barefooted and some bare-chested, each holding a cutlass and several knives stuck in his belt.

Earlier I had been afraid of McGregor and Hutchins—or thought what I felt then was fear. It was nothing compared to the stark horror that swept over me at the blood-curdling sight of those men waiting, eager for action. Stories of the ways of pirates came back to me, their killing and maiming, slicing off noses and ears and fingers of their victims and laughing all the time they did it, using women so viciously that their savage animal passions became a living death for the captives.

I closed the porthole and the cabin door, my hands shaking. There was no bolt on the door and no place in Captain Hagen's quarters where I could hide to be completely safe. I crouched on the floor beside the chest which had been my seat earlier. Anybody merely glancing in from the passageway might miss me. Might. . . . I hoped it would be like that. The cabin was warm, almost stuffy, and I was freezing.

The ship lurched as the grappling hooks landed on deck, each making a sharp *clunk!* followed by the splintering noise of wood giving way when the metal barbs chewed into the planking. Shouts turned into screams and groans. An occasional pistol shot cracked. Footsteps changed to the frenzied jumping and thrashing of hand-to-hand combat. I put my hands over my ears, but it didn't shut out the gruesome noises.

The silence, when it came, was as eerie as the sounds of the fighting. It wasn't a complete quiet. Pain-wracked cries mingled with a jumble of voices and groans. I could not understand any of the spoken words coming from the deck or recognize a voice.

If we had won, the *Queen Anne's Revenge* would be leaving. I had to know. Standing up, I crept to the porthole and looked out. The pirate ship was very close to us, the grappling lines intact with men from the *Revenge* crossing them to reach the *Solace*, balancing on the ropes like cats on a tree limb. They were laughing arrogantly. We had lost.

A piercing cry reverberated through the air. New cries followed, each one shrill with panic and agony. The crew of the *Revenge* must have found the women! *Dear God,* I whispered, not knowing if I spoke aloud or not, and at that instant two men came into the room.

One of them went immediately to the desk, shuffling through maps. I shrank against the wall as if that would make me invisible.

"Must be the Captain's quarters," the man at the desk said. "Here's his logbook."

"And here's his wench!" The other man jerked me up. "Aye, a fine looker, too. I didn't know Hagen had such good taste."

His hand shot out to grab my breast. I choked with pain and indignation as his fingers pinched my nipple.

"Small tits but the rest of her looks all right," he went on. "Willie, don't you think she's too good for a Captain who wouldn't even give us a nice welcome when we came aboard to relieve him of his cargo?"

Their coarse laughter followed the jibes. They were enjoying my fear and discomfort. The man dropped his hand from my breast. I took a step backward to get away from him, my shoulders hitting the wall behind me. The two of them laughed, coming nearer. I was cornered.

One man was tall with a swarthy complexion and dark hair plastered to his forehead. A blue cord circled his brow just above his slanting eyes, ending with a knot tied over one ear. The other, the man called Willie, had heavy features and his bare chest was a lattice of scars, lumpy pits and blotches. I noticed all that vaguely as my eyes were glued to the red smears on his hands and the drops of blood clinging to the knife in his fist.

"How about it, Willie?" the tall man cocked his head toward me. "Shall we have a go at her?"

"Why not? Who's to know? Hagen won't mind. He's in no condition now to object even if he knew."

I caught my breath. "What about Captain Hagen?" I asked in a ragged voice, the first time I'd made a sound. The room was whirling around my head. Was it Bates Hagen's lifeblood on the knife waved in front of me?

"Well, I ain't rightly knowing what Teach plans for Hagen." Willie stuck the knife into his belt and began unbuttoning his trousers. "I'll take her now. I'm damn ready. The nearness of her done that to me."

He shoved me to the floor. I struggled as he fell on top of me and somehow I managed to cross my legs at the knees. Willie cursed, crushing my mouth in a slobbery kiss, and then twisted my legs apart while the other man grabbed my hands and held them above my head. I was still struggling against the two of them when Willie entered me.

"She's a wild one, she is," he panted and grinned as he finished.

"Damn it, Willie! Move away from her! Give me a chance to find out for myself!"

The second body fell down on me like a rock, the man's weight crushing the breath from me. I tried to fight him, but he only laughed and then clamped his hands on my neck. "I'll throttle you good if you don't be still!" he hissed.

He would kill me. I knew that. I forced myself to go limp and he loosened the grip on my windpipe, starting the ferocious stabs between my legs that tore at my body as if he was cutting me in half with a knife. I had thought there would never be anything as terrible as what McGregor made me endure in the tunnel, but this was worse.

When he had satisfied himself he stood up, yanking me to my feet. I tottered, my knees buckling. The other man grabbed my arm and forced me to remain in an upright position.

"Teach will open his eyes damn wide at the sight of us bringing in the Captain's wench," Willie said in a triumphant voice. "Come on, woman. You can walk."

I did not move. He slapped me hard on the buttocks with the flat of his hand, sending me reeling across the cabin. I was too wrung out to fight them any longer, but I hung back once more. They dragged me down the passageway to the deck, one of them on either side of me clutching my arms.

The glare outside was blinding. My nostrils filled with the sickening stench of fresh blood. I looked down at the deck planking, bright red and slick. A foot severed above the ankle slid past us and caught in a coil of rope, the bone protruding from the flesh. I gave a desperate cry. Jarvis was sprawled in front of us, his unseeing eyes wide, the whites showing and the eyeballs rolled back in his head, his stomach slashed open and his organs spilled out in a gory pulp. Nausea rose into my throat, into my mouth, and I trembled with horror. The two men tugged at me, shoving me past Jarvis' body. Wounded sailors lay everywhere, some of them attempting to tend their own wounds, others huddling glassy-eyed waiting for help or death, whichever arrived first.

When I saw Captain Hagen tears of thankfulness welled into my eyes. He was alive and apparently not critically injured. Then I realized he was a prisoner aboard his own ship. He stood tied against the main-mast, both his hands and feet bound. Dry blood crusted on a small cut across his chin; his shirt was in shreds, a reddish stain running the length of one sleeve. His face seemed to have been chiseled from gray stone. As he caught sight of me I thought I detected a brief softening around his mouth, the expression disappearing so quickly I did not know if I imagined it.

"Captain, see what we brought you," Willie said.

At his use of the term "Captain," I thought he was addressing Bates Hagen. The two of them holding my arms jerked me forward and I found myself in front of *their* captain, a strange hulking man with features so fiendish that I shuddered. He was huge, tall as well as robust, with a great mane of bristly black hair under a broad-brimmed black hat. His long black beard started under his eyes and fell halfway to his waist, the ends in little braided pigtails, each tied with a ribbon. His trousers were black, stuck into knee boots, and he wore a long-skirted coat of emerald velvet, the wide cuffs turned back to his elbows showing a lining of yellow silk. In the leather belt strapped around his waist were an assortment of pistols, daggers and an oversized cutlass.

"Real nice, ain't she, Captain Teach?" Willie's tone begged for praise.

The strange man swerved his eyes the full length of my body in a stare which made me feel stark naked before him. "Just where did you find this pretty lass?" he asked. "Wasn't she with the other wenches?"

"She's the captain's lady." Willie, strutting, broke into a self-satisfied grin. "That's what me and Tyson figure because she was in Hagen's quarters and right much at home there, too."

"Well, well, Bates. You never told me you'd ac-quired a wife." Teach spoke to Captain Hagen without taking his eyes off of me. "She's a looker, although I must say you don't provide her with much of a wardrobe. I don't like my women in rags. I make sure that they're decked out with a bit of finery and that they have jewels. This one no doubt is a nice bundle in bed. I can see why you want her."

My face was burning. He walked around me slowly, looking me up and down, murmuring, "Hmmmmm," from time to time. His right hand was on the hilt of the huge cutlass and his left hand fingered one of his beard pigtails.

"This complicates your future, Bates," he added in a sniggering voice. "At the moment I've no time for a hanging because I'm going to be late getting to New Providence Island as it is. Anyway, your men claim you've treated them well and I have the gunpowder, which is what I came after. I have something else, too." He gave a raucous laugh. "I have the *Solace* and a sweet bunch of wenches to keep my men happy. I'd take this wench of yours for myself if my new wife wasn't waiting for me aboard the *Revenge.*"

He hushed briefly, tapping the cutlass with a grimy, long fingernail. "So I don't need you, Bates," he went on. "If I put one of my mates in charge of the *Solace* to sail her to New Providence and sign what's left of your crew on with my men, should I dump you over the side with your limbs still bound? Or," he rolled his eyes, "should I set you adrift in a dinghy and let the sea deal with you at a slower pace?"

Captain Hagen did not speak. I swallowed hard, unable to tell if Teach was serious or if he was playing a cat-and-mouse game, taunting Bates Hagen. The pirate seemed to be enjoying himself immensely. I hoped his brazen banter was for the benefit of his own men and the battered crew of the *Solace* rather than a declaration of what he meant to do.

But I couldn't be sure. The only thing I knew positively was that I was frightened. My teeth bit into my lower lip as I willed myself not to scream.

"You men, y   lower a dinghy," Teach spoke to some sailors   nding near him and looked at Captain Hagen once more. "I think I'll be generous with you, Bates. I'll send your wife along. For company, of course." He threw back his head and laughed. "I'll give you two oars and because I always like to do right by a lady, you can have a bottle of water. A small bottle, mind you. Oh, and a pistol with one shot. You can decide if you're a gentleman and have the guts to kill her when her agony becomes unbearable in the sun with no food and the water gone, or if you'll be selfish and turn the weapon on yourself."

"Leave her out of it, Teach!" Hagen said roughly. "She—"

"Don't you tell me what to do! You're my prisoner," Teach cut in, his voice sharp. "Lower away, men. Get that dinghy afloat in a hurry so we can be on our way while the wind is strong. Unbind Hagen and put him over the side."

Turning to me, Teach removed his hat in a sweeping gesture and bowed from the waist; the knives and pistols in his belt clattered. "As for you, my pretty one," he said, "allow me to conduct you to the railing so you can join your husband. I trust your voyage to nowhere will be a pleasant one, Madame."

I cringed at the thought of his touching me and refused his outstretched hand. Shrugging, he responded with a menacing smile and promptly clamped his palm under my elbow, tightening his hold as I tried to move away from him. I didn't want to get into the dinghy. Eventually I would drown or die of thirst, but that seemed less awful than what lay ahead if I did not obey Teach. The agonizing treatment by Willie and

Tyson was too fresh for me to risk a repeat. It was easy to guess what lay in store for the other women if Teach handed them over to his crew.

The dinghy seemed very small and very far away as it bobbled on the surface of the ocean. Climbing down the ladder was like repeating a nightmare. I clutched the rough ropes, remembering that it was a mistake to look at the water, hearing the waves slap the hull of the *Solace*. Wind gusts shook the ladder and my hands curled around the rope. Just a few more rungs, I told myself desperately. Just two more . . . one more. . . . I almost fell on reaching the dinghy. Captain Hagen, standing in the tossing boat, caught my arm and steadied me. Once I was on the plank seat he took the oars, pulling the tiny boat away from the two ships.

"You can row harder than that, Bates," Teach yelled from the deck of the *Solace*, laughing as he spoke. "I'm five years older than you and I can row twice that fast and never lose my breath. Stretch your muscles, man! No doubt I'll meet you in Hell—but you'll get there first!"

A sob caught in my throat and I squeezed my eyes shut to keep tears from rolling down my face. When I finally opened them again it was to look back at the *Solace* and the *Queen Anne's Revenge*, both under sail now, dark silhouettes against the dazzling pink and amber sky. The fog had evaporated at last and the air was clear. The late afternoon sun was a semicircle of vivid light on the western horizon, its fiery rays streaking the sea with gold.

"Looking back is a mistake, Marley," Captain Hagen said quietly.

"Where else is there to look? It may be our last sight of any human beings."

"I don't think so. We probably aren't more than a hundred knots from the Carolina coast. With any luck, the current will carry us in, although I don't know where we'll land."

My eyes widened in astonishment. "You know this—and that awful pirate captain didn't? He thinks he's putting us out in the ocean to die!"

"Oh, he knew. He's too good a sailor not to know where he is."

"Now you're praising him? After what he did to you? To us?" I couldn't believe what I was hearing.

"Praising that scoundrel? I certainly am not! But he's an able navigator even if he is mean as hell."

"You know him? Before today, I mean?"

"He came from Bristol originally, just as I did. He likes that nickname of Blackbeard, but I won't call him that. I won't give him the satisfaction. He likes prancing around in those foppish clothes, threatening everybody but the Lord Himself, and he'll kill in a hurry to capture a ship. But if the crew he's robbing surrenders without too much of a brawl, he's apt to spare their lives. Knowing that, I couldn't stand by and watch my men being slaughtered uselessly when we were outnumbered and bound to lose. Teach was hellbent on getting the gunpowder and he'd have taken it no matter how many men died or if he'd had to sink the *Solace* in the process."

I'd heard of the pirate Blackbeard. Seamen who frequented the inn tavern at New Bedford spoke about him with awe. A shiver raced up my spine.

"Was he telling the truth when he said he had a wife on the *Queen Anne's Revenge?*" I asked. "What woman would want him?"

"There's no accounting for tastes, Marley. I suppose he had a wife. He's had plenty of them—gets his quartermaster to perform the marriage. When he's tired of that particular woman he drops her off at the next port, or if he's ashore he'll sail off and leave her there. He claims he's good to his women. Maybe he is, or maybe it's another of his lies."

"Does he lie often?"

Captain Hagen gave a harsh chuckle. "Almost every time he opens his mouth. He'll tell anybody who'll listen that he grew up an orphan, but he came from a decent family. He's educated, too. My family has been acquainted with his for two generations, but I doubt if people in Bristol know how he earns a living now. I don't believe he planned to kill me, just to make me sweat. He'll get his satisfaction out of my misery at losing the *Solace* and if we ever meet again, he'll taunt me about that."

"You didn't lose the ship, Captain Hagen," I said. "It was taken from you by a large force and after you defended it. You ought not to blame yourself for what happened."

His eyes darkened, smouldering as he squinted at the sunset. Wind whipped at the sea, splattering spray from the foaming waves into the dinghy. "I lost it all right," he muttered. "And don't keep calling me 'Captain' when I don't have a command. Can't you say 'Bates'? It's my name."

There was a fierce rebuke in his tone and the words stung until I realized they were not aimed at me as an individual. I happened to be the only person in hearing. He actually was chastizing himself. Not knowing what to say, I remained silent and he continued to row. It seemed to me we were moving in a line at right angles to the two ships which now were blurs in the distance.

"Marley," he rested his arms on the oars, giving me a long look, "what happened in my quarters? Did those thugs who brought you on deck harm you?"

"They—they raped me."

"My God! Both of them?"

Shivering at the memory, I nodded. His lips thinned out into a hard line. "Are you hurt much?" he asked.

"I'm all right." Waiting a minute, I said, "What about the other women?"

"They were treated as despicably as you were and then forced to board the *Revenge*. I don't doubt every man on that ship will have a time with them tonight. I hope the women can survive."

As brash as Prudence Hall was, she'd survive if anyone did. So would some of the others, but not all. "Did you see Nellie Matthews?" I asked.

"Only a glimpse of her. After Teach discovered there were women passengers I told him they were heading for Charles Town. I'd like to think he'll drop them off there because I don't imagine he'll want to drag them all the way to New Providence. That many more mouths to feed and that many more ways to divide the water, not to mention taking the crew's thoughts off their work. By the time he passes Charles Town his crew should have satisfied their lust for the time being."

"If they're allowed to go ashore at Charles Town, will McGregor still be in charge of them?" I asked unsteadily. "Will they have to marry the men he tells them to marry?"

"I don't know if McGregor is dead or alive. Jarvis is dead. So is Hutchins. I guess by now Roark is; both his legs were lopped off by a cutlass. If he doesn't bleed to death they'll kick him into the sea to be rid of him."

I remembered my first night on board the *Solace* when Roark led me to the Captain's cabin and helped me into the hammock. Bates Hagen's clipped manner of speaking must have been to hide how he felt about the deaths of his men. For a moment, he seemed a stranger to me.

I stole a look at him. There was almost nothing to

remind me of the man who had kissed me lovingly hours before. This man whose shoulder muscles rippled under his torn shirt as he swung the oars back and forth in the dinghy had aged years since then. His eyes were troubled and his mouth was too stern. I had survived a terrible day and I didn't doubt Bates Hagen had been through physical pain in the fighting, but he was suffering now in the anguish of losing his ship and knowing he had been unable to stop the pirates from their bloody carnage. My heart went out to him, but I didn't know what to do or say to help.

He settled the matter with a terse order to me. "Don't waste your strength talking too much, Marley. That will just keep your throat dry and we have to stretch the drinking water as much as we can. Don't lick your lips any more, either. I know the salt bothers you and your skin may crack because of it, but licking your lips uses up saliva and puts salt on your tongue. That just makes you more thirsty. We'll each take a sip of water later on tonight."

I opened my mouth to answer him, closing it and nodding instead. But there was one more question I had to ask. "Do you honestly think we'll make it to land, Captain Hagen?"

"I'm going to have to call you Miss Lancaster if you refuse to use my first name."

I drew a long breath. "Bates . . ."

"That's better." He actually smiled. "Yes, I think we'll reach land. Now, no more talk for the time being."

Chapter 8

AFTER DARK I slept a little, lying cramped on the bottom of the dinghy, the night air chilling my bones. Bates had announced we would take turns sleeping; one of us should be awake at all times to watch for passing ships.

"Then we might be rescued?" I asked, hope making my voice unnaturally shrill.

"It's unlikely until day. A ship's lookout won't spot us in the dark, but if we see a vessel on the horizon we'll have time to get out of its path—with luck." The final two words were spoken half under his breath. "Lie down, Marley. It won't be the most comfortable bed in the world, but you'll feel better for some rest. I'll wake you around midnight."

"How will you know the time without an hour glass?"

"By the movement of the stars." He uncorked the flat green bottle of water, holding it out to me. "Only one sip, mind you," he ordered. "Don't swallow it immediately. Swish it about in your mouth and hold it against your tongue as long as you can and then let it trickle down your throat as slowly as possible. That will make you feel you've had a bit more than one taste."

I did as he ordered, savoring the partial relief from thirst. The water disappeared from my mouth as if it soaked into my dry flesh; there was never a sensation of swallowing.

The bottom of the dinghy was wet from sea spray. Although I was half out of the wind, the damp cold was raw. I doubted I could get comfortable enough to doze off, but fatigue must have taken care of that for after a time I slept, dreaming fitfully. After what appeared to be only minutes I felt a hand on my shoulder. Bates was shaking me gently.

"Think you can stand watch for a while?" he asked.

I yawned, dreading to move. "Is it midnight yet?"

"Long past midnight. I didn't have the heart to rouse you sooner. Call me at sunup, which should be in about three hours. Or call me earlier if you sight a sail. Marley, if you find you're having trouble staying awake, pinch your thighs or flex your fingers hard. Sometimes that helps."

We changed places and from his steady breathing I decided he must have gone to sleep immediately. I lifted my skirt, pulling the tattered mauve material around my shoulders, tucking my petticoat under my knees and hugging my arms to my body in the hope of finding some warmth.

The sea was calmer than it had been at dusk with long swells replacing the choppy white-capped waves. Above me a billion stars blinked and glittered in the black heavens. I felt very small, very forlorn. When I was a little girl my mother used to say, "God will take care of us no matter what happens, Marley." Would He? I had my doubts as I looked up at the sky. God had not taken care of my mother when she was wrenched from her home in London and from the man she loved. Coming to the Colonies meant hard, hard work and very little pleasure for her. God hadn't protected Jarvis. Or Roark. No Divine Presence stopped Willie and Tyson from ravaging me or kept McGregor from taking my virginity.

I was determined not to think about those matters, reminding myself instead that I was fortunate to have inherited an independent streak and that my mother also had endowed me with the capacity to love, a trait obviously not given to everyone. Blackbeard lacked it. So did McGregor. My mother had survived her ordeal—and I meant to survive mine. Suddenly, I wanted my mother so much that my throat closed up and an ache filled my chest. I wanted to be able to put my head in her lap as I'd done when I was small and to feel her fingers smoothing my hair away from my forehead. With a soft word and a hug she had been able to give me peace then, and although I had a woman's body now, I needed that sense of security.

I caught myself sharply, sitting very erect. *I'd almost dozed off!*

Gripping my thighs with numb fingers, I pinched the flesh until burning pains zigzagged into both legs, and at the same time, I was scanning the horizon in every direction. No ships were in view. There was nothing but the water, the sky and the stars. Bates Hagen was correct. Pinching got rid of the sleepiness.

At daybreak when I awakened Bates we each had another sip of water. My stomach was pulsating with hunger. To avoid thinking about it, I did arithmetic sums in my mind. Two and two equal four; four and four equal eight; eight and eight equal sixteen. My mother had drilled numbers into me so that I would never forget them.

The dawn was surprisingly misty after such a starry night, but once the sun was in full view most of the dampness left the air and I could feel warmth return-ing. It became unpleasantly hot as the morning wore on. Without protection from the sun, our heads and shoulders were baked. My swollen tongue pressed against the dry roof of my mouth. If the weather was so miserably hot in May, I didn't know if I wanted to live in the South. July and August would be worse. Still, I knew I could make myself satisfied to live anywhere as long as it was on solid ground.

The dinghy drifted. I couldn't decide if Bates had stopped rowing to save his strength or if he considered the effort futile.

"Marley," his voice cut into the silence, "look to the west. That's to your left. What do you see?"

He was pointing. Shading my eyes with one hand, I followed the direction of his forefinger.

"Birds!" I gasped.

"Seagulls."

"Does that mean we're near land?"

"I expect so."

Wild relief enveloped me and I laughed out loud. Bates smiled, too. It wasn't the glowing grin I remembered on the *Solace*, but the two tiny vertical lines between his eyebrows eased as his lips curved. I watched the gulls, seeing one bird dip to the surface of the water and rise into the air with its wings spread wide. Bates grabbed the oars and began to row, sweat shining on his forehead and dripping to his chin where a night's growth of whiskers put a honey-colored fuzz across his jaws.

It was midafternoon before green smudges were visible on the horizon. Vegetation, Bates remarked, resting his arms on the oars as he spoke.

"The tide's going in and the current will carry us," he added. "We're in luck to move with the flow."

As the sun went down the wind became stiffer and the green blur definitely resembled trees, although they were lower and squatter than the huge oaks and elms I knew in New Bedford. We were approaching a broad sandy beach dotted with driftwood and dunes and trees in the distance. I searched the landscape for a house or a wisp of smoke, but there was no sign of life except the gulls who soared and screeched.

Darkness was falling when one of the oars touched bottom. It was Bates' turn to laugh out loud. He yanked his boots off, taking out the knife which was still in the metal sheathe and sticking it into his belt next to the pistol. I had forgotten that knife. It seemed centuries since I'd stood in the Captain's quarters on the *Solace* and seen Bates Hagen arm himself for the inevitable fight.

Barefooted, he jumped into the ocean and grasped the side of the dinghy, pulling it toward land.

"I'll help," I said, removing my shoes and easing over the opposite side.

I was thigh-deep in water and the Atlantic was cold to my feet and legs, but it was a lovely coolness after the burning heat. My toes dug into the sandy earth. We tugged the dinghy to shore and across the wet beach to a dry spot beyond the water line, both of us panting as we collapsed beside it. The exertion and the lack of food and water and rest had been exhausting.

The sand was very white and finely pulverized, still warm from the sun. I picked up a handful, letting the grains slide through my fingers. Then I lay back, stretching my arms over my head, thankful to be on a surface which didn't toss under me. A few stars were visible against the darkening sky, the heavens a rich blue-black. The seagulls had disappeared and the only sound came from the foaming and splashing waves.

"I think I could sleep forever," I murmured.

"Both of us could use some rest. It's too near night to forage for something to eat. I don't know what might be behind those trees, but I'll give it a go in the morning."

"Bates," apprehension showed in my voice, "could Indians be hiding in the woods past the dunes?"

"If anybody was nearby and had seen us—one small dinghy with only two people and one of them a woman and no larger ship anchored off shore—we'd be surrounded by now. Don't worry about animals, either. There may be deer and rabbits, but they aren't flesh-eating creatures. I doubt if snakes would come in this direction toward the sea. They'd be more inclined to head for the woods and the marshes."

"Snakes—Ugh!"

"I didn't mean to alarm you, Marley."

He reached into the dinghy for the water bottle. Despite the pirate's generosity and our careful sipping, now only a scant three inches of liquid remained. "Just one swig," Bates reminded as he handed the bottle over. It was all I could do not to gulp every drop. As before, I held the sip in my mouth as long as I could, rolling it under my tongue.

"Do you know where we are?" I asked.

"On the northern coast of Carolina, but I don't know exactly where. These outer banks are a sandbar with more water on the other side separating the banks from the continent. If we don't find any settlers here, we'll be sure to reach them once we're further inland. I'd like to think we're near enough Bath Town to take refuge there. If that's the case, we shouldn't have any trouble getting passage out because plenty of ships sail into Bath Town for fresh water and food or to make repairs."

What he said could be true, I reflected silently, or he could be trying to calm my fears. I shivered involuntarily, but Bates was too busy recorking the bottle and returning it to the dinghy to notice.

He lay down beside me, three feet of space between us, and I would have given anything if he'd put his arms around me or if he had just held my hand for a little while. The touch of another human being would have been more comforting than all the talk in the world. But he did nothing.

Turning on my side toward him, I saw that he was on his back, his feet spread wide with one hand resting across his stomach and the other arm crooked under his head. His lips were parted ever so slightly and his chest moved rhythmically with the steady, silent breathing.

I had never known anyone who could doze off so quickly. Probably, I mused, it resulted from all those years at sea with four hours on watch and four off so that sleep was taken in snatches. Pulling my feet up under my skirt, I closed my eyes and yawned, knowing I, too, would be asleep soon.

Chapter 9

IT WAS WELL into the morning when I awakened, the sun high and the air warm despite a sea breeze. I turned over, expecting to see Bates—and finding nobody. Panic rippled over me and I jumped up, looking in every direction.

"Bates!" my voice was so hoarse the sound could not have carried far.

The only answer was the raucous cawing of the gulls and the steady roll of the surf. No footprints were visible to show where he had gone. The wind was already pushing sand over the shallow imprint of his body beside me. Over the spot where I'd slept, too.

He's left me, I thought desperately. *Oh, God* . . .

Bates wouldn't. I could not actually believe he'd do such a thing. Yet thinking about the possibility turned the panic into pure terror. I remembered he had commented that the pirates might get rid of the women eventually since that would mean fewer ways to divide the water supply. Perhaps pirates weren't the only men to reason like that. If Bates went alone—without me—he could move faster and the water would last twice as long.

The dinghy was in the spot where we had beached it. So he'd left on foot! I peered over the side of the boat. The oars were on the bottom, but the water bottle was missing.

He really had abandoned me. I clutched the side of that small boat and tried to think. Above the beach the dunes shimmered and shifted in the sunlight, behind me the Atlantic stretched to eternity. From where I stood on the beach the trees Bates and I had seen when we were afloat in the ocean weren't visible, but I knew they lay past the sand hills and I had to get to them. I couldn't remain where I was and do nothing. The sand would swirl over me as it had done over everything on that barren beach but a few pieces of driftwood and some shells—and they would be covered before long.

Slogging up the dune, I slipped backward a foot in the soft sand for every three steps forward. Halfway to the top the scent of food cooking hit my nostrils. It was my imagination, of course. I had heard that hunger did weird things to people. In an involuntary action my tongue flicked across my salt-caked lips and the taste burned my mouth, making my thirst even more unbearable.

Glancing ahead, I saw Bates coming over the top of the dune carrying the green water bottle in his left hand. He paused, grinning at me as he'd done so many times on the deck of the *Solace*. It was a mirage! Seeing him had to be wishful thinking born of aloneness and fear mixed with the dazzling reflection of the sun on the white sand.

But I blinked and lifted my head to look again. He was moving toward me, the breeze whipping his hair and his torn shirt. *He was real!* A strangled sound came from my throat and suddenly, unexpectedly, I began to sob.

"Marley, don't!" he called. "It's all right." He was scrambling down the dune. I stayed where I was, both my hands pressed to my face. There were no tears in my eyes. My body must have been too drained of fluid to put moisture on my lashes, but the sobs wracked me until I felt Bates' arms circle my waist. I leaned against him and pushed my forehead into his shoulder until the wild weeping ended.

"Which do you want first?" he asked. "All the water you can drink? Or breakfast?"

"D-Don't tease m-me. I—I thought you'd g-gone."

"Without you? I wouldn't. Here—" He raised the water bottle, removing the cork with his teeth. "Drink every drop you want, Marley. It's fresh and there's plenty more where this came from. I was bringing it to you."

The bottle was full, the water sweet and clear in contrast to the brownish liquid Blackbeard had given us from the ship. Almost as a reflex I held the first mouthful against my tongue and let it slide slowly down my throat, but then I gulped hungrily, swallowing so fast a trickle came from the corner of my mouth and dripped off my chin. Bates, chuckling, caught the droplets with his fingers.

"I figured with as much greenery as showed on the far side of these dunes that fresh water would have to be nearby and I was correct," he said. "I found a spring. Come on with me and I'll show you."

He took my hand and we continued the climb together. I no longer slipped backward with every third step. The water had relieved part of my weak sensation, but my real strength came from being with Bates. When we reached the crest of the ridge, a plain of coarse gray sand dotted with patches of scraggly grass lay before us. Some forty feet beyond was a green forest. These woods were a thicket of tall bushes with twisted branches and tiny, glossy leaves. All of it was so dense no one could have walked through that growth without hacking out a path.

I took in the landscape with one sweeping glance, but what I really saw was the fire and the meat. The smell of cooking food had not been my imagination, after all. Wood burned in a shallow hole which Bates had made in the sand and lined with large shells. Forked logs of driftwood were placed on either side of the fire, and another strip of wood braced into the pronged forks held two small fowls, the meat an amber brown. As I watched, a few drops of fat fell to the fire, spluttering and sizzling in the hot ashes.

"I caught a seagull," Bates explained. "It was in a flock on the beach. I walked amidst them and grabbed it. Another bird had a broken wing and couldn't fly, so I got that one too."

"How did you start the fire?" I asked wonderingly.

"With the flint from the pistol. It wasn't too hard to get a spark and ignite some dry grass and wood chips. The driftwood is as dry as parchment. Do you want more water before we eat?"

"Yes," I smiled. "I don't think I'll ever get enough water."

The spring was nearby, water gurgling from the earth into a miniature pool no wider than a well bucket, its sides covered with green moss. I lay on the ground on my stomach with my face over the water, drinking as much as I wanted before scooping up handfuls to splash on my face and neck. Bates watched me, standing three or four feet away. I could feel his eyes on me and finally I stood up, shaking water from my hair and swinging my hands to and fro to dry them.

"It's heaven," I said.

"I know. You can come back to the spring after we eat."

We sat on the sand. With his knife Bates divided each gull in half. The meat was tough and stringy, but that didn't matter. I would have welcomed anything.

"Eat slowly," he cautioned. "Your belly has been without food and if you gobble too fast, like as not you'll vomit."

I wanted to make each bite last forever. Neither of us spoke until all the meat was consumed and we'd gnawed the tiny bones. Holding up my greasy fingers, I told him I was going to wash.

"If you'll turn your back, I'll bathe my entire body," I added.

"And if I won't turn my back?" There was a bantering note in his tone.

I tossed my head in a saucy manner. "I thought you were a gentleman, Bates Hagen!"

"It depends entirely on the circumstances."

"That's a letdown." My voice mimicked his in the same light way. "I thought the captain of a ship was always a gentleman."

It was the wrong comment for me to make, or perhaps my reference to his ship would have brought the same reaction from him. His mouth hardened and a smouldering expression of controlled anger came into his face, the same look I'd seen when he demanded that I no longer call him "Captain" since he'd lost the *Solace*. My off-handed remark must have stirred something he was trying to ignore. And besides, what I said was not true. Blackbeard had been a scoundrel instead of a gentleman and I did not doubt there were other sea captains who could be crude if not actually evil.

"I won't spy on you, Marley," Bates said gruffly. "That's a promise."

"I didn't mean—"

"Be quick about your bathing," he interrupted. "We're not more than a mile from what I believe is Ocracoke Inlet. If we can make that we'll be into Pamlico Sound and away from the ocean. Pamlico will take us to Bath Town."

"Will we be there by tonight?"

"Probably not, Marley, but with luck we may make it by tomorrow night. Rowing will be easier once we're in the Sound."

He threw sand on the fire before walking a short distance to wait with his back toward me. Keeping my eyes on him, I went to the spring and hesitated only briefly before removing my dress. If he whirled around in spite of his promise, I could hurl sand in his eyes, but I vowed to have my bath, such as it was. Even without soap or a towel or privacy from a man's gaze, the thought of being clean was far more enticing than worrying about Bates' taking a peek.

Lifting my petticoat, I pulled it over my head and crouched naked by the spring, splattering my entire body again and again until I was completely wet. The wind dried me and the streaks of salt disappeared from my skin. Even the taste of salt was out of my mouth.

"Are you almost finished?" Bates called without moving.

"Almost." I put on my petticoat, wishing there was time to wash it and my dress.

"We'd best be on our way, Marley. The current is right to take us toward the inlet."

He had not looked my direction. I got into the dress and said I was ready, waiting while he had a final drink from the spring and filled the green bottle. He washed his knife and dried it on the seat of his trousers before returning it to the sheathe in his belt, never glancing at me once.

The midday sun was scorching as we got the dinghy into the Atlantic. Bates rowed hard, following the shore line, and I would not have realized when we rounded a point of land and entered Pamlico Sound if he hadn't commented that we were passing Ocracoke Inlet. Soon the waves appeared smaller and we no longer moved parallel to the coast, but headed northwest across the Sound. The water was incredibly blue. I put my hand over the side of the boat, licking one finger and promptly making a face.

"It's still salty," I mumbled in a disgusted way.

"It will be for some time. Sea water comes in with each tide."

Land was visible on the horizon a long way off. Bates rested on the oars, allowing the current to carry us forward. His eyes were on me now, lingering on my hair and mouth, sliding slowly across my breasts and the length of my body. He said nothing, but somehow I could feel his approval. I hoped I looked as good as I felt.

"Do you think we'll get to shore by night?" I asked.

"Would you rather remain on the water, Marley?"

My chin came up and I cringed at the memory of that miserable sleep in the dinghy after we left the *Solace*. "I most certainly would not," I came back firmly.

Bates flashed a quick smile and resumed rowing. He had been teasing me again, although I hadn't realized it at first. That was an indication he must feel better about our circumstances. Twenty-four hours earlier he could barely talk, much less joke.

"I'll give you my word we'll sleep on land tonight, although it may be pitch dark before we get ashore," he said. "That will give us a haven and a chance to look for something to eat in the morning—if we're lucky."

"If we're lucky," I swallowed a sigh. "If . . . if . . . if . . ."

"Don't feel defeated. You've been damned great about all of this. Most women would have bawled or screamed from the instant Teach put them over the side and I'm forever grateful to you for not doing either."

"You're forgetting I cried this morning."

"That was more my fault than yours. I never meant to frighten you. I wanted to be able to give you a full bottle of fresh water as soon as you were awake—and I needed a drink myself. It never occurred to me you might think I'd left you."

The sun went down, the sky glowing with bright pinks and crimsons which reflected on the surface of the water until the colors faded into a pearlish gray-blue. A thin new moon, just a wisp of light, appeared and a gentle breeze blew my hair across my cheeks, the wind taking the last traces of the day's heat so that the air was deliciously cool.

"Another half hour of rowing," Bates said.

We were rapidly nearing land and I could not tear my eyes away from the strange sight. The sandy beach on the water's edge was narrow with scattered clumps of tall grass and salt-stunted bushes. Behind that were the unbelievable trees which seemed to be growing in black water instead of soil. Those trees were huge, the trunks gnarled and the branches filled with something soft and gray that blew silently without falling and that clung like newly carded wool.

"What is it?" I asked.

"The stuff on the trees? It's called Spanish moss and it flourishes on the coast from here South. It's all over the area. Likes the salt air and the dampness, I suppose. The mild winters, too. You can tell there's a bog where the trees are, but the tide from the Sound has peaked and the beach is still dry. We'll be all right."

When his oar scraped bottom, Bates and I got into the water to guide the dinghy ashore as we'd done the previous night. Darkness had set in, the moon paler than before although now stars filled the sky. The trees were bigger and more eerie as we neared them. A ground fog swirled through the marsh, making the trees appear to float; the moss added a ghostly touch. Insects buzzed and hummed, a bird or tiny animal called and shrieked.

"Tired, Marley?" Bates asked.

"A little. But not as tired as I was last night. The water and the food helped."

He uncorked the bottle and after I had my swallow, he took one. We stretched out near the dinghy. Suddenly, a crackling noise came from behind us, from the trees.

"What was that?" I whispered hoarsely, sitting up. "Indians?"

"I doubt it. I'm told you only worry about Indians when you hear nothing at all. They're that silent when they want to be. The woods are always full of night noises. Some animals sleep all day and roam after dark, but I suspect the creatures we're hearing would rather stay in the marsh than come to dry land where we are."

He meant to be reassuring, but I was nervous and tense. Easing down once more, my body felt rigid. The sand was unbearable. I looked up at the stars, trying to count the brightest ones to force myself to think of other things and finally I gave up.

"I wonder if I'll ever sleep in a real bed again," I mused aloud. "I'd love to lie on clean sheets which smelled like sunshine and were smooth to my skin. Not gritty like this sand." My voice ached with longing. I hadn't intended to sound pitiful, but the emotion was strong and Bates apparently realized it for his hand found mine and he fitted his fingers over my palm.

"Sure you will, Marley," he answered. "We both will. We've done the hardest part; we're out of the sea now. When we move on tomorrow, we'll be out of the Sound and into the Pamlico River. We'll have land in sight on both sides all the way to Bath Town."

A tingle shot up my arm from the gentle pressure of his fingers. I didn't pull free and he made no move to let my hand loose. Water rippled onto the shore in a muted rhythm. The hum of insects grew duller until it was nearly gone. The stars glowed and glistened over us. I thought Bates might have fallen asleep, but I wasn't sure. I closed my eyes, forcing myself to relax. It was impossible to do with his warm hand on mine.

After a little while he turned on his side, facing me, still holding my hand but putting his other arm over my waist. That sent the tingle from my arm all the way through my body.

"Marley . . ."

His voice was so low I might have thought I was dreaming if it had not been for his arm resting just under my breasts.

"Yes," I murmured.

"Are you asleep?"

"No . . . are you?"

"No." He waited a long minute, breathing deeply. "I want to make love to you, Marley. But only if you'll be pleased. I'm not going to push myself on you."

The nearness of him forced my heart to beat faster than normal. *If I would be pleased.* . . . Was this how a decent man approached a woman? Asking? Even pleading slightly?

I didn't know. The three men who had taken me had not asked. They demanded and were brutal in their hurting assaults. My virginity was gone. Whatever reasons I'd had for keeping it no longer mattered. Having Bates possess my body could not be more painful and humiliating than what McGregor and the two pirates had done.

I remembered the way Bates kissed me just before
the fight with the pirates. The sweetness of that kiss had
been intoxicating. Besides, I reminded myself, I owed
him a debt. He could have dumped me into the Atlantic
and rowed away. Or left me on the beach. Or consumed all the water in the bottle when we were at sea.
Or eaten both of those birds without sharing the
life-saving food.

"Marley, for God's sake!" he burst out. "If you find
me repulsive, say it!"

"Oh, no!"

"What does that mean?"

What could I say when my head was spinning and
strange new fires were beginning to burn in my body? I
fought for words.

"Marley . . . ?"

"I don't find you repulsive," I whispered. "Not
ever."

His hand tightened on my waist. "Do you want me,
Marley?"

The idea of repaying a debt to him vanished. I did
want him. I wanted him so much I could think of
nothing else. Turning toward him, I touched his cheek,
feeling the rough stubble of beard, inching my hand
toward his mouth. He opened his lips so his tongue
could taste my fingers.

"Yes, I want you," I answered softly.

Bates slid an arm under my shoulders and raised
himself to lean over me, his other arm still circling my
body. His mouth was tantalizingly gentle and at first he
barely brushed his lips against mine, but the kiss
deepened until I was aflame with sensations I'd never
known before. My hands locked at the back of his neck
while his mouth moved to my cheeks, my forehead,
coming back to my lips with his tongue touching mine.

He kissed my throat and I trembled as he pulled the

bodice of my dress aside and began to kiss my breasts. This person with him did not seem to be me, Marley Lancaster. It had to be somebody else. I was floating rather than lying on the sand on a remote beach in the Colony of Carolina. The heat which blazed inside my body was turning my blood to molten lava.

I strained closer to him, never wanting him to stop the languorous caresses. He lifted my skirts and eased my legs apart, stroking my thighs tenderly before finally lowering his body on mine. I forgot about McGregor and the terrible men from the *Revenge*, forgot about the sand and being hungry. The past and the future no longer existed. There was only the now with Bates and me alone in the star-studded universe. I dug my fingers into his back, my body rising and falling with his.

Chapter 10

THE DINGHY SLID around a bend in the Pamlico River early in the afternoon. I caught my breath at the sight of another human being. The man was on a low bluff three or four feet higher than the water. He sat on a fallen log with his back against the tree stump, a wide-brimmed hat pulled low over his eyes so that his face was half hidden. His bare feet were extended, a fishing pole braced between his knees.

"Bates, look!" I sang out, pointing.

At that instant the man either spotted us or he heard my voice, for he gave a yell. Bates, his mouth curving into a broad smile, hollered and began to row harder toward shore. The man was already scurrying to the water's edge to meet us.

The day had seemed endless as the dinghy glided along. The river was no longer bright blue but a muddy grayish brown under a dark sky. For the first time since we left the *Solace*, a hint of rain was in the air. I found the scenery monotonous. The land was flat and the river banks edged with sandy strips or marsh grass, the inevitable woods in the background. Tree limbs drooped with masses of hanging moss. The growth was strangely attractive, but the silent, swaying, gray masses gave me a spooky feeling.

When I awoke that morning Bates had a driftwood fire going. He was cooking a fish which he said he speared with his knife.

"I waded into the water to get it and had the devil of a time," he went on. "There were plenty of fish, but they moved in a hurry."

This time he was cooking over embers. He held out a charred piece of fish; the white flesh was thick and moist inside. Even the taste of wood ash couldn't kill the flavor.

"I haven't been able to find any fresh water here," he said.

I took another bite of fish, chewing slowly to make it last longer. "That won't matter if we reach Bath Town tonight, Bates," I answered.

"Well, I'm not taking any chances. We'll continue to ration what's left in the bottle."

As soon as we finished eating we pushed the dinghy into the Sound. Bates hadn't referred to our lovemaking or even given me more than a casual look. That was surprising! It was uppermost in my mind. I was disappointed. I had expected to be kissed awake and then cuddled, maybe to be loved passionately again, and when he caressed me I was ready to tumble into his arms. There were no kisses or caresses. If he had a desire for me in the daylight, there was no indication.

Without the sun it was cooler and in the calm water, rowing didn't seem to be much exertion for him. Studying his face with secret glances, I longed to run my fingers through the mass of light brown hair which curled about his face. I wanted to feel the muscles in his back as he moved the oars. We were quiet for the most part—until we saw the man. I'd discovered Bates was right about talking. Conversation helped my spirits and made the time pass a little quicker, but it drained my mouth of its scant saliva.

As we neared shore I had a good look at the stranger. He was shorter than Bates, sturdily built with powerful shoulders and hair that was almost white. His features didn't seem old enough for that. I couldn't guess his age. Thirty-five, perhaps. No older than forty, because he moved with the nimbleness of a young man when he scrambled down the river bank and waded out to meet us.

His face was a triangle, the wide forehead sloping to a narrow chin, a scar going from his left ear across his cheek to his mouth. The mark could have come from a knife; the line was thin and only slightly raised, but it pulled the corner of his upper lip enough to make a perpetual smile. His brown leather breeches were fringed at the bottoms, and he wore a loose collarless shirt of brown homespun.

"You folks having a boat ride or you been shipwrecked?" He grasped the side of the dinghy and guided us to land.

"Neither," Bates said. "We had an encounter with some pirates at sea. You're a mighty welcome sight, Mister. You're the first person we've seen since we got into this dinghy."

"The name is Josh Harding. I'll be right proud to have you and your missus stop with us."

I sucked my breath in, waiting to hear Bates explain that we were not married. That didn't happen.

"We would be pleased," Bates answered. "I'm Bates Hagen, Captain of the *Solace* out of the Colony of Massachusetts. We could use some food and water. A bar of soap, too."

"Pirates, huh." The man nodded and shoved his hat to the back of his head. "Do you know which pirates? These waters are full of them most of the time."

Bates' lip curled. "Teach."

"The *Queen Anne's Revenge?*"

Bates nodded and Harding glanced toward me. "I'm surprised that old lecher would let a pretty lady escape. Blackbeard's a mean 'un, all right. He usually wants every woman he sees for himself along with any booty to be plundered."

"He had a new wife on board the *Revenge*—at least that's what he said," Bates came back. "What he wanted was my cargo and he got it. Got the ship and the crew—those of my men who survived."

The three of us climbed the sandy bluff, Harding leading the way down a path through the woods. To my relief we were on dry soil. The trees were so thick their branches entwined over us, shutting out the sky and putting us in a shadowed light. The gray moss was everywhere. I touched some, finding it like a vine with short tendrils, airy and porous though not as soft as it appeared.

Our walk couldn't have taken more than five minutes when we came to a clearing with a log house. Smoke, pale and misty, rose from the chimney. A woman stood in the yard.

"We've got ourselves some company, Dorcas," Harding said, introducing us as "Captain and Mrs. Hagen." Once again Bates failed to explain that I was not his wife. My face felt hot from blushing.

Dorcas Harding was thin and gaunt. Her coarse black hair was braided and pulled away from her face, the plaits wound tightly around her head and held in place with a comb made of metal, its intricate design encrusted with gleaming red gems. Her skin, a pale coppery color, was stretched taut over her bony face.

She had the blackest eyes I'd ever seen, eyes devoid of expression. It was impossible to know if she was happy to see us or irritated or indifferent.

She nodded and so did I. I found it difficult to tear my gaze from the startling clothes she wore in that wilderness. Her dress—badly tattered—was a fancy ball gown of turquoise blue silk with tiny silk buttons extending from the neck to the waist, the bodice made with a low vee filled in with blue embroidery on white silk. It must have been exquisitely beautiful once, but now the full skirt was stained and spotted, the skirt hem was torn and loose threads dangled against her bare feet.

Bates was astonished at the sight of her, too. I could tell by the way his eyebrows lifted. He bowed and said he was glad to make her acquaintance, adding, "Mrs. Harding." Her husband promptly said, "She's Dorcas and I'm Josh. We don't hold much with titles hereabouts."

Bates' reply gave our first names, and it dawned on me I must look just as ragged and filthy as Dorcas. My mauve dress had faded gray and was stiff with dried salt water.

"Sit if you want," she spoke for the first time. Her voice was curiously toneless.

"We need water more than rest," Bates replied. "And food if you have any to spare."

"Aye, we do. Come in the house," Josh said. "A swig of rum might not do you any harm."

The thought of rum in my empty stomach sickened me. Bates remarked quickly that we had eaten so little the past three days he didn't believe we should touch spirits until we had food in our bodies.

The log house contained one small room with a sod floor. It was sparsely furnished: a pine board bed in the back corner, several wooden chests against the wall and in the center a table with two plank benches. A wooden bucket of water on the table held a strange dipper which seemed to be fashioned from the leg bone of an animal and tied by a leather thong to a large round shell. Bates and I drank eagerly. The fire was low and Josh promptly threw a new log on it. The wood blazed up, intensifying the odors from a black pot on the hearth.

"Rabbit stew," Dorcas said. She filled two bowls and put them before Bates and me. There was bread made from coarsely ground cornmeal, the pones so dry they crumbled. When I saw Bates mash his bread into the stew gravy, I did the same with mine, eating it with a wooden spoon.

"So it was Teach," Josh muttered. "Did you ever see him before he attacked you?"

"Yes." Bates clipped the word out. "I knew him."

"Humph, so did I." Josh made a snorting sound deep in his throat. "Sailed with the bastard once and once was enough."

"You're a sailor?" Bates asked.

"For nigh to twenty years I was. But I couldn't take Blackbeard's bloody ways and never knowing when his temper would explode and he might turn on me. Once I saw him slice off the quartermaster's ear for no reason except that he'd honed that big cutlass of his and wanted to see if the blade was sharp."

I shuddered, believing Josh was telling the truth. I could believe anything about the pirate.

"I never minded a fair fight," Josh went on. "But Teach is something else. I only sailed with him on one voyage. He was first mate on the *Windblown Lady* when I signed on and I didn't linger on that sloop long. When we put into the harbor at New Providence Island I'd had my fill of Teach. A few months later when I was heading north on another ship, we hit heavy seas off

Hatteras and went down. I made it to shore holding to a piece of the mizzenmast. She—" he nodded to Dorcas, "found me half dead on the beach and took me in."

"How long ago was that?" Bates inquired.

"Five years, give or take a month." The scar on his forehead twitched, but Josh obviously was enjoying talking. "Dorcas needed a man since she was alone and I figured I was ready to quit the sea and stay on land for a spell and take myself a woman." He shrugged his shoulders. "It's not bad here. When sloops come into the Sound I make some money because I was a ship's carpenter and I haven't forgotten how to use tools. Sometimes I get paid in goods instead of gold, which is all right by me. A barrel of rum or a keg of sugar comes in right handy and a captain will part with those if supplies are plentiful."

His eyes circled the room. "It's how Dorcas got her comb and her dress," he said with an air of pride. "I laid new floor planking on the deck of Stede Bonnet's brigantine and he gave me a chest of finery along with some other items. If your missus needs a change of clothes, she's welcome to help herself."

"Both of us need clothes," Bates told him. "We don't have anything except what we're wearing."

Dorcas crossed the room to a chest, swinging the heavy lid open to reveal a mass of gowns. The sight dazzled me. I'd never seen so much elegant clothing at one time in my entire life. The six dresses she took out were a rainbow of colors, all of them made from rich cloth and lavishly trimmed. In the bottom of the chest were nine petticoats, some plain and others ruffled and laced.

"Take your pick," Josh looked at me and immediately glanced at Bates, mumbling, "I like the way a woman glows when she examines finery."

The two men chuckled as if they shared a private

joke. I paid no attention to them, more engrossed in holding the dresses up. After a full inspection of each one, I chose a rosy brocade which had dozens of tiny tucks across the bodice, the stitches so small they were invisible. The sleeves were edged with ecru lace and a lace frill bordered the low, square neck. The dress might be slightly large, but I didn't think it would be too big to be used. Because I felt guilty about accepting such a fabulous garment when I had no money and nothing to give in return, I selected the plainest petticoat.

"Do you know who these things belonged to?" I asked.

Josh pursed his lips. "Bonnet must have got them off a ship he captured and whoever had them was rich. That's real China silk. Like as not the chest they were in belonged to a passenger whose luck ran out."

So they were stolen. I thought about Blackbeard, clasping my hands together to keep them from shaking.

"Is this Bonnet a pirate?" I asked, not relishing the idea of using the clothing of some poor woman who might have been tortured or raped or killed at sea. At least the French lady whose belongings were in Seneca Irving's house had died a natural death.

A grin split Josh's face. "Well, you might say Stede Bonnet's a pirate." Bates joined in the laughter.

I said nothing and neither did Dorcas.

"Nobody likes the English trade laws," Josh added, "and smuggling's no sin as I see it. Pirating's not, either, if you aren't cruel about it. People in Bath Town would lack for just about everything except cornmeal and a slab of pork if pirate sloops didn't come into the harbor there and nobody questions where the goods come from." His eyes slid the full length of my body before returning to my face. "So you take your new dress and dike yourself out, pretty as you please,

Marley. A pretty lass always deserves to have pretty clothes to my way of thinking."

"Marley's a great one for bathing," Bates grinned. "She probably wants to wash first."

It was embarrassing to talk about a bath in front of strangers, but I could have hugged Bates on the spot for doing it. Josh told Dorcas to take me to the creek. She got a bar of dark soap and a rough homespun towel from the shelf over the bed, motioning for me to follow her outside.

She was as quiet as Josh was talkative. Dorcas walked soundlessly on bare feet through the brown pine needles which cushioned the path. I must have stepped on every twig and stick, every footstep crackled. Nothing had been mentioned about heating the water and I didn't ask for that. The new dress and petticoat were over my arm. How strange that I'd always dreamed of owning a pink brocade gown and now that I actually had one, the lovely garment wouldn't be worn in a drawing room but in a log house, and it would soon become as faded and soiled as Dorcas' blue silk.

The sky remained overcast and there was a slight chill in the air. I heard the creek before we reached it, water rushing softly against stones. Where Dorcas stopped the stream was barely ten feet wide, clear enough to see the sand and pebbles on the bottom. A flat boulder jutted out from the bank, and she dropped the towel and soap on it, turning to go.

"Wait!" I must have sounded frantic. She stopped and her eyes widened. I didn't want to be left alone in the woods.

"Is it safe for me to be here by myself?" I asked her. "Could Indians be nearby? Hiding behind those trees . . ."

She straightened her shoulders. "I am Indian," she

answered in a tight, hard voice. "Are you afraid I'll scalp you because your skin is whiter than mine?"

"Oh, no, Dorcas! I never—"

"I saw Josh watching you," she said fiercely. "His eyes don't shine and grow soft that way when he looks at me. Are you after him?"

Her anger showed in her words and in the way her mouth twisted. Her black eyes glittered like an animal ready to pounce.

"I have my own man, Dorcas." I said the first thing that came into my mind and it was true. "I don't want any man but Bates. It's just—just that everything is so different here from where I used to live."

She didn't speak. I had no way of knowing if she believed me or not. "I'm very grateful to you and Josh for helping Bates and me, and Bates is, too," I continued. "If you'd rather I didn't take your dress and petticoat, I can understand."

"Josh wants you to have the clothes," she muttered.

"Some time I hope we can repay your kindness. I certainly don't think evil of you because you're an Indian and that shouldn't keep us from being friends. Maybe I ought to have realized from your coloring that you're one of them, but I never thought about that."

I was rattling on, saying too much, saying more than was necessary. Stooping to pick up the soap from where she'd laid it on the rock, I opened my mouth to address her again and she was gone. I hadn't heard a thing in that brief second. The dried twigs along the creek bank had not snapped under her feet.

Slipping out of my dress and then my petticoat, I knelt on the rock, leaning over the water to wash both garments before going into the stream to bathe myself. The water was icy cold. There was no point in dawdling. It would be impossible to have the leisurely bath I'd anticipated. The frigid water reached my ribs, goose pimples appeared on my arms and my breasts. My teeth chattered. Ducking my head under, I came up quickly to soap my hair. I might freeze, but I'd be clean.

The air seemed colder than the water when I climbed to the rock and dried off hurriedly, donning the new petticoat and then the pink dress. I'd have given anything for a looking glass. I tried to gaze into the stream, but my image was a contorted and blurred reflection. I felt good, though. Like a new person. The breeze caught my hair, light and fluffy again. My hairpins were long gone, probably having dropped into sea, and now I combed the long black tresses with my fingers.

"Well, well," Bates' voice sounded from behind me. I jerked around to see him coming down the path from the house. He stopped walking, his eyes on me. "My God, you're beautiful, Marley."

"It's the dress," I said, smiling.

"It's you more than that."

Coming to me, he put his two hands in my hair, playing with it a moment before pulling me close and holding me tightly against his body. "You're cold," he whispered.

"Not any more. Not when I'm with you."

I lifted my mouth for his kiss and it was as sweet as I expected it to be. The pressure of the lower part of his body on mine let me know he was aroused and that same desire burned in me, but he dropped his arms and stepped back.

"Not now, Marley," he said. "We'll have time for that later."

"Bates, why did you tell Josh and Dorcas we were married?"

He gave a mischievous grin. "I didn't tell them."

"Josh assumed it and you didn't correct him. It's the same as telling him."

"You don't relish being called my wife? Maybe I ought to feel insulted."

"Bates, please don't make fun right now. Answer me truthfully. Please!"

"I was afraid of what Josh might think or do." The light note was gone from his voice. "If Josh had been a Puritan or as straight-laced as the religious people in Massachusetts, he might have refused us even a cup of fresh water. The strict ones don't accept a man and woman laying together without some holy words spoken over them, but after I saw Dorcas, I knew Josh had no religious convictions. Leastways, not strong ones."

"She's Indian."

"Of course. Didn't you realize it the instant you saw her? That's what I meant about knowing Josh wasn't a churchgoing man. Not many settlers look kindly on a white man who takes a squaw."

"You had another chance to tell them about us while we were eating, Bates."

"Does it matter so much to you?" he came back. "Does it make so much difference? Why? We've been together as husband and wife and I hope we will again."

He was watching me carefully and I wasn't sure how to reply. I loved him dearly and the last thing I ever wanted was to hurt him, but this was the time for truth.

"Yes, it bothers me," I admitted. "My mother wasn't a Puritan, but she believed in marriage and she paid for not having a legal husband. She was looked down on and talked about. She always told me to be sure what I did with a man was right in the eyes of God and thechurch . . ." My voice trailed off and tears came into my eyes, not rolling down my face but lingering on my lashes. "I love you, Bates Hagen. To me, that keeps what—what we did on the beach last night from being a sin. But I don't like living a lie."

He cupped his warm hands around my face. "Will it make you feel any better if I tell you we'll go to a preacher as soon as we're in Bath Town?"

"Oh, Bates—You never mentioned anything about marrying me. I—"

I couldn't finish whatever I'd been about to say because he kissed me once more, his tongue probing my mouth, one of his hands slipping inside the low neckline of my dress to caress my breast. Ignoring what he'd said earlier about our waiting until night to make love, he didn't bother asking if I wanted to do it. He just led me a few feet from the creek to a big oak tree whose branches reached the earth in a circle. He eased me to the ground, unbuttoning his breeches and quickly lifting my skirts. He entered me at once and it was over in a moment, but it was heavenly.

"That should hold us until bedtime," he grinned as he got to his feet. "I hope it was right for you, being so hurried, but I couldn't help myself. God, you're beautiful!"

"You said that before," I whispered and smiled.

"You don't like my repeating it?"

"I love your repeating it. I love you . . . everything about you."

I still lay on the ground under the tree and Bates sat beside me. There was a tenderness in his eyes and he picked up one of my hands, holding it between both of his. "I used to wonder . . . if I really ever fell in love . . . if the woman would love me," he said. "I never thought I'd be lucky enough to have a beautiful woman love me . . ."

Reaching up to his face, I traced the outline of his mouth with my forefinger. "Bates, when are we going to Bath Town to find that preacher?"

"I'll be going tomorrow. Josh and I. You're to stay here until I see what the situation is in town."

"Why? I don't want to stay here without you! I want to go when you do!"

"Shhhh, Marley. It's all right. I'm planning to be back here by sunset because Josh says it's only a two-hour trip by water. If you're scared about the Indians, don't be. I asked him about that and he said the Tuscarora have been quiet in this area since they were put down five or six years ago."

I wasn't convinced. "What—What if something happens to you? What if you don't come back for me?"

"I'll be back. Don't you worry your pretty head on that score. Now, do you intend to watch me have a bath or will you join me in the water?"

The way he asked the question made me giggle. "I've had my share of cold water today," I told him. "But I might watch. I've never seen a man take a bath."

"You stand there looking rapturous and maybe I'll take you into the creek with me, clothes and all, lass." He pretended to be considering the idea. "No, I like you better naked," he went on. "I'd let you undress first."

"You've never seen me naked, Bates Hagen!"

"Oh, I've seen enough." He gave a broad wink. "And in case you'd like to know, the view was wonderful."

I was blushing, but I wasn't angry and I didn't feel embarrassed. It surprised me. Besides, I had seen enough of him to like that view, too.

Bates pulled off his clothes and jumped into the creek, submerging and surfacing immediately to move his head and shoulders in a massive shake which sent water showering in every direction. I jumped away to keep dry.

"Whew! It's cold!" he gasped. "Why didn't you warn me?"

Laughing, I ignored his question and blew him a kiss as I started up the path to the house.

Just before dark we ate again, the four of us sitting on the benches with bowls of rabbit stew and corn bread before us. The room was dim except for the pale yellow light from the fire. Josh talked constantly, describing sea voyages he had made and faraway ports he had visited. I had the feeling he was thrilled to be able to carry on a conversation with someone whose background was similar to his. Most of his remarks were addressed to Bates. I wondered what he and Dorcas talked about when they were alone or if they spoke at all except about necessary matters.

Dorcas had remained quiet. She had not looked at me when I returned from my bath, although Josh had given a low whistle. He told me I must be a queen since only royalty was "like that." I didn't dare ask what "like that" implied. I knew Dorcas had heard his remark, although she didn't let on. I could feel her dislike of me and it made no sense. I had done nothing to give her cause. She sounded jealous when we were at the creek. Even though she'd busied herself stirring the stew when I came back to the house, there was no warmth in her. I'd bitten my tongue at the creek to keep from asking her how in the world she could think I'd be attracted to a rough character like Josh Harding when Bates was younger, more handsome, smart enough to command a ship and all the man any woman would ever want.

There was a change in Bates' appearance when he came back to the house. He had shaved off the stubby whiskers, his jaws now a trifle paler than his sunburned cheeks and forehead. He looked different in the buckskin trousers and brown homespun shirt that belonged to Josh.

"I'll pay you for these clothes and for Marley's when I get my hands on some money," he said. Josh nodded without giving a reply.

During the meal I was seated beside Bates on one bench. Dorcas and Josh ate opposite us. My thigh touched Bates'. Once I moved my foot, putting an inch of space between us, and he promptly wrapped his long leg around mine under the table. We were touching once more and I couldn't have moved that leg if I'd tried. All the time he and Josh were talking about being in the south of France, the men agreeing that Marseilles was a fascinating port and a great place for a sailor to have shore leave.

I wanted bedtime so Bates and I could make love again. I smiled inwardly. How quickly I'd discovered the pleasure of being in a man's arms! But I dreaded the idea of the four of us in one room, with Josh and Dorcas aware of what we were doing. As much as I longed for the feel of Bates' body on mine, I wondered if I could respond to his caresses without complete privacy.

"You two can use the bed," Josh remarked, as if reading my thoughts.

"Nonsense," Bates came back. "We've accepted your food and clothing, but I won't deprive a man and wife of their rightful sleeping spot. Marley and I will be fine on the floor."

Dorcas stepped outside and returned with a large basket of woven grass, filled with dry pine needles. She scattered pine in a corner diagonally across from the bed. This was to be a mattress for us. Opening a sea chest, she removed a woven coverlet and handed it to me without comment. The wool felt soft and was thick enough to be warm.

Perhaps Josh had caught the determination in Bates' voice and knew it was useless to argue with him. No further mention was made of where we would sleep. The fire was banked with ashes, fully hiding the red embers. I heard the bed creak as they got into it, but even if I'd glanced in that direction I wouldn't have seen them. The room was pitch black, far darker than the beach and the sea where Bates and I slept under the stars.

Rain began to splatter against the wooden shutters. It muffled the sounds of undressing. I took off the pink brocade dress and folded it carefully. I kept on my petticoat. I lay down first, next to the wall. The pine needles were a rough bed, prickling slightly, but they were better than the gritty, blowing sand.

Bates slid down beside me. He was naked and I swallowed a gasp of surprise. He put his arms around me and brought me close to him. I savored the warmth of his flesh and the clean smell of his skin. Without asking if I'd also like to be naked, he lifted my petticoat over my head and tossed it aside. I didn't protest. He brought me against him once more, his hands moving across my body, touching and caressing, finding little secret spots which he tantalized with his fingers. He kissed my nipples, first one and then the other, until they were as hard as river rocks. I could sense his smile as he brought his mouth to mine, his tongue probing, searching. The desire he was arousing became a pain in its intensity, a good pain, the best pain in the world, but I never wanted his caressing strokes to end. Finally, when neither of us could endure the sweet agony of waiting, he entered me, possessing me as if we had one body for the two of us.

I forgot we weren't completely alone and if the bed

across the room strained or creaked, sounds were lost in the drizzling rain and the wild way my heart was beating. Neither Bates nor I spoke, not even a whisper. We didn't need words.

He didn't move away from me immediately as the passion in us died. His body was a dead weight on me, his breathing rough and uneven. Then slowly, gently, he raised himself on his elbows, our legs still locked together, and his face was suspended over mine, his lips finding my mouth in a lingering kiss so incredibly sweet I lost myself in it. As he slid onto the pine needles he wrapped both his arms around my body. I went to sleep with my head on his shoulder, the steady muted sound of his heartbeats a lullaby in my ears.

Chapter 11

THE MEN LEFT for Bath Town shortly after sunup. It was a radiant morning. The golden sun shone through raindrops on the trees, the gray moss glistened like brilliant gems. I walked with Bates and Josh to the river and watched them get into the dinghy and row off.

When I returned to the house Dorcas was coming through the door with a basket over her arm. "What can I help you do?" I asked. She hadn't spoken when she dished up the last of the rabbit stew for breakfast. And Josh had not bothered to tell her goodby. I had noticed, though, that Josh never took his eyes from me when Bates kissed me on the mouth just before they put the boat into the water.

"I'm going to work my vegetables," Dorcas said.

"You have a garden? I can dig weeds."

She threw me a suspicious glance. "First I'm going to gather salad."

I wasn't sure what "gathering salad" involved, but decided she must be picking greens. My idea was correct. She didn't seem particularly happy when I insisted on going with her. She grudgingly got a basket for me. We walked silently to the creek and followed it upstream to an open area carpeted with small, leafy plants. She said they were salad, pronouncing it more like "salit."

"How do you cook it?" I asked after she showed me what to pick. I was hoping to draw her into conversation.

"Boil it with salt pork."

Dorcas, I decided silently, spoke only when she had to and never added an extra word.

When our baskets were full we washed the greens in the creek and carried them to the house. She put them in the big pot, adding a strip of meat which she cut from a large hunk suspended on a hook from the ceiling. The meat was white, caked with salt, and mainly fat.

When she went outside once more I hurried after her, making up my mind to follow and do whatever she did. We headed away from the creek, down another path through the woods to a cleared field where rows of plants were growing. I recognized corn and potatoes, but not the rest. Some plants barely broke the surface. I questioned Dorcas. She pointed out squash, beans and tobacco. She squatted down to yank up weeds. I did the same, kneeling in the next row so that she and I were facing each other.

The sun was hot on my back. I was glad I'd put on the mauve dress after the men left. I would save the new brocade for when Bates returned. Perspiration appeared on my face and between my shoulder blades. Finally I couldn't stand the quiet any longer. I'd had enough silence since leaving the *Solace* to last me forever. I vowed to have a conversation with Dorcas even if I had to bombard her with questions. If it came to that, I reflected ruefully, she'd probably be a master at one-word answers.

"You have a lovely name," I said. "Were you named after your mother?"

"Dorcas is not my true name." Lifting her head, she murmured an Indian word which I didn't understand, the syllables rolling off her tongue. "That is my name," she went on. "It means 'First Star In The Sky At Evening.' Josh didn't want me to have an Indian name so he calls me Dorcas."

"I suppose your people still use the Indian name whenever you're with them, though."

"I have no people now." Her voice was stony, expressionless.

"Nobody?" I gave her a sympathetic look. "I have no family, either, Dorcas. Not a relative that I know, although my mother may have had some kin in England. It's very sad."

"I have kin but they don't want me."

She fell silent, continuing to yank up weeds. I asked the question I had to ask. "Why don't they want you?"

"You will not understand," she replied in the same toneless way. "You're white."

"Tell me and see if I don't understand, Dorcas. I want a friend—a woman friend. You don't know how good it is for me to be with you."

Her black eyes bore into me and I held her gaze. She must have believed me. She began to talk, the words coming out haltingly. She said her mother had been the daughter of a Tuscarora chief, that the Indian tribe had twenty villages near Roanoke Island, each with its own chief.

"Where is Roanoke Island?" I asked.

"Near where we are. The white people call all this land Carolina now. When the white settlers first came, my people tried to help them. My mother, especially. She showed the white women from the ships how to plant crops, how to make mats and baskets from grass and rushes. They didn't even know how to make clothes from animal skins. She taught them that. They taught her their language and she told me how to speak it. Sometimes I would go with her into Bath Town. When the white people came down with fevers, she sent the Tuscarora medicine men to cure them." Dorcas stopped. When she spoke again her voice was hard. "My mother bore a white child. The chiefs had her and the baby killed as punishment."

"Oh, Dorcas, how awful! How old were you then?"

"I'd had eleven summers."

"You were just a child. Who took care of you?"

"The year after that when I reached my maidenhood I was given to a man in my tribe. But I couldn't conceive and he didn't want me any longer."

I ached to reach out and touch her. Knowing she might not want that, I did nothing, sure she would stop talking, but she didn't. Once she started the story, she had to finish it. All the pent-up emotion she'd kept locked away was bursting from her at last.

"The white settlers didn't keep their promises to the Tuscarora," she said bitterly. "They took our hunting grounds and our home sites. After a time the tribes banded together to make war on the town. It was bad for everybody. There were raids every night. Days, too. That lasted a long time and many whites were killed, even the women and babies. My people died, too, and some were taken prisoners and were never seen again." The bitterness deepened until she fairly spat out the rest of it. "Finally the settlers got a cannon and we couldn't win against that."

Pausing once more, she straightened her shoulders. "The Tuscarora are mighty warriors, but they couldn't fight with so many men lost. It was decided to go North and join the Iroquois. All the women who could conceive were gotten with child to rebuild our tribe, but I was still barren so I was left behind."

"You mean—abandoned?" My eyes widened.

"I don't know that word."

"Abandoned means they went without you, just didn't care what happened to you."

To my surprise, she took up for the Tuscarora. "They had little enough food and not enough horses for everybody to ride," she said defensively. "They didn't take a woman who would eat but who couldn't give them children. No man would want her."

"You sound as if you believe it was all right for them to leave her behind, Dorcas. I think it's awful. I should think you'd hate the Tuscarora even if they're your family."

"I didn't expect *you* to understand. You're white." She stared past me at something in the distance, her mouth twitching. "The Indians don't want me because I am barren and because my mother gave birth to a white child. The whites don't want me because I am a Tuscarora. People in Bath Town don't trust any Indians now. I belong nowhere."

"You stayed here—by yourself—until Josh came?"

"I had a teepee. There's plenty of fish and I know how to make arrows and hunt."

"Did Josh build the log house?"

She shook her head. "White people lived there before the fighting. They were one of the first families killed and the house was set afire, but a hard rain fell so only the roof burned. When Josh came I took him into my teepee. When he was strong enough to work, he fixed the house for us. A ship was on the river in a cove near here, a square-rigged ship, and he knew some of the sailors. He worked for the captain to get tools."

I'd thought my background was pitiful, but it could

not compare to what Dorcas had suffered. Small wonder that she didn't fully trust Bates and me since we were white. Yet she trusted Josh and he was as white as we were.

"Josh seems like a good man," I said. "You're lucky to have a husband who will provide for you."

She started to speak but changed her mind. She clamped her lips together, her face a blank. We continued pulling weeds in silence. After a few minutes I tried one or two other topics in the hope of another conversation, but my efforts were useless. Still on our knees, we inched along the garden rows, our heads low over the plants, the silence broken only by songbirds.

Late in the afternoon I went to the creek for a bath. I put on the new petticoat and the pink brocade. I felt suddenly very good. It was marvelous not to be hungry or thirsty and I was clean all the way to my toes. I hummed a song which the sailors at the New Bedford Inn sang after they'd downed many mugs of ale. I didn't know the words to the tune, but I remembered the merry melody.

Dorcas shook her head when I asked if she would come with me to the river to wait for the men. I went alone, sitting on the fallen log where we'd first seen Josh. The midday heat had dissolved into a comfortable coolness. The Pamlico River flowed lazily in front of me, a deep blue reflecting the cloudless sky. Wild flowers, yellow with velvety brown centers, were growing near the log. I picked one, sticking it in the front of my gown so that the stem lay between my breasts and the blossom nestled against the lace ruffle.

For a little while I felt more at peace than I'd been for some time, but as the sun went out of sight it was hard not to be apprehensive. At last the dinghy came into view. Bates waved and yelled, "Marley!" I waved, unable to answer him in the rush of relief that he was all right and that he'd come back. The men beached the boat and climbed the bluff. Bates put his arm around my waist as we started down the path toward the house.

"Tell me about Bath Town," I said.

"Later. We'll talk after we eat. What have you been doing all day, Marley?"

I explained about gathering the salad and working in the garden with Dorcas. "Oh, and I had a bath," I added.

"I might have known," Bates chuckled. "You're going to wash the skin right off your bones one of these days, lass."

Josh joined in the laughter and so did I. Except for greeting me when he and Bates came ashore, Josh had kept quiet. But he listened to what Bates and I said to each other and he pulled his eyes across my body every now and then. That stare made me flush. When Bates joked about my taking so many baths, Josh turned, looking over his shoulder at my breasts. I snatched the yellow blossom from my bodice, not wanting to call attention to the low neckline. Did Bates notice those suggestive leers Josh was giving me? I remembered Dorcas' acid tone when she remarked that Josh never looked at her with his eyes "soft."

We ate as soon as we were in the house. The greens were delicious, but I couldn't swallow the fat pork. The others wolfed it down. Dorcas mixed meal with water, rolling the paste between her palms into round balls which she dropped into the pot with the greens and the pork. The meal balls were a sickly green color, but the taste wasn't bad.

When we got up from the table Bates motioned me outside and we walked a short distance from the house to the edge of the woods. I realized he must have something important to say and decided he didn't want to speak in front of Josh and Dorcas. Daylight was turning into silvery lavender dusk. The gray moss swayed noiselessly, the trees loomed black ahead. I clung to Bates' hand, fearful because he seemed strangely aloof. Two tiny vertical lines showed between his eyebrows. He was almost frowning and his mouth was set in a rigid line.

"Marley, I found a place for us to live in Bath Town and there's work for me. For you, too," he said. "The schoolmaster died three weeks ago and his house is empty. The people are mighty eager for the children to continue their studies. You and I can live in the house without paying any rent in return for teaching classes."

I looked at him incredulously. "Are you trying to tell me that *I* would have to teach school?" I gasped. "I wouldn't know how to begin!"

"You can read and do sums. That's enough."

"Doing them myself is one thing, Bates. But teaching another person is something else."

He stood in front of me and tucked his thumbs into his belt just as he had done on the *Solace*. "We have to be practical, Marley. You and I don't have a coin between us, much less a bar of gold. I'm a seaman—not a schoolmaster. But I know numbers and navigation and I can teach those subjects if I have to do it. You can teach reading and writing because you have to do it whether it suits you or not."

He wasn't asking what I wanted to do. From his tone I knew he was issuing an order to me. This was the voice he had used on his ship when he commanded the helmsman to change course or when he wanted a sailor to act in a hurry.

"If only we had some money," I sighed. "Money can solve every problem."

"Not every problem, Marley, but I grant you money will make life easier. Well, we're without it so we'd best consider ourselves fortunate that the Bath Town schoolmaster died when he did. Even if we didn't have a place in town, we couldn't stay on here and expect Josh to take care of us indefinitely." He moved his tongue across his lips. "I thought we'd leave first thing in the morning if the weather is good. If it rains, we'll sit tight another day. I don't hanker to be in a dinghy in a cloudburst if I can avoid it."

It wouldn't have mattered if I'd disagreed with him because his plans obviously were made.

"Bates, can we be married as soon as we get to Bath Town?" I asked. "Certainly before dark tomorrow night?"

In the misty light I saw his jaw muscles tighten. "There's no preacher," he said thinly.

"You mean—no preacher in the entire town?"

"Nor anywhere near. Bath Town doesn't even have a church."

A knot came into my throat. "There has to be a preacher with that many people," I muttered. "What do they do when a couple wants to get married or when somebody dies or when a baby is to be baptized?"

"Any person can read Scripture and say a prayer at a grave, I reckon. As to baptizing, maybe they're not church-minded as folks are where you grew up in Massachusetts."

"But for marriages—"

"They have common law marriages."

I twisted around so he couldn't look into my eyes, doubt and terror making me tremble. I could almost see my mother, almost hear her voice telling me to be sure I was married legally in the sight of the Church and of God.

Bates put his hands on my shoulders and forced me to turn so I faced him again. "A common law marriage is all right," he said gently. "I'd be willing to bet half the couples in Bath Town were wed that way and plenty more will be in the future."

"Did you ask Josh if that's how he and Dorcas were married?"

"I don't have to. A white man wouldn't take a squaw to a preacher. He'd be laughed into the ocean if he did that."

Tension turned to anger. I resented Bates making all the decisions, resented the way he uttered slurring comments about Dorcas. "Why do you keep calling her a 'squaw' like that?" I snapped. "You make it sound dirty. She can't help the race she was born into and she's never done anything to harm you—or me, either."

"I'm not slandering her. An Indian woman is a squaw. A lot of men might use a squaw for their own pleasures in bed, but not many would live openly with one. I doubt if I would even under the same circumstances Josh has. I suppose it suits the two of them and it's convenient for them. What they have is a common law marriage. Now about us . . ."

He was waiting for me to reply. I longed to say anything was all right as long as he and I were together. I hesitated. My mother's teachings remained strong. "Bates, if we went to another town we might find a minister."

"There are no other towns nearby."

He answered as patiently as if he'd been explaining to a child. Neither of us spoke immediately. I could see his chest rising, the tempo of his breathing quickening. A hundred different emotions pulled at me.

"Marley, you and I care about each other," he said in a low voice. "I love you and I hope you love me and want me. You've said you did and I believe you. Isn't love enough?"

"I do love you. Believe me . . ."

"A common law marriage is just as sound in the sight of God to my way of thinking as if a preacher in a black coat was standing before us in a church reading from the *Book of Common Prayer*."

"Maybe—But—"

"I'm not going to beg you to do something against your will. But we've already been together as though we were husband and wife. I could tell you were as pleased and satisfied about it each time as I was. That's sufficient for me, but if you need words spoken, I'll speak them. All I want is to have you with me always and for you to be happy."

The night wind blew softly against us, ruffling my hair and swirling the pink skirt around my ankles. The moon had risen, its saffron light making Bates' eyes as velvety as the center of the flower I'd picked on the river bank that afternoon. My heart seemed to burst with the love I had for him. Stretching out my hand, I touched his face, his chin and mouth, tracing the line of his eyebrows. Some of the tension went out of him. He circled me with his arms so that my body fitted tightly against his, my thighs on his thighs and my breasts on his firm chest.

"What words do we say?" I asked.

"We'll have to make them up."

"You go first."

He broke the embrace, but took both of my hands into his, standing very tall in front of me, his eyes never leaving mine. "I, Bates Hagen, do take thee, Marley Lancaster, to be my lawfully wedded wife from this night on. Amen." Smiling, he added, "Now it's your turn, Marley."

My voice was so faint I could scarcely hear myself speak as I repeated the vows. "I, Marley Lancaster, do take thee, Bates Hagen, to be my lawfully wedded husband from this night on."

"You didn't say, 'Amen,' Marley."

"Amen, my darling."

His hands tightened on mine and both of us broke into joyous laughter. I was almost drunk with exhilaration. Bates, his gray eyes dancing in the moonlight, said mischievously, "How do you like being a married lady, Mrs. Hagen?"

"*Mrs. Hagen*—why, that's me! I like it. In fact, I like it a great deal."

"Your new husband is a fine fellow, I hear." He gave a wide grin.

"Oh, yes." I used the same teasing tone. "However, being married must have made him a trifle shy. He hasn't kissed me since I became his wife, but that's all right because it's made me bold. I just might kiss him if he doesn't hurry. After all, I've been married to him for at least two minutes and my new husband is just standing there."

"So I've taken myself a brazen wench!"

I pretended to be annoyed at his choice of words. "For your information, Captain Bates Hagen, I am not a wench. I'm now a married lady—and don't you forget it."

"You bet I won't forget," he grinned again. "Even if you're acting surprisingly brash all of the sudden. A bit saucy, too."

"Are you complaining already?"

"Lordy, no. I like for a woman to have spunk." The laughter left his mouth and the mocking note went out of his voice. His tawny hair formed a burnished halo around his head in the soft moonlight. I'd never seen him more serious.

"I like for her to have the sweetness you have," he whispered. "And a beautiful body like yours as well as beautiful features and a beautiful soul. Marley . . ."

He wrapped his arms around me and put his mouth

on mine. The kiss made my senses reel. I felt weak and strong at the same time. I could neither think nor breathe. Desire for him became a white hot fire in my veins. He wanted me with the same intense passion that made me ache for him. I could tell by the growing hardness of his body, by the urgency of his kisses increasing as he slid his lips down my throat to my breasts. Still holding each other, we moved from the moonlit clearing into the murky shadows of the trees, his hand tugging at my skirt—and at that moment Josh yelled, "Bates!"

The rough sound came out of the darkness. Bates and I sprang apart instinctively. Neither of us had realized Josh was standing in the doorway of the house. He was silhouetted against the pale orange glow from the hearth.

"Yes," Bates called. "What is it?"

"Are you all right?" Josh strode into the yard, turning his head to peer in the direction of Bates' voice. "You and Marley have been outside so long I thought something must have got you. Meeting a polecat in the night is no happy event. I figured if you'd strolled off, you might have lost your way in the woods."

"We're coming in now," Bates said. "We—uh—took a walk and—uh—went further than we intended."

Apparently satisfied that we were not in danger, Josh stepped inside without closing the door. The splash of light from the fireplace made a path for us across the yard. Bates put his arm around my waist as we started to the house, twigs and pine cones snapping under his boots and my skirt swishing softly against the uneven clumps of grass. The delicious moment we were sharing when Josh interrupted had passed, but passion continued to smoulder in us and I knew we could recapture the ecstasy once we were lying on our pine needle mattress.

"I'll see you in bed, Mrs. Hagen," Bates whispered.

My heart was too full for me to speak, but I nodded. My husband suddenly swooped me into his arms, picking me up as if I'd been a child and cradling me against his chest, not letting my feet touch ground again until we were at the door.

It was almost an hour before we could lie down on the pine needle mattress. Josh was in a conversational mood and he started on a long sea tale. I stole a look at Bates, knowing he was as bored as I was, seeing the pulse in his temple quicken. His mind was a long way from Josh's ramblings. Finally he yawned and Dorcas jumped to her feet to bank the fire.

Bates and I reached eagerly for each other once we were in our bed. The waiting had kindled our passion until our bodies trembled with desire so fierce we didn't take time for many kisses or caresses. We came together violently, straining against one another, my fingers digging into his back while his hands were on my buttocks, lifting me so that I felt swallowed by him. We were panting hard as the lovemaking ended, exhausted with a marvelous all-engulfing fatigue. I kissed him before nestling against him, savoring the warmth of his loving embrace. That night he went to sleep before I did. I lay quietly, inching my body into a new position so his head was against my breast, my chin resting on his hair.

Chapter 12

I<small>T WAS</small> <small>MIDMORNING</small> on a muggy, humid day when we left for Bath Town. Instead of leaving shortly after daybreak, as Bates wanted, we were delayed by a thick fog that completely covered the Pamlico River. From the dinghy it was impossible to see the water, although it was only a few feet away. We returned to the log house to wait for the sunshine, which Josh maintained always followed a bleary overcast morning.

All of us were strangely silent. I didn't want to linger any more with Dorcas and Josh, but I couldn't help being apprehensive about a new place, not knowing what the town was like or what sort of people I might find. The idea of teaching school sent shivers up and down my spine. I was terrified at the prospect. Bates had said I didn't have a choice about teaching. I knew I would attempt it, but I had not been fibbing when I told him I didn't know how to begin.

We four made a strange contrast. Dorcas sat cross-legged on the floor, weaving a basket, her coppery fingers darting first to the left, then to the right as she twisted and braided long strips of grass. She was seldom idle and she seemed to keep an endless supply of grass soaking in a bucket of water behind the chimney. The grass tightened as it dried, she'd told me, but the baskets and mats she wove were not sturdy enough to last long. The supply had to be replenished constantly.

Josh moved a bench from the table, putting it nearer the hearth and settling himself. He was whittling a spoon from a chunk of oak, the pinkish yellow chips falling into the fire as his knife clicked faintly against the wood. He was intent on his task, pausing now and then to hold the spoon up or turn it over and lick his tongue across the surface of the wood in search of a rough spot.

During those pauses, his eyes glanced in my direction, always lingering on my breasts. I would have given anything to be clothed from my ears to my toes instead of the low-cut pink brocade. The mauve dress was just as revealing. I'd purposely worn the better one, hoping to make a good impression when we reached Bath Town. A shawl might have helped, but I didn't want to mention it and have Josh command Dorcas to give me more of her clothing—if she possessed a shawl.

Bates was the enigma. He could not be still. He walked the length of the log house, turning at the wall and retracing his steps, his face knotted into a fierce frown. The restless pacing was interrupted occasionally when he made a fist of his right hand and banged it into his left palm. I found it hard to believe that this was the same man who had whispered marriage vows to me so tenderly, who had cradled me in his arms while we were making love on our pine mattress.

After peering outdoors for the hundredth time, Bates decided the fog was beginning to lift. I couldn't see much change, but when we reached the water the visibility was a little better. The men pushed the small boat into the river. I took my familiar seat, stepping over a rolled bundle of grass mats and a basket holding corn bread and two slices of fried salt pork. I was grateful for the food, remembering hunger and not knowing where we would get our next meal. I couldn't help wondering if a couple ever started married life with fewer worldly possessions than Bates and I.

The men shook hands. I made a move toward Dorcas, but something about her defiant expression and the rigidity of her body kept me from hugging her. I wasn't about to embrace Josh, not with his lusting gaze sweeping up and down my body whenever Bates' attention was elsewhere.

"I hope you'll come to see us soon," I said after thanking them for their kindnesses.

"Sure will," Josh answered quickly. "I get into Bath Town real often."

"You'll come, too?" I looked at Dorcas.

"Maybe," she muttered and shrugged.

Her face remained as inscrutable as ever and I had the feeling her reply meant no. With what she had told me about Indians being unwelcome in town, I doubted that she would set foot there. Yet I didn't want to lose her friendship. In her way she had been very kind to me. I didn't understand her, but I liked her. With our backgrounds we had something in common, both of us losing our mothers, both of us being alone. I sensed the bond between us although I couldn't tell if she did.

A few of the tension lines smoothed out of Bates' forehead when he took the oars, but he remained aloof. After half an hour scattered patches of blue appeared in the sky. Finally a thin shaft of sunshine broke through the clouds, lighting the water with a silvery sheen. The mist was evaporating enough to give occasional glimpses of the river banks, the trees heavy with the shaggy, dripping moss.

Bates rowed with a steady rhythm, bending forward and pulling the heavy oars back, not speaking. I endured the silence until I wanted to scream, racking my brain to know what I could have said or done to irritate him so much. We didn't need to save our throats by not talking, since drinking water was no longer a problem, but Bates was lost in a world of his own and I might have been back at the log house with Dorcas and Josh for all he noticed me.

"Bates, what's wrong?" I blurted out.

"Wrong?" His head jerked up, but he didn't miss the stroke as the oars sliced through the water. "What do you mean?"

"You've scarcely spoken a word at all this morning and you haven't uttered a sentence to me."

"For God's sake!" he snapped. "Don't begin acting like a woman and expecting attention every second!"

Blood shot to my face, making my skin burn. I felt as if he had slapped me. "I *am* a woman." I attempted to keep my voice calm but didn't succeed very well. "I do not expect constant attention, but I would appreciate an occasional remark from you."

"If I had anything to say to you, I'd speak. Since I don't, there's no point in your pouting like a spoiled brat."

He tossed me a scowling look. I didn't reply, wishing fervently I'd never spoken and had let him continue the trip in absolute silence if that was his choice. It would certainly have been better than the unpleasant words we'd exchanged.

"Oh, now I see what's wrong, Marley." His lip curled. "You were hoping I'd lift your petticoat and lie on top of you in the dinghy or pull into a cove for a quick fornicating spree on shore this morning. You're disappointed that it hasn't happened! Well, get this into your head, lass. There are more important things for me to do at the present time than perform like a stud horse."

Rage put an acid taste on my tongue. If we hadn't been in the boat I'd have turned on my heels and left. "Going to bed with you is the last thing I want right now, Bates Hagen!" I came back. "The very last thing! How dare you speak to me in such a hateful way? You're insulting!"

"So I'm insulting, am I? First you accuse me of not talking to you and that made you mad. Now you're upset because I did talk. You're not satisfied whether I try to please your silly whims or not. That's nothing but a wench's selfish play for attention."

We glared at each other. I was furious and hurt, confused at the change in his personality and at the same moment I was amazed at the fury boiling within myself. It hadn't occurred to me that Bates and I would have an argument. I didn't want one, especially on this first day of our marriage when we should have been wildly happy just to be together. But neither did I want to sit quietly and allow him to make those ugly, hurting insinuations about me.

A terrible new thought spun through my brain and it was a fear. If Bates regretted taking me for his wife. . . . If he no longer needed or wanted me now that his physical desires were satisfied and since he'd found a house and a position . . .

Shuddering, I hugged my arms across my ribs. Bates saw the movement and his eyebrows went up. "Are you cold?" he demanded roughly, sounding as if he was accusing me of a crime.

"No."

"You're shivering. Damn it, Marley, that means you're cold! I don't know how you can deny it."

"I—I'm all right," I said stubbornly. "I—I'm j-just upset."

I wasn't all right and all of the sudden I was freezing. Anxiety and the harsh words we'd said to each other did that to me. Bates let the oars hang slack as he leaned forward to open the bundle of grass mats, tossing one into my lap and removing my mauve dress from the center of the roll.

"Put the mat over your knees and wrap the dress around your shoulders," he said. "I don't know why you'd be cold in this weather. Are you getting sick?"

"No." I sucked my breath in. "I just don't like being addressed in such a hateful voice. It might not matter much if it came from McGregor or a brute like that awful Teach because I wouldn't expect more from the likes of them. But it hurts coming from my husband. Last night you were gentle and loving and I felt you honestly cared about me, but today you act as if I'm a dog you'd like to kick or a burden you wish you could drop overboard."

"That's not true, Marley. I love you and—"

The sentence hung in midair as the bristling anger left him. He touched his lips with his tongue and picked up the oars once more, but his eyes remained on me, their smoky depths bottomless.

"If you want to know what's on my mind," he sighed, "I'm not sure I'll be much of a success as a landlubber. I've been at sea most of my life and in these last nineteen years I've never stayed ashore longer than a few days at a stretch. To be truthful about it, I simply don't know how to live on land."

I wanted to reassure him. "You had to adapt to living at sea, Bates. You can do an about-face now."

"There's a big garden already plowed and planted behind the schoolmaster's house. Some of the townspeople did it for the old man when he got sick. We could take it over. I haven't the slightest idea what to do to bring in a good harvest and I'm not really interested in finding out, except that under the present circumstances, the alternative would be starving and I don't hanker for that."

I could feel myself growing warm in the relief that he was telling me about it at last. His voice was ragged, the sentences coming quickly now that he had admitted to having worries.

"I don't know much about farming, either," I said, choosing my words carefully. "But my mother always had a few vegetables growing and I do know how to chop around plants with a hoe to get air under the soil. You ought not to worry, Bates. Any man smart enough to command a ship can surely learn to pick beans and corn."

His lips curved into a smile, the first one I'd seen since the previous evening. "I reckon you have a point," he said. "It appears you've got plenty of brains and common sense under that gorgeous black hair."

The compliment gave me a glow and a mellow feeling. His tension was dwindling, his face no longer frowning and his voice sounded easygoing and peaceful, a sign he had returned to being the man I'd grown to love instead of a brooding stranger.

As the sunshine pushed away the last of the clouds the air was noticeably warmer and my eyes scanned the river banks in the hope of seeing buildings and plenty of activity, evidence of a bustling city. I said as much to Bates and he gave a low laugh. Bath Town was a hamlet of two or three hundred people, he said, definitely not a city.

"Right now we're in a small bay," he went on. "It

was well chosen for a town since two creeks meet here and Bath Town has been placed on the east bank of one of them. In spite of not having a church, surprisingly enough, neither does it have a jail and I didn't see any stocks. Maybe that means the lack of a preacher keeps the citizens less sinful than if they had to listen to a hellfire-and-damnation sermon every Sunday."

When at last we had a glimpse of Bath Town in the distance, four boys about eight or nine years old were sitting on the edge of a wooden pier dangling their bare feet into the water and apparently watching for us. They jumped up and shouted. Immediately several men and women walked to the water's edge, one man stepping in front of the others. We were still too far away for me to make out anyone's features.

"That's Amos Martin," Bates said in an undertone. "He made the bargain with me about teaching and he'll be our neighbor. In fact, he built the house we'll live in. It seems his first wife died and he remarried a widow with four children. He already had six of his own, so he built another house, a bigger one, and rented the original place to the schoolmaster."

"Rented?" The word rolled around in my mouth. "How will we pay rent when we have no money?"

"We'll earn money. The townspeople will pay us for their youngsters' schooling. Amos knows Teach stole my ship and all our belongings. I told him what happened to us and he's so anxious for a school he doesn't care that we're penniless. He said he wouldn't charge us rent if his children could come to school free, and I agreed."

"Did you also tell him we weren't married, Bates?"

He clamped his lips together. My question had irritated him and I wished I hadn't asked it.

"No, I didn't tell him that," Bates muttered between clenched jaws. "Besides, we're married now."

While Bates rowed near enough the pier for one of the men to throw a line into the dinghy, I studied Amos Martin. He stood with his hands clasped behind his back and his feet wide apart, a middle-aged man of average height with a stolid body and curly red hair pulled into a queue at the nape of his neck and tied with a black string. He had pale blue eyes under thick red brows and his nose was slightly humped as if it had been broken, but there was no real disfigurement. Although he certainly wasn't handsome, his features blended together to give a good appearance. He wore work clothes just as the other men on the pier did, all of them in buckskin or dark sailcloth breeches and collarless homespun shirts. Amos had his sleeves rolled up to the elbows, revealing muscular arms covered with a reddish fuzz of hair.

"You said he has a store?" I asked Bates.

"He sells ships' supplies. That's his business just beyond the pier."

I stole a look at the women, finding them staring at me. I felt overdressed in the pink brocade; their clothing was simple. Their dresses were made of homespun or calico, mostly without trim. The older women buttoned the garments to their throats while the younger ones had deep square or rounded necklines like mine, the colors somber blues, browns and grays.

Children of assorted ages were everywhere, little ones clinging to their mothers' skirts or hands and older boys and girls giving curious glances toward Bates and me as if they were sizing us up. Several of the women were pregnant. One who didn't look older than I had a baby in one arm, a toddler by the hand and she was expecting again.

My age . . . I realized suddenly that I'd had a birthday since leaving Massachusetts and had not been aware of the particular day. I was eighteen now, old enough to have had one or two babies of my own. I didn't want it to happen yet. I didn't want to wonder if my child was McGregor's or if it had been fathered by one of the two pirates. When I did have children I wanted to be positive they resulted from the marvelous love Bates and I shared, not from rape.

"Looks like most of the town is here to meet us," Bates said in that same undertone.

He leapt from the dinghy to the pier and helped me out. Once I was standing on the dock, he greeted Amos Martin with a hearty handshake.

"We figured the fog must have delayed you," Amos said. "I'm thankful you didn't see fit to change your mind about coming."

"Aye, the fog was the reason," Bates answered. Turning toward me, he added, "This is my wife."

I stepped forward—*and sprawled!*

If I'd been knocked from behind I couldn't have gone down harder. A strangled cry came from my throat and a collective gasp went up from the throng. I found myself lying full length in front of Amos Martin with my nose resting on the toe of his boot and my pink skirt apparently halfway up; a faint wind fanned my petticoat against the back of my knees.

Bates quickly put his hands under my arms and set me on my feet. "Marley, are you hurt?" he asked, the worry lines in his face once more.

I was attempting to smooth my skirt and get myself together, so embarrassed I wanted to die on the spot. Looking down, I couldn't find anything which I might have tripped over.

"Only my pride is hurt," I murmured and all those strangers laughed.

Bates smiled, too, adding to my humiliation, but I decided that was better than if he'd made a big thing of my tumble. He had a firm grip on my hand and his touch was reassuring.

"It's good you have a sense of humor," Amos chuckled. "You folks won't believe what a great moment this is for Bath Town. We don't get many new residents, much less a pair of schoolteachers. People who live nearby come to town to get supplies and go when they have what they want. As for the ships, the captains sail in to sell their goods and take on fresh water and supplies, and maybe give the sailors a romp, but they leave quickly. We lost a lot of people in the fighting with the Tuscarora and we need new residents."

I hoped I didn't show surprise at the phrase, "a pair of schoolteachers." I deliberately ignored Amos' mention of the Indians, not wanting to dwell on that. Amos began to make introductions. The men came to Bates and me as he called their names, then the women, the individual faces and names blurring in my mind to be sorted out later. I did make a mental note of Hannah Martin, Amos' wife. She was a thin brunette with a sweet smile, too frail to have had four children, not to mention now being in charge of the rearing of six others who belonged to her husband. Small wonder that there were blue shadows under her eyes.

Despite their plain manners, something about the townspeople made me like them at once. I wasn't sure why, for their simple clothing, weathered complexions and work-scarred hands gave them a rough appearance, men and women alike, but they had open faces and genuine smiles without the harassed expressions I'd seen on the Puritans in Massachusetts. They spoke to their children in normal tones, without being overly stern, and they laughed and talked to one another with a zest which was contagious. It surprised me to feel at ease among them so quickly. I glanced at Bates, seeing that he grinned and acted more like himself than he'd been all day.

"You probably want to inspect where you'll live," Amos said. "The house has been closed since Professor Denton's death. Yesterday after we knew you'd be coming here, my missus and some of the other ladies got in there and cleaned it up. Cleaned up the schoolroom, too."

When he paused, both Bates and I thanked Hannah. Before she could speak, Amos was talking again.

"It's ready for you to start classes tomorrow," he went on. "These children have been out of school so long they may forget what they've been taught if they keep their brains idle many more days. This time of year they only attend classes in the mornings. That's so they can help with the crops and chores in the afternoons."

We left the pier and walked into the heart of town. Some people tagged along, although most of them returned to whatever they'd been doing. My first impression was of flat land and lush green growth. There was not a hill or knoll in sight. Leaves, bushes, uneven grass and a variety of colorful flowering plants softened the starkness of the buildings, which were the ugliest structures imaginable.

A street ran the length of Bath Town, the sand road marked with wagon ruts and animal tracks, the breeze swirling a fine spray of sand a few inches off the ground so that what might be a hole one second would be smooth later. The trees were enormous; gray moss hung from every limb. Amos pointed out the inn, which he referred to as "our ordinary," the two bars or publick houses next to it, a blacksmith's forge, the customs house, a general store and his own store opposite.

His business had a split log nailed to the front with "Martin," whittled into it; under his name in smaller block letters was, "Naval Stores Sold Here." The buildings were made of rough sawed boards, unpainted, the same material used to make the houses. I saw brick chimneys but not a single brick structure.

As we continued to walk I counted twelve dwellings, none large by New Bedford standards which was all I could compare them with. A few had two stories and several were designed with a story-and-a-half. Most had small front porches as well as shed additions, the shed chimneys broad enough to make me think they served as kitchens. The yards were small, some enclosed with fences, and every house had a big garden behind it. Livestock pens for a horse or a mule were behind the gardens, and pig pens were on the edge of the woods as far from the houses as possible. With such flat land it was easy to see a long way off in the distance. Cows and sheep grazed in a green meadow. Chickens, geese and dogs were everywhere. I wondered how the owners could tell their own fowls.

"Here we are," Amos said as we stopped before a house much like the others. It was a square building with a shed on the side; the unpainted boards were weathered gray from the salt air and the wind, and the windows had heavy wooden shutters. He pushed the door open, standing aside for Bates and me to go in.

I'd braced myself for the same sort of log house which Dorcas and Josh had. But we were to fare better! I let my breath out slowly as my eyes circled the room. It had a plank floor rather than sod. A table and four chairs were in the center; two cupboards and a clothes press made from pine boards stood against the wall.

The bed was the real surprise, an honest-to-goodness bed which stood high off the floor; it had a carved headpiece and four carved posts, each with a smooth round knob on top, the dark wood polished until it gleamed. The mattress was covered with a quilt fashioned of tiny diamond-shaped swatches of blue and cream homespun in an intricate sunburst pattern.

"It's beautiful," I said, seeing Hannah smile at my comment.

"Professor Denton brought that bed with him in a wagon when he came," she answered. "He never said where he got it. I've always thought it must have been made in England because he was from Albemarle County in Virginia, just as we were. The only furniture like that I've seen was made in England. The bed and his books are all he owned when he came. He got the other furnishings as payment for his teaching."

"The quilt, too?"

A faint pink color came into her cheeks and she laughed a trifle self-consciously, putting one hand to her mouth and deliberately turning her back toward Amos and Bates who were across the room inspecting the chimney. "That quilt was made by Zeke's mother—Zeke was my first husband," she whispered. "After I married Amos I made the error of telling him my first mother-in-law pieced up the quilt as a wedding present for Zeke and me, and Amos refused to sleep under it. He claimed the ghost of Zeke would haunt him if he had to look at the quilt, much less wrap up in it."

She lifted her fingers to her mouth, suppressed laughter deepening the lines around her eyes. "So I brought the quilt over to Professor Denton who needed it. But I profited in the bargain," she went on, still whispering. "After that Amos put the bed he'd used with Agnes, his first wife, in the loft for the children. Agnes was my cousin. I'd been having a little trouble with her ghost whenever I got into her bed with Amos even though he was my husband then. I could almost feel Agnes watching us. She was a great one for finding fault and I could practically hear her telling me what Amos and I did wasn't the way she and Amos took care of their lives when she was with him. I must say she produced six fine children, but she nearly nagged Amos out of his senses."

We giggled together and joined the men at the hearth. Hannah apologized for the lack of a fire and I told her I was delighted not to see a roaring blaze. The air was heavy with humidity and I was beginning to feel sticky with the midday heat.

"Most of us do our cooking early and get finished with it during hot weather," Hannah said. "That way, the house cools off before dark. Nights can be steamy hereabouts."

The shed room attached to our house was the school; one chimney served both rooms. Amos said the rocks for our chimney had been used originally as ballast on a ship. The schoolroom was long and narrow with a table and chair at the far end and nine backless benches for the students. Each bench could easily hold six or seven youngsters.

"Are there that many children to come to school?" I asked with my eyes on the seating space.

"Thirty, more or less," Amos replied. "We don't have many houses or families in Bath Town, but one thing we know how to do is bring babies into the world."

"Look at the books, Marley," Bates exclaimed, pointing to the shelves. "Amos says some were Professor Denton's and the others were donated to the town by an English clergyman to start a library." He turned to the Martins with a question. "Didn't Professor Denton have any heirs to claim his possessions?"

I'd been wondering the same thing. Hannah said no, that the schoolmaster had been a loner and close-mouthed about his background. "He was a good teacher, but the little ones were terrified of him," she added. "He'd rap them on the tops of their heads with a ruler when they made errors and he hit hard, maybe harder than he meant. Many's the time my children have come home with lumps as big as pullet eggs. I believe in punishment, but not in injuring."

I took down a small volume in dark leather, discovering it was a selection of religious treatises. The book next to it was titled *The Fables of Aesop.* I was familiar with that one. My mother had taught me to read with the Bible and a copy of Aesop's *Fables.* A sailor had given both books to her when he discovered she could read. Like the rest of my belongings, those books had been destroyed when Susan James' house caught fire.

To Bates and my surprise, we had a steady stream of callers during the afternoon, each one bringing a welcoming gift of cooked food or clothing or making payment for their children's schooling. All of them seemed to know of our meeting with Blackbeard at sea, the information supplied by Amos, no doubt. I was amazed to discover two of the men had been shipwrecked and had stayed on in the area as Josh had done. By dark we had more than enough food for several days. I had two homespun dresses and a petticoat and Bates had a new pair of sailcloth trousers and one slightly worn pair. We had two gold coins. One couple brought towels and four bars of yellow soap. Another, Mary McGurn, whose husband, Seth, was the blacksmith, presented us with a battered wooden cradle. Bates looked as if he would explode when he saw the baby bed. With a rosy face I managed to thank her, wishing I could do what my husband was doing, which was to vanish into the backyard. Bates stayed there, pretending to be inspecting the garden, until he made sure Mary McGurn was gone. By the time he returned to the house I'd tucked the cradle out of sight under the bed.

"Where is it?" he demanded.

"It?" I pretended not to know what he was talking about.

"The cradle, damn it! I'm not ready for that," he growled.

I pointed to the hiding place, assuring him I wasn't ready for it, either.

We ate at dusk, sitting at the table in our new home and sampling the food we'd been given. There was a pot of greens which made me think of Dorcas; they looked and tasted like the ones she cooked. I didn't mention that and Bates made no reference to her or to Josh. Bates couldn't get enough of something Hannah called "syrup bread," which was made of cornmeal and eggs sweetened with molasses and was a rich brown color. We had fish, fresh and fried that morning, and plenty of salt pork.

When we finished the meal Bates brought in a pail of water from the spring, watching as I poured some into a pan and washed our plates.

"There's water left in the bucket," he said, merry-ment making his eyes glow. "Aren't you going to take a bath?"

"I will at bedtime."

"Why, I thought you had to wash yourself every few hours or you'd corrode or turn green or grow barnacles or something," he teased.

"So you thought that, did you?" I answered and laughed. "Maybe you're correct, but right now I'm going to sit on our porch. All the other people are sitting on theirs."

We settled ourselves on the stoop, my feet scarcely reaching the ground while Bates had his long legs stretched out in front of him. As far down the street as we could see children were playing in the yards, running and laughing, while the adults on the porches rested from the day's work.

Night was coming fast, the sky misty with soft violet shadows. The leaves rustled gently in the faint wind and some bushes with small white flowers gave off a tangy scent. Group by group, the children were summoned indoors and the hum of voices and laughter ceased. Amos and Hannah waved from their steps and called a goodnight to us, gathering their youngsters together.

Bates and I fell silent. His arm was lightly around my shoulders and I couldn't help wondering what he was thinking, but I didn't ask although I hoped he felt as peaceful and secure as I did. Even my fears about teaching school were dimmed now that I knew how friendly the townspeople were. I watched the moon rise, seeing the color turn from gold to amber and then silver against the blue-black sky. The crickets had started their singing chirp and an owl gave occasional hoots from a tree branch.

"I guess we'd better go in, too," Bates murmured.

"If you're a gentleman, you'll wait here until I have my bath."

"What's with the 'gentleman' talk? What have I ever done to you that wasn't gentlemanly? We're married now so what's the difference if I see you wash or not?"

"If we were in a river or a creek I wouldn't mind, but washing in the house is—is not the same. Please, Bates. It matters to me. In a week or so maybe I won't be modest about bathing in front of you, but now—Well, I'd rather you waited outside until I finish."

"Whatever pleases your fancy, Marley." He gave a chuckling laugh, kissed me and pushed me into the house, settling himself on the stoop once more.

I undressed and washed quickly, finding the water

left in the pail tepid and the soap rough but mildly
fragrant from herbs or flower petals. Amos had given
us candles, but they weren't necessary. Moonlight
beamed through the open window. I put on the new
petticoat, loving the feel of the sheer linen next to my
skin.

"Bates," I called softly.

He came into the house and folded his arms around
me. "You feel so good, Marley," he whispered.

We held each other close, my cheek against his.
Finally we kissed again and stepped apart. Bates began
to undress and I removed the quilt from the bed,
folding it carefully and putting it on the table.

"Bates, look!" I said, grabbing his arm and turning
him around so he was facing the bed which now
glistened white in the moonglow. "Sheets! Clean
sheets!"

His laughter reverberated around the room and he
put his arms around me again. He was naked now. I
moved my hands across his smooth shoulders and
rested my palms flat on his chest against the thick mat
of tawny hair.

"That's what you wanted, isn't it?" he asked. "Seems
to me I recall when we lay on the sand that you doubted
you'd ever sleep on sheets or in a real bed again. Well,
there's the bed and here we are."

I laughed, too. Reaching my hands up to his face, I
touched his lips and traced the outline of his eyebrows.
The desire in me flamed and I clutched him fiercely,
kissing him with my tongue probing his mouth and my
hands sliding to the lower part of his body. He was
caressing me, touching me everywhere, kissing my
breasts, his hands moving from my hips to my thighs
until I thought my body would explode. We fell across
the bed and began the torrid, pulsating lovemaking as
though we had only that one night for passion.

When it was over both of us were exhausted. After a long time I murmured, "Bates, I love you."

His reply was a sleepy, "Mmmmmm . . . love you," and he tightened his arm around me. I nestled against him, warm and clean, my body so satisfied I felt as if I was floating high on the clouds. On that first evening in our new home I didn't know how short-lived those happy nights would be.

Chapter 13

By the middle of August the days were slipping by easily. It gave me a jolt to realize Bates and I had been residents of Bath Town for three months. I'd succeeded in putting the past to the back of my mind and I didn't worry about the future because the present was delightful. I had the man I adored and a home. Even if we had almost no money, we were surrounded by good people who made us feel welcome, and teaching school was less of a burden than I'd anticipated. There were moments when I actually enjoyed it. We must have been doing the job well since the parents asked that classes go on in the mornings during the entire summer to make up for the no-school days during the previous schoolmaster's illness and death in the spring.

On our first day Bates announced to the students that he wasn't tapping anyone on the head with a ruler. Every youngster perked up, listening intently.

"If you deserve punishments, you'll do extra lessons," he went on. "If you continue to misbehave or fight or hurt another individual and the lash is called for, I'll personally deliver you to your parents and let one of them take care of the whipping.

"Meanwhile, I hope you'll discover that learning isn't necessarily a chore and that the more knowledge you acquire, the more successful you may make your lives. Mind you, all learning doesn't come from books. Some of it does, which is why everybody in this room is going to learn to read and do numbers."

He instructed the older students in mathematics and the boys in navigation first thing each morning. I had reading and writing lessons for the little ones. We didn't have paper or chalk boards, but in good weather I would take the children outside, furnish each one with a stick and let them do their letters and numbers on the sand.

After a week of four consecutive rainy days, Bates conceived the idea of bringing sand indoors and spreading a thick layer on a flat board so writing could be taught regardless of the weather. He put legs on the board to form a table and added four sides around it to keep the sand from sliding to the floor. With a satisfied grin he said that he should have been a ship's carpenter. That word *ship* crept into his conversation often.

Bates was a hopeless gardener. He detested doing it; it showed in his face and his moody silence every time he touched a hoe or a rake. Although he was graceful and adept with other tools, his awkwardness in the garden was a joke. I watched him tend the plants clumsily. Finally I suggested that I take full responsibility for the garden. He looked as if I'd just handed him a bucket of gold. Other women did their family gardening and our plot wasn't nearly as large as most, but we just had two to feed. There was only one other family in town without children.

"That would be fine, Marley," Bates said when I

offered. "Amos needs help with his naval store and I can work for him every afternoon cutting and mending sails. He'll pay me in coins instead of goods and it'll sure be a safe feeling to know we have some money."

And you'll be near the water and can see the ships coming across the bay before they dock, I thought silently.

I knew he missed the sea and I'd noticed the wistfulness in his face when he watched a sloop riding at anchor or when he talked to the sailors. Two or three ships came into Bath Town harbor every week and the residents of the town rushed to the pier to buy, sell and barter. The seamen were anxious for fresh food and just as eager to sell some cargo, and apparently nobody questioned the source of those goods. Once when I asked Bates about it, he shrugged and commented that booty was booty until it changed hands and became the property of whoever paid for it.

"Hannah told me that the *Sweet Glory* was a pirate ship." I mentioned a brig which had left Bath Town the previous day.

"No questions were asked about that so no answers needed to be given, Marley. I heard that rumor, too. Heard they flew the black flag at sea. But the men behaved themselves in port. If I'd had the money to buy you a bolt of China silk, I'd have brought home enough of the blue material to clothe you for the next two years. I daresay you wouldn't have objected—*if* I'd had the money."

I changed the subject, knowing he'd spoken the truth and wishing we could have afforded the lovely silk. I wouldn't have uttered a word of protest if Bates had been able to present me with that shimmering cloth. I'd been envious of Hannah, of the dresses she was sewing for herself and her girls from the material Amos bought

for them. It was pale yellow shot with threads of white
and cream; the silk was iridescent, changing color in
each different light.

There were opportunities to dress up and life wasn't
all work for us. Bates went to the cockfights, but I
couldn't abide them—they were such bloody specta-
cles. I saved my recreation for Saturday nights. Bath
Town came alive then. Seth McGurn, the blacksmith
who was a native Scot and also a bagpipe player, and
William Chapman, a farmer who could fiddle, made
music. Pine resin torches were put up near the pier and
young and old danced to the merry tunes. Rum, brandy
and punch flowed freely in the publick house. When
our legs were too tired to continue dancing, we'd sit in a
circle around William and Seth.

The frolicking ended when the torches burned down.
Bates and I walked home hand in hand, laughing and
pausing to kiss, occasionally stumbling over a courting
couple hiding behind a tree or under a bush bordering
the road. At least we didn't have to resort to that for
our loving, I reflected thankfully. As soon as we were in
our house we'd come together with a passionate
sweetness which was as intoxicating as the drink had
been.

Josh paid us a quick visit when we'd been in Bath
Town about three weeks, arriving at noon just as school
was dismissed for the day. It was an extremely hot
morning. His homespun shirt was dark with perspiration, but he was freshly shaved and looked as clean as if
he'd scrubbed himself before leaving the log house. I
was glad to see him even though I noticed his eyes
raking over me, his gaze focused on my hips and breasts
so boldly I felt he was undressing me in his mind. But
on that particular day I was wearing a blue homespun
which buttoned to my chin and it didn't give him much
of a view.

"I wish Dorcas had come," I told him. "Is she all right?"

"Dorcas? Sure. She's scrawny but she never gets sick."

"Josh, Bath Town people are friendly and they wouldn't hate her or insult her for being an Indian. Please tell her I said that and the next time you come, insist on her making the trip."

"Wouldn't do no good," he shrugged. "She's got her own notions. Anyhow, I might not always let her know when I do my coming and going."

Bates gave me a warning look which meant I'd better hush. He had been about to head for his afternoon job at Amos' store when Josh arrived, but he waited. I brought out a plate of corn bread and some fried fish left from breakfast. Like the other wives, I'd learned to do my cooking early in the day and then kill the fire so the house would stay as cool as possible. In the summer heat it didn't matter that we ate many cold meals.

The men talked mostly about ships while I mended one of Bates' shirts. Josh remarked that he had sailed through the inlet to the Atlantic after a storm some days earlier because he thought he heard human cries.

"If it was a shipwreck, the sea must have swallowed up the victims," he said. "I didn't see anybody and no big pieces of a ship's hull or planking on the beach. I guess those voices must have come from a careened sloop in one of the coves."

"What's a 'careened sloop'?" I asked.

Bates explained that when there was no dry dock and a ship needed repairs below the water line or was so caked with barnacles it lost speed, it was "careened," which meant it was lifted out of the water by ropes and turned slightly so the bottom was exposed. The mammoth trees, especially the pines, were excellent for that as they could handle the weight of a ship. There were plenty of inlets along the Carolina coast ideal for the purpose as the sailors could work without interruption.

"Why don't they come into town to do it?" I asked innocently.

Josh and Bates looked at each other and laughed.

"It appears you don't know much about the ways of pirates, Marley," Josh replied. "When Blackbeard or the likes of him makes a run into Bath Town, it's apt to be a quick visit and he's gone again before a cry is raised. In a cove a captain can take his time about the ship's repairs and give his crew a chance to wash off some of their crud. Used to be when the Tuscarora were here that the sailors had their fun with the squaws or some of those 'trade women' the tribes kept to satisfy their own lust and rent to any man with the price."

"You said *when* Blackbeard comes to Bath Town." My voice was thick with apprehension. "You didn't say *if*. Do you mean he might come here?"

"Sure. He's in and out of Bath Town a lot. Teach thinks Ocracoke Inlet is his own private waterway."

I was so unnerved I couldn't be still. Dropping my mending on the table, I murmured something about needing to get to the garden. I was attacking the weeds with vengeance when Bates called out that he was going to the store. I was still jittery over Josh's comments about Blackbeard and didn't wonder what the two men had been discussing. Ships, no doubt. Bates doted on anything pertaining to the sea.

Josh came around the house to the garden and waited at the end of a row where I was working, his straw hat pulled almost to his eyebrows. "Need some help with that, Marley?" he asked in a lazy tone.

I made the error of glancing up. The sensuous invitation in his eyes was unmistakable.

"Thanks, but I can manage," I said.

"Two can handle a task in half the time it takes one. Come on back to the house and we'll plan about it." He laughed as he spoke, a low, sultry laugh. I was instantly afraid of him. He wanted me and I didn't know how far he might go to satisfy himself if I gave him half an opportunity.

Bates was too far off for a scream to bring him back. I couldn't call to Hannah; she'd packed her younger children into a wagon and hitched up the mule for an afternoon of berrypicking some distance from town. Besides, Josh had befriended Bates and me and I didn't want to do or say anything to embarrass him or myself.

"Taking care of this garden isn't just a wifely chore, but it's my pleasure," I said in what I hoped was a light-hearted manner. "I wouldn't want another soul to help. Anyway, my husband would be irked if he thought I'd let a guest work, especially a friend like you. Remember what I said about bringing Dorcas when you come to see us again, Josh."

I hoped the reference to "my husband" and "wifely chores" along with the mention of Dorcas would let Josh know I wasn't interested in a romp with him. He must have gotten my message because he said goodby and trudged off down the road toward the dock where he'd tied his dinghy. If he turned to glance over his shoulder at me, I wasn't aware of it. I clutched the hoe and kept my eyes on the ground until I was positive he'd had ample time to be all the way to the publick house.

That night Bates told me I shouldn't have harped on Josh's bringing Dorcas to visit us. "Let him decide if he wants to do it," Bates snorted. "You seem to forget she's a squaw although nobody else does."

"I wasn't harping, to use your word," I came back defensively. "I like Dorcas and I'd enjoy seeing her."

"I like her, too. But—"

"She must lead the most desolate life in the world," I interrupted him. "A trip any place would be some variety for her."

"That's not your responsibility, Marley. I don't doubt that she's living as she wants and it's probably the only way she knows. Josh is a rough character, but he's all right and he has some pride. It would humiliate him to drag an Indian here. Next time he comes, you inquire after Dorcas if you want, but don't make an issue of it."

Bates and I seldom disagreed and I didn't want even a small fuss. Busying myself with setting out the food for our supper, I let the topic of Dorcas drop.

It was a month before we saw Josh again and that time he made a quick, rushed visit. He had broken his knife blade and came to Bath Town for a new one which he bought at Amos' store, stopping at our house just long enough to eat. He was in such a hurry to get home before night that he didn't waste time giving me any of those dreaded leering looks. It wasn't until after he had gone that I realized Dorcas' name wasn't uttered.

That evening while Bates and I were sitting on our porch I said, "How did Josh pay for his new knife?" We had such a small amount of money I was always interested in the way others managed without spending their coins.

"Josh had some gold in his pocket," Bates answered.

My eyebrows went up. "How did he get gold out there in that wilderness?"

"He'd been doing some carpentry work on a ship careened near his house and he was paid well for his work."

I dared not ask if it was a pirate ship. I didn't want to know.

*　*　*

Josh wasn't the only man in Bath Town who gave me suggestive stares. But Josh was a mature man. Calvin Martin was sixteen. Calvin was Amos' oldest son, a tall, gangling chap with red hair and a square face, his features softer than his father's. He had tremendous hands and feet which always seemed to be in his way. Once when I said something about it to Bates, he chuckled and commented that all boys went through such a period. What I didn't mention to my husband was that sometimes I'd catch Calvin staring at me and if our eyes met the boy would turn away quickly, his face flushed. Calvin didn't attend the school; he helped Amos in the store instead.

"Calvin's like a colt. He'll grow out of it eventually," Bates remarked. "I used to be the same way."

I decided my imagination might be working too much if I was concerned about a boy giving me looks. As if he could read my mind, Bates added, "I don't blame Calvin for enjoying feasting his eyes on you, Marley. After all, you're the prettiest lass in Bath Town."

So Bates had noticed. I made light of all of it. "Maybe the boy will get over his awkwardness, but he'll never be handsome like you, darling," I said.

"Oh, ho! Flattering me, eh? What am I supposed to do in return for such a pretty speech?"

"Well," I pretended to be thinking, "you could kiss me. Or make love to me. Or—"

"Stop right there," he grinned. "I like the second suggestion about making love."

He came to me, kissing me and slipping his hand inside my dress. My nipples hardened under his touch and the moistness between my legs let both of us know how ready I was for his caresses and his body. All thoughts of Calvin Martin and the way he stared at me were forgotten.

Chapter 14

THE SUMMER HAD been a scorcher and I was happy to see September. While the days remained hot and muggy, the nights were more comfortable. By the middle of the month it turned cool enough toward dawn for Bates and me to pull the bedsheet over our bodies.

I slept in a petticoat. It amused him that I removed it when we were making love and put it on again before going to sleep. I was no longer modest about letting my husband watch me bathe or see me undressed, but I'd been brought up to sleep in a petticoat and it seemed natural to continue doing it. Bates got into bed as naked as the day he was born and woke up that way. On those cool autumn nights he snuggled close to me and I certainly didn't object. I loved opening my eyes in the morning, his arms holding me close and our bodies curved together.

During the summer I'd have given anything to bathe in the creek as the men and boys of Bath Town did. Despite all the water surrounding the community, women were supposed to be satisfied with a pail of water for their personal washing while the males went upstream to a spot that was absolutely off limits to girls and women at any hour of the day or night. When a bunch of men were there at the same time or when the wind came from that direction, I'd hear splashing and yelling. Bates would come home from the creek with his skin shining and a contented, relaxed air.

"I'm clean all the way to my bones without having to bother with soap," he usually remarked.

I was clean all the way to my bones, also, but I used soap of necessity and it never ceased to irk me that I had to make do pouring water from the hearth kettle into a shallow pan if I wanted a bath. Hannah had showed me how to make soap, combining tallow, wood ashes and pine resin and boiling the mixture until it was thick and bubbly. Like her, I cooked it in a pot over a fire in the yard and then spread it on a wooden trough to harden. The soap was yellow and strong, the odor rank. She suggested saving back a little in the pot and adding crushed flower blossoms to give it a pleasant scent for bathing, while the plain soap was used for scrubbing clothes.

One afternoon at the end of September I went with Hannah and three of her children to gather wild grapes on the edge of the woods. I had never tasted such grapes, small and green-colored and deliciously sweet. The vines had spread into the nearby trees, attaching themselves to the bark and branches and sending out long tendrils laden with fruit. We filled our baskets, nibbling and chatting as we picked.

When we returned to Bath Town I was in a wonderful frame of mind. Hannah went into her house promptly while I lingered on our porch to gaze at the glorious sunset. The sun lay on the rim of the horizon, a glowing circle against the vibrant red-orange sky. *Red sky at night, sailor's delight,* I murmured to myself. It was an old saying that Bates often repeated and I'd discovered it held plenty of truth. When the sun went down in a scarlet blaze, we could count on fair weather the following morning.

A good half hour of daylight remained and Bates probably wouldn't be coming in until dark, so I decided to have a bath and get rid of the dust and sticky juice from the grape-picking. Our food was already prepared, the last harvest of beans from the garden, boiled eggs, corn bread and the grapes.

The autumn crispness in the air was changing to a chill as night approached. On impulse, I built a fire, striking a spark with Bates' flint to ignite the dry kindling on the hearth. Flames quickly shot into the chimney, sending out a pleasant spurt of heat. I added an oak log and shoved the pot of vegetables suspended from a spit nearer the fire, wishing I could have a hot bath but not wanting to wait to heat a kettle.

When the cold water touched my flesh I shivered, hurrying the bathing. Bates probably wouldn't have complained if our meal had been delayed, and he could have teased me about using the hot meal as an excuse for a hot bath. I had a mental picture of his devilish smile when he commented that he was surprised I hadn't washed my skin off. Yet he enjoyed my being clean as much as I did. He was always telling me how good I smelled and how wonderful I felt against him, burying his face in my hair or against my throat while he murmured the loving phrases I adored to hear.

Footsteps sounded on the porch as I was pulling a fresh petticoat over my head. "Bates, is that you?" I called out, not wanting to be caught half dressed by anybody else. I grabbed my dress and hurriedly got into it, relieved to hear his familiar, "Aye."

He flung the door open and stalked into the house without even glancing in my direction.

"All right, so I've had another bath, but your supper won't be late," I laughed. "Don't you like the results?" I danced toward him, my skirts swirling. "If you'd enjoy a clean kiss, I happen to have some that are just waiting for you . . ."

The saucy words trailed off and I stood still. I'd expected him to smile and hold out his arms, but he was in front of the wall cupboard with his back to me, his shoulders hunched up while he removed clean shirts and trousers from the shelf and began to roll them into small, tight bundles.

"Bates—" Suddenly my tongue seemed too large for my mouth. "Bates, what are you doing?"

He turned slowly. I caught my breath, frightened at the expression on his face. His features were set into a steely mask, his jaws clenched and his eyes like chips of gray rock. The only sign of life was the throbbing pulse in his temple. I had seen him look that grim only once before, the afternoon on the *Solace* when Teach's men dragged me from below to the deck and Bates, his hands and feet bound to the mast, was Blackbeard's prisoner.

"I'm going to sea," he said in a strangely hoarse voice.

I was too stunned to believe him.

"You mean—we're leaving here?" I gasped.

"*I'm* leaving, Marley." He flicked his tongue across his lips. "You're staying."

My knees buckled and I swayed, holding to the edge of the table for support. Bates got to me quickly, clutching my arms and pushing me into a chair, then stooping in front of me which put his face on a level with mine.

"It's something I *have* to do, Marley," he said in that ragged, unfamiliar tone. "I've fought it ever since we came here to Bath Town and I'd have been long gone from here months ago if it wasn't for you. I don't want to leave you, but the sea is my work and my life and I can't stomach the thought of teaching school forever or farming or being a storekeeper."

I found my voice. "Bates, take me with you!" I begged frantically.

"That's not possible."

He stood up, walking a few paces to the hearth and resting his hands on his hips. The fire made one side of his face rosy. The other cheek was shadowed.

"But we're married!" I burst out, looking at him with desperation. "Don't you love me any more?"

"God, yes! I love you so much you're a fever in my blood, Marley."

"Then why—?" I swallowed hard. "How can you think about doing this? How can you go away without me if you love me? I could never leave you. Nothing would make me do that. Nothing."

A long, strangled sigh tore from him. "Try to understand, Marley. I have to go for another reason. I lost Seneca Irving's sloop. Lost it through no fault of my own, but I lost it, just the same. I have to get back to him and tell him my version of what happened."

"But that was months ago. Why is it so necessary now?"

"Unless I do, I'll never command another ship."

The sputtering of the fire was the only sound in the room. I was so near tears I trembled. The expression on Bates' face was unreadable, his eyelids half closed as if he wanted to shut out the sight of me, one corner of his mouth twitching ever so slightly.

"Does it matter that much for you to command another ship?" I asked when I could get myself under control.

"Damn right, it matters!"

"Why, Bates? I just don't understand any of this."

"A man has to do what he thinks is right. I only hope Irving won't slap me into debtors' prison. I'll rot there for sure if he does because there's no way I can raise enough to pay him for the *Solace* and the cargo—if he demands payment—unless I earn it at sea."

"Prison!" The wretched word seared my mouth. "Don't go to see him if there's the slightest chance he could put you into prison! We can have a good life here. We have friends and a house. . . . But if you want to live some place else, it's all right with me. I'll live anywhere on earth and make myself satisfied as long as you and I are together."

He shook his head, his hands which had been on his hips now hanging limply at his sides. "I can't, Marley."

"Why? Why can't you?"

"I'm signing on a ship as first mate. I wouldn't have the job if I dragged a wife aboard."

It was all I could do to breathe. I ached all over, my heart thudding against my ribs with such grinding beats that each one was a knife jabbing into me.

"Marley, I plan to come back for you. I mean it when I say I love you—and I've never told that to another woman."

"W-When w-will you come b-back for me?" I asked shakily.

"Whenever I can. Just as soon as I can. I don't know what the future holds so I can't set a date on the calendar, but I'll come, Marley. That's a promise. We'll be together again."

I wanted to believe him and was afraid to do it. Bates reached up one hand to run his fingers through his hair, the tawny locks falling over his forehead again. I was suddenly engulfed in an icy fear at the prospect of being left alone.

"Bates, what about me until you return?" I said.

"You'll be all right."

"Am I supposed to sit here and wait until it suits your fancy to drop by Bath Town and see if I'm still alive?" My voice was shrill with fear which I covered up with ugly sarcasm. "What if Amos doesn't want me occupying this house by myself or what if he finds another schoolteacher? Where am I supposed to go then? What am I supposed to do?"

"I've spoken to Amos and told him my plans. He's not happy about my leaving. I'll admit as much, but he knows I'm a sailor and I think he understands my feeling about getting in touch with Irving. Amos said all the parents are pleased with the way you've gotten the children to reading. He knows you can't teach navigation like I was doing, but you can show the students how to do simple sums and continue the reading classes. He wants you to stay on here and run the school."

Bates' eyes were boring into me, not the eyes of the man who kissed me so tenderly and who could laugh with me over silly little incidents. This was the sea captain, accustomed to giving orders and having them obeyed instantly, accustomed to making decisions which would be executed without question. Nothing I said was going to change his mind. I knew that as surely as if he'd spoken the words.

Misery churned inside of me but it was all mixed up with a burning anger that he could have used me so dreadfully. With his promises and his kisses Bates Hagen had made me fall in love with him, and now I was shattered to learn his feeling for me obviously was a casual, shallow emotion. It had to be that way or he wouldn't be leaving, casting me aside.

"Our marriage—our so-called marriage—must have been a joke to you," I stormed at him. "You claimed a common law marriage was as binding as if we'd stood up in front of a preacher, but that apparently was a convenience to save you the trouble of having to coax me—or rape me—every time you wanted a woman in your bed!" My head jerked up, my voice reeking with bitterness. "I believed you! I honestly did, and that makes me a dunce, doesn't it? I—"

"Marley, for God's sake—"

"You hear me out! I've been faithful to you. I've tried to be the best wife I could and I did everything I knew to make you happy. Now all I have to show for it is a broken heart. Maybe I'd have been smarter and a lot better off staying with the other women on the *Solace* even if those pirates had used me terribly. If I'd made it to Charles Town and married the man who paid Seneca Irving for a wife, only my body would have been hurt. Not my heart or my soul. I wouldn't have loved that husband, whoever he might have been. I was already in love with you! If he'd finally rejected me the way you're doing, it wouldn't have been the end of the world for me."

The blood left Bates' face, making him as gray as the ashes on the hearth. Veins in his neck stood out on the surface of his skin like twisted ropes and his lips were shut in a forbidding line. Without bothering to turn his head in my direction, he fixed his eyes on the door and strode across the room to it.

The fury and the fight went out of me.

"Bates—" His name was a sob.

"I have to go, Marley. My ship will sail with the tide and I don't want to be left on the dock."

He continued to stare straight ahead toward the door, but he stopped walking abruptly. I could hear his ragged breathing.

"What ship, Bates?"

"The *Sweet Glory*."

"What is its port?"

"She's bound for Boston this trip."

The choking panic rising in my throat made me reel and sent the room spinning around my head. "Bates, isn't the *Sweet Glory* a pirate ship?" The question came in a tortured whisper, although I felt as if I were screaming.

He cleared his throat but didn't reply. Opening the door, he stepped out into the twilight.

"Bates, please . . ." My voice broke, loving him so much I doubted that I could live without him. "Aren't you even going to kiss me goodby?"

"I can't," he groaned. "If I touch you now I won't be able to go and I have to do it. I have to."

He disappeared into the shadowy dusk, his boots clattering briefly on the porch and the steps, the sound dulled as he reached the sand road.

Part Two

Chapter 15

IT WAS NOT difficult to pick out the captain of the *Roxanne*. His fancy clothes separated him from the crew. The ship lay at anchor in the Bath Town harbor, a graceful brig with two masts and an unusually long bowsprit, her sails furled and the decks cleaner than those on most of the vessels which tied up at the pier to sell cargo and take on fresh food and water.

On the point of land overlooking the bay several planks had been laid across sawhorses to form tables for the merchandise. Anybody who came to buy could not only see the goods, but could look onto the deck of the *Roxanne* at the coils of rope, lifeboats and the six cannon. Although the big guns were covered with sailcloth, their shapes were obvious. The crewmen hawked their wares in loud singsong voices with a variety of accents: "Come-a and see-a what we have-a for you," rang through the village.

The afternoon air was brisk, the October wind whipping at my skirts and tossing my hair into my eyes. I pulled my cloak close and adjusted the hood, tucking my hair inside it. The cloak was strictly utilitarian, made of plain gray wool, and I had bought it cheaply from just such a group of sailors on a cold morning not very long after Bates left Bath Town thirteen months earlier.

During the long year without him I had lived one day at a time, hoping constantly that each hour would bring him home to me or at least bring a message from him. The school kept me busy during the daytime. I tended the garden in spring and summer, and the spinning and sewing in winter. Some townspeople paid for their children's education with clothing and food; a few others gave me money. I'd spent the coins for such necessities as the cloak and items I couldn't make. The few remaining coins were hidden in a small wooden box stashed behind a loose brick in the chimney—for Bates when he returned.

During the busy days I managed not to think about Bates every minute. But the nights were a special agony. I would close my eyes, aching for sleep. Instead, I'd see my husband and relive the hours we had together, seeing him in the dinghy afloat on the Atlantic, feeling his tenderness the first time we made love on the sand, hearing his whispered marriage vows in the moonlight.

I could almost feel his warm lips sliding over my face, moving to my breasts, almost feel his hands on my body. Then I would open my eyes in the darkness and shudder. Bates' half of the bed was empty, his pillow smooth and cold against my cheek. Instead of his deep breathing and murmured love words, there was only the creaking of the house timbers and the rattle of a tree branch against the roof.

If Bates had died I could have accepted life without him better than the torture of knowing he left me of his own free will. Death was an act of God. I'd still have grieved, but it might not have been as hard to go on living. Maybe I'd even want a new love if my husband couldn't come back from the grave. As it was, the hurt of his going alone was shattering, and his not returning was a fresh torture. I needed him. Needed to talk to him, needed to see him coming through the door of our house at dusk. Needed the security of a man's arms around me.

But not just any man. Bates Hagen. I did not realize that he had become my entire world until he was gone.

I'd had opportunities to be with other men during that year without my husband. I'd rejected all of them with a firmness which made enemies for me. The first was Josh Harding who came into town a month after Bates left and made no bones about his intentions.

He ate the food I offered, and caught me by the shoulders as I was clearing the table, trying to kiss me. I averted my face and his mouth grazed my hair, but he wouldn't let me go.

"Josh, stop it!" I hissed and twisted. His grip remained firm.

"Marley, aren't you hungry enough for a man to want me between your legs?" he asked boldly.

"How dare you? No. No! Leave me alone!"

That time I jerked free, and when he persisted, I opened the door and gave him a shove, ordering him not to come near my house again until Bates was back. Josh was physically stronger than I and he could have planted his feet on the floor and refused to budge despite the push I gave him, but he stepped out on the porch and whirled around to face me.

"You really think Bates Hagen is coming back here?" he gave a snarling laugh. "Not on your life. For a long time before he left I knew Bates was ready to go, that he was just waiting for the right ship to tie up at the pier." Josh's eyes moved over me again in a lewd look, his lip curling. "You must have thought being a sailor's wench was permanent, but you ought to have learned by now that no woman ever replaces the sea for some men."

"Go, Josh! Just go and stay gone!" I barked, banging the door shut in his face and leaning against it until I stopped shaking. I had not seen Josh again, although he must have come to Bath Town for supplies.

Sam Drake, the tanner, a man who had outlived four wives, came to call one night and announced that he was "ready to begin courting." Shocked, I reminded him that I was married, a fact which he sloughed off. He acted genuinely amazed that I turned down his advances.

The biggest surprise had been Calvin Martin. He kept my woodbox filled, which I put down to an act of neighborliness or perhaps to an order from his father. If he saw me fetching a pail of water, he'd run over and take it from me. I always thanked him. To be truthful, I was glad if he lingered to talk. Chatting with him was like chatting with one of my students, only Calvin was taller, and he still had the boyish awkwardness which Bates had sworn would vanish.

One summer night after Bates had been gone nearly a year I walked out into the yard for a breath of air. Calvin approached my house in darkness. He walked silently, his footsteps soundless on the soft earth.

"Marley," he said and for a moment I was stunned. I recognized his voice, of course, but in the past he'd always said, "Mrs. Hagen," never using my first name.

"Oh, it's you, Calvin." Just to be saying something, I added, "Nice evening, isn't it." The night was clear and a fresh breeze blew off the river. Down the street as far as I could see, the houses were dark, the townspeople having put out their candles and gone to bed.

"Real nice," Calvin whispered. "Especially if I'm with you."

Something in his tone put me on guard. I didn't like the idea of being alone with any man—except Bates—in the night. Even though Calvin was a youngster, he was standing very close to me, his breathing unnaturally fast.

"I—I have to go in now," I said quickly.

"Aw, Marley . . . don't do that. Stay out here and let's watch the stars."

I couldn't believe what I was hearing. Floundering for an excuse to leave, I said, "I—I have to—to study my lessons. I can't teach the children if I don't prepare," and I ran indoors. Waiting, I half expected him to follow, but he didn't. He must have returned home.

But a few nights later he was back. That time he came into the house. He tried to kiss me immediately, and attempted to put his hand under my skirt. I pushed him away and he came at me again.

"Calvin, what in the world is wrong with you?" I barked angrily at him. "Amos and Hannah would be furious if they thought one of their boys was annoying a neighbor! You're making a pest of yourself acting this way. I'm ashamed of you because I know you've been taught to behave better. If you don't leave me alone I'll have to speak to your father!"

He opened his lips to speak and closed them in silence, bolting out of my house. I sat down limply in the nearest chair. Maybe I ought to have felt flattered, but I didn't. There were plenty of men in Bath Town but no unattached women except some very young girls and two elderly widows—and me. I didn't consider myself unattached and I wanted no man except Bates. Calvin Martin had best find one of those young girls if he wanted to put his hand under a skirt.

After the first six months without Bates I began going to the harbor whenever a ship arrived in the hope of gaining information about my husband. It was no easier that day in October when the *Roxanne* was tied at the dock than it had been the first time. I still had a fluttery sensation in the bottom of my stomach at the thought of approaching strangers with questions.

I'd never received any news. Mulling everything over in my mind, I couldn't decide if I was afraid to pose the questions or if I feared the answers. I returned home distraught after each experience, feeling very much alone and fighting new desolation, bracing myself to go back to the dock for the same questions when the next ship anchored.

The crewmen of the *Roxanne* were a rugged group in mottled calico shirts and sailcloth breeches. They were barefoot and most of them wore loose jackets which failed to hide the inevitable knives and pistols stuck into their belts. Several had tied gaily hued scarves around their foreheads; some wore jewelry, heavy gold chains being the favorite. One burly seaman had an opal cluster clipped to his head scarf with at least fifty stones in the pin, their iridescent colors sparkling in the chilly sunlight.

I didn't doubt that most of the jewels and many of the wares had been stolen, that once everything was the property of some unfortunate passengers or had belonged to the victims of raids at sea. The *Roxanne* did not appear to be a pirate ship, but it was impossible to know for certain, as no captain would be stupid enough to hoist a black flag as he sailed into port. Buying stolen goods was of no concern to the townspeople, not even to Hannah and Amos. Hannah merely smiled and shrugged when I once inquired how she felt about it. I recalled Bates' comment that "booty is booty."

On that October afternoon I had no intention of

making a purchase, but I pretended to be looking over
the wares until I was positive I'd spotted the captain of
the *Roxanne*. Getting into conversation with members
of the crew seemed to give them the idea I was flirting,
which they accepted eagerly. I was determined to avoid
that. Months earlier when I questioned a sailor about
Bates, he followed me halfway home and would have
gone further if Seth McGurn hadn't come along and
sent him running. After that episode, I put my questions only to the ship captains, making sure there were
plenty of people nearby if I needed help.

Chapter 16

WALKING SLOWLY IN front of the *Roxanne*'s displays, I went past a table laden with pewter plates and fine porcelain china cups, moving on to the small kegs of molasses and loaves of brown sugar, sniffing the tangy odor of the sweets. I paused before the cloth. Ribbons and strips of rich fur trim lay next to bolts of worsted, silk and calico. There were a number of dresses and cloaks, some ornate and others rather plain. Most of them showed signs of wear.

I held up a turquoise satin gown decorated with tiny bows of silver ribbon. As I twirled it around, I noticed a lanky man emerging from the publick house across the street. He waited a moment on the steps, wiping his mouth with the back of his hand and letting his eyes sweep over the tables as if he was checking to determine how much had been sold. His trousers were pale tan, tucked into black boots gleaming with a high polish, and his white silk shirt was made with a stock at the throat and long full sleeves gathered into cuffs at the wrists. Over it he wore a knee-length jerkin of brown velvet with a design of scrolls and leaves

182

embroidered in gold thread. He wasn't a local resident—I knew all of them on sight—and he was dressed far too well to be one of the *Roxanne*'s crew. He had to be the captain.

He came toward the tables, walking lazily. A gust of wind caught the hem of his velvet jerkin and tossed it back to reveal a gleaming russet satin lining. I studied his face while appearing to inspect the turquoise gown.

He was of average height, slender, but with broad shoulders. His hair was as black as mine and his eyes equally dark. He had a lean face with chiseled cheekbones and a straight nose, his wide mouth curving in a slightly sardonic manner as if he was laughing at a secret joke. Yet there was an air of authority about his erect carriage, and his clean-shaven chin was firm. Like Bates, this man could make an order stick once it was delivered.

Strolling the length of the sawhorse tables, he turned and started back with the same leisurely strides. I was aware that he was watching me. A few townspeople were milling about the merchandise. I'd already nodded to Mary McGurn and Leah Powell. They stood near the molasses table, Mary pinching off a bit of sugar loaf from time to time and sneaking it into her mouth when she thought nobody was looking. Leah was the worst gossip in Bath Town. Heaven only knew what she might think—and relate afterward—if she saw me engage a stranger in conversation. But it was now or never!

Drawing a deep breath, I waited until the man was about three feet away before saying, "Captain?"

He hadn't expected me to speak. I caught the flicker of amazement on his face. It vanished quickly and he bowed, tilting his head a little to the right. Those black eyes slid from my forehead to my toes before he swung them to my face again.

"Captain Luke Nance of the *Roxanne*, m'am," he said. "I'm sure we've never met or I would have remembered such a charming lass."

His voice was pleasant, his manners gentle. He was a man of some breeding. I ignored the compliment and tried to fend off his stare, although it made me self-conscious. I didn't bother to explain that I was a married lady and not a lass.

"Captain, I wonder if you know of a man named Bates Hagen or if you've seen him recently?" My words came out in a jumble. I was always breathless when asking that question.

Mary and Leah crept closer, undoubtedly eavesdropping. Like the other people in Bath Town, they'd long since stopped inquiring if I'd heard from my husband and I felt they had jumped to the conclusion that he'd abandoned me. Pretending not to notice them, I turned all my attention to Captain Nance.

"Bates Hagen commanded the *Solace* until it was seized by Blackbeard, the pirate," I went on in a low voice to make it difficult for the women to hear. "Now he's first mate on the *Sweet Glory* out of Boston—or he was aboard that ship last fall."

"Hagen . . . hmmmm." He pursed his lips. "Now a mate after having been a captain?"

"I told you the pirates took his ship! Those awful men from the *Queen Anne's Revenge*—ugh!" I shivered at the memory.

He gave me a penetrating look. "You sound as if you'd dealt with the pirates yourself, m'am."

I started to relate the entire story, hoping it might make him more inclined to talk, but changed my mind. Instead, I merely told him that the *Solace* carried cargo as well as passengers. I didn't let on that I was one of the passengers and had been raped, although I added that Bates was set adrift in a dinghy. Captain Nance's face darkened and he listened without interrupting or asking questions. Somehow I had the feeling he knew my husband and he certainly hadn't given an immediate denial the way other captains had done. They might have been lying, of course, but this man seemed to be a different sort. My heartbeats quickened in anticipation of what he was about to say.

It came in the form of a question.

"This Hagen is a friend of yours?" he asked. "A sweetheart? A fellow you met when his ship was in port here?"

I drew myself up as tall as possible. "He is my husband, Captain Nance!" His dumbfounded expression would have been comical if I'd been in the mood to laugh.

"Bates Hagen—*married?*" He shook his head slowly as if he did not believe me. "That's something of a shock. I'd never have thought Hagen, of all men, would—"

Leah's sharp intake of breath grated behind him. Captain Nance broke the sentence off as he glanced back at her. Her cheeks flamed and she ducked her head, suddenly very interested in sorting ribbons. He wasn't fooled; he gave her a blistering stare for a full thirty seconds.

"Well, yes," he turned to me again, his voice firm and loud enough so Leah certainly didn't have to strain to hear. "Why don't you and I go over to the publick house so I can answer your questions fully and *without an audience.*"

Those final three words were enunciated distinctly. Leah knew they were directed at her; red streaks shot down her throat and neck, and she looked as if she had a high fever.

Under other circumstances I might have declined to go to the publick house with a man other than my husband. I was anxious to be away from Mary and Leah and I fell into step with Captain Nance. I had to trot to keep up with his long strides. When he realized I was running he grinned and slowed. At that instant the wind turned blustery, pushing my hood off and spinning sand from the road into our faces. My hair tumbled free and I could feel it fanning about my head in a wild black mass which must have made me look like a freak. With one hand I tried to get my hood on again, using the other hand to clutch at my skirts so they wouldn't fly up.

"You do have plenty of problems," he murmured, pulling the hood into place for me. "Let's get out of this gale and that'll solve one of them." Cupping his palm under my elbow, he hurried me across the street.

I hadn't been inside the publick house since Bates left. Nor had I gone to the Saturday night frolics since then. Nothing in the common room of the publick house had changed. It was a large rectangle with a fireplace in one corner, the low blaze giving off a comfortable warmth. A bar stretched across the back wall; two kegs of spirits at the far end and a row of pewter mugs hanging on pegs were the only decorations. The plank floor, pine tables, chairs and benches had been scrubbed almost white.

Beyond the common room, the kitchen was visible through a wide door. The Oglesby family lived upstairs. Tom Oglesby owned the publick house and four Oglesby children came to my classes. Meg, the oldest, was a precocious fourteen-year-old who had not returned to school in September. Now she helped tend bar, building something of a reputation for herself as a flirt. I could easily understand why the boys snickered at the mention of her name. I noticed the suggestive way she looked at the captain of the *Roxanne*.

He led me to a table for two near the hearth. It was the only table in the room which didn't seat four or six or eight. There were a handful of customers, all of them on the far side of the room at a long table; guffaws sounded from time to time. Meg sauntered over to us, her yellow calico dress cut low enough to show a good deal of her budding breasts as she swiped at our table with a feather duster and flashed a saucy smile at the captain.

"'Evening, Captain Nance. 'Evening, Mrs. Hagen," she said. "What can I fetch you to drink?"·

"A mug of ale for me and bring the lady whatever she fancies."

I said I didn't care for anything, but he refused to let me beg off. "Bring her a glass of your best wine, lassie," he told the girl, winking at her. Meg giggled, returning the wink and leaning forward so that he had a chance to stare down her dress. From where I sat opposite, I couldn't tell if he was doing it or not.

"You don't approve, Mrs. Hagen?" he asked as Meg walked away.

"Approve of what?"

"Of my having a laugh with that barmaid. You're frowning as if you think I've taken her to bed and I assure you I haven't although I daresay she wouldn't mind. She's hardly more than a child. I prefer my women to be full grown and—" his eyes moved to my head, "full blown."

I'd been attempting to smooth my hair and undo the wind damage. Now I dropped both hands to my lap, suddenly self-conscious. His remark could have been interpreted in many ways, but I let it pass.

"I noticed the barmaid call you 'Mrs. Hagen,'" he said. "So you actually must be his wife."

I was so irked I wanted to slap Luke Nance.

"Captain, if you aren't going to give me any information, there's no reason for me to sit here and listen to your crude jokes." I stood up, ready to leave.

He motioned me down again and sounded apologetic. "I'll give straight answers," he said. "What do you want to know?"

"When did you see Bates?"

"In the spring. The end of March or it could have been the first week in April."

"Where?"

Meg approached with the drinks. Under the rim of the table I clasped my hands together in my lap, not wanting to talk in front of her and scarcely being able to contain myself.

"Where was Bates when you saw him?" I demanded as she left us. "Is he all right?"

"I don't know if he's all right or not." Captain Nance took a long gulp of ale. "I only had a glimpse of him and maybe it wasn't Hagen but another chap who looked a little like him from the distance. I was taking the *Roxanne* out of the Charles Town harbor and another brig was coming in and we passed and hailed one another. There'd been a bad storm the night before, one of the worst I've ever experienced, and I was damn thankful to be on land with my ship anchored. The other brig's mizzenmast was sheared off and they had a snarl of lines. The result of that gale, I'm sure. The sailors weren't paying much attention to us and I saw a man on that deck who seemed familiar and I thought at the time it was Bates Hagen, but it was a misty morning and I could have had my vision blurred."

"What was the name of the ship?"

"I don't recollect."

My hands and feet turned cold and the rest of me was burning. If Bates had been in Charles Town he was only a short distance from me . . . and he hadn't come near me or sent a message . . .

"You're white as a ghost, Mrs. Hagen!" Captain Nance picked up the wineglass and held it to my mouth. "Taste some of this. Are you going to be sick?"

The wine was strong and too sweet, but it put a little strength in my body. After the first sip I took the glass from him, cupping my fingers around it and draining every drop.

"I—I'm not sick," I managed to mumble. "It's just—just that I would have thought . . . if Bates was in a Carolina port . . . that he'd have gotten in touch with me."

I was thinking aloud, speaking as much to myself as to him. Captain Nance moved his tongue over his lips and answered quickly, "Perhaps it wasn't possible for him to do that."

"I know," I sighed. "If Bates wasn't in command he would have no say in the ship's destination. But a lot of vessels have come into Bath Town since last spring and if he'd only sent a letter . . . or a message . . ."

"Listen, Mrs. Hagen. A sailor makes plenty of sweet statements to a pretty lass when he's in port and knows he'll be at sea shortly and the words won't catch up with him. I reckon Hagen's no better and no worse than the rest of us. If he gave you the impression you were the only one he'd ever had a fancy for or if he told you he was coming back to see you or planned to take you with him or—"

"But we're married!" I cut in.

He cleared his throat. Meg came by with several lighted candles in tin saucers, putting one on our table. I hadn't realized how dim the room had become. The flame was reflected in the captain's black eyes; tiny pinpoints of light gleamed.

"Married by a preacher with a legal license, Mrs. Hagen?" he asked quietly.

I shook my head, so miserable I wanted to die.

"Well, you wouldn't be the first common law wife to find herself left by the shore," he went on in a strangely gentle voice. "You said Hagen has been gone a year and that's a long time for you to sit and wait and worry. It's right hard for a man to remain faithful to one woman that long when he's not near her, too. Life's for the living—not for promises. Maybe it's time you thought about yourself rather than him. I sure don't enjoy seeing a lovely lady like you wasting herself over a sailor long gone when a perfectly able replacement is sitting in front of her yearning to know her better."

Choking back a gasp, I jumped to my feet.

"I've made you angry," he muttered. "I certainly didn't intend to do that."

"I'm not angry, Captain Nance," I lied. "I'm just not interested in your—uh—offer. Thank you for your time and the information."

"Hey—wait! If Hagen won't come to you, why don't you go to him?"

I'd been about to leave. I stopped, an old sensation inching up my spine. Me . . . go to Bates? It was a thought I'd never considered.

Immediately common sense set in. "Even if I knew for sure that Bates was in Charles Town, I couldn't do that," I answered. "I can't afford passage aboard a ship and I don't have a horse to go overland."

"The Roxanne is sailing South. We'll hoist anchor tomorrow morning and I could drop you off in Charles Town."

"Didn't you understand what I just said, Captain Nance? I don't have that much money!"

Those black eyes never wavered. "You wouldn't have to pay money," he replied softly.

"How—? What?"

I caught my breath. A mystical smile pulled at the corners of his mouth and something stirred inside of me. I'd never thought of trying to locate Bates, but if my husband found it impossible to come to Bath Town, why shouldn't I search him out? The love he and I shared was so deep I would never believe he had stopped wanting me unless I heard it from his own lips. If we could only be together again, everything would be just as it was before.

My breasts rose and fell as the tempo of my breathing increased. I looked at Captain Nance. "You'd let me have *free* passage on your ship when you never set eyes on me until an hour ago?" I asked. I was remembering the way I'd been tricked aboard the *Solace*. This time I intended to be sure. Of course, Captain Luke Nance was a far cut above McGregor.

He drained the ale and spun the mug in a circle on the table. "The *Roxanne* isn't designed for passengers. There's only sleeping space for the crew and a cabin for the captain." He hushed, giving me an impish smile. "Yes, I'd gladly let you have free passage, but the only way my ship can accommodate another person would be for that one to share my quarters."

The implication hit me and I exploded. He didn't care about finding Bates or helping me. All he wanted was a woman in his bed. He'd been poking fun at me the entire time and I'd been too stupid to catch on. "I hope your precious ship sinks and that you go down with it!" I hissed at him. "The last thing I ever plan to do is to get involved with the likes of you! I don't even want to have to say, 'Good morning,' to you in the future!"

Tears of fury filled my eyes and I grabbed my cloak. To my consternation, he reached out, his fingers closing around my wrist. I tried to yank free, but his grip tightened until I felt as if a chain was binding my arm.

"My 'offer' as you call it was sincere," he said in a serious tone. "And it still goes if you care to sail aboard the *Roxanne*. I'm sorry not to have been of more help. Perhaps Blackbeard will have some information when he moves to Bath Town. From what you've said about the events aboard the *Solace*, I gather the pirate knows Hagen well or he'd never have given him a dinghy."

"Blackbeard's coming—*here?*" My question was a rasping whisper.

"Didn't you know?" Nance's face showed surprise. "I thought it was common knowledge that he's building a mansion between Bath Town and Plum Point."

Stunned, I shook my head.

"The dwelling is on the east side of Bath Creek, up on the cliff with a view of the bay," the Captain said. "I hear tell he's bringing in mahogany panels for the walls and a hand-carved black walnut bannister and a load of fine French furniture—all stashed in the Bahama Islands just waiting to be brought here when he's ready for them."

"I don't believe you!" I choked the words out. "You're just saying this to frighten me!"

"Why the hell should I want to frighten you?"

He made a growling noise under his breath and for the first time he seemed genuinely annoyed with me. "So you think I'm making up a tale, do you? Do you also believe I deliberately scare children and jump on old people?"

I might have replied if I could have found my voice. Heaven knows what I'd have told him. His eyes were blacker than ever and his mouth hardened. I had the feeling that not many people dared to question what Luke Nance said.

"Meg!" His voice boomed out with her name.

Every head in the room jerked around. The girl came to our table. "You want more wine and ale, Captain?" she asked and picked up our empty glasses.

"No, we don't." He addressed her, but his eyes remained on me. My wrist throbbed from the strength of his fingers which held me in an iron grip.

"I want to ask you a question, Meg," he went on. "Have you heard anything about the pirate Blackbeard coming here to make his home?"

"La, sure." She gave a big smile, replaced at once with a quizzical expression. "Why are you asking me that, Captain Nance? Last night you were sitting right over there—" she gestured to a table near the bar. "You were drinking rum punch when everybody here was talking about Blackbeard coming to stay as soon as his new house is finished."

The Captain said nothing. His gaze was fixed on my burning face.

Meg began to giggle, twirling the hem of her skirt as she beamed. "Won't it be nice when he moves here?" she said in a bubbly voice and she was all smiles again. "More money for the publick house! That man is always rich and his sailors will be bringing in fancy finery and jewelry and everything. Every time he comes he gives me a present. See this petticoat?" She held up her dress to show an undergarment with a lace ruffle. "He brought that to me last winter."

Blackbeard had come to Bath Town since Bates left? I was glad I hadn't known about his visit. An acid taste came into my mouth. I felt so sick I thought I might vomit on the spot.

At that moment Meg must have become aware that Captain Nance was holding my arm. She glanced down and gave an odd, "Oh!" part exclamation, part question. In the split second that followed I realized the common room was silent. The laughter and chatter of the townspeople and men from the *Roxanne* had hushed. All those eyes were staring at Meg, Captain Nance and me.

I didn't say a word. I couldn't. His hold on my wrist loosened and I stumbled to the door.

Chapter 17

A SAFFRON MIST blended with the twilight, giving an eerie glow to the landscape, shrouding the trees and buildings in murky yellows and grays. The sunset colors were gone, and the sky was patched with purplish clouds that hid the first stars. I didn't realize I'd been in the publick house such a long time talking to Captain Nance.

I wasn't accustomed to being in the heart of the village at dusk. The quiet was spooky. Small waves splattered the dock. The *Roxanne* swayed back and forth on the water. The trees shook in the wind, the bare branches rattling, but there were no human sounds. Businesses had closed for the day and the sailors' merchandise was gone, the sawhorse tables dismantled and the planks piled on the ground.

Not a seaman nor a resident was in sight, and I didn't see a dog or a barnyard animal. Bath Town lived by the sun, not an hourglass. Autumn and winter nights, some people dropped into the publick house, but most stayed home.

Trudging along, I shivered and held my cloak snugly. The shock that Blackbeard was building a house at Plum Point less than a mile from where I lived had passed. Now I was tense with a gnawing, pulsating fear. *It can't be . . . that awful man wouldn't come here to live among decent people.* I repeated that over and over to myself.

Teach had gall as well as power to do whatever he chose. It was unlikely that such a detailed report of his plans would be known unless there was truth to the rumors. If I believed Meg Oglesby and Captain Nance . . .

I would not believe it until there was verification from someone else, I decided desperately.

Bates and I hadn't been in Bath Town a month before we discovered that Blackbeard often paid visits to the harbor. What was even more astonishing, the residents welcomed him. They admitted he might be a robber at sea, but they swore he'd never done evil on land. Apparently the pirate possessed a flamboyant charm and showed it when he wanted to. The townspeople bragged about entertaining him in their homes. His stories of voyages to far-off places enchanted them. He also brought extravagant presents—bolts of silk, a pair of leather boots, a set of porcelain. There was scarcely a house in town that didn't have at least one of his mementoes—except mine.

I couldn't imagine how anybody would take up for the man. Bates had reminded me these people had never seen Teach doing his dastardly work at sea. They had no evidence of his cruelty. I'd never told a soul how he planned to turn the women passengers from the *Solace* over to his crew. I didn't want to talk about those painful events. Nor did I want anybody to know I'd been raped by two of Blackbeard's sailors. The Bath

Town men would shrug. Most of the women seemed to think no one could be taken against her wishes, that if she was attacked she would have to cooperate for a man to possess her. I knew differently. I knew a woman could fight like the devil and still not be a match for a man's physical strength.

Bates tried to reassure me when we first heard of the pirate's visits. He quoted Amos to say that Teach hadn't come to town often since he acquired the *Queen Anne's Revenge*. The ship was too large to navigate the shifting sands of Pamlico Sound's narrow channel. The *Revenge* would have to be anchored within Ocracoke Inlet and Teach would proceed the fifty miles to Bath Town in a smaller vessel. The nuisance of such a maneuver apparently cut down on his visits. He hadn't put in an appearance since I'd lived there—at least, not that I'd known about.

After leaving Captain Nance at the publick house, the tangy odor of food drifted to my nostrils. On any other evening I'd have been ravenous from the good scents, but eating was the last thing on my mind. I couldn't stop thinking about Blackbeard. I knew Meg Oglesby wouldn't be the only person to give a warm greeting to the pirate and his crew.

If Blackbeard built his house and moved to Bath Town, I wouldn't stay, I vowed to myself. I didn't know where I'd go or what I would do, but I could not get up each morning with the terrifying prospect of coming face to face with Teach or one of his sailors.

The twilight had turned into a gloomy darkness. As I neared the Martin house I saw the faint outline of a man several paces ahead. I recognized the set of Amos' shoulders and his way of clasping his hands behind his back so that his elbows protruded at right angles. I called to him and he waited for me to catch up.

"Something wrong, Marley?" he asked. "You're not out this late very often."

"I—" The bland answer I was about to give froze on my lips and a question burst from me. "Is it true that Blackbeard is building a house at Plum Point?"

"I hear it's so." He sounded as matter of fact as if he'd commented on the weather.

"Amos, do you realize how awful that man is?" I said frantically. "Can't you keep him away from here? He steals and kills and does all kinds of unspeakable deeds!"

"Simmer down. Teach has taken an oath to give up piracy. He's received a certificate of pardon for anything he might have done in the past."

I couldn't take my eyes off of Amos. "How do you know that?" I demanded hoarsely.

"Everybody knows it, Marley. You keep to yourself so much you aren't aware of what's going on."

"Who on earth would pardon that criminal? I can't believe a pirate's sins can be wiped away as if they'd never happened."

"The Governor on order from the King of England." Amos seemed a bit exasperated at my questions.

"I don't care if the angels themselves pardoned him!" I came back hotly. "*I* know how evil Teach is! Know firsthand! He doesn't deserve the time of day, much less forgiveness! What about all the people he's killed or maimed? What about those he's stolen from? Pardoning him isn't going to bring back the dead or return his victims' belongings!"

Amos' normally placid face was showing anger. "Teach spared you and Bates, didn't he?" he snapped. "He set you two adrift in a seaworthy dinghy and gave you oars and a bottle of water. Put you out near shore, too. Bates told me that himself. It doesn't make Teach sound very bloodthirsty to me."

He was defending the pirate! I swallowed hard. In the dim twilight I could barely make out Amos' features, but his abrupt tone indicated he was becoming more annoyed with me by the second. I was equally upset with him.

"You're forgetting that Blackbeard stole the *Solace,*" I said. "God knows what he did to the women who were passengers."

"Every ship is up for grabs at sea whether taking it is legal or not. You're a sailor's wife. You ought to realize that as much as I do."

"Stealing is stealing, Amos Martin! No wonder there's no church or preacher here—or even a jail. Everybody in this town condones lawlessness. All of you must be sick to want a man like Blackbeard living here—just because he buys your friendship by giving out prizes. You don't even mind that those gifts were taken by force!"

His body stiffened and he squared his shoulders. "Hush! Enough of that," he stormed at me. "You listen to what I'm saying, Marley! You'd best get yourself calm about this because Teach is coming whether you like it or not. And there's nothing you can do to stop him. I grant you he's earned himself a reputation at sea, but if he wants to live peacefully on land, there's plenty of space around here for him. Governor Eden is his friend and has given him the property on Plum Creek, and since Teach has the pardon, he must be ready to settle down on land. I suspect—" Amos took a rasping breath, "I suspect if people hereabouts had to choose between Teach and you, a goodly portion of them might prefer having him in their midst."

I recoiled as if I'd been slapped. "Are—are you trying to say the school isn't—hasn't been satisfactory?" I managed in an unsteady voice.

Brushing past me, Amos took several steps forward

and stopped. I felt as if I was choking to death. My fingers curled into such tight fists that my hands throbbed.

"The children appear to be learning their letters and numbers so I reckon the school must be all right." There was a raw bitterness in his tone I'd never heard before. "You're not making any friends for yourself here, though. You don't mingle much and you've given a mighty hard cold shoulder to every man who has tried to pass a little sweet talk with you."

"I'm married," I said defensively. "I remember it even if the men of Bath Town don't."

We'd reached the lane leading from the road to his front door. A short distance ahead I could see my house.

Amos cleared his throat. "I've said this much so I reckon I may as well say the rest of it, Marley. Bates has been gone for more than a year. You're a comely woman. It seems mighty strange your not wanting a man since you've been a wife. You're young and of child-bearing age, too. At first I told the others that Bates Hagen would be back in a few months because that's what he told me. Now I think it was just a tale he was spilling out and I know full well nobody else in Bath Town thinks he's coming here again."

A lump the size of a pullet egg formed in my throat. Amos paused briefly, perhaps waiting for me to speak, but I didn't.

"Of course, Bates may be dead," he continued in a gutteral tone. "But if he's alive, it appears to me his not returning here is on purpose. Folks hereabouts prefer a schoolmaster to a lady teacher; he can maintain discipline. They liked the school better when Bates was running it, especially since he could teach navigation. But that's not the sole reason some of us are dissatisfied. We've already got more men than women—young women, that is—in Bath Town. It doesn't seem right for some of the men to need wives and you're ignoring them."

A searing pain shot through me. I touched my tongue to my lips, attempting to say, "Good Night, Amos." But no sound came from my throat. I walked away from him without uttering a word, my heart about to burst. The night mercifully closed around me. I heard Amos' door open, the hinges creaking, and then the door slammed shut. It was only two hundred feet from the Martin house to mine. Every step seemed a mile long.

My house was dark and the fire almost gone. I lit a candle and put a fresh log on the embers in the fireplace, throwing in a handful of oak chips to make it blaze up quickly. I felt encased in ice. The chill was partly from the nippy autumn wind, mostly from what Amos had said.

The Martins had been Bates' and my closet friends. Had been—I reflected wryly. With a hurting need to be realistic, I wondered how true that friendship was now. I couldn't imagine what had prompted such strong accusing language from Amos . . . unless . . . unless . . .

The thought crystalized and I sat down heavily. Unless Amos knew I'd turned down his son. Calvin! That had to be it. Calvin must have told him. I pressed my cold fingers against my eyes and then extended both hands to the fireplace. Calvin was over a year younger than I, but I'd rebuked him sternly and treated him like a child, threatening to tattle to his parents if he didn't quit dropping in and making suggestive remarks. Remembering how he'd tried to kiss me and get his hands under my skirt, I realized now that those actions hadn't been boyish overtures but a fumbling effort to begin a serious courtship. No doubt Calvin confided in his father. Amos had managed to cork up his rage at me until it erupted when I angered him by protesting Blackbeard's plans. I gave a hollow sigh, aching to put all of it out of my mind. That wasn't possible with so much horror and fear churning inside.

Mechanically I moved the kettle nearer the fire and stirred the pot of stew. I had no desire to eat. Soon the room was warm. I removed my cloak and was hanging it on a peg when I heard footsteps across the porch, the tread so heavy it had to be a man's boots.

Amos might be coming over to salve his conscience and apologize for speaking to me in such a hateful fashion. Well, let him come, I thought. I'd be polite but nothing more. It would be hard to forget his ugly remarks.

"Marley." The voice was a rough whisper, so low I scarcely heard my own name.

I unbolted the door. It wasn't Amos. Josh Harding strode into the room.

"Surprised to see me, lass?" he grinned. "You must be! You look like you're staring at a ghost, but it ain't so. I'm all flesh and blood. You can feel for yourself if you need proof!" He put out his hand, coming nearer.

There was something menacing in his manner and I backed off as I got a whiff of his foul breath. He had been drinking, although he wasn't drunk, for he stood upright. It had been months since I'd seen Josh. I was relieved to see anybody who would get my mind off of the encounter with Amos.

"Would you like some supper, Josh?" I asked. "I only came in a few minutes ago and the food's cold, but it won't take long to heat. I made the stew fresh this morning."

"I know you just came in. You walked right by me in the publick house without so much as a nod or a wave, but I saw you and Luke Nance holding hands as bold as anything."

"We were not holding hands!" I gasped. "Captain Nance had seen Bates and—"

"Don't tell me to deny what I witnessed with my own eyes, Marley," he interrupted, his mouth twisting. The scar on his cheek shone scarlet from the firelight. "I know what I saw. Nance had his hand on you! I said to myself that if you were over your haughty airs and dishing out favors these days, Josh Harding ought to rate a few. And I don't mean settling for a bowl of food, either."

His eyes fixed on my breasts. I jerked backward and my shoulders touched the wall. Both of us were breathing heavily. He came toward me, his face inches from mine. A bubble of saliva caught in the corner of his mouth and a strange glitter made his pale eyes burn as they shot from my breasts to my hips. I tried to slip sideways and get away from him, but he was too quick. He braced his hands against the wall on both sides of me, leaning forward and pinning me with his body.

"Josh, get hold of yourself!" The words were strangled.

"Luke Nance might be younger than I am, but I've had more experience with loving than he'll ever see. I know how to make a wench happy and have her squealing and begging for more. You'll hate for us to be finished, Marley. Right now we're going to get in your bed and take it slow and easy until morning."

"We'll do no such thing! Get away from me, Josh!"

He threw back his head and laughed. "You keep putting me off and you'll have me real excited. Y'know that? I never was much for turning down a dare, especially when it was made by a pretty wench."

Violent fear rocked me. I managed to get my hands

on his chest, but I couldn't push him away. His body pressed so hard against mine it was impossible for me to lift my knee. I'd have slammed it into his groin if I could. The more I squirmed and twisted, the more he laughed like a giant cat tormenting a mouse. I knew I'd never summon enough physical strength. If I stopped him, it would have to be with a mental weapon to stifle his lust. I searched my mind desperately, hoping the mention of Dorcas would get his attention away from me.

"How is Dorcas?" I managed in a frenzied voice.

"Dead."

"What—?"

His expression never changed and he did not loosen his hold on me, his thighs continuing to mash mine and his hands clawing at my shoulders.

"That's right. Dead," he answered. "She took a fever and died in the summer. I've been too long without a woman. I mean to have you tonight! I've always had a hankering for you, Marley, ever since I saw you sitting in the dinghy. You ought to be finished with your grieving for Bates and be ready for some fun."

"No, Josh! No! I—"

His wet mouth came down on mine. I gagged and jerked my head and his lips slid across my cheek. He clutched the front of my dress and gave it a savage tug, ripping it and my petticoat to my waist, the material shredding to expose my bare flesh. Still holding me against the wall with his thighs, he put both his hands on my breasts, squeezing and kneading them until a wretched sob tore from me.

"I'm going to have you one way or the other, Marley," he grunted.

"You're hurting me, Josh! Stop it! Stop!"

He continued squeezing, pinching my nipples. "You

can make it pleasant for us or you can give me a hard time. I don't want to hurt you. I might have to if you keep pushing me back."

I knew it was useless to resist him. He would have me even if he killed me in the process.

"Just do it and be finished with it," I moaned.

"By damn, you'll like it!" His voice was fierce. "I swear I'll make you like it!"

Grabbing my arm, he pulled me across the room to the bed, yanking off what was left of my clothing. Lying there naked, I closed my eyes so I wouldn't have to watch him remove his shirt and trousers. The bed sagged when he sat down, kicking off his boots. He hurled over beside me, sliding one arm under my body and the other over me to bring me against him while he covered my face and my breasts with rough kisses.

I submitted. I had no choice. All I wanted was for him to be through and to get out of my house forever. But that wasn't how he intended to have it. This was different from those terrible moments with McGregor and the men from the *Queen Anne's Revenge*. It was deadening. Those three hurried, anxious to spend their hot passions quickly. Josh had no need to rush. He deliberately dawdled, toying with his own emotions, teasing himself, almost satisfying his lust and then holding back.

"Prolonging it is real nice," he whispered. "Makes the last part be that much sweeter when I'm ready for it, but I ain't ready yet. You're right delicious, you are."

If he expected an answer or a reaction from me he must have been woefully disappointed. I was past speaking, but determined not to give him the pleasure of hearing me cry out. Begging him to leave me alone did no good before he started his hurting caresses. Pleading wouldn't stop him now.

I had no choice. I let him do what he wanted until finally it was over. Snorting and hassling like a frenzied animal, he rolled off my body at last. I thought he would sleep from exhaustion, but he got up immediately and sat on the edge of the bed with his back toward me and scratched his nails across his stomach and chest.

The room was dim. The candle had burned down; the fire was a mass of embers. Josh stretched. He ambled over to the hearth and took two logs from the wood box. He threw them in the fireplace, jabbing at the coals with the poker until flames spurted up and the pale embers glowed orange-red. Pulling the sheet over my naked body, I looked at him through half-closed eyes, so battered I throbbed. I hadn't spoken since he threw me on the bed. I didn't intend to make a sound.

He got into his trousers and buckled his belt, sliding his shirt over his head. "Where do you keep the spirits, Marley?" he asked. "I could sure use a drink."

I forced myself to breathe deeply with a steady rhythm, hoping he would think I was asleep. Maybe he did think it. He dragged a chair to the hearth and sat down to put on his boots. Then he prowled the room in search of rum or brandy. A futile effort—I didn't even have a flask of wine. He was muttering in an undertone, words too faint to catch. When he found nothing in the cupboard, he squatted to look under the bed and yanked the wood box away from the wall to see behind it.

Except for the fire hissing and sputtering, the house was silent. I was afraid to peep at him for fear he'd realize I was awake. I kept my eyes closed, listening to his movements to learn what he was doing. There was a low chuckle, and then coins jangled as if he was bouncing them up and down on his palm, the silver ringing like a chime. He had discovered the money I'd hidden under a loose brick in the chimney.

"Reckon now I can buy myself whatever I fancy to drink," he murmured and laughed.

That pitifully small sum of money I earned teaching was all I had. I'd never intended using it for myself except in an emergency. It was for Bates when he returned. Asking Josh to put the coins back would be a joke even though they were rightfully mine. I couldn't take them from him by force. No matter what I did, I knew I'd never see that money again.

He walked to the door, his footsteps quickening. *Let him go! Let him go!* I prayed desperately.

But Josh paused beside the bed. "You enjoy our loving, Marley?" he asked softly.

Lying there, I cringed under his gaze but refused to move a muscle or reply. It took all the willpower I could summon to continue the even breathing and to hold my eyes shut without allowing the lids to flutter. My heart was pounding.

"All right, lass, you get your rest," he chuckled, opening the door. "That way you'll be real eager and anxious for me in the morning. I'll be back."

The instant he was outside I got to the door and put the bolt in place. Shivering so much my teeth rattled, I wrapped up in my cloak and crouched on the hearth before the fire.

Josh would return as he'd said. I didn't doubt that at all.

But I wouldn't be there.

Chapter 18

I emptied the kettle into the washbasin and scrubbed every inch of my body with scalding hot water as if that would wipe away the memory of Josh Harding. It didn't, of course. But I made hasty plans while I bathed, determined to be gone from the house before sunup.

Standing on the hearth in a clean petticoat, my skin smelling of soap instead of Josh's putrid sweat, I put the bedsheet and the clothing he'd ripped off into the fire. The flames licked at them. The material scorched and turned brown, then caught ablaze. I stared until nothing remained. Cloth was scarce. Deliberately destroying so much was an extravagance. The sheet could have been laundered and the dress and petticoat mended. But I wanted no part of anything the man touched.

Luke Nance's offer of "free" passage, which seemed insulting and preposterous yesterday, had now become a lifesaver. Sailing with him regardless of the circumstances appeared far safer than lingering in Bath Town. Josh would take me to bed whenever the whim struck now that he'd proved he could overpower me. Without the friendship of the Martins, I felt isolated. Amos turned against me. And Hannah, dutiful wife, would follow suit.

If I didn't leave Bath Town, the only way to keep Josh away would be to marry any man who would have me—and I could not endure that. The only husband I wanted was Bates. Unless I had proof he was dead, I still considered myself his wife. I still loved him no matter what the people in the community thought and gossiped and whispered.

The trip aboard the *Roxanne* wasn't going to be free. I had no illusions about what was in store for me. Since I couldn't buy my passage with money, I would pay with my body. At least I'd be gaining something in return: finding my husband was worth any price. I was sick with fury at what I'd just endured from a man who was supposed to be my friend—and Bates'! Captain Nance had decent manners and he looked clean, almost elegant. He couldn't be more brutal or repulsive than the men who had forced themselves on me.

If only I had money! Lots and lots of money. That *if* burned into me. If I'd had money, Seneca Irving would have long since been repaid for the *Solace* and Bates and I wouldn't have been separated. If I'd had money, I could have bought the *Roxanne* or any ship in the Bath Town harbor, ordering the captain to take me where I wanted to go. If . . .

Drawing a ragged breath, I shoved those dreams aside. Someday I vowed to have more than enough gold, but at the moment too many things had to be done before dawn for me to waste time wishing.

It seemed wrong simply to vanish and have the townspeople wonder what happened to me. I had a mental picture of the students arriving at an empty house and immediately shoved it aside. They were no longer my responsibility. I'd done the very best I could by them. If what Amos told me was true, my efforts weren't appreciated.

I decided against paying a visit to the Martins to tell them my plans because I didn't want to have to answer their questions. I sat down to write a note, wondering how much to state. Not much, I decided, remembering the conversation with Amos. Besides, what difference would it make after I was gone?

More than a year earlier Bates sharpened goose quills for pens and made pokeberry ink for writing lessons. But paper was expensive and the parents refused to spend money for it when their children could write on sand. So we had no paper. I'd never defaced a book in my life, but this was a crucial circumstance. Tearing a blank page from the back of one of the books in the schoolroom, I dipped my quill in the brownish ink and wrote:

> I am going to Bates. Thank you for your kindnesses to me. Goodby,
>
> > Marley

After laying out a blue homespun dress to wear the next day, I spread a blanket on the table, putting my other dress and two clean petticoats in the center of it along with a towel and a bar of soap. This time I meant to have more than just the clothes on my back when I began a journey. Everything else would be left in the house. Some items had been given as payment for holding classes. The next teacher would find a use for them, just as Bates and I had done with the belongings of the former schoolmaster.

The pink brocade which Dorcas had given me was in the cupboard since Bates left. I lifted it out, the folds of silk rustling and the rich sheen of the rosy fabric glowing. I ran my hand over it, immediately thinking of Josh and shuddering at the recollection of the day he told Dorcas to find something for me to wear. That brocade reminded me too much of him. I shoved it back into the cupboard. Then I drew it out slowly and added it to the other garments on the blanket. Homespun dresses were drab. I wanted to look my best for Bates. With my husband holding me in his arms once more, surely I'd be able to forget the ordeal with Josh Harding. I needed that fine gown.

Suddenly, unexpectedly, the day's events caught up with me. Misery and soreness combined into an overwhelming fatigue. I felt as if I was falling down into the bottom of a well . . . falling and falling and falling . . . and could never find the strength to climb to safety. My hands reached out and found the back of a chair. I clung to it until the dizziness passed and I could get across the room to the bed. Collapsing, I closed my eyes.

I slept at last, but it wasn't a restful sleep. Vague, unpleasant dreams bordered on nightmares. The slightest sound roused me. The familiar branches rattling, the shrieks and hoots of night animals seemed weird and loud as thunder. I found myself startled, wide-eyed, sitting up in bed with my heart racing and the covers clutched to my chin. A dozen times I got up in the darkness, cracked open the shutter and looked out to make sure what I'd heard wasn't Josh coming back.

Chapter 19

BY THE TIME the first pale glimmers of gray light showed on the eastern horizon I had dressed. The blue homespun was plain, made with long sleeves and a square neck. My hair was twisted into a bun to fit snugly under the hood of my cloak, although little tendrils already were brushing softly against my cheeks. I wasn't hungry, but I forced down a bowl of stew, discovering thankfully that the food eased the hollow sensation in the pit of my stomach.

Forget Josh—forget Josh—forget Josh, I repeated to myself like a refrain. I knew I could never completely wipe away the memory of his ruthlessness, but I was determined to try, especially now that I'd be rid of him. After smothering the fire with ashes, I tied the four corners of the blanket together into a bundle, picked up the note and stepped outside.

The sky was overcast, the landscape a blur of shadowy predawn blacks and grays. The gusty wind had died and the damp air smelled of rain coming. Not good weather for going to sea, I thought as I crossed the porch of my house for the last time.

To my relief the Martin house was quiet, an indication that nobody was awake there. I tiptoed up Amos' steps and put the note under the door. Once on the ground, I almost tripped in haste to get to the road and out of sight. I don't know what I might have said or done if Amos or Hannah had seen me and called out.

The finality of what I was doing struck me. A lump of pure panic formed in my throat. Awful questions nagged at my brain. What if Captain Nance was now delaying his departure until the weather cleared? What would I do—come back to the house? What if he refused to permit me to come aboard his ship notwithstanding his promise about my sailing free? What if the *Roxanne* had already gone?

I broke into a run, unable to believe any situation could be worse than to reach the dock and discover the *Roxanne* sailing away, a tiny speck off in the distance. Captain Nance had mentioned leaving "in the morning" without giving the actual hour. I didn't keep up with the tide charts. If "in the morning" implied any time after midnight, he could be miles away. Clutching the blanket bundle I ran as fast as I could, panting and gasping for breath, my sides aching. Not a soul was in sight, although smoke curled from the chimneys of a few houses. The sky was becoming lighter, with no hint of a sunrise, and the clouds billowed overhead, the darker ones thick and ominous.

A low, involuntary cry tore from me when I came to the heart of town and saw the ship at the dock, her gangplank not yet raised. I slowed to a walk, trying to get my breathing back to normal. The *Roxanne* was a hubbub of activity. Men on the cross masts unfurled sails and another group of sailors rolled huge barrels from the pier to the ship's deck, cursing as they strained at their task. The smell of tar and resin was so penetrating I guessed those barrels held naval stores.

Some of the seamen leered at me, grinning suggestively, and one made a pointedly obscene gesture. My eyes scanned the deck in search of the captain.

I noticed two men standing near the bowsprit talking, but it wasn't until one turned and I had a glimpse of his face that I recognized Captain Nance. His eyes and hair were black as ever. His lean face with high cheekbones was not quite handsome, although he could not be called ugly. Dressed in sailcloth trousers and a dark loose jacket, his appearance was very different from the man I'd seen the day before wearing a silk shirt and brown velvet jerkin embroidered with gold thread.

Just as I spotted him, he saw me, his eyebrows lifting slightly. A mocking smile spread over his face and he sauntered to the deck rail to stare down to the dock where I stood.

Our eyes met and my cheeks felt uncomfortably flushed as I waited for him to speak. He didn't. He just stood there.

I moved my tongue nervously across my lips. "Captain, I—I—" I floundered, finally settling for, "Good morning."

"You're saying 'Good morning' to me, Mrs. Hagen?" he came back. "That's a big surprise. Seems to me I remember the final comment you made to me yesterday in the publick house—loud enough for plenty of people to hear and that includes some of these men—" he gestured toward the crew, "was that you hoped you'd never have to say 'Good morning' to me. No . . ." he gazed up at the sky and gnawed his lips as if he was concentrating. "No, I'm wrong. What you said was that you hoped the *Roxanne* would sink and that I'd go down with her. Then you added that you never wanted to say 'Good morning' to me. And here you are doing it anyway and on such a bleak morning!"

The sailors snickered audibly. My face was no longer merely flushed. It was burning.

"Captain Nance, I—I would like to—to take you up on your—uh—offer," I said shakily.

"What offer is that, Mrs. Hagen?"

He knew what I meant. I could sense it. His mocking smile deepened and those black eyes bore into me. The crewmen were drinking in every word, enjoying my discomfort. I had the feeling I'd embarrassed him before his sailors in the publick house and now he was relishing the chance to humiliate me.

"Captain," my voice cracked, "would you come to the dock so I don't have to shout?"

"Anything to oblige a lady. Well . . . almost anything."

That brought more snickers. But he walked down the gangplank and jumped lightly to the dock, stopping two or three feet in front of me. "About that offer you referred to," he went on and to my utter relief he spoke too softly for the sailors to overhear, although his voice still carried a derisive tinge. "Is that what brings you out so early in the day?"

"Yesterday afternoon you said I could sail to Charles Town aboard the *Roxanne*. Sail free. I—I didn't think at the time I'd be interested but I am."

His eyelids flickered, but his expression did not change. He was looking at me so intently I wondered if he could see the bones inside my body. "Do you also remember my telling you yesterday that the *Roxanne* has no quarters for passengers?" he asked.

Mumbling a yes, I nodded.

"That would present problems, wouldn't it, Mrs. Hagen?" he went on in the same sarcastic way. "I should hate to think of your propping your eyes open to stay awake the entire voyage—unless you're like a horse and can sleep on your feet. But where in the world would you bed down? Perhaps the crew could make a spot for you in their section. I don't know how comfortable you'd be there, but it would be an educational experience."

He was deliberately making this as awkward for me as possible and he seemed determined to embarrass me as much as he could. I was just as determined not to flinch. I forced myself to meet his eyes, trying to will my voice steady.

"Yesterday you said I'd sleep in your cabin, Captain," I managed, although the sentence sounded as if I was choking.

"Did I actually say that?" He pretended to be surprised. "What do you think of such a plan, Mrs. Hagen?"

"Captain Nance, please don't taunt me this way! If you—"

A voice from the ship boomed out, interrupting me. "Cargo stored, Captain. Ready to weigh anchor whenever you say."

"Ready now," he answered and turned his back on me, starting up the gangplank.

I felt as if I was dying. Watching him, I wanted to scream but my vocal cords were paralyzed. Tears of frustration came into my eyes and I blinked hard to be rid of them. I couldn't bear to give him the satisfaction of seeing me cry.

Halfway up the plank he paused to glance over his shoulder at me. "Well, aren't you coming aboard?" he asked. Maybe it was my imagination, but his tone sounded normal. The mocking look seemed to have left his face.

I came to life and ran after him.

Chapter 20

As I reached the deck of the *Roxanne* on the heels of Captain Nance, he spoke to a runty sailor coiling rope near the lifeboats. "Dobbs, take Mrs. Hagen to my cabin and hang another hammock there," he said.

The man was short and bleary-eyed, his "Aye," accompanied by a lewd stare and a toothless smirk which made me feel extremely thankful not to be sharing the crew's quarters. He continued to coil the rope, flinging the heavy line about as easily as if it had been sewing thread.

"Damn it, Dobbs! Do it now!" The bruskness in Nance's voice gave evidence that he expected to have his orders carried out instantly.

Dobbs dropped the rope and scowled, moving to a wooden chest nailed to the deck. He lifted out a rope hammock.

"You—" Captain Nance looked at me, "go with him and stay out of view until we're away from port. It'll take the men's minds off their duties to have a wench in sight until we're safely into the channel."

He didn't have to issue his order to me a second time.

The last thing I wanted was to arouse his anger and make the voyage more difficult. I had another personal reason for not wanting to be seen. If any of the townspeople realized the ship was moving and paused to watch her sail, questions might be shouted from land if I was spied aboard.

Amos was in my mind. He opened business early and would pass near the dock to reach his store. Captain Nance might put me off the *Roxanne* and leave port without me if any questions made him think I'd committed a crime. Although I wasn't guilty of anything, no doubt he would deposit me on shore rather than take the risk of being accused of helping a criminal flee.

Dobbs didn't speak. Neither did I as I followed him. The *Roxanne* was smaller than the *Solace*, with narrower decks and a sleeker hull, but the passageway was just as dim. I'd forgotten the chilly dampness, constant swaying and dank odor. A familiar throb made the ship pulsate; the pumps were being put into action. A heavy thud on the deck and the lunging movement of the ship let me know the anchor was up and that we were under way.

Captain Nance's cabin was a surprise. It was far more ornate than I expected. It was located in the deckhouse above the water line; the porthole at eye level made it possible to see out while standing erect. The walls had been stained a warm golden brown. All along the ceiling joining the walls was a molding six or seven inches deep, the amber wood carved in an intricate design of ropes and anchors. The floor planking, I noted with relief, was completely dry. I hoped it would remain like that.

Two large chests and three wall cabinets occupied one side of the cabin. Across stood a heavy oak desk and a round-backed wooden chair flanked by benches which must have been fastened to the floor. The real surprise was the long green velvet cushions covering the two benches. I sat on one and watched Dobbs put up my hammock in the corner across from the Captain's. The seat was comfortable and the cushions delightfully soft.

Still scowling, Dobbs finished his task and left. After a short time I went to the porthole and looked out at the gray sky and the brown-gray Pamlico River, seeing the heavily wooded far bank. The wind must have become stronger; the moss-laden oak limbs flailed when gusts struck them, and the majestic pines bent slightly, straightening to sway again.

Bath Town was not in my range of vision. I knew it to be behind us, probably visible from the other side of the *Roxanne*. I wondered vaguely if Amos was on the pier . . . or if Seth McGurn was opening his blacksmith shop for the day . . . if Calvin had walked down with his father. The Martins must have discovered my note by now. Amos might have sent one of his children to my house to make sure I wasn't there . . . or he could have gone himself or dispatched Calvin. It made me mad that I couldn't stop thinking those thoughts.

Rain began to fall, the big drops splashing on the deck and making needle pricks on the surface of the water before becoming a drizzle and then a downpour. I missed the fire from my hearth, missed the familiar room, even the schoolroom.

Catching myself sharply, I pushed those thoughts away and closed the porthole, surveying the cabin again. My body no longer ached from Josh's violent lust, but I'd slept so little the previous night that I was dead tired. The hammock looked very inviting. I crawled into it, setting the blanket bundle at my feet and wrapping my cloak snugly around myself. I must have gone to sleep immediately.

A faint scraping noise sounded nearby as I came back to consciousness. I opened my eyes and saw long shafts of rosy light surging through the open porthole, the cabin awash in oranges and crimsons. The air smelled clean and crisp. My hammock swung so gently I barely realized the ship was under sail.

Turning my head, I saw Captain Nance seated at the desk writing in his logbook. When he paused to dip his quill into a bottle of ink I realized the scratching noise came from his pen against the paper. He finished writing and closed the log, recorked the ink and put the bottle and quill into a desk drawer. Pushing his chair back, he stood up and stretched before glancing toward me, his mouth spreading into a grin when he saw I was awake.

"So you don't plan to sleep both day and night until we dock," he said. "I was wondering about it."

"What time is it, Captain Nance?"

"Nearly five and the sun's on its way down. You slept right through two squalls, but it's faired off and I was debating with myself about rousing you as supper's being dished up. You won't have another hot meal until this time tomorrow. So if you're hungry, you'd better come along topside."

"Yes, I'm hungry." I got out of the hammock and smoothed my creased skirts. For some unknown reason the silence was embarrassing. To break it I said, "I didn't mean to sleep so long, Captain Nance."

He continued to hold his gaze on me. "If you and I are to share these quarters," he muttered dryly, "it seems you could say Luke, which is my given name, instead of calling me Captain Nance."

"All right, Luke."

"Well?" There was a trace of irritation in his tone.

"Well, what?" I came back, puzzled.

"Aren't you going to give me your first name or am I

to continue to say Mrs. Hagen even though our relationship promises to be a bit cozy? That seems a trifle ridiculous to me under the present circumstances."

Hot blood rushed to my cheeks. "It's Marley," I told him.

"What th—?" His eyes widened and a startled expression slid across his face.

"Marley," I repeated, spelling it out. "M-a-r-l-e-y. I'm not surprised you haven't heard the name before. It's unusual."

"I've heard it." His face darkened. "Or rather, I've seen it."

It was my turn to be amazed. "Seen it where?" I asked eagerly. "I'm interested because I've never known another person with the name. When I asked my mother about it, she couldn't remember where she'd got it, just that she'd liked the word."

"I don't recollect. No matter."

He was almost growling and I couldn't imagine why there was such a change in his personality. I didn't think I'd said or done anything to annoy him.

But when he spoke again, it was in a normal way without any irritation. "Since this is your first night on the *Roxanne* it will be best for you to eat with me, Marley. I'll wait for you on deck. Do you think you can find your way there alone?"

I nodded and he continued. "Don't you linger in here because the men are already lining up for food. In the future you can have the run of the deck during daylight, but after dark and in bad weather you're to stay in this cabin. I have enough on my mind during a squall without worrying you've been washed overboard."

Again I nodded. He went out, immediately opening the door again to poke his head into the room.

"By the way," he said, "I brought two buckets in for

you. The one under your hammock is for your necessaries; mind you keep it tied to the wall peg so it won't tip over and spill. Don't let it get too full before it's emptied, either. The other bucket," he looked toward a half-full pail set into a wooden frame between the two chests, "is for when you want to wash. That's river water right now and damn muddy, so you might prefer waiting until we're past the channel and into the sea where all you'll have to reckon with is salt."

The memory of the stickiness of bathing with salt water came back to me. Cold salt water, at that. It had been May when I was on the *Solace* and the air was warm most of the time. Now, at the end of October, the thought of washing in cold water in the cold cabin was anything but inviting.

As if he could read my mind, Luke said, "The Atlantic is mighty chilly this time of year, but I don't know of any harm in your heating a pail at suppertime when you need to do it if there's a blaze for cooking and some heat left in the firebox on deck. Not tonight, though. The men are agog enough over discovering that there's a female on board without you flustering them further by making too many movements your first evening."

Luke Nance was a decent man, I decided as he closed the cabin door a second time. He had considered my personal needs without my having to ask.

Chapter 21

Following Luke to the forward end of the *Roxanne* a few minutes later, I tried to ignore the frank stares of the sailors. Most of them leaned against the rail or squatted on deck while eating, their bowls held under their chins to catch any food they spilled. Luke handed me a wooden spoon and bowl. A sailor who apparently was the cook dished up a ladle of beef in gravy and added a square of corn bread. I said, "No, thank you," when he offered a piece of lemon, but Luke quickly took the lemon from the plate and tossed it into my bowl.

"Everybody on my ship eats a ration of lemon daily unless we're South where we can get different fruit," he said. "Keeps down scurvy. Chew it up, peel and all, Marley. I guarantee you won't like the taste, but it's a sight better than an attack of scurvy and your teeth falling out as a result."

I dutifully bit into the lemon and gagged at the sourness, making such a dreadful frowning face that a roar of laughter went up from the crew and Luke. He motioned for me to take a seat on the chest which held the hammocks. He sat on the floor in front of me next to two of the ship's officers, introducing them as Garlow, the quartermaster, and the first mate, Frenchy. Both men were nondescript and dressed in the customary seamen's clothing.

"Frenchy is a nickname," Luke went on. "He's from Marseilles and his real name is so long no one bothers to try to pronounce it."

The man called Frenchy gave a shrug and grinned, attacking his food as if he hadn't eaten in ages.

The mention of Marseilles stirred me, bringing back memories of the night Bates and I spent with Josh and Dorcas. The men amused one another talking about ports they'd visited and agreed that Marseilles was a place to have fun on shore, that it was the best port in France for a good time. A feeling of wistfulness overwhelmed me. Because I didn't want the aching for Bates to show in my features, I tried to think of other things. The men near me ate without speaking and I wondered if this was their usual custom or if they were ill at ease because I was there.

"The meat is a nice surprise," I commented finally. "I'd tried to prepare myself for pease porridge, never expecting beef."

"You'd prefer porridge?" Luke's tone was solemn while his eyes twinkled.

"Definitely not! The only reason I force myself to swallow pease porridge is to keep from being hungry!"

Frenchy and Garlow chuckled. I had the impression they were sizing me up to see if I would fit into shipboard life. Luke was doing that, also. I vowed silently to make a noble effort. Was he sorry he'd allowed me to come aboard? Did he wish he'd never extended that offer of passage, even as a joke? I had no way of knowing.

"I'm not overly fond of the porridge, either, but it's a staple once we're away from shore," Luke said. "I don't doubt that you'll get a bowl of it tomorrow or the day after that. By then the fresh vittles from Bath Town will be consumed."

Luke and Garlow talked about the ship and the weather. Like the others, I washed my spoon and bowl when I'd finished eating, dunking them first in a bucket of soapy river water and then into the rinse pail which looked as thick as the Pamlico River itself.

The wind was steady and the red and orange colors were completely gone from the sky. Darkness was coming fast. Luke crossed the deck to give instructions to a sailor. I decided to go below, recalling what he had said about my having freedom to roam the deck during the day but not at night. I didn't want to do anything to irk him, especially on my first night on the *Roxanne*. I didn't want him to think I was ignoring the rules he'd stated.

Holding my cloak close in the chilly air, I crept down the passageway and opened the cabin door. I stepped into a room of misty violet shadows, the porthole a pale circle against the far wall. Memories engulfed me. I thought about Bates once more, reliving my first night on the *Solace* when I'd been cold and wet and desolate and Bates had allowed me to sleep in his hammock. I knew exactly how the porthole in his cabin looked that midnight long ago. I'd never dreamed then that someday he and I would become husband and wife.

With a determined effort I pushed Bates out of my mind, not wanting to dwell on him when Luke Nance would be coming any moment to claim payment for my passage aboard the *Roxanne*. On impulse I left the cabin door ajar as if that would make me feel less alone. I sat down on one of the green-cushioned benches to wait, trying to compose myself.

It would be wrong for me to rebuff Luke. He had allowed me to sail and I meant to keep my part of our bargain. After his reference to what he termed our "cozy relationship" I felt positive that he intended making love to me that evening. I was braced for his advances.

Darkness fell and the stars were visible, the violet shadows becoming black so that the far side of the cabin was a blur. I must have waited the better part of an hour. Small waves lapped against the *Roxanne,* an indication that we were out of the river and into Pamlico Sound. The planks of the ship creaked and the ever-present throb of the pumps had settled into a dull rumble. Occasionally a voice from the deck reached my ears, one sailor yelling to another or a guffaw of coarse laughter. My heart began to beat very hard.

I did not hear Luke's soft footfalls, but I saw the glow of a lantern in the passageway before he reached the cabin.

"You sitting here alone in the dark, Marley?" he asked as if he thought I should be surrounded by a throng of people and a hundred candles. "I suppose it's rough on you to be the only wench among so many men."

"I'm all right." My voice had a squeaky sound.

Coming across the cabin, he held the lantern near my face, its warmth on my cheek. "Oh, lordy, but you're beautiful," he whispered and let his breath out slowly.

The compliment was unexpected and it flustered me. Blood flowed into my neck, all the way to my forehead. Luke saw the blush, smiling as he set the light on the desk. He took a seat beside me on the bench, turning slightly so we were facing each other.

Because I could not bear the silence I said, "How long will it take us to reach Charles Town?"

"Some days. Not as long as a week if we get a decent breeze."

One week. One week at the most before I'd see Bates, I thought. Just one more week . . .

"Marley, you'll be bored aplenty just sitting and waiting for the voyage to be over," he said. "We'll have to find some way to keep you occupied, but I won't have you taking on any of the chores assigned to the men. Can you sew? My clothes could use some patches and darning."

"Yes, I can sew. But I don't have a needle or thread with me."

"I have both."

"I'll need a thimble, too."

"Well, I don't own one, but maybe something can be rigged up for you to use. Frenchy is forever carving to pass the time. I'll see if he has a whale's tooth or a bit of wood he can whittle into a thimble. How big is your finger?"

Before I could reply he picked my hand up from my lap and murmured, "Hmmmmm . . . small."

His flesh was rough and warm against mine. Although his touch was light, I trembled. I must have forgotten that a man could be strong and gentle at the same moment.

Quickly returning my hand to my lap, he fixed his eyes on me. "You scared of me, Marley?" he asked. "You're quivering."

"Of course I'm not! Why should I be afraid of you?" I spoke with a bravado I didn't feel.

"What changed your mind about sailing with me on the *Roxanne?* In the publick house you made it plain you didn't like me or my ship, and then the next morning there you stood on the pier seeming desperate and fairly begging me to let you come on board. It doesn't make sense to change so much overnight."

He deserved an answer and I didn't want to lie, but I could not bring myself to tell him about Josh or about my final bitter words with Amos.

"There were—were circumstances." I cleared my throat. "I—I didn't w-want to be near Blackbeard or any of his pirates when—when he comes. It seemed—seems—like a good time for me to leave Bath Town," I stammered, with the sentences coming out in jerks and no way for me to know if my reply satisfied him.

"The barmaid in the publick house—Meg is her name, isn't it? She told me you taught school, Marley."

This was a safer topic and I spoke more normally. "I don't think I gave satisfaction teaching. Not the way Bates did, although I really tried. But—but I didn't know the parents weren't pleased until—until recently. The people in Bath Town appeared to feel a man would keep better discipline even though I didn't have any problem making the children obey. They thought a man could teach navigation—which I couldn't do. Bates taught navigation and I only knew how to give classes in reading and writing and numbers."

"That should be learning enough," he said tersely. "If the town lads want navigation, they can go to sea and get it properly on a ship."

He seemed to be taking up for me! I was dumbfounded, but his next remark was just as startling in a different way.

"No doubt it will be a blow to the men of Bath Town not to have you to feast their eyes on," he murmured, continuing to stare at me with a small smile playing about his mouth.

I blushed again. Luke was leading up to the lovemaking by giving me compliments. I knew that must be the way it was. I grew tense, my hands twisting in my lap until I forced them to be still, hoping he wouldn't notice my nervousness. Trying to relax was impossible, but I didn't want him to know that I was becoming more distraught every second.

His breathing quickened. After a silence which seemed to last forever, although I suppose it was only two or three minutes, I made myself look at him, finding that he was gazing rather tenderly at me. The reflection of the lantern glimmered in his eyes; tiny golden flecks of light danced under his black lashes. He parted his lips. I was sure he was going to kiss me. Or tell me to undress. Or perhaps reach out for me and rip my clothes off as Josh had done.

Instead, he clamped his mouth shut and got to his feet. A mask dropped over him, killing the warmth in his smile and leaving his nose and jaw in such finely chiseled lines that he seemed more a marble statue than a living man. "I have some duties topside," he muttered. "If you're cold there's a cover in the chest to your right, and the needle and thread are in a wooden box under the blankets. My clothing is in the wall lockers. Tomorrow you can stow your belongings in that chest as it's only partially full."

Picking up the lantern, he barged out of the cabin. Apparently he could not wait to be away from me. His footsteps, which had been silent before, clattered on the floor of the passageway, the light wavering and then vanishing as he reached the deck.

I was stunned. I felt rebuked, as if I was not good enough for him or attractive enough or passionate enough for him to want to make love to me. When he'd said I was beautiful, he sounded sincere. While I hadn't sought his advances, the obvious rejection in his voice and his manner stung as though he had slapped my face.

I didn't want to admit being disappointed, admit it even to myself, but my hand burned from the brief touch of his fingers on my skin. My mouth, awaiting a

kiss, was left tingling with anticipation. It was Bates
Hagen I wanted, I reminded myself, not Luke. I
wondered vaguely why I had to force myself to think
about my husband. Yet Luke Nance was a virile,
attractive man and I had been thankful for it as I tried
to prepare myself mentally and emotionally for his
caresses. Now, suddenly and unexplainably, when
those caresses didn't materialize, I felt bereft and more
alone than ever.

Chapter 22

THE *ROXANNE* SLIPPED through Ocracoke Inlet into the Atlantic Ocean early the next morning. By suppertime there was no sight of land. The following day the weather changed drastically from cool to very warm. The wind died, leaving the sea as smooth as a china plate.

Some of the crewmen grumbled about the inactivity, but Luke didn't appear perturbed. When I commented to him that I didn't believe the ship had moved an inch in the past four hours, he merely chuckled. "We should be thankful not to be bucking a gale," he said. "In autumn hurricanes and heat can be expected off the Carolina coast one minute and cold and clouds the next."

That remark was typical of the conversations he and I'd had since my first night on the ship. He was polite, friendly and somewhat aloof. He would pop into the cabin, make a casual comment to me and fall into his hammock, going to sleep at once. As if he possessed a secret inner timing device, he awakened barely a second before the gong rang for a change of watch. The instant his eyes were open, he was wide awake and fully alert.

I passed the hours mostly sewing and sleeping, going on deck each morning and afternoon for a walk from one end of the ship to the other. The men had ceased to ogle me. They'd stopped snickering at dusk when I put my washpail over the firebox to warm water. I figured they must be taking my presence for granted.

Time dragged. I tried to read the books on Luke's desk, but all of them had to do with navigation and they were so technical I didn't find them interesting. The sewing was a blessing. Luke was right about his clothes needing repairs; I discovered innumerable rips and holes. I didn't mention the thimble again, not knowing if he'd forgotten it or wasn't able to have one made, although putting stitches in the heavy trousers left my fingertips sore.

Perhaps those first days and nights I slept too much because by the fourth evening aboard the *Roxanne* I was wakeful. Supper that night was anything but appetizing, the tasteless pease porridge, a hard ship's biscuit and the ever-present slice of lemon. I choked it down because Luke would have reprimanded me and mentioned scurvy. As usual, I sat with Luke and the officers on deck during the meal. When we finished eating I rinsed my bowl and carried my pail of warm water to the cabin for a bath while enough daylight remained to see across the room.

I undressed and washed quickly, drying off and slipping into a fresh white muslin petticoat, feeling clean despite the salty water. The bar of soap I'd brought from Bath Town had a faint flowery scent which lingered on my body. The warm, damp air made my hair curl softly around my face.

Night fell, the stars brilliant in the deep indigo sky.

The room was too warm for more clothing. I didn't feel immodest about not wearing a dress in the darkness, knowing that by dawn it would be cool enough for me to need a light blanket. Luke wouldn't have a glimpse of me in my underwear.

Lying in my hammock, I tried to doze but couldn't lose consciousness. The bell rang to signify a change of watch. I turned restlessly, wishing I was in a real bed with a real mattress, wishing that I was lying on cool, fresh sheets dried in the sunshine. After a long time Luke came in, a blurred figure in the dim room as he moved past my hammock and got into his. Neither of us spoke and I closed my eyes. His breathing became steady and he seemed to be dead to the world.

More wide awake than ever, I started to count to myself but the numbers didn't bring drowsiness, and neither did silently repeating Bible verses which my mother made me memorize when I was a little girl. An eternity went by. My eyes were propped open. I eased out of the hammock and tiptoed to the porthole, seeing the full moon coming over the horizon as red as blood in the starry sky. The ship was motionless and so was the red-gold surface of the sea.

"Gorgeous night, isn't it?" Luke's voice was low.

He startled me. I wouldn't let myself turn and I continued to look at the view.

"Yes . . . gorgeous," I murmured. My heartbeats seemed louder than the whispered words.

"You wakeful, Marley? Usually you're sleeping at this time of night."

As he spoke he got up and came to me, standing behind me to look past my shoulder at the stars and the moon and the water, warmth from his body permeating my back.

"I seem to be saturated with sleep," I said. "I didn't mean to wake you, though."

"You didn't. Maybe I'm saturated with sleep, too."

The moon had moved above the rim of the ocean, paler now with the red changing to an exotic apricot color. The sea was covered with a flaming golden sheen. Luke slid his arms around my waist and clasped his hands together under my breasts. I began to tremble. Instantly, he stiffened.

"There you go quivering again," he said and winced, dropping his hands to his sides. "Do you find me so repulsive, Marley? You object so much if I'm near you or if I touch you?"

I had to answer him and oddly enough my reply was truthful. "No, Luke, I—I don't object."

He put his hands on my shoulders and spun me around fast. His mouth came down on mine with a tender firmness. I responded to the kisses in spite of myself, my lips opening under his and my arms going to the back of his neck. I'd thought I must steel myself to endure the caresses of any man but my husband. But now every nerve in my body was vibrantly alive, my breasts swelled against his chest while he stroked my back with amazingly gentle fingers. The kiss lasted until both of us were gasping. When he drew his mouth away, his embrace tightened.

"You want me," he said in a husky voice. "I can tell. Thank God for that."

I could not deny it. I was aroused, too swept up in the sweetness of his caresses and the stormy passion in my own body to wonder if I wanted *him*, Luke Nance, or if he was a stand-in for Bates. He was not forcing himself on me as Josh had done, hurting me and using my body disgracefully. In the moonlit darkness I could have been in Bates' arms. Luke's touch was tantalizing, his strength encased in a special loving tenderness. His muscles rippled under my hands and his mouth was delicious.

"Ever do it in a hammock, Marley?" he whispered.

I knew what "it" meant. "No," I said quickly.

"Well," he gave a soft laugh under his breath, "there's a technique to keep us from tipping over. A technique on my part. You just put your thoughts on enjoying."

Two of us in one hammock would mean a lot of weight on the ropes. If we didn't tip over, the line could snap and we'd fall, just the same. It surprised me that I could be practical when I seemed to be afloat in the moonlight, my breasts burning and my body pulsating with a white-hot desire.

"We could spread a blanket on the floor, Luke," I said.

His laughter rang out again, wild and joyous. "You're my kind of lass," he answered and kissed me as he put one of his hands into the top of my petticoat to touch my bare breasts in an enrapturing way. I could taste his tongue in my mouth and I clung to him, never wanting the kisses and the embrace to stop.

Both did stop for a brief moment while he thrust me away long enough to take the velvet cushions from the benches and toss them to the floor, covering them with a blanket from my hammock. He opened his arms and I went into them.

"Will you get naked for me, Marley?" he whispered.

My answer was to pull the petticoat over my head. There was no sensation of embarrassment. I stood nude before him, my breasts firm and the rest of me quivering with passion as I watched him remove his clothes. We didn't search for a dark spot to do our loving. The cabin was aglow with moonlight which turned my flesh luminous and made my nipples a deep rose color. I could see the black hair covering his chest forming a thin black line down the length of his stomach, the skin of his body paler than his windburned face and arms. A half-smile made the corners of his mouth turn up and his eyes were hooded and misty.

Maybe the mist was more in my vision than his. I moved into his arms again with my body curved to fit his, drinking in his maleness and the good feel of his nakedness against me as we sank down on the cushions. While he was caressing me I touched him everywhere, exploring his body, straining to get closer to him and bring him closer to me, gasping with the sheer joy of the fulfilled need burning every inch of my body. He was stroking my thighs and hips, kissing the hollow of my throat, nibbling at my breasts with his tongue, doing wild things to me until finally he lowered himself onto me and I arched my back to meet him, gasping at the fury of the explosions within us.

Chapter 23

THE KISS WOKE me, but I was too groggy with sleep to open my eyes immediately. Snuggling against Bates under the blanket, I could feel my body coming alive and I hoped we'd have time for a little lovemaking before getting up to go into the schoolroom and begin the day's classes.

"Love you, darling," I murmured.

The next kiss was fantastic. I lost myself in it, feeling his mouth on mine, feeling it slide to my throat and my breasts. I forced my eyelids apart and a small strangled cry tore from me. The dark hair brushing my cheek belonged to Luke Nance—not to Bates.

"What's wrong, Marley?" Luke asked lifting his head from my breast.

"Nothing. I—I must have been dreaming."

"A good dream or a bad one?"

"Good." It had been better than reality. In the dream I was in my husband's arms. To change the subject I said, "It's already morning, isn't it?"

"A beautiful dawn and there's a freshness in the air

237

which makes me think we'll get some wind before night." Leaning over me, he cupped his hands around my face. "A moment ago I could have sworn you said you loved me, Marley. And you called me 'darling.' Did you mean that?"

My mind was all mixed up. In a way I meant it. And in another way, those words had been intended for Bates. "Yes," was the easiest answer and I gave it because I didn't want further questions.

Smiling, he pulled me close and began those enticing strokes which rekindled the desire I'd felt on awakening. I didn't have to be coaxed to make love. While this was quicker than our time together the night before, it was just as enjoyable. When it was over Luke gave me a final kiss and rolled his body off of mine.

"Go back to sleep if you want," he said as he put on his clothes. "No need for you to be up this early in the day. Besides, I like to watch you sleep."

"You like—for heaven's sake! When have you ever watched me sleep?"

"Lots of times." His grin became mischievous. "Some occasions when the moon shone on you and other times I watched you in the daylight. Watching wasn't simple for me, either. It was all I could do to keep my hands off you and to hold back from kissing you."

Now that he was dressed I was conscious of being naked and I wrapped the blanket around my body. "You're not making sense, Luke," I said. "If you wanted to kiss me that much, why didn't you?"

"And get myself slapped on the face for my effort? No, sirrreeee. I figured you'd already let me know you didn't welcome any advances from me so I decided to wait until you were ready and showed it. Appears I was right, wasn't I?"

I felt hot all over. He saw my face flush and laughed.

"Aren't you going to put the next question to me, Marley?"

"What next question? I think I may already have asked too much."

"Don't you want me to tell you how I knew last night that you'd done an about-face and wanted me?" His eyes were sparkling and he gave a teasing laugh.

"Oh, if you're so eager to tell me, I might listen. But I don't think I'll beg for it," I came back in a saucy voice. I was dying to hear, though.

"Very well, I'll keep silent."

That wasn't what I wanted. Not at all.

"Luke—"

He stooped and with a swift movement of one hand flipped the blanket aside to expose my nakedness. Before I could protest, he kissed one rosy nipple and then the other, my flesh firming under the touch of his lips.

"Proud pouting beauties, both of them," he whispered. "They gave your inner feelings away last night when I saw you standing at the porthole in that white petticoat looking like a fairy princess. I'm glad they gave you away, too. I've been half crazy wanting you ever since you sat opposite me in the publick house. You don't know how happy it makes me for you to enjoy our lovemaking and to show you want me without my having to plead for it."

I moved my tongue over my lips. Suddenly my mouth and throat were uncomfortably dry. I was about to let him know those words I'd uttered before I was fully awake hadn't been for him. But I could not do it. There was no need for me to hurt him deliberately. I settled for a smile.

With a final lingering kiss, Luke picked up the blanket and covered me, his hands as gentle as if he'd been tucking a baby into a crib.

During the four remaining days before the *Roxanne* reached Charles Town Luke and I laughed and talked and kissed and made love. I savored every second.

I hadn't forgotten that I was Bates Hagen's wife and I still wanted my husband, but it would have been a lie to claim I didn't welcome Luke's attention and enjoy being with him. Time no longer dragged for me. His footsteps would sound unexpectedly in the passageway and my heartbeats promptly quickened.

He presented me with an exquisite ivory thimble which Frenchy had made. I thanked Luke, then said another thank-you to Frenchy at supper that evening. I continued to sew while Luke wrote in his logbook or studied the charts or had short naps or merely sat beside me on the bench. We talked and talked, and at night we lay in each other's arms on the velvet cushions.

It bothered me a little that I was giving myself so completely to Luke. I tried to analyze my true feelings for him. I knew I hadn't fallen out of love with Bates—I could never do that. But I'd been thirteen long months without any show of affection from another human being and I was starved for love. Calvin Martin's fumbling attempts to caress me served only to make me livid. Josh's crude attack aroused my hatred. Luke was as gentle and sweet with me as Bates had been. My blood ran hot in my veins when I was near him.

When Luke wanted to know about my childhood I told him of my mother's background. Compassion showed in his face as I described life in New Bedford with my solitary leaving. I sluffed over the part about McGregor and how I happened to board the *Solace*, merely saying I'd sailed South and would have landed at Charles Town if Blackbeard hadn't intervened.

"So Teach did put you in the dinghy with Hagen,"

Luke said, making it more of a statement than a question. "He must have had a wench of his own aboard his ship or he'd never have let you out of his sight."

"He did. A new wife, he called her."

"Wife—nothing," Luke snorted, but he was serious again quickly. "Marley, what did you plan to do when you reached Charles Town?"

I could not bear to tell him the truth, that if Irving and McGregor had their ways I'd have to marry a stranger. "Look for work and try to make a home for myself," I answered, and to change the subject, I said, "What about you, Luke? Where did you live when you were a little boy?"

"Right here on the *Roxanne*. I was born in this cabin. She was my father's ship and he named her for my mother. I've never 'lived' on land in my life except when the ship was in drydock or tied to a pier for loading cargo."

I looked at him in amazement. "Where is your family now?"

"Dead, God rest their souls. My younger brother, Stephen, died with smallpox when I was twelve. There were some babies who didn't live to be a year old, but Stephen and I were the only ones of my parents' children who survived longer than a few months. We were sailing off the coast of Italy and we'd just unloaded cargo at Naples when Stephen came down sick and my mother nursed him and caught the pox. She died, too. A week after he did. She was so ill and out of her head with fever I don't even think she knew he was gone. After that, there was only my father and me."

"Your father is dead, too?"

"He was killed in a fight with a drunk sailor."

Bitterness came into Luke's voice. "I was on shore that night. We were in Liverpool with the *Roxanne* berthed in the Mersey River. Burnley, the bum who killed my father, came aboard the ship. He'd sailed across the Atlantic with us, but he wouldn't do his chores and my father put him off as soon as we docked. The man filled his belly with spirits and came back to the ship when most of the crew had gone ashore to frolic."

Luke closed his eyes and opened them again. "I walked up the gangplank close to midnight and stumbled over both bodies. Burnley was dead and my father was dying, but he lived long enough to tell me what happened. He said he was alone in the cabin when Burnley sneaked on the ship and stabbed him in the back of the shoulder. The fight must have been hellish. Blood was splattered from one side of the cabin to the other and the length of the passageway and across the deck. My father succeeded in strangling the man, but Burnley got one last swipe with that knife and hit Father's chest. The last words he spoke to me were to tell me to take command of the *Roxanne*."

The memory hurt Luke. I could see the suffering in his face and I reached out to put my hands over his. The gesture must have surprised him, but when I tried to pull away he twined his fingers through mine and would not let me free.

"Marley, I've never been able to talk about it to anyone until now . . . to you," he said.

"How long ago did it happen?"

"Six years. I was twenty then."

"It must have been terrible for you. I know the feeling of being completely alone, of not having a soul to—to belong to."

"Those first months were . . . terrible," he sighed. "I wouldn't hanker to live through them again. The voyage after my father's death was the worst I've ever endured. Some of the crew questioned my authority since they were older than I."

"What in the world did you do?"

"Hoved into the nearest port and dumped them. Then signed on new seamen. That's a maneuver I'd learned from my father. Luckily, we were in the Mediterranean heading toward Greece and near enough land so several ports were close."

"Don't you tire of—" I caught my breath, searching for the right term, "of just sailing and sailing?"

His eyebrows lifted in astonishment. "Why should I, Marley? Being afloat comes as naturally to me as breathing."

I did not doubt it for a second. Bates Hagen had been cut from the same cloth.

Another time, on a sunlit morning when the *Roxanne*'s sails were filled with wind and we were moving at a steady clip, Luke came to the cabin shortly before noon and took a seat on the bench beside me. I was patching one of his shirts. While I continued to sew, I could feel his eyes glued to my face.

Looking up from the mending, I smiled at him. "You're staring," I said, my voice light and teasing.

"It's nice to stare at you. One of my favorite occupations."

"But you already know how I look."

"You're very beautiful with that black hair shining and that mouth of yours as red as a ripe strawberry and—" He burst out laughing. "All right, lass, blush! You always blush if I say any personal remark or give you a compliment. God knows your blood must be in a perpetual state of movement. Boiling hot, too."

Very mindful of my crimson cheeks, I mumbled

self-consciously that I'd give anything not to blush. I couldn't remember a time when I hadn't done it or been teased about it.

"Don't stop it. Not ever," he came back quickly. "I like to see you all rosy and quivery."

Lifting the sewing from my lap, he put the partially mended shirt, the needle, thread and thimble on the desk. "With a bit of urging on your part, Marley," he added in a soft voice, "I know something we can do this minute that I like more than watching you blush. You give me the word and I'll take off my britches and bolt the door and put the cushions down."

Desire swept over me, making my body tingle. Luke's nearness aroused me in an intense way, my breasts throbbing and the lower part of me on fire. "At the rate we're using those cushions day and night we'll wear them out soon," I murmured, smiling.

"We can get some more cushions made in Charles Town. Come to think of it, I'll have the ship's carpenter make us some sort of bed or bunk to go in the corner of the cabin and we'll be able to remove the hammocks. My parents used to have a built-in bed, but I took it out after my father's death when I moved into these quarters and I was used to sleeping in a hammock. Now, though . . . with you . . ." he pulled me close, "instead of buying more cushions, I'll get us a mattress."

Swallowing hard, I burrowed my face into his shoulder to avoid his eyes. I'd be leaving the *Roxanne* in Charles Town and Luke knew it, of course. He'd known from the beginning that the journey was to take me to my husband. We would reach the port any day and it hardly seemed worthwhile to have a bed built for just one or two more nights.

Perhaps I should have said as much to him. Before I could he put one hand under my chin and raised my face to his, his hot mouth coming down on mine, his tongue probing and his searching, exploring hands everywhere on my body. When the long embrace ended I helped him put the cushions on the floor and spread the blanket. The lovemaking began, savagely sweet in its intensity, and I strained against him.

Sudden noise loud as thunder filled the cabin, two heavy fists beating on the door. Luke and I froze instantly.

"Land ho, Captain Nance!" Dobbs' gutteral voice rang out from the passageway. "The lookout's sighted Charles Town!"

Chapter 24

LUKE SPRANG UP and hurriedly got into his clothes, apologizing wryly for not being able to complete the act of love. "That interruption coming when it did sort of killed my mood," he said with a twisted grin.

"I know. It killed mine, too," I agreed. "I'm thankful you'd bolted the cabin door or Dobbs would have barged in."

"Tonight we'll take up where we left off, Marley. I need to be topside now. With land in sight we may make port in a couple of hours in this breeze. We're not very far out in the channel." His final sentence was flung over his shoulder as he left the cabin at a run.

My heart was pounding so hard my ribs felt ready to splinter. In a few hours I would be with Bates! The realization was overwhelming and for a moment I was dizzy with excitement. Some strange mystical instinct made me positive my husband was in Charles Town. Bates had to be there . . . *he just had to be there!*

Dressing as speedily as Luke had done, I went to the forward end of the ship and stood at the starboard rail where several sailors were gathered to await orders.

The sky was a vivid blue and the water a mass of white-capped blue waves. In the distance the land was a hazy green streak across the horizon.

With the strong wind the *Roxanne* moved rapidly and Luke sent men into the rigging. Before an hour went by I could make out the colors flying on the other vessels in the Charles Town harbor and some buildings were clearly outlined.

It was difficult to tear myself away from the deck rail and the excitement of approaching land, but I went to the cabin to gather my belongings. *Bates*, I whispered and a surge of anticipation filled my mind. *Bates* . . . Leaving Luke wouldn't be easy because I was genuinely fond of him, but Bates was my husband, the man who owned my heart and soul.

Humming softly, I folded dresses and petticoats, tying the corners of the blanket to form a bundle just as I'd done that final morning in Bath Town. The pink brocade hadn't been out of Luke's sea chest since my first night on board the *Roxanne*. The silky material rustled and shimmered as I shook out the folds of the gown, sunlight giving the brocade a glowing sheen. The dress felt wonderful against my skin. I fastened the tiny buttons down the front of the bodice. The lace frill brushed my throat and my breasts lifted until they seemed about to burst from the low-cut neck.

I wanted to look just as Bates remembered me. Maybe . . . I mused, after the hours in Luke's arms which turned me from a wraith into a real woman once more . . . maybe I'd be more beautiful than Bates remembered . . .

Luke had a small mirror he used for shaving and which he kept in the wall locker. I found it and stared at my reflection, amazed at the change since the last time I'd seen myself twenty-four hours earlier. My cheeks were as pink as the brocade and my eyes sparkled like blue jewels. Continuing to smile simply because I felt so happy, I wrapped my cloak around myself so the dress would be hidden. I returned to the deck.

We were very near land and most of the *Roxanne*'s sails were furled as the ship glided toward shore. It was warmer, the gusty breeze replaced by humidity and the smell of fish and rum drifted to me. I don't know what I expected, but the scene on land in front of me was startling. Throngs of people milled about near the dock, the raucous sounds of their rowdy laughter and chatter coming to my ears. They weren't elegantly dressed. Most of the men wore buckskins, while the women wore homespun or calico dresses with shawls around their shoulders and some wore sunbonnets which hid their faces. They appeared to be having a marvelous time. The fish odor came from a sailcloth tent set up near the water's edge. Food and drinks apparently were sold there. A fiddler roamed through the crowd playing merry tunes. Dogs of all sizes, shapes and colors barked and grabbed for tidbits of fish. A few people danced. Every now and then a shrill burst of laughter split the air. I decided a carnival must be in progress as everybody was in such a gala mood.

Luke stood near the ship's bowsprit with his hands on his hips and his head cocked slightly to one side, a stance I'd noticed when he was tense or had a lot on his mind. I moved aft to join him and instantly was aware of the silence on the *Roxanne,* an eerie quiet, in contrast to the clamor on land. Sailors clinging to the masts and rigging were not uttering anything, but when I'd left the deck earlier the men had laughed and exchanged salty remarks as they went about their chores. Now they riveted their attention to the shore as if they were hypnotized and incapable of stirring.

Luke must have heard me or sensed my presence for he turned abruptly when I was some eight or ten feet behind him. With a flying leap, he was beside me, grabbing my arms and jerking me around so that my back was to the land.

"Don't look, Marley!" His tone was gruff. "Go below and stay there!"

He was already hustling me toward the deckhouse entrance, his fingers biting into my flesh. Puzzled, I glanced over my shoulder in spite of his stern admonition—and the sight made me choke.

Lifeless bodies swung from a wooden gibbet which had not been within my range of view until I neared the bowsprit of the *Roxanne*. Although I closed my eyes in horror, I saw the hideously distorted corpses with eyes bulging almost out of their sockets and the swollen tongues blackened and dangling in what must have been final gasps for air.

"It's a hanging," Luke said grimly. "I didn't want you to have to witness the sight. That's not a pretty way to die."

Trembling, I clung to him, pushing my face into his chest. Nausea boiled into my mouth and my stomach heaved. "I wish I hadn't looked," I moaned.

"Try not to think about it, Marley."

How could I not think about it? I felt as if the terrible sight was engraved on my mind to haunt me forever.

"Is that why so many people are over there on land? They came to watch the hangings?" I shuddered again, unable to believe such a thing.

"Some folks seem to get pleasure out of executions. I happen to find them sickening." Luke drew a long, ragged breath. When he spoke again, he appeared to be thinking aloud rather than addressing me. "I can't imagine why so many would be hanged at one time unless they committed a crime together."

"How many?" I'd looked away too quickly to count. "Nine."

A fresh tremor shot through my body and Luke's arms tightened. He held me until I could raise my face and meet his eyes.

"You go to the cabin and wait there until I come for you, Marley," he said gently. "I have no idea how long that will be, but I should think the bodies would be cut down before dark. You don't want to see that happen and you will see it if you're on deck."

I managed to nod, past objecting to anything he said, and he walked with me to the deckhouse, giving my hand a little squeeze. The shock was ebbing slightly, but I was still overwhelmed with the gruesomeness of those bodies. It wasn't just because the men were dead; it was because their deaths must have been so agonizing.

I had seen dead people before. My mother. Two friends in New Bedford, one a girl my age named Elizabeth who died with a fever and the other a child struck by lightning. The crewmen from the *Solace* who didn't survive the fight with Blackbeard's pirates. But I had never seen anyone who was strangled to death by hanging and I never wanted to look at one again.

The cabin was just as I'd left it, the blanket bundle on my hammock, Luke's logbook and charts in their accustomed places, my sewing on the desk where he laid it when he took if from my hands. An eternity had passed since he and I were beginning our lovemaking only to be interrupted by Dobbs and the news that land was sighted—an eternity which was only half a day but to me it was a century.

Nothing had changed—except me. I sank down on a bench with my fingers pressed to my mouth and tried to

think about Bates instead of the grisly corpses, but that
didn't bring me any peace of mind. My joyous mood
was gone. In its place I felt shock and a hurting
disappointment that the search for my husband must be
delayed further. After so many months of longing for
Bates, even a few extra hours seemed unbearable.

Chapter 25

I WAITED A very long time for Luke to come to the cabin. At first I attempted to sew, but my hands shook and the stitches were so uneven and ugly that I put the mending aside. The afternoon shadows lengthened, sunshine no longer coming through the porthole. The room took on a chill. Footsteps, the seamen's muffled voices and heavy objects being dragged sounded from the deck. After what seemed hours a bell rang to call the crew to supper. I knew it must be four o'clock. Sitting alone was becoming more and more frustrating. Although I wasn't hungry, I considered joining the men—an idea I speedily vetoed for fear of getting another glimpse of those bodies on the gibbet.

Twilight was near when someone finally came down the passageway, the yellow glow of a lantern cutting through the grayness.

"Luke—?" The single word was a question.

I jumped up as he came through the door. He sat down heavily in the desk chair, so haggard my heart went out to him. I knew he was tired and just as horrified seeing those bodies as I was.

"Sorry I'm late, Marley," he said in a thin voice. "I had business in town and it took longer than I thought it would."

"Are the bodies still there?"

"No. I expect they've been buried by now. Or dumped into a salt marsh or the sea."

"Who were they, Luke?"

"Pirates. The port of Charles Town has been plagued so much by pirates that the Governor of South Carolina took personal command of four armed vessels and went on the high seas to destroy any pirate ships he found hovering near the entrance to the harbor. From what I heard this afternoon, plenty of men were killed in the fighting. The other sea robbers were put in irons and brought back to land for trials. Today was the second mass hanging this week. Another one is scheduled day after tomorrow."

"Was Blackbeard among them?" It was hard to keep my voice steady as I asked the question.

"No, but I daresay the Governor and the residents of Charles Town would have liked it if he had been. Teach blockaded the Charles Town harbor some time ago and took a number of local people hostage in the process. Nobody here has forgotten."

Luke must have become aware of my consternation. He leaned over to pat my arm. "Quit worrying about it, Marley. You're actually turning pale. You get to looking like that every time you hear the word 'pirate.'"

"I just don't like anything about piracy. Not anything."

"Well, if it will comfort you, this is probably the safest port on the Atlantic coast right now. After the punishment being dished out here to pirates, it's unlikely Charles Town will be troubled by them in the near future. The news of these hangings will be passed along in every port in a hurry. Hey—look—" The frown lines eased out of his forehead and his mouth curved into a smile. "Let's stop talking about that and get to something more interesting. How would you like to eat dinner tonight in a mansion?"

His eyes moved over me as though he'd just noticed the pink brocade. "You seem to be dressed for a special occasion," he added. "Where'd you get that gown? I've never seen it before."

"I—I had it." I didn't want to say I'd put it on for Bates.

"I was going to dispatch one of the men to the hold to fetch you that blue dress with the silver ribbon you were fingering when I saw you the first time in Bath Town. No matter now, though."

"Luke, please don't make me eat with those people celebrating the hangings!"

"Not on your life. Anyhow, that crowd's gone. The fiddler and the dogs, too. You and I are invited to the home of Welbourne Richards. Believe me, you'll be impressed!"

I was still apprehensive and I'd reconciled myself not to search for Bates until morning. "Who is this Welbourne Richards?" I asked.

Luke rubbed his hand across the stubble of beard. "How about getting out my best clothes for me while I wash and shave?" He peeled off his shirt and trousers. "Richards is a merchant, the man I do business with in this port. He contracted for the wool and silk and the nails I brought in on the *Roxanne* and he's sending a carriage to pick us up. I wouldn't be surprised if it's not waiting on the dock already."

"He came to the ship this afternoon?"

"No, I went to his office in the back of his store. It's only a couple of squares away. He's the one who gave

me the information about the pirates and the hangings."

"And we're going to his home for his celebration of
the executions?" My lip curled slightly.

"That's not true, Marley. Get your mind off the
pirates. This isn't a party. Just supper with Welbourne
and his new wife. I'll wager it'll be a fancy enough
meal, though. This second wife of his is younger than
any of his three children. They're grown and married
and in their own homes. She's a great one for putting
on airs—a hell of a good looking woman in a bold way.
I suppose Welbourne figured she'd brighten up his bed,
and no doubt she does, and her reward is a damn easy
life and a pile of money to spend."

Luke, lathering his face with soap, smiled in my
direction. He seemed in much better spirits and it was
obvious he looked forward to the evening. I was
growing more ill at ease by the minute. It wasn't that I
didn't long for a change from the ship, but I'd never
been to a social event in my life and wasn't sure how to
act, something I didn't want Luke to discover. With a
long intake of breath I decided to stay close to him and
do whatever he did during the evening.

I took his polished boots from a chest. I removed
clothing from the wall cabinet, laying the white silk
shirt with the stock, the creamy tan trousers and the
brown velvet jerkin on his hammock. While he dressed
I bathed my face and brushed my hair, coiling it on top
of my head.

"Ready?" he asked as he put my cloak around me
and picked up the lantern. "You're ravishing in that
pink gown. It's a shame you don't own a better wrap.
I'll buy you one tomorrow."

Every muscle and nerve in my body went taut. This
was the chance to remind him I would be leaving the

Roxanne permanently in the morning. I could not do it. Sliding my tongue across my lips, I said nothing and the opportunity slipped by.

A pearly dusk had set in as we reached the deck. Lights shone from the windows of some of the buildings on shore and laughter came from taverns along the waterfront. A few sailors lounged nearby, but the throngs were gone. In spite of myself I glanced toward the gibbet. Bodies no longer hung there; stubs of rope remained on the crossbar, macabre markers of the execution.

"Don't stare in that direction, Marley," Luke said in a rough voice. "You'll spoil your evening if you keep dwelling on what you saw earlier. Spoil my evening, too."

That was one thing I didn't want to happen if this was to be my last evening with Luke Nance. I managed a determined smile, tucking my hand through his arm while we were walking down the gangplank to the waiting carriage. It was a luxurious vehicle painted black with green trim and green upholstery, and the two men in the driver's box wore green uniforms with shiny brass buttons. One man held the reins of a team of sleek roan horses and the other jumped to the ground as we approached, opening the carriage door for us.

"Welbourne paid a pretty penny for this rig, I'll bet," Luke whispered in my ear. "It must have been imported from Europe."

"Captain Nance?" The footman in green spoke with a pronounced Scottish accent. Luke nodded and we settled ourselves in the carriage. I wondered if the driver and the red-headed footman could have been Mr. Richards' sons and decided not. Probably they were his employees or indentured servants whose passage he'd paid to the Colonies. Both were young and muscular.

The dirt road was reasonably smooth as we drove through Charles Town, the horses' hooves keeping a steady clopping rhythm. Luke pointed out various sights to me.

"That's Welbourne's business," he gestured to the right. "The Customs House is on your left and next to it is a tavern which serves excellent punch and won't tell all the ingredients. Here," he pointed toward a house and chuckled softly, "is the best brothel this side of the Bahama Islands. Miss Amy's place, although some claim that's not the actual name of the wench running it, that it's 'Miss Aimee' or something French and has to do with the French word that means love."

It was a frame building painted white with a second-floor porch on one side. I could make out several misty figures leaning against the porch railing. Two lanterns suspended from twin posts in the yard swung gently. As we passed a woman's voice called out a greeting which I assumed to be intended for the men in the driver's box. They didn't acknowledge it or slow the horses. Luke laughed again.

"Was she giving *you* a welcome?" I asked him, half-teasing, half-serious.

"I didn't hear her say my name, did you, Marley?"

I really wanted an answer and didn't know why it seemed to be important, but I kept my voice light. "In New Bedford people whispered about brothels and pretended they didn't exist. I take it things are different in Carolina. It would seem you're so knowledgeable about Miss Amy's that you feel right at home."

He grinned, his teeth flashing in the dim twilight. "You fishing for facts about my past, Marley?"

"I suppose I'm getting those facts in a roundabout

way without fishing. You didn't deny knowing the path to that house!"

After I spoke I was afraid he might get irritated, but he laughed again and I joined in. Instantly he became serious. Leaning toward me, he picked up my hand and held it between both of his, speaking too softly for the men atop the carriage to overhear.

"Sure, I've been to that house, Marley, and to some others like it in other ports, but not any more. You're all the woman I'll ever want or need. I'm so much in love with you I'm fairly intoxicated with your presence. I want us to be together the rest of our lives."

His hands holding mine were extremely warm. I hoped he didn't notice the iciness which swept through me. *Don't talk this way, Luke Nance,* I thought desperately. *Don't do this to me when you know I love my husband.*

Frantically changing the subject, I asked Luke who would be in charge of the *Roxanne* in his absence during the evening. Any topic would be better than his feelings for me.

"Garlow," he·replied. "I've given three-fourths of the crew shore leave tonight and the others will get their time off tomorrow from noon until midnight."

"When will you unload the cargo?" I didn't care when, but I had to keep him talking about the ship.

"This afternoon we unloaded some cargo and we'll finish in the morning and begin reloading at once. Water and food supplies, of course, and we'll take rice and rum to Philadelphia. I anticipate being at sea again in forty-eight hours, more or less. It's a mighty short time in port, but the men had a fling in Bath Town and we made minor repairs there so the ship's in fair shape. There's a need for major repairs and I may have to put her in dry dock this winter. I mean to get North and stay put while the winter storms are raging. South of the Virginia capes it doesn't make much difference except in a real gale, but sailing in northern waters in the dead of winter invites trouble. So if there's shopping you need to do here in Charles Town, you'd best get at it tomorrow before we sail, Marley."

He seemed waiting for me to speak and I said nothing. This was another chance to remind him I'd made the trip to Charles Town for the sole purpose of finding Bates. Once again I let the moment go. It was hard to believe he'd forgotten I was married. Yet he seemed to be taking for granted that when the *Roxanne* sailed North, I would be aboard.

The carriage left Charles Town, moving along a road cut through woods. The trees were huge and loaded with the familiar gray moss. We were farther south than Bath Town and the air was balmier in late autumn than I had expected. I realized somewhat ruefully that snow probably had fallen in Massachusetts.

Occasionally we glimpsed water which Luke identified as the Ashley River. The carriage was comfortable and the drive pleasant. I felt myself relaxing slightly and Luke stopped talking but whistled a low, tuneless song. Despite the darkness I could make out the excitement in him. I'd never thought of him as handsome in the way that Bates was, but his winsome smile and sheer masculinity made him very attractive.

The horses slowed and turned through a wrought iron gate, the red-headed footman jumping down to close it as we passed. We went down a lane. I spied a house in the distance, stunned at the size of the dwelling as we approached. It was, as Luke had said, a mansion—a long pink brick structure, the center section flanked by wings on either side, windows in the central section ablaze with candlelight. As we neared the building the horses' hooves clattered on a paved circle and as if that was a signal, the front door of the house opened and a man and a woman came out.

With the lights from the house behind them, they were silhouettes. As the carriage stopped the man moved forward to take the lantern from the footman and Luke jumped to the ground. The two men shook hands. This stranger, who had to be Welbourne Richards, put his head inside the carriage to greet me, still holding the lantern.

"Welbourne, may I present Miss Marley Lancaster," Luke said.

I caught my breath. He was not calling me Mrs. Bates Hagen! I bit down hard on my lower lip, managing to nod. I was incapable of speaking at the moment.

If the tall man in front of me noticed my silence, he didn't give any indication. "I'm happy to have you in my home, Miss Lancaster," he said and put out his hand to assist me.

The lantern shone on his face. He was tall, taller than Luke, and elegantly dressed in a black silk suit with black velvet trim. His gray hair was thin on top, his scalp showing, and his round face had apple cheeks oddly out of place on a person of what I guessed his age to be. Luke had mentioned three grown Richards' children, so this man could not be young.

"May I present my wife, Nicolette, Miss Lancaster," Welbourne led me across the paved courtyard where Luke was talking to the lady who turned toward me. She was slender and pale, her auburn hair fashionably dressed with curls piled high and one long lock curling over her shoulder. Her dress was gorgeous—ecru satin with tiny blue velvet bows scattered over the skirt and a wide blue velvet sash, the ends coming past her knees.

I saw all of that subconsciously—the man who was

our host, this woman and her fine clothes. Yet I actually saw nothing but her face. My eyes were riveted to it, my breath coming in tiny gasps. I was so stunned I thought I might collapse.

The woman's husband called her "Nicolette" and so did Luke. I knew her as Prudence Hall! Prudence who had been aboard the *Solace* with me, Prudence who accepted favors from McGregor and repaid him with her body, Prudence who had laughed uproariously the day McGregor tied me to the mast and would have flogged me with a cat-o'-nine tails if Bates hadn't intervened.

She must have recognized me, too. She didn't let on. Her gray eyes looked squarely into mine without a flicker. Her expression never changed as she curtseyed and answered, "I'm happy to make your acquaintance, Miss Lancaster. Shall we go inside and have a bite of supper?"

Chapter 26

PRUDENCE LED THE way into the house. We entered a foyer with a curving staircase to the second floor, then passed into what she called "our red parlor," an octagonal room with elaborate brass sconces holding clusters of candles on each of the eight walls. The red fringe on the white damask drapes matched the deep crimson carpet and the ruby satin upholstery on the furniture.

A servant, dressed smartly in black cotton and a starched white apron, brought us cups of wine punch. We drank quickly, not lingering, and then were ushered into a gold and white dining room. A round table was covered with an embroidered linen cloth and the places set with silver and bone china. To my astonishment, Prudence seemed ladylike and mannerly, a vast change from the sassy girl on the *Solace* who slurped her pease porridge and made coarse jokes with the sailors.

The serving was deliberate and calm. The roast pork and vegetables looked delicious. The men ate with relish, but I might as well have been chewing a rag for all I could taste. The same was true of the elegant dessert, something Prudence called "tipsy pudding"—a cake sprinkled with rum and covered with a rich custard. I noticed she didn't eat much more than I did and her smile seemed etched into her face like a doll's. The tautness of her mouth made me wonder if she also felt tense, but she could hide it better than I.

I scarcely spoke. While we were in the red parlor and in the dining room, Luke tossed several questioning glances my way. Once he attempted to force me into conversation by saying, "What do you think about it, Marley?" I was engrossed in my own thoughts and had no idea what the others had been discussing. When I murmured, "I don't have an opinion," it put a scowl on his face. He was furious and it showed.

Then he turned all his charm on Prudence—or Nicolette—or whatever her name was. He laughed and chatted and drank in every remark she uttered.

Welbourne Richards attempted to draw me out and eventually gave up. I didn't blame him. I realized I must seem rude, but I'd had one shock after another. Luke had hurt me badly by introducing me as Miss Lancaster. I had been numb seeing Prudence and having her pretend we weren't acquainted. All I wanted was for the evening to end.

When the final bites were taken, Mr. Richards turned to Luke and said, "Shall we walk out on the terrace for a view of the river and let the ladies have a little while to themselves?"

Prudence rose at once, and so did the two men. I got to my feet. "Come with me, Miss Lancaster," Prudence hadn't spoken to me since the courtyard introduction.

I followed her in silence through the foyer and up the circular stairs to a small sitting room with yellow walls and comfortable furniture. A large embroidery frame on a stand was near the hearth where a log fire burned.

Two low rocking chairs were covered in flowered tapestry. Candles were everywhere. She closed the door and whirled around, her skirts swishing with the quick movement.

"Marley!" she burst out, her eyes no longer expressionless but large and filled with awe. "Marley, you must wonder why I didn't say you and I know each other, but I couldn't! I simply couldn't! Some of the things I've told Welbourne about my background are lies and I'd die if he ever found out how I came to Carolina! He's happy with me and I'm going to do everything on this earth to keep him happy. I've never had it so good. I've got a wonderful life here, better than I ever knew or expected before, and I just don't want anything to upset all of this!"

She flung one arm out in a broad gesture which included the entire house. "Not *anything!*" she repeated. "Can you understand?"

Her proud manners had vanished and her skin was chalky white. Even her tone of voice was more Prudence Hall than Nicolette Richards.

"Don't worry, Prudence," I said and sat down in one of the rockers. "I won't let anybody know."

A little of the desperation drained out of her face. "I should have realized I could count on you, Marley," she sighed. "You were the best of the girls on the *Solace*. I've wondered real often what happened after Teach set you and Captain Hagen adrift, but no matter what it was, it couldn't have been much worse than what we went through."

"Blackbeard turned all of you over to his crew?"

She nodded and cringed. "Did he ever! We could scarcely eat or sleep. Every time the watch changed on the *Queen Anne's Revenge* the sailors going off duty lined up. No sooner would one get off of me than a new one was taking his place. When they finished, another batch of men who'd been in their hammocks sleeping wanted a fresh turn. They acted like they'd never had a woman or thought they'd never have one again. It was—" her voice grew flinty, "plain awful. But I fared better than most of the others. I guess I'd known enough men to be able to put my mind on something else while I was enduring, but I'd never in my life had one man right after another that way. A few of the girls simply couldn't take it."

My throat went dry. "What about Nellie?" I asked.

Prudence held her hands out to the hearth, staring into the blaze. "She was your closest friend, wasn't she?"

I said yes, wanting her explanation and almost afraid to hear it.

"Nellie lost her senses and turned raving mad. It wasn't surprising, Marley. Two days and two nights of those men and no rest, and she'd been a virgin before, which I guess made the shock greater. She began to scream in the middle of the night and ran on deck in her petticoat and jumped overboard."

"They didn't rescue her? Or try to? Oh, Prudence—"

"She went down and never came up. One of the sailors who was standing watch on deck when it happened told me about it, but I'd heard her scream and it was the most terrible noise." She closed her eyes and reopened them. "Well, maybe she's better off dead."

"What about the others?"

"Everybody else survived except Rebekah Peale. She was bitten by a rat and died real quick. I was scared Teach would kill the rest of us just to save food and water once the novelty of having women aboard wore off. But about that time he put into a cove to move the gunpowder off the *Solace* and onto the *Queen Anne's*

Revenge. His men were more interested in whoring than working and he went wild. He shot the first mate in the belly for not obeying his orders and whipped those who didn't hustle. Then he said any of the women who wanted to walk to Charles Town could leave. You've never seen women move so fast in your life."

"*Walk* to Charles Town?" I was thinking about the day I walked away from New Bedford. "How far did you have to go?"

"Only seven or eight miles. I reckon that lousy Blackbeard had the last laugh, though. He put McGregor off at the same time—that could have been to keep us women from getting lost although I didn't think of it at the moment. When we reached Charles Town, McGregor said we'd have to hold to our marriage bargains."

I gave her a sympathetic look. "That seems too much, Prudence. Didn't any of you raise protests?"

"Why should we?"

"It wasn't fair after all you'd just been through."

"We'd come South all along to get husbands and somewhere to live." Her mouth twisted. "Anyway, after all those men pawing us and crawling over us, being with just one man sounded like heaven."

"So Welbourne Richards got you?"

She laughed and seemed to relax slightly. "It wasn't like you think, but I was lucky. Welbourne's wife had been an invalid a long time and his housekeeper had just died. He needed a person to run the house and be in charge of the servants. He heard that a group of indentured women had been brought into the harbor. Actually, it was another group, only he didn't know that when he approached McGregor. That no-good McGregor sold my supposed 'indenture' to Welbourne for twice what the other men paid for wives."

Glancing at me with her cheeks suddenly rosy, she

laughed again. "Don't think I'm complaining," she went on. "Mrs. Richards was unconscious and died in a month, but it was weeks before anything happened between Welbourne and me."

"You were living here in the house?"

"I sure was. One night Welbourne came to my room late and got into bed with me. I guess by that time I was good and over what took place aboard Teach's ship because I was ready for a man, and Lord knows Welbourne needed a woman. He'd been a long, long time without any loving, he said, and I believed him after the way he acted. It was nice for both of us . . . real nice . . ."

Her eyes were now sparkling and she was smiling as if she'd never known a somber thought. "The next morning he told me he wanted us to marry. I was eager to become Mrs. Welbourne Richards, but I knew I wasn't good enough for him or able to act like a lady. I told him so and then he said he had to go to England on business and wanted to take me along, and he promised to find somebody in London to teach me how to talk and what to do in a drawing room. He kept his word, too. Marley, I was a whore in Massachusetts. Welbourne doesn't know—nobody here does, but I came South to get away from that kind of life. Being here is like being in fairyland. All the fabulous places Welbourne took me in England . . . the clothes he bought for me . . . and the gifts. He couldn't do enough for me. We were married in London and came back here three months ago."

"I'm glad it turned out right for you." I meant it. "But why did you change your name to Nicolette?"

She had the grace to look flustered. "That's another matter I lied about to Welbourne. I let him think 'Prudence Hall' was the name I gave McGregor for my indenture paper so I wouldn't disgrace my family, that

my real name was Nicolette Perdrix and that my father
was French. Oh, I made it a good tale, that he'd
married my mother in Massachusetts and then
abandoned her when he returned to France."

"Did Mr. Richards believe the story?"

"I hope so. He's never let on if he didn't. Perdrix is
the French word for partridge. A French sailor I used
to know rather well in Massachusetts taught me a few
words of the language and that was one."

Warm and comfortable in the rocker and some of my
tension gone, I marveled at the change in Prudence. I
felt a rush of thankfulness because I had not been taken
aboard the *Revenge*. I wondered if I would have
survived as Prudence had or if, like Nellie, I'd have
become a maniac. At least I'd been spared the horror.

"Marley, you must be bored with me talking so much
about myself," she said. "What happened to you? You
and Captain Hagen were the lonesomest pair I've ever
seen when you were sitting in that little dinghy with the
ships sailing off and leaving you."

"We were lucky. We were near land and made it to
Bath Town."

"And—? What happened then? Can't you see I'm
dying to know?"

Everything I'd bottled up inside myself exploded. I
began to talk and couldn't stop, the words tumbling
out. I told her how Bates and I fell in love and had a
common law marriage because we weren't near a
minister, about teaching school and how he left to go to
sea. My voice broke when I mentioned the endless year
of waiting for him. I added that the two men I'd
thought were my friends because they'd been Bates'
friends had turned against me.

"One was angry because I refused to have a romance
with his son—and all the while he knew I was married,"
I sighed grimly. "The other man—" remembering Josh,

I choked. "The other one raped me. Luke's ship was docked in Bath Town at the time and he offered to give me passage on the *Roxanne* so I could look for Bates. Well, here I am."

Her eyes widened in surprise. "But I thought you were Luke Nance's woman! Welbourne said—"

"No!" I interrupted her. "I want my husband!"

"Marley, do you mean you've never slept with Luke Nance? Never let him touch you? I can't believe that."

I gave a mirthless, embarrassed smile. "I didn't have any money and I was frantic to leave Bath Town. Luke and I made a bargain for my passage and I'm—uh—sharing his quarters, but it doesn't mean anything. There's nothing serious between us."

"The man's in love with you, Marley. It's written all over his face."

"He's known from the start that I'm in love with Bates. That I want my husband."

"You could do worse than Luke," she shrugged. "Welbourne thinks a lot of him."

Somehow I was on the defensive and I didn't understand the sensation. "It's not—not what—not that I don't *like* Luke." I floundered for the best words. "Maybe 'like' isn't strong enough because I'm really fond of him. He has been kind to me and I respect him—but my husband is the man for me."

Prudence took an iron poker and jabbed at the fire. Small flames arose from the half-burned log on the andirons. "Are you sure Hagen is in Charles Town, Marley?" she asked.

"I hope he is. We only docked this afternoon and I haven't had a chance to look for him, but there are an awful lot of ships in the port. I'm going to make inquiries tomorrow."

Standing up, she began to move restlessly around the room, brushing a speck of dust from a table, blowing out a candle which had burned low and was dripping wax onto its silver holder.

"Maybe I shouldn't tell you this," she measured each word out, "but I saw Captain Hagen."

"When? Where?" I gave a gasp. "How is he? Is he all right?"

"I wasn't able to speak to him, Marley. And I doubt if he saw me—or perhaps he did and didn't recognize me. Or didn't want to. It was in London last July and he looked fine. Welbourne and I were eating at an inn with some of his friends and their wives. We were in a private room on the second floor. It was awfully stuffy and we opened our door to try and get a little air, and there was another private dining room across the hall with several men eating there. They'd opened their door, too, and Bates Hagen was in that group. I recognized him and I was dying to ask him about you, but—I couldn't do it."

"Oh, if you only had! Why couldn't you ask?"

"And have Welbourne want to know how I'd known Hagen?" She shook her head. "I was sitting where I could see him and get a few snatches of the conversation, though. They were talking about a ship."

"What ship?"

"I don't know. I don't think they ever mentioned the name. But I gathered Hagen was to be the captain."

"Do you know when it was leaving and from what port? Where was it heading?"

"I don't know. What makes you think you can find him here in Charles Town?"

"Luke saw him in this area. But that was months ago, too."

"Then all you need do is to ask Luke, Marley!"

"It wouldn't do any good. I've already asked and he doesn't remember. At least, that's what he said."

"Then what—"

"I'm going to inquire everywhere. Surely somebody has seen Bates here."

She looked disbelieving and my own confidence was fading, but I refused to change my mind. I'd come to Charles Town to locate my husband and I meant to do it.

"You can't very well visit the ships anchored off shore," she sighed, "and I don't know that it would be wise for you to go aboard the ones at the dock—unless you can talk Luke into accompanying you."

"I couldn't ask him to do that."

"I don't blame you. It's a bit much to ask a man who loves you to help you find some other man who'll cart you away. I suppose your only choice is to make the rounds of the taverns. You may have to work for answers but—"

"Work?" I cut in.

"Work at coaxing the sailors to talk. Flirt a little, Marley, and keep smiling instead of being irked if some bloke pinches your backsides or tweaks your boobies. The barkeeps should remember if Hagen has been in recently. Or," she paused and smiled, "you could go to Miss Amy's. That's the whorehouse and the old wench who runs it has probably met every seaman in the Colonies at one time or the oth—"

"Nicolette!" Welbourne Richards' voice echoed up the stairs. "Please don't deprive Luke and me of the company of two charming ladies any longer."

"We're coming down now, dear," she answered, dropping the old accent and using her new refined voice as if she'd suddenly remembered she was the wife of a wealthy merchant and not a Massachusetts whore.

Our eyes met, both of us self-conscious in the knowledge that we had shared some extremely personal confidences. I had not cared for her when we were on the *Solace*, but it dawned on me she was very different

from the person I'd known then. It wasn't only because
she had learned manners and acquired a cultured way
of speaking. With a rueful smile I realized that I, too,
was different from the child-woman who walked out of
New Bedford on an April morning.

"I hope I don't slip up and call you Prudence," I
whispered as we started down the curving stairs.

"You do and I'll forget I'm a lady," she giggled. "I'll
boot you right past the back door of this house and into
the river!"

Luke and I stayed another hour. The second half of
the evening went better than the first, or maybe it
seemed better to me because I was more at ease and
making an effort to be pleasant. Luke had little to say
and he refused the invitation for us to spend the entire
night, explaining that he had ship's business to handle
early in the morning. Good-byes were exchanged and
the Richardses walked out to the paved courtyard with
us, urging us to visit again. Prudence and I gazed
deeply into each other's eyes and both of us knew our
secrets were safe.

The carriage rocked along the sandy road in the
moonlight, the roan horses maintaining a steady gait. A
faint breeze off the river made the night air cooler; the
gray moss on the trees took on an ethereal appearance.
It had been an eventful day and I was tired. At the
same time I was swept up in a special exhilaration at the
news about Bates having been in London. That would
explain why he hadn't come to Bath Town for me. If
what Prudence overheard was correct, he was acquiring
his own ship and from July until November would have
allowed him ample time to finish outfitting the vessel
and cross the Atlantic. Tomorrow he and I might be
together . . . tomorrow . . .

Luke seemed disinterested in chatting. It was more

fun to think about Bates, to realize the end of my waiting was near. I leaned my head back and closed my eyes, not actually dozing but relaxing, and without being aware of it, I slid over on the seat toward Luke until my head was against his shoulder.

"We're almost at the ship, Marley!" His voice roused me.

I straightened up, my eyes wide open. The unusual crispness in his tone was harsh and we weren't even in sight of Charles Town, much less the waterfront. I turned sideways to look at him, finding his eyes fixed on something straight ahead. He hadn't put his arm around me as he'd done in the past when I swayed toward him. His manner seemed strange. I attempted to draw him out. "Welbourne and Nicolette are nice and their house is a palace," I remarked. "I've never set foot in such a beautiful home."

His yes was a snort and he hushed. We rode the rest of the distance in a puzzling silence.

Garlow was on deck when we reached the *Roxanne* and Luke paused to speak to him. I went to the cabin and found it filled with shimmering silver moonlight. Removing the pink brocade, I spread it on one of the hammocks. I was standing at the porthole in my petticoat taking the pins from my hair when Luke stomped down the passageway, his footsteps so heavy that I was startled by the sound. He banged the door shut and stood before me, glowering, his hands on his hips and his burning eyes on me.

"Just what the hell were you doing tonight, Marley?" he stormed. "You insulted my friends! You insulted me with your rude behavior and God knows what Welbourne thinks! I'd told him earlier you were gentle and sweet and a lady even though you hadn't had the advantage of money or heritage. Now he's sure I was lying! As for Nicolette, you acted like the food she served was poison. You didn't eat enough to be polite and I know damn well you weren't sick! I'm due an answer, Marley, and I mean to have one!"

Luke had never used that furious tone to me. For a moment I was too shocked to believe what I was hearing. My mouth dropped open, my breasts rising as I came to my senses and found my voice. Anger overwhelmed me.

"Don't you owe *me* an explanation and an apology, Luke Nance?" I said between clenched jaws. "*I'm* the one who should be hurt and mad! Why did you introduce me as Miss Marley Lancaster instead of Mrs. Bates Hagen, which you know is my name?"

"I was trying to spare your reputation, Marley. A married woman accompanied by a man not her husband—that would cast doubt on your character—not on mine."

"I have nothing to be ashamed of! I'm proud of being Mrs. Bates Hagen and don't you forget it! I thought it revolting to be called Miss Lancaster when you were deliberately leaving a false impression!"

"Regardless of what you feel about it, you may as well begin using your maiden name. A common law marriage isn't worth an owl's hoot when the two people involved don't stay together."

His sarcasm hurt and I wanted to hurt him in return. "You're just jealous," I came back. "You don't want to accept the fact that I'm married."

"You *think* you're married and maybe you were—in the past. At least, that's what you claim. But whether it was common law or with a preacher and a legal certificate, it must be over or you would be with Hagen instead of standing here in your petticoat with me."

"I'll be with Bates tomorrow!" I said fiercely.

Luke's head shot up. "Just what do you mean by that? Quit daydreaming!"

"All I asked was for you to bring me to Charles Town so I could locate Bates." I uttered each word distinctly, trying to force myself to be calm enough for him to get exactly what I was saying. "In return, I agreed to sleep with you. Oh, I know you didn't spell that out in so many words when we were talking in the publick house, but it's what you meant and I've done my part of the bargain. I must say you've done yours and done it rather nicely. You've made me like you and respect you and enjoy our time together, but I don't owe you another thing and there's nothing I want from you— least of all a lecture!"

The bluntness of what I said surprised me. I hadn't meant to sound so heartless. Luke and I stared at each other, the moon's rays turning his white shirt and my petticoat silver. I could see him as plainly as if it had been noon, see the black hairs which formed his eyebrows, see his teeth bite into his lower lip, see the muscles of his neck standing out like ropes.

His expression changed, his eyes softening as a pleading look crept into them. "I love you, Marley," he whispered. "I want you here . . . with me. It can be any way you choose. We can be married by a preacher while we're in Charles Town. If I give him enough money he'll overlook the necessity of proclaiming bans in church in advance. Or it can be common law or just the two of us like it's been these past days. I reckon that's all right with me. Nothing has ever been as perfect for me in my entire life as this time with you."

I gave a ragged sigh because it seemed impossible to make him understand. "But I'm already married," I said frantically for the hundredth time. "Bates is my husband. I can't marry one man while I'm the wife of another."

The softness in his face died and he slammed his fist against the desk top. The wood cracked as if it was kindling. "For God's sake don't say that again!" he blared out. "You haven't been listening to what I'm saying! I love you and I want you but it's got to be him or me, Marley! I guess I want you enough to let you break your heart over him and I'm still opening my arms to you, but you've got me dangling and that's as sure a way to kill me as if I'd been strung up with those men on the gibbet! What's your choice? Bates Hagen or me?"

Tears came into my eyes. I didn't want to hurt Luke and I had done it already. The suffering in his face tore at me, but my answer was the same as it had always been.

"Bates," I mumbled brokenly. "Luke, I'm sorry. I'm so sorry."

He yanked the door open and went out, leaving me alone. A thin wispy cloud passed in front of the moon and instantly the silvery light became a mass of blue shadows.

Chapter 27

I WAS STILL awake when dawn broke. The night had been endless. Luke never returned to the cabin. I lay in my hammock and ached for sleep, hearing the bells mark the hours and the change of watch for the sailors, seeing the moonlight fade and the sky turn black before a milky grayness signaled an overcast morning. Twice I got up and paced the length of the room only to crawl into my hammock again and lie there fighting torment.

At the hour I should have been getting up I finally fell into a heavy dreamless sleep. It was afternoon before my eyes were open again. Befuddled, I sat up too quickly and had to grab the sides of the hammock to keep from falling. Not once in my life had I stayed in bed until midafternoon except that first day when I boarded the *Roxanne*. It took a few minutes for my mind to shove away the sleep fog.

Everything began to come back. The visit to the Richardses. The bitter quarrel with Luke. I glanced at his empty hammock and shivered.

With the jolting realization that half a day had been wasted when I could have been making inquiries about

Bates, I began to dress, putting on a plain blue homespun. I wanted to look my best when Bates and I met, but I'd be trudging from one tavern to another and it seemed stupid to wear an enticing outfit. I was willing to do almost anything to get news of my husband, but I drew the line at giving my body to those uncouth smelly seamen who no doubt would be half drunk by the time I questioned them.

Luke was not in sight when I reached the *Roxanne*'s deck. I was relieved to avoid another scene. The blanket bundle and the pink brocade dress were left in the cabin. I could say good-bye to him when I returned for my belongings, and God willing, Bates would be with me.

Crewmen were busily loading cargo, rolling barrels up a wide plank ramp which temporarily replaced the gangplank. Some of the men cursed routinely. I nodded to them instead of stopping to speak as I made my way to land. Under threatening clouds the air was raw and I hoped the rain would hold off for several hours. People were in evidence near the pier but not the throngs of the previous day. I saw very few women, everybody hurrying as if they wanted to finish their errands and head home. No one paid attention to me, for which I was thankful.

Five taverns were in the dock area. I'd save Miss Amy's for later and maybe I wouldn't have to ask my questions at the whorehouse. I neared The Blue Goose, a rowdy looking place with a large blue fowl, its wings spread wide, painted over the entrance. The sounds of coarse laughter came from inside and I had to make myself open the door, wishing desperately that I had some money and could buy the information I needed instead of begging for it.

The tavern was dim, smoky, the walls made of unpainted boards and the windows so high they offered

little light. A fire burned on the hearth and several men
sat close to it. Two men leaned against the bar where a
burly man with several days' growth of whiskers was
pouring ale into clay mugs. Silence fell instantly when I
stepped in, every pair of eyes staring at me. I could feel
my face growing hot and I held my head high, not
gazing to the right nor the left as I approached the man
behind the bar to ask my questions.

"I—I am l-looking for—for Captain Bates H-
Hagen," I said shakily. I'd started speaking normally,
but by the time I finished my voice was scarcely more
than a whisper.

"You don't need him 'cause you can have me with my
britches open," a voice rang out from the group near
the fire. The men roared with laughter and my forehead
felt redder than ever.

"Lass, I'll give you some memories that'll make you
forget that other bloke," one of the chaps at the bar
commented.

"Don't know anybody by that name," the barkeep
muttered. "What's he done that you want him? Put a
child in your belly?"

They were making fun of me. I wanted to turn and
run, but I refused to do it. Remembering what
Prudence said about my having to "work" for the
information, I tried to speak in a lighter tone. I could
scarcely breathe my heart thundered so much.

"I am Mrs. Bates Hagen," I said. "Some of you—" I
swallowed hard, "nice sailors are bound to know my
husband." With great effort I forced a small, trembling
smile.

"Can't say as I do, but he sure has great taste in
wenches," a husky voice said. "You come here by the
fire and sit on my knee and I'll get your mind off of him
by letting you hold onto—"

I fled. I couldn't stand there and listen to any more.

Outside the wintry air cooled my burning cheeks. It was a small consolation that none of the customers in The Blue Goose had touched me, but I wasn't that fortunate in the next place.

It looked like the first tavern, only smaller, the same smoky dimness and stale odors of beer and sweat and filth. I heard the type of lewd remarks and received the suggestive stares I'd just endured in The Blue Goose. All the men denied that they'd ever heard of Bates. A man dressed in sailor's clothing left his seat and sauntered up to me. I turned away and he grabbed me, holding me against his body while he tried to kiss my mouth. When I finally managed to twist away, he gave me a swat on the backsides which sent me reeling against the far wall. Another man seated at a table stretched out his arm and circled my waist, setting me down on the bench opposite him. I jumped up and started for the door.

I tried to tell myself they meant no harm, that the ale and rum put them in a frolicsome mood. But that didn't make me feel better or bolster my courage. I couldn't give up, though. I had to find my husband.

The next two taverns were similar, the no answers just the same. My self-confidence was fading as I left the fourth place. I didn't have any inkling whether the men I'd approached were telling me the truth or not. It was inconceivable that the barkeeps didn't know the names of all the ship captains. There was a chance that the men I'd questioned knew Bates, knew where he was at that very moment. Their silence might be to protect a friend since they weren't sure why I was seeking him.

It was dark by the time I approached the final waterfront tavern, a place called Toby's, located across the square from The Blue Goose and about a thousand feet from the dock where the *Roxanne* was berthed. Of all the taverns I'd seen in Charles Town, I dreaded most having to go into Toby's; it was the rowdiest. I'd overheard some of the *Roxanne*'s sailors joking about going there, making cracks under their breath about the women they'd meet at Toby's. I was aware that any women who were regular customers of that tavern would have to be prostitutes in search of a night's business.

The door to Toby's was bright red, a strange contrast to the building's rough pine boards which had never been planed smooth, much less painted. I heard a woman's laughter inside as I stood outside the door, working up courage to enter, and another woman was singing. Easing the red door open, I stepped into a large room, not as dim as the other taverns. Four lanterns hung from wall pegs. The room was jammed with men, all of them watching the far end of the room where a buxom girl in a low-cut yellow dress and a ruffled petticoat stood on a table and twirled her skirts higher than her knees while she sang a bawdy song.

None of the men looked my way. Even the barkeep was intent on the girl and didn't realize I'd come in. My eyes circled the room—and pure horror rippled over me!

McGregor stood against the far wall!

My knees buckled. He was gazing lustily at the girl in yellow. I felt sick at the sight of him, sure that when he spotted me he would expect to sell me to some strange man as fulfillment of Seneca Irving's awful marriage agreement. But first he might rape me again!

A lump of pure terror formed in my chest as I stumbled out of the tavern and ran through the night toward the *Roxanne*. I had to get away from Toby's before McGregor saw me. My lungs felt scalded and a jabbing pain tore at my sides. Panting hard, I brushed past a seaman leaving the *Roxanne*. I was almost at the top of the gangplank when a pair of iron-muscled hands reached out to grab me.

"No!" I screamed, unable to see in the darkness and sure it was McGregor who had me. "No! No!"

"Marley—for God's sake!"

It was Luke's voice. "What's wrong?" he demanded. "What's happened to you? Are you hurt? Where have you been?"

I tried to answer him and couldn't. No words would come. I felt as if I was dying, as if my lungs would never be full of air so I could breathe normally again. If he hadn't been holding me, I'd have fallen into a crumpled heap at his feet.

"Marley . . . Marley," he whispered brokenly, the fury gone from his voice. He pulled me close, folding me in his arms.

Trembling, I buried my face in his familiar chest and clung to him. His hands began to move up and down my back, the gentle gestures a comfort. If we were being watched by sailors or even by McGregor, I was too distraught to be conscious of it—or to care.

After what seemed a long time I managed to make a sound. "I want to come back to the *Roxanne* and be with you if you'll let me," I murmured in a choked voice.

There was nothing else for me to do.

Part Three

Chapter 28

LUKE BRUSHED SNOWFLAKES from the shoulders of his dark brown worsted coat as he came into our room and laid a package in my lap. I was seated in a low chair near the window, knitting a pair of knee stockings for him and trying to utilize the final bit of daylight. I was turning the stocking heel and needed to see the stitches. It was the end of February, the winter days still short and cold, but a fire burned in our hearth and the room was cozy.

"What's this?" I laid the knitting aside and looked at the package, lifting my head, seeing the way his eyes sparkled. "Not another gift, Luke?" I chided. "You really shouldn't. You're spending all your money on me."

"You let me worry about how I spend my money, Marley." Stooping in front of my chair, he gently rubbed the knuckles of his right hand across my cheek. His flesh was cold from the outside air. I reached up and sandwiched his hand between my palms until it was warm.

"Aren't you curious to know what's in the box?" he asked.

I untied the string and removed the lid, catching my breath at the sight—a cape of heather-colored wool lined with pale lavender silk! The material was soft as goose down and beautifully sewn; woven braid of the same wool bordered the neck, the sleeves and the front opening.

"Oh, Luke . . ." I held the cape up, running my fingers across it.

"Try it on, Marley."

I did. The garment was gorgeous and it fit me perfectly.

"I never thought I'd see a wrap as lovely as the blue velvet," I said, thinking of the exquisite cloak trimmed with gray fur and the matching muff which Luke bought for me shortly after we reached Philadelphia.

"But this is just as elegant," I murmured.

"Beautiful women should be dressed in beautiful clothes," he answered and his smile broadened. "I was at the docks a couple of weeks ago when a cargo of cloth was being unloaded from a French ship. One carton had a loose board on the side so the contents were in plain sight. I saw that fabric—" he gestured to the cape, "and knew it was right for you. So I bought the bolt on the spot and took it over to Gundst. He finished the cape this morning."

Herr Gundst was the German tailor who made Luke's best clothes. Frau Gundst, his wife, a tiny little woman who sewed so fast her needle whirred like a hummingbird's wings, had made the blue velvet coat and muff and several other garments which Luke bought for me. For the first time in my life I had lots of clothes and more than enough petticoats and several pairs of shoes.

Luke had showered me with other things, too.

Sapphire earrings which he said matched my eyes. Books. A tiny leather purse with a real ruby in the clasp. A looking glass with an ivory handle. A lace shawl. I told him once I was almost afraid to exclaim over a bauble or comment on ribbons or gloves or admire an object in a shop for fear he would present it to me an hour later.

Now he was giving me the cape. "Do you like it, Marley?" he asked.

I smiled at him. "How could anyone help liking it? I've never felt such cloth and the color is luscious."

"I told Gundst not to use a heavy inner lining since you'll need something lightweight when we go South next week."

His "next week" startled me. In our three-and-a-half months in Philadelphia, Luke often referred to the coming voyage of the *Roxanne* without mentioning a specific time to sail other than "in the spring." The ship had been put in dry dock for repairs. He'd said nothing about the work being completed and with spring some time off, I was dumbfounded at the news.

"You mean we'll go in just a few days, Luke?" I inquired.

"Yes. Probably by the tenth of March. My ship doesn't make money unless she's hauling cargo. Wait until you see the *Roxanne!* I have a real surprise for you aboard the ship."

"What sort of a surprise?"

"Just you wait and see for yourself. Hey—" Frown lines marred his forehead. "You don't seem very excited."

"I—I guess I've begun to think of this room as home. It's so pretty and comfortable. I don't want to leave it . . ."

My voice trailed off and a sudden mistiness blurred my vision. During our stay in Philadelphia we'd lived in a boardinghouse on Walnut Street in sight of the Delaware River. For me, it had become home.

"Home is the ship," Luke replied.

A strange expression swept into his black eyes and he cupped his hands around my face. "Are you trying to say you've been happy here with me, Marley?" he asked in an oddly urgent voice. "That *I've* made you happy?"

"Of course I'm happy." I caught my breath. "Luke, what's wrong? You look so—so different."

"Say it!" he demanded, his tone thick. "Tell me *I've* made you happy!"

I searched his face, trying to read his thoughts and feeling that I was almost with a stranger.

"You've made me very happy," I said.

Instead of the smile I anticipated, his frown deepened. "Can't you say the rest of it, Marley? For once can't you say you love me?"

Pinpoints of fire danced in his eyes. He deserved to hear what he was begging me to say. No man could have been kinder or more loving toward a woman than Luke Nance had been to me. Months before, I'd promised myself to repay him with all the affection I was able to give.

But he wasn't Bates Hagen and I couldn't pretend that he was. Only God knew where Bates was.

Despite the new cape around my shoulders and the log fire on the hearth I was instantly chilled to my bones. A quick tightness developed under my breasts as I stared into Luke's pleading face. Thanking him was not enough. I had to force myself to say the words he longed to hear even if they were a lie.

"I love you," I whispered and closed my eyes to avoid watching the glow of happiness surge into his.

"Oh, God, I love you so much, Marley. So much

. . ." Holding me close, he buried his face in my hair.

The dinner bell clanged outside our door, accompanied by running footsteps. Luke loosened his arms and managed a twisted smile.

"Damn that Arthur," he muttered. "He's the most punctual lad I've ever seen. I wish I knew how many times that blasted bell of his has interrupted you and me during a personal moment."

I laughed and smoothed my hair into place. "Don't blame Arthur," I said. "His mother would give him a paddling if he wasn't on time with the bell. Anyway, we can take up that kiss later in the evening. I'll mark the spot we left off." With my forefinger I pretended to put an X in the air.

"That's a lass after my own heart. Sweet and practical at the same moment," Luke came back with an impudent wink, his somberness disappearing.

Arthur Hawthorne was the nine-year-old son of our landlady. Every morning at seven and again at quarter to five in the afternoon he raced up and down the corridors of the house ringing the bell to announce meals. Mrs. Hawthorne had more boarders than roomers and she had two seatings for each meal. Luke had warned me that the best food went first and if we waited we might find gravy without any meat, so we made a point of eating as soon as Arthur rang the bell.

The hall was chilly when we left our room. The lone candle in a wall bracket on the landing gave off little light. I clung to Luke's arm as we went down the narrow stairs to the first floor. The dining room was a cheery place with a bright fire on the hearth and four tables, each set with eight places. The two Hawthorne girls, Mollie and Kate who were thirteen and fourteen, put bowls and platters of food on the tables. Their young faces shone rosy from running to and from the basement kitchen where their mother and an unmarried aunt cooked in a cavernous stone fireplace.

No seats were assigned. Luke and I found places at a table near the fire. The food was plain but well seasoned—venison stew, hominy and corn bread with a crock of rich golden butter so fresh I knew it must have been churned that day. Luke talked to the man sitting opposite us, a Mr. Duncan, an Englishman who had come to the Colonies several weeks earlier to buy furs. Now he was stating that he would be leaving soon with a boatload of animal skins for which he hoped to get "a pretty penny" in London.

I paid scant attention to the men while I ate, more engrossed in my own thoughts. I wasn't over my surprise at Luke's fierce demand that I say I love him, but then I'd had a lot of surprises about Luke Nance in the past three-and-a-half months.

Chapter 29

MY MIND WENT back to the night I stumbled aboard the *Roxanne* after seeing McGregor in Toby's tavern. I'd braced myself for a flood of questions after I sobbed out to Luke that I wanted to stay with him on his ship. Those questions never came. That night he gave me what I needed most at the time, tenderness and security.

He had guided me to the cabin and wrapped a blanket around my quivering body, insisting that I take a few swallows of brandy. "Have you eaten today, Marley?" he asked.

I shook my head.

"Not since last night?" His face darkened. "You barely ate a crumb then. I'll send a man out to get you something hot."

"Don't bother," I mumbled. "I—I'm not sure I can eat."

"You can jolly well try."

He walked to the cabin door and bellowed for Dobbs. He pressed money into the sailor's hand and

ordered him to find me a dish of hot food with meat or
eggs and bread. "Fruit, if there is any," he added. "Just
be quick about it and I want the victuals hot. There'll
be a coin for you after you return."

I avoided Luke's eyes. He prowled around the cabin,
I huddled on one of the benches. Dobbs was back in
half an hour with a china plate covered with a napkin,
the sailor panting from running. "Captain, I have to
return the plate," Dobbs said in an undertone with a
sidelong look at me, apparently not realizing that I
could overhear. "Only way Miss Amy would let me
take her dish was 'cause I said you wanted it. I
promised her I'd bring back the plate and the cloth to
her tonight. She sent you a message, Captain. Said she
hadn't seen you in a long spell and—"

"Go get your ale," Luke cut in, hushing him.

I wasn't supposed to know the food came from a
brothel. At that point I was too drained to care.
Because Luke took a seat beside me and insisted that I
eat, I swallowed most of the wild turkey meat and a
little of the bread and stewed apples sweetened with
molasses. The food—and probably Luke's presence—
got rid of some of my fearful dizziness.

"Feel better?" he asked. "You don't look so pale
now. You're still trembly, though. Think you can get
some sleep? I need to be on deck because we'll be
sailing shortly. The cargo and supplies are aboard and
there's no reason not to catch the next tide."

"I—I'm all r-right," I managed.

He lifted me in his arms, blanket and all, and gently
put me in my hammock. Picking up the lantern and
Miss Amy's plate and napkin, he started for the door.

"Luke . . ." my voice was a sob.

He turned and waited, the glow from the light not
reaching his face.

"Luke, I—I—Thank you," I finished lamely.

A little softness came into his eyes. "You get your rest," he said and went out, carefully closing the door.

To my amazement, I did sleep. The next morning I awakened to find Luke in his hammock burrowed under a blanket, and the *Roxanne* moving in a stiff wind with no view of land from the porthole.

During the voyage to Philadelphia I waited for Luke to ask about my time on shore in Charles Town and what happened to make me return to the ship in tears, shuddering with fright. He didn't ask. The days were routine. He was busy with his duties and I dawdled with the mending to make the work last longer. We were careful and polite to each other when we were in the cabin. Occasionally he mentioned a port he'd visited or he asked about my childhood. At night we crawled into our separate hammocks.

Five days and four nights went by before we became lovers again. I had the feeling Luke expected me to make the first move if we were to resume the relationship. I knew I owed him something, but since seeing McGregor I'd been too distraught to want any man to touch me. A sense of guilt wore me down eventually. I was taking from Luke and giving him nothing in return. I resolved to uphold my part of our arrangement.

On our fifth night out of Charles Town when I returned to our quarters after supper, I spread the green cushions on the floor and took off my dress, lying down in my petticoat with the blanket over me. The room was very dark, only a few stars visible through the porthole. The pumps droned and waves slapped the ship in a measured rhythm. After a time Luke came in without a lantern and stumbled when his foot touched one of the cushions.

"What—? Marley?" he sputtered as he regained his balance.

I heard his quick intake of breath when he realized I was on the floor. He knelt beside me, his features blurred in the darkness but his eyes smouldered.

"Marley?" A million questions were uttered in that one word.

"I—I thought . . ." I began. "If you want . . ."

He gathered me into his arms and stretched out beside me on the cushions, holding me tightly before his hands and his mouth touched my face, moving to my breasts. His caresses were feather-light at first, as if he was almost afraid to love me. Then they grew bolder, his fingers between my legs, stroking, fondling . . .

He yanked his shirt over his head and I found the buttons on his trousers, helping him open them. When his trousers were off he removed my petticoat, his naked flesh hot against mine as my body arched to meet his. We kissed, each of us planting kisses all over the other. There must have been as great a need in me as there was in him, for I responded ardently. We came together in a fiery burst of passion which let me know he had been harboring a deep desire but possessed enough willpower to keep it in check.

Afterward I felt good, my body soft and relaxed, the tension gone, my mind at peace. We slept snuggled together on the green cushions as we'd done so many other nights. I didn't hear the bells for a change of watch, but later I found Luke gone. At daybreak when I awakened once more he was there, and we made love again, slowly and more deliciously that time, as the pink and gold sunrise flooded the cabin.

Even then there were no questions from him. Everything was wonderful between us in the days and nights that followed. We laughed and chatted and made love as if there had never been a crisis. I thought about Bates—I knew I could never stop thinking about my husband and wanting him. But if he was in Luke's mind, there was no indication.

The remainder of the trip North was uneventful. We stopped once at Hampton Roads off the Virginia capes for fresh water and a supply of food. That day it was pouring. Since the dock area was a rough section of town, Luke suggested that I stay on the ship. I didn't protest despite the longing to set my feet on the shore. In about three hours we were at sea again. I didn't have another glimpse of land until the *Roxanne* sailed down the Delaware River to Philadelphia on a blustery November afternoon.

Luke had told me he was putting the ship into dry dock to have the hull overhauled.

"Will we sleep on the *Roxanne* while the work's being done?" I asked.

That made him smile and he shook his head. "Hardly. You really don't know much about ships, do you, Marley? The keel will be hoisted and turned at an angle. If you tried to sleep, you might have to stand on your head in the process. We'll stay at Mrs. Hawthorne's. Last summer when I was in Philadelphia I told her I'd return during November and I gave her a month's rent in advance at the time to be sure of a room."

"Mrs. Hawthorne's? Is she another Miss Amy?"

He doubled up with laughter. "Definitely not," he said when he could speak. "She's a widow—a respectable widow—who runs a boardinghouse on Walnut Street, which is one of the best areas in the city. It's an easy walk for me from there to the dry dock to oversee the job on the ship. You'll be near enough shops and houses to roam as much as you want during the days. All right?"

"Of course."

It was not four in the afternoon when the *Roxanne* weighed anchor, but already nearly dark as Luke and I walked the short distance to Mrs. Hawthorne's. Our belongings came behind us in a wheelbarrow pushed by a young boy. Luke had stripped the cabin of all our possessions, commenting sarcastically that despite the Colony of Pennsylvania being founded for religious purposes, the people there were no more honest than anyone else. Nothing he owned would be left intact once carpenters and dock workers were swarming over the *Roxanne*.

The air was icy and the wind sharp although the snow flurries had ceased temporarily. I glanced at the gray sky through the leafless tree branches and pulled my cloak tighter.

"Cold, Marley?" Luke asked.

"A little. But it feels good to be on land."

"You can see Mrs. Hawthorne's from here. The house on the northeast corner two squares away."

The house looked just like the other dwellings in that section of Walnut Street, tall and narrow, made of red brick with white marble steps. As we neared it a faint yellow glow appeared in the window beside the front entrance. Someone inside was lighting candles and it seemed a sign of welcome.

"Mrs. Hawthorne has three children—three living, that is," Luke said. "The two girls are in their teens and Arthur is the apple of her eye because he was born a month after her husband's death. He is eight or nine now. Mrs. Hawthorne's sister, Miss Tyson, lives there and helps cook. It's about the best place I've found to stay in Philadelphia. I hope you'll be satisfied there, Marley."

I assured him I would be, and I was. But a small shock was in store for me that first afternoon. I discovered I had become Mrs. Luke Nance.

One of the Hawthorne girls answered Luke's knock and made a curtsey. "Glad to see you again, Captain," she said and gave me a curiosity-filled look while she spoke to him. "I'll fetch Ma. You can wait in the parlor where it's warm."

The girl sped off and Luke opened the door to the right of the entrance. The room was small. Two candles glowed from a stand near the window. A low fire took some of the chill out of the air, although the room couldn't be called warm. The furniture was dark and forbidding, especially the horsehair settee on which I made the mistake of sitting. I could feel the prickle of the upholstery through the layers of my cloak, dress and petticoat.

Mrs. Hawthorne bustled in, a plump woman with curly gray hair tucked under a white cap and a mammoth white apron covering her black dress. She chattered so much Luke gave up trying to get a word in until she paused for breath, her shoe-button eyes darting everywhere. Her face was red and shiny with perspiration despite the cold, something she apologized for by informing us that cooking was hot work in winter as well as in summer.

"Mrs. Hawthorne," Luke said at last, "I'd like to present my wife."

I swallowed a gasp, knowing my cheeks must be as scarlet as hers. Luke did not look at me. I managed to get to my feet and nod. I doubted if I could find the strength for a proper greeting. It wasn't necessary, because Mrs. Hawthorne began talking again.

"La, Captain Nance," she beamed at Luke. "So you got smart enough at last to find yourself a wife! Good for you and high time. Come along with me to your room, Mrs. Nance. You're a bride, I take it, as the Captain was here last August and single then. I was going to put him in the back of the house on the third floor. I'd saved that spot for him, not knowing exactly when a seafaring man would arrive and never dreaming he wouldn't be alone. But it's lucky my best room happens to be vacant. Second floor front, right over this parlor. Mr. and Mrs. Haynes moved out of that one the first of the week and it's been cleaned. You can see the river from the front window and it has the most comfortable bed in the house—except mine."

She laughed heartily at her joke and picked up a candle, motioning for Luke and me to follow her.

The stairs were steep. On the second floor we went down a long narrow corridor. She entered the room first, lighting a candle on the mantelpiece with the flame of her candle. Then she touched her flame to the kindling on the hearth. The dry wood caught quickly and Luke tossed on a log from the woodbox.

My eyes circled the room which was to be our temporary home. The walls were cream-washed with blue drapes at the windows and blue curtains around the bed, a high four-poster which stood in one corner. Two wing chairs were near the fireplace with a candle stand between them, and a low straight chair was placed next to the window. The walnut clothespress and an eight-drawer highboy with brass pulls would give us ample space for our belongings. No rug covered the floor, but the wide oak planks had been polished until they shone.

Mrs. Hawthorne turned to me, holding her hand before her mouth as if that would keep Luke from listening, and said the necessary bucket and the wash-stand were behind a screen in the corner opposite the bed.

"We start dishing up food at quarter to five," she went on. "You'll know because Arthur will ring the dinner bell. I'd best be off to the kitchen. You people make yourselves at home, Captain, Mrs. Nance."

As the door closed behind her I whirled on Luke, a knife edge in my voice. "When did I become 'Mrs. Nance'?" I asked coldly. "You might have warned me that you were going to tell her we were married!"

He stood with his back to the fire, his feet wide apart, and he looked squarely into my face. "I rather think you became my wife in Charles Town that night we sailed, when you asked me if you could stay aboard the *Roxanne,* Marley."

A little of my rage vanished but not all of it. "I never said I considered myself married to you," I came back. "Aren't you curious to know why I returned to the ship that night?"

"Not unless you want to talk about it."

That remark left me speechless. Luke's eyes did not waver.

"I know why," he went on. "You didn't find Hagen because he wasn't in Charles Town. I'd made sure of that."

"You knew—and you let me go out looking for him?"

"You didn't ask me if you should go—or could go," he said dryly. "In fact, you didn't even tell me when you were leaving the ship. I discovered that later when I didn't find you in the cabin and some of the crew said they'd seen you going down the gangplank." He sucked his breath in. "I don't know what little incident sparked your return in such a miserable state, Marley, but I suspect some drunk sailor tried to get his hands under your skirt and got irked when you rebuffed him. Or maybe you weren't able to fend him off." Luke's face was suddenly contorted with fury. "If a man forced himself on you against your wishes and you'd pointed him out to me, I'd have broken his damn neck!"

I could not make myself tell him about McGregor and why I was so terrified of the brute. Even though what happened between that man and me wasn't my fault, I was ashamed of any contact with him.

"N-Nobody d-did that to me in C-Charles Town," I stammered.

The fire hissed, sparks shooting up the chimney. Luke poked at the blaze and put another log on the andirons. Straightening up, he looked at me once more.

"Marley, would you have preferred for me to tell Mrs. Hawthorne that you are, 'Mrs. Hagen, the lady I'm sleeping with'?" he asked. "After all, you got mad when I told Welbourne and Nicolette you were 'Miss Lancaster.' It seems impossible for me to please you on that score. I'm positive Mrs. Hawthorne, who happens to be mighty religious, would refuse to let us occupy the same room and the same bed in her house if she didn't think we were married."

I felt deflated because I was sure his reasoning was correct. Sinking heavily into a chair, I gripped its arms to steady myself.

"Would you like for us to stand up before a preacher here in Philadelphia?" he asked softly. "I'll arrange it whenever you say."

I'm Bates Hagen's wife, I wanted to scream out at him. I tried to say it and couldn't, could not remind him of what he already knew because the mention of Bates' name was guaranteed to infuriate him. If I repeated that I was already married, Luke would claim a common law marriage meant nothing when the man and woman weren't together. God knows he'd said that to me often enough.

The two candles on the mantelpiece didn't give off enough light to illuminate the corners of the room. The shadows were blue-black as twilight became darkness. Luke continued to watch me, his mouth drawn into a grim line.

"Do you honestly think of me as your wife?" I asked when the silence became agony.

"I want to do it, Marley. We're living as though we're married. Is that such bitter medicine for you to swallow?"

"No. It's just . . . just . . ." I lifted my chin, meeting his eyes. "Thank you for accepting me . . . under the circumstances."

"Damn it to hell!" he burst out. "Marley, at times you're the most exasperating woman I've ever known! What do you mean by 'under the circumstances'?"

Gnawing my lower lip, I was unable to tell him again that I was married and in love with my husband. The pulse in Luke's temple had a staccato rhythm and he was breathing faster than normal.

"I—I guess there aren't any circumstances," I mumbled. "I'm very grateful to you and I hope I'll be worthy of—"

A bell clanged outside our door. The unexpected sound made me jump. After a second the tension lines smoothed out of Luke's forehead and his mouth spread into a grin.

"That's Arthur," he said, chuckling. "The lad must be growing up because he's ringing louder and I thought he was loud enough last summer. Let's get to the dining room, Marley. I'm hungry enough to eat the

spoons and anxious for something more palatable than
pease porridge and dry biscuits."

His surly mood was gone and the subject of our
relationship wasn't discussed any more that evening.
After dinner several roomers settled themselves in the
parlor. Luke whispered to me that their rooms were
without fireplaces so they would do their sitting where
it was warm. That let me realize he must be paying
dearly for our well furnished place with the chimney
and comfortable wing chairs. We went upstairs, un-
packed and undressed. The bed, as our landlady had
blithely proclaimed, was quite comfortable for sleeping
and for lovemaking.

The stay in Philadelphia was delightful. I made
friends with the other roomers and gave a hand to
Mollie and Kate with their chores. Mrs. Hawthorne
discovered I'd taught school and asked if I would help
Arthur with his sums. The youngster and I had an
hour's session each morning right after breakfast
before he left for school. He was bright but not
particularly inclined to study more than necessary.
Remembering the students in Bath Town, I decided
most boys must be alike regarding lessons no matter
where they lived.

In good weather I walked all over the city except the
dock area. Luke didn't feel it was a proper place for any
woman unless she had business there and no man in her
family to handle it. The rest of the time I sat by the fire
in our room, reading the books he bought for me or
knitting for him. A neighbor of Mrs. Hawthorne had
wool yarn to sell and I bought both black and white.
Luke's stocking supply was woefully skimpy and so was
mine. I also knit him a red ribbed stocking cap to cover
his ears from the cold weather at sea.

Luke went out each morning and returned late in the afternoon. That gave us an hour of daylight together before the dinner bell rang. It was our time to talk and I looked forward to it. He would come in tired and cold from supervising the work on the *Roxanne,* warm himself before the fire in our room and describe the progress of the overhauling or mention any vessel which had just come into port or left. I'd cite things I'd seen on my walks or tell him of amusing incidents in Mrs. Hawthorne's house.

Occasionally he'd fall silent and I'd lift my head from the knitting expecting to find him dozing. Instead, he was watching me, a special tenderness in his face. Our eyes would meet and inevitably he told me I was beautiful, the compliments all the more meaningful because they were spoken at a time when we weren't kissing or in bed. His love enveloped me like a soft fluffy blanket. I responded to him both physically and emotionally.

But I still missed my husband. Bates Hagen was a fever in my blood. Sometimes when I was alone in the bedroom at Mrs. Hawthorne's I'd relive the days and nights with Bates, asking myself over and over why it was impossible for me to accept the fact that he was gone. As much as I tried, I couldn't shove him out of my thoughts.

Perhaps part of it was because he was the first man I'd ever loved, the first man I'd given my body to of my own free will. I remembered the way his arms felt around me and the sweet-salt taste of his lips and how his eyes glowed in the twilight when we whispered our marriage vows. I knew exactly how he looked when he came down the dune to meet me after we'd landed the dinghy, all smiles because he'd found a spring and we could drink as much water as we pleased, and how he'd

held me against his heart our first night in Bath Town
and said, "This is what you wanted, isn't it, Marley? A
real bed with clean sheets?"

The longing for him pulled at me, making me ache as
though I had a raging fever. Yet those months in
Philadelphia moved very quickly. By the time Luke
announced that we'd be sailing South in a matter of
days, I'll admit I actually had begun to think of myself
as Mrs. Luke Nance.

Chapter 30

ON OUR LAST afternoon in Philadelphia Luke was so late coming to Mrs. Hawthorne's that I began to worry. It had been a sparkling, sun-drenched day with the sky very blue and the March air cold but not raw. Good sailing weather! I packed our belongings, putting my things into the new trunk and canvas satchel which Luke bought for me some days earlier, and getting his clothes into one sea chest and his spyglass, logbooks, charts and maps into another.

After finishing I glanced around the room as if I hadn't already memorized every inch of it, wishing longingly we weren't leaving. I preferred living on land, but the idea of *not* accompanying Luke was beyond my comprehension. I was eternally thankful that he took for granted I'd board the *Roxanne*.

When the sun went down and Arthur's dinner bell rang, I went to the front window and anxiously looked toward the Delaware River. A shadowy blue-gray twilight was setting in and the evening star was rising, a brilliant speck in the pale hyacinth sky. *If something had happened to Luke* . . . The thought sent a surge of panic into me. I grabbed my cloak, ran down the stairs and out into the street, hurrying toward the dock. Halfway there I saw Luke walking very fast and he must have spotted me at the same time I recognized him.

"Marley!" he called out. "What are you doing here? Is something wrong?"

I felt embarrassed at worrying for nothing, but I told him the truth. "You were late and I thought you might be hurt or sick."

He reached me, taking my hand and tucking it through his arm as he slowed his pace to match my shorter steps. We started up Walnut Street to Mrs. Hawthorne's.

"This is a new experience for me," he grinned. "I'm not accustomed to having the most beautiful lady in Philadelphia scared for fear I've stumped my toe."

"You're making fun of me, Luke."

"Not one bit. I'm pleased that you care."

"You've never been so late before," I said defensively. "No wonder I was concerned."

"We were stowing the last of the cargo and supplies on the ship so none of that will be left to do tomorrow morning. Just as I was ready to leave about an hour ago, the *Edinburgh Lass* arrived and tied up next to the *Roxanne*. That's Jack Chaddock's ship and he's an old friend of mine. Used to be first mate with my father years ago before he got the *Lass*."

With my hand still through his arm, Luke put his free hand over my fingers and squeezed them gently, excitement rippling through his voice. "Jack had just come from New Providence in the Bahama Islands with a layover in Bath Town on his way here, Marley, and he gave me a piece of news that will interest you."

News of Bates! That had to be it. My heart began to pound.

"Tell me!" I said urgently.

"Jack said Teach is dead!"

I made a strangling sound deep in my throat. That was good news, of course, but not what I expected or longed to hear. Apparently Luke misinterpreted my reaction, thinking I was so shocked at the word of Blackbeard's death that I was gasping.

"That's one pirate you can quit worrying about," he went on, the same lilting note in his voice. "With him gone and the mass hangings in Charles Town along with Royal Pardons being issued right and left to any pirates who repent and swear off robbing, it wouldn't surprise me if the seas aren't a heap safer in the future than they've been in the past."

Pushing aside my disappointment over not hearing anything about Bates, I tried to collect my wits. "Are you sure Blackbeard is gone?" I asked.

"Jack Chaddock is trustworthy. Besides, he talked to the man who killed Teach and then he saw Teach's head."

"His *head?*" my voice rasped. "Not all of him?"

"That's right, Marley. Teach's head. Jack told me there was a fierce battle off Ocracoke Inlet between Teach's *Adventure* and one of the two ships from His Majesty's Navy. It had been stationed in Virginia waters for some time at the request of Governor Spotswood to keep the pirates from invading that colony the way they've taken over the Carolina coast. Spotswood heard a rumor that Teach was tired of being a so-called 'gentleman' in his fine house near Bath Town and tired of that latest wife, too, and was ready to set sail and plunder his way North. So Spotswood ordered one of the Navy ships to search out the pirate and get rid of him."

"Was Blackbeard killed in the fight?"

"Aye, and it must have been a bloody one. Jack said

the Navy ship that found Teach didn't have any big guns, just small arms on purpose, because when Teach was sighted, the Navy didn't want Teach to know they meant business. Teach only had eighteen or twenty in his crew and he'd anchored the *Adventure* on the Sound side of the southern tip of Ocracoke Island. Lieutenant Robert Maynard was in command of the Navy ship—I don't know the chap but I'll lift my hat to him if we ever meet—and Maynard put some men in a rowboat to take soundings so he wouldn't get grounded on a shoal. Well, Teach fired on the rowboat and that started the action. Then the tide changed and both Maynard's and Teach's vessels got stuck on sandbars."

Luke drew a long breath, obviously relishing the story.

"Teach was too near to use his big guns so he ordered his men to hurl whiskey bottles filled with shot and lit by fuses onto the deck of Maynard's sloop. I suppose Maynard remembered some tricks he'd learned in the Navy. He sent his men below, all except himself and two other officers, and made the crew stay in the hold while the bottles were hitting the deck and exploding. Those bottles cause a heap of smoke and when the air cleared and Teach didn't see many men, he must have figured he'd killed everybody. He called for grappling hooks and he and his men boarded the Navy vessel. That's when Maynard's crew poured out of the hold with their pistols cocked and their swords ready, and they surprised the hell out of the pirates."

All I cared about was knowing for sure Blackbeard was dead, not learning the details of the battle, but I couldn't get a word in to stop Luke.

"Jack said Maynard told him there was so much blood on deck that the floor planks were red and slick and even the sea around the ships turned red," Luke went on. "It was kill or be killed, and Maynard and

Teach were face to face before it ended. Teach had that huge cutlass of his and he snapped off Maynard's sword blade with it. Then Maynard threw the hilt in Teach's face and stepped back to take his pistol from the sling and fire it. A shot hit Teach in the guts, but the bastard just kept lunging forward. I guess Teach thought he'd finish Maynard off with the cutlass, but a British sailor came at Teach from the rear and hit him in the back of the neck with a sword. Cut his head halfway off. Teach was still swinging that cutlass when he went down. He grazed Maynard's knuckles in the process."

We stopped at the corner to let a carriage go by. Luke hushed briefly until the sound of the horses' hooves was off in the distance.

"Maynard ordered the head completely severed and the body dumped overboard," Luke said, "but he took Teach's head to port as proof of the victory. Tied it to the bowsprit of his ship and sailed into Bath Town to let the people there see it before he went back to Virginia with his trophy, grisly as it was. Jack Chaddock was in Bath Town at the time, which is how he got all of it firsthand and saw Teach's head. Maynard had prisoners, too. All of Teach's men who weren't killed in the fight."

I found myself shuddering, but I'd listened to every sentence. "When did this happen?" I asked.

"I didn't find out the exact date. Come to think of it, I didn't inquire. Some time ago, I suppose, as the *Edinburgh Lass* has been from Bath Town to the Bahamas and back here since then."

We walked a short distance in silence and reached the white marble steps leading to Mrs. Hawthorne's house. It was completely dark outside, but candles were burning in the hall and I welcomed the light as Luke opened the front door.

"Marley, without the danger of an attack from

Teach, I think I might take the *Roxanne* to the Bahamas after I unload cargo in Charles Town," he said. "Rum and sugar are bringing fantastic prices in the Colonies as well as in London and I can buy both cheap in New Providence and resell at a good profit."

I didn't reply. Luke still had my arm through his and with his free hand he picked up a candle from the hall table, holding it nearer my face.

"Are you all right, Marley?" he asked. "You don't look like yourself."

"It's the news about Blackbeard. The man deserved to die and I'm glad he's gone, but hanging his head from the bowsprit seems so gruesome. I'm thankful I didn't see it."

"That's probably better treatment than he gave some of his victims," Luke said dryly and continued to stare at me. "I wouldn't have related everything Jack said if I'd realized it was going to upset you so much."

Everything Jack said. The phrase echoed through my mind. Either there was no word about Bates—or Luke had been too swept up in the news of the fight and Blackbeard's death to bother to ask.

The following morning we were up early. Before the sun, in fact. Splashes of rose and apricot colored the eastern sky, promising a sunny day, and the tree branches swayed enough for me to know there was some wind.

Luke brought in the pitcher of hot water, which daily was set outside our door. I bathed first, hurrying so he could shave and wash while his half of the water was warm. I put on a clean white muslin petticoat with a wide ruffle across the hem and began to brush my hair. Luke was lathering his face, more talkative than usual. When he wasn't speaking, he whistled softly, a sign he was in very good spirits. It was clear that he looked forward to going to sea, something I couldn't say for myself.

"Four months on land at one whack is more than my quota," he commented. "But there is one thing about being on land I hate to give up. Shaving with warm water sure beats a cold shave."

"Beats a cold bath, too," I murmured.

"Once we get to the Bahamas we'll have warm water all around us, Marley. A warm ocean and a beautiful beach and a beautiful climate—except when a storm strikes. These past three or four years I've purposefully stayed away from that part of the world because the pirates took over New Providence and were in control of the islands. Now I don't have any qualms about going there. There are other pirates, but Blackbeard was the leader and set the pace. The rest tried to keep up with his devilish actions."

"Luke, please don't talk about pirates!"

My voice was thin and shrill. Luke stepped around the screen which separated the washstand from the rest of the room. Bare from the waist up with water droplets clinging to his shoulders, he was patting his freshly shaved face with a towel. I stood in front of the highboy, still in my petticoat, ready to put on my dress which lay across a chair.

"I won't mention anything else about pirates," he answered. "I never realized until last evening how much it upsets you."

"I detest everything about pirates! Everything!"

"Shhhhhh, Marley. Don't get yourself so riled up. I daresay there's not a pirate within twenty miles of Philadelphia at the moment. Besides, you're the one talking about piracy now after I promised not to do it." He came to me, smiling. "Want a kiss from a man whose face is as smooth as a baby's bottom? You'd better give a speedy reply since these cussed whiskers will start sprouting again any second."

His merry mood was making my gloom evaporate and I pushed away the thoughts of Blackbeard and his men. Moving my fingertips over Luke's cheeks, his upper lip and chin as if I was testing to see if he'd told the truth, I nodded my approval.

"It really is nice and smooth," I said. "Yes, I think I'd like a kiss. Maybe more than one. A dozen kisses."

"Sorry, lass. One is all you get at the moment because I don't have time to take you to bed and I'd be mighty tempted if I kissed you a dozen times. The tide won't wait. Not even for loving."

I made a face at him to show my displeasure and then I laughed. "Well, if it has to be just one kiss, Captain Luke Nance, make it a good one. I'm ready."

Closing my eyes, I pursed my lips and lifted my face to his. The light, casual kiss I expected didn't materialize. My lips felt as though they'd been touched by a firebrand and his tongue plunged into my mouth as one of his arms circled my waist and his other hand pushed my petticoat off my shoulders to expose my breasts.

"Oh, Luke . . ." I breathed his name, desire rising instantly in my body. His palm was warm against my flesh and the kiss didn't end until both of us were breathless.

"What the hell—let's do it!" He grinned and took my petticoat off, then removed his britches and with his arms around me and our bodies pressing tightly together, he guided me across the room to the bed. "The *Roxanne* can't sail without her captain, that's for sure," he whispered. "If we miss the morning tide, we can jolly well catch the afternoon one."

Chapter 31

LUKE AND I didn't get to Mrs. Hawthorne's dining room for the first breakfast seating. We laughed about being late for the first time on our final morning, our bodies still tingling from the delicious moments in bed. As soon as he ate, Luke left for the ship with an order for me to follow within the hour. I was to come to the dock with the man he would send for our belongings. We had acquired too many worldly goods in Philadelphia for a boy with a wheelbarrow; we needed a man strong enough to handle a pushcart.

Luke gave me three coins, one for each of the Hawthorne youngsters when I told them good-bye. They thanked me profusely. I turned to their mother, my eyes filling with tears as I hugged her.

"You'll be back soon, I hope," she said.

"I hope so, too, Mrs. Hawthorne," I managed in a choked voice.

"I feel like you're my own family, Mrs. Nance. You've changed the Captain for the better. He was always polite in the past and never caused any trouble in the house the way some men do, but sometimes he could be abrupt. Only now that he's married to you, I haven't noticed any of that. The love light fairly shines in him when he's with you. And no wonder!"

A familiar warmth in my face let me know I must be blushing. "Luke's a good man and he's been very good to me," I told her. "I wish we weren't leaving today. I'd much rather stay on here, but sailing is his work. His joy, too."

"You're doing right to go with him when you can, Mrs. Nance. I came across the Atlantic with my Roger because he wanted to settle in the Colonies and I cried for four days after we left Liverpool behind. I've never regretted the move because it kept us together. My Roger is dead, but I stuck with him when he was alive, and now I've got enough good memories stored up to do me until I meet him in Heaven. Here—" she handed me a package. "That's for you and Captain Nance. Cornmeal muffins and sliced meat. You go now, my dear, before I cry all over my clean apron."

With a final hug I stepped out into the morning sunshine and would not allow myself to look back at the red brick house.

The pushcart bounced down Walnut Street toward the docks. The man maneuvering it, a thin, muscular fellow wearing a patch over one eye, talked constantly to himself: "Avoid that bump," "Mind the rut or I'll lose the Captain's sea chest." It was a golden day, a remarkable contrast to the snowy November afternoon four months earlier when Luke and I arrived in Philadelphia.

I was as much changed as the weather. I'd become more at ease among strangers with the discovery that I could carry on a conversation with just about anyone. I'd have had to be blind not to have noticed the admiring glances from the men roomers and boarders at Mrs. Hawthorne's. I even looked different, my body still slender, but my breasts and hips curved more and my hair was thick and glossy black from being washed often in hot water with good soap.

Luke's loving gentleness had given me a sense of security and it hadn't taken me long to become accustomed to the beautiful clothing he provided. The blue velvet cloak and matching muff were elegant. Under it that morning, I had on a pale gray worsted dress trimmed with bands of blue silk braid in the same shade as the cloak.

The *Roxanne* gleamed with fresh paint, quite a contrast to the last time I'd seen her. Luke was on deck and he came down the gangplank to meet me, giving one of the sailors an order about our luggage. I nodded to Dobbs, Garlow and other men I recognized. There were many new faces. Luke had mentioned that he was signing on crewmen to replace a few who wanted to leave and two who were, as he'd put it, "too lazy to step out of the way of their own spit."

"The ship looks lovely," I told him, seeing his quick smile.

"She should sail like a dream. Come and see the surprise I have for you, Marley."

We went down the dim passageway to our quarters. The surprise was a bed, an honest-to-goodness bed! The hammocks were gone. The bed had been built by the ship's carpenter, made of the same polished wood as the walls of the cabin with the headboard carved to match the molding around the ceiling. The bed was pegged into the wall to hold it stationary. Luke proudly showed me that there were latticed side rails which could be raised or lowered by a rope attached to a hidden lever.

"That's so you won't roll out if we hit foul weather," he grinned. "You don't even have to get up to raise the rail, either. You can do it lying down with your head on the pillow. Feel the mattress, Marley. It's goose down and so are the pillows. No more cushions on the floor for us."

"No more hammocks, thank goodness," I laughed. I never felt safe in a hammock and Luke knew it.

"You like the bed, Marley?"

"I love it."

"This way you'll be comfortable and I can sleep with my arms around you like we've been doing on land. You're a hard habit to break and I don't aim to do it."

Meeting his black eyes, I caught the depths of intense feeling reflected in them, the dancing fire and the glow. Mrs. Hawthorne's comment flashed through my mind. Luke actually did have an inner glow in his face when he gazed at me—except . . .

Except if I mentioned Bates. That was guaranteed to make Luke Nance livid. He would clamp his jaws so hard together that I marveled his teeth didn't crack. Sometimes it would be hours before the tension was gone from him. Standing in the cabin beside the new bed, I resolutely promised myself to push Bates Hagen from my thoughts, the same vow I'd taken silently so many, many times, and all the while I doubted that I'd be able to do it. I'd tried—heaven knew I had. But I still thought about my husband.

"We're ready to hoist anchor so I'm going topside," Luke said. "Come along if you want a last glimpse of land for a spell. There are enough supplies on board to take us all the way to Charles Town without a layover at Hampton Roads, barring something unforeseen." He cleared his throat. "I'm not planning to stop at Bath Town, either."

I didn't know if he threw that last sentence in to get my reaction, but it didn't matter. I kept quiet because I had nothing to say. Luke turned at once, going to the

deck. I followed him, thinking that the sailors of the
Roxanne must be taking my presence for granted now.

Standing at the deck rail, I saw the houses and trees
of Philadelphia slip by. Four red-headed children
standing on the river bank waved and I waved back at
them. A small sloop going into port passed us and then
we passed a flat-bottomed skiff with two men rowing.
The town faded from view, and both river banks were
woodsy with occasional pieces of cleared land between
scattered farmhouses.

"Marley, it's a plumb gorgeous morning for starting
out, isn't it?" Luke appeared beside me and put his arm
lightly around my shoulders. "Know something?" he
went on in an exuberant tone. "I don't believe I've ever
felt happier in my life than I do this instant. You're the
cause of most of it, but the *Roxanne* can take some of
the credit. The ship is in great shape."

His eyes roved from my hair all the way to my feet,
coming back to my face and he chuckled softly. "Your
shape is mighty nice, too, lass."

Overhead, the sails billowed out in the wind, glistening white with newness against the cloud-free sky. The
pumps began, the first throbs rocking the *Roxanne*
slightly until the spurts became a steady rhythm. I
leaned against Luke and reflected silently that a
guardian angel must have tied my life to his. Not only
had he been kind to me, but he'd given me fascinating
experiences. In spite of not being eager to leave
Philadelphia, I had to admit to a quick excitement at
sailing. It was as if Luke's zest was contagious.

"Captain! A frayed line!"

The rough voice came down to deck from the
mizzenmast and I looked up in that direction just as
Luke was doing. One of the new sailors had spoken.
Luke hurried off, barking an order to Garlow. I could
not tear my eyes from the mizzenmast and I clung to the

deck railing with hands which clawed the wood like talons. The seaman who had yelled down was tall and lean. With the sun shining on his tawny hair he was so much like Bates that a lump rose into my throat. I shut my eyes quickly—looking at him was too painful to endure, and then I opened them because I had to see him once more. I continued to watch him, hypnotized, my heartbeats so intense that my chest ached.

The man swung down from the rigging on a rope, landing on deck not far from where I stood. He wasn't Bates, of course. Now that I had a closer look at him, his features didn't resemble Bates' at all. He lacked Bates' broad brow and square-jawed chin and his eyes were pale instead of a smoky blue-gray like Bates', but for a second I'd thought I was gazing at my husband.

Luke's voice at my elbow startled me. I hadn't been aware that he'd returned to my side until he spoke.

"That was MacVey, one of the new men and he seems to be a good one," Luke commented. "I hired him two weeks ago, and when Jack Chaddock and I were talking yesterday, MacVey came by and they hailed one another. Jack gave him a good recommendation. MacVey and Jack sailed together at one time. You can sure tell MacVey is a Scot from that brogue of his."

I was too dazzled looking at the man to notice his accent, but I made a mental note to avoid any more glances in his direction when he was in the rigging on a sunny day. I didn't want to put my heart into an unceasing state of bittersweet agony from memories.

Chapter 32

IT WAS WHAT Luke smilingly termed "an uneventful voyage—Thank God." Each day when he wrote in the ship's log he commented to me that he'd never seen better sailing. The wind was steady and we didn't get into a squall, much less a spring snow.

"Nothing for me to record except our location and that's an amazing situation," he said one morning as he closed the logbook and put it in a desk drawer. "I haven't even had to discipline the crew and it's a minor miracle. Maybe the long breather on shore let them get the kinks out of their systems. No doubt they had enough drinking and whoring to make them ready to return to work."

"What about the captain?" I asked mischievously. "Did he have enough drinking and whoring to satisfy him?"

"I like my rum but I was never much for getting drunk. The cost is too dear the next day—and that's a fact I learned from experiencing it. As to whoring," he reached over to touch my cheek, "I've become a one-woman man and don't you forget it. I'll always be hungry when it involves wanting you."

A somber, smouldering look came into his black eyes and his voice took on a more serious note. "Marley, I wish we'd been married when we were in Philadelphia," he added.

I let the remark pass, commenting on the good weather to change the subject. If I hadn't done that, I'd have been forced to remind him again that I already had a husband.

The further south we sailed the more pleasant the days became. I gloried in the warm sunshine. After becoming accustomed to the fire in our room at Mrs. Hawthorne's, it was hard to readjust to the damp chill in the cabin. Herr Gundst had put Luke's clothes in order so there was no mending to be done, but I managed to stay occupied reading or knitting or taking walks on deck.

We were off the Carolina coast when I became sick. It started one night with a hard chill which made my teeth chatter. By dawn I was burning with fever. Every bone in my body ached and my stomach was churning. Luke hovered over me, worry lines cutting into his face.

I didn't want him to know how awful I felt. "I'm all right. Honest, I am," I insisted. "You know how these diseases are. They have to wear themselves out in their own sweet time."

"If they don't wear you out first," he muttered. "Marley, I hope you haven't got scurvy."

"Don't be silly," I answered with a forcefulness which took all my effort. "We had a varied diet at Mrs. Hawthorne's and we haven't been at sea long enough for me to get scurvy. Besides, I've eaten my lemon slices every day since we sailed."

He put his hand on my forehead and wished aloud that we had ice to make the fever go down. I'd already wished it longingly, although I didn't say as much.

"A cold towel on my head will do the same good," I

murmured, and to try to get his thoughts off of me and onto something else, I asked how far we were from Charles Town.

"Three or four days if this good wind holds. I'm going to make you a strong rum toddy, Marley. It'll cause you to sweat and get some of the poison out of your body. If you're not all right by the time we dock in Charles Town, I could leave you with Welbourne and Nicolette to recuperate and stop off for you on the way back from the Bahamas."

I shook my throbbing head. "I'd rather stay with you, Luke. Please."

What I couldn't bring myself to say was that I didn't want to see too much of Nicolette. To me she was still Prudence Hall. I could close my eyes and see her snickering the day McGregor tied me to the mast, enjoying my predicament instead of attempting to coax him to let me go. With her newly acquired manners and her elegant clothes, she was different now. But I didn't relish the idea of being in her debt and I would be if I was a guest in her home. I had no real security with her. I did have with Luke.

Luke made the rum toddy and held the cup to my lips, making me drink every drop. The spirits burned my throat. Just as he'd told me, I began to perspire.

He sat on the side of the bed and held my hand. After a time he gave me a searching look. "Marley, could you be with child?" he asked.

"No! Definitely not. I had my woman's time last week—remember? Don't be so concerned about me, Luke. It's just some sort of ague. I feel better already so you go on about your duties."

The part about being better was a lie. I'd never been more miserably sick. But by the time we reached Charles Town three days later, the fever had broken. I was weak from the illness and from not being able to eat, but the terrible aching had stopped. I managed to sit up in bed with pillows at my back for support when the call came. The "Land ho!" cry from the lookout in the crow's nest was loud enough to reach my ears. An eternity later the pumps stopped and I listened for the *clunk!* of the anchor hitting the water. When it came, the hard splash made the ship heave slightly. She straightened at once.

Throwing a blanket around my shoulders, I went to the porthole on very wobbly legs, anxious to see a view other than water and sky. A green fuzz of new leaves showed on the tree branches near the dock. If the gibbet was still standing, it wasn't in my range of sight. I saw The Blue Goose, the painted bird's wings still outspread, although the colors looked dingier in the sunlight than they were on the gray afternoon when I went there. Remembering that awful experience, I found myself shuddering. Was Bates in Charles Town now? If I wasn't strong enough to look for him myself, how could I find out? I certainly couldn't ask Luke to do it. And McGregor? Was he still in Carolina?

The thought made me shudder again as I gazed through the porthole. Several men in sailor's clothing who seemed to be half drunk lounged near the door of The Blue Goose. Further down the street in front of another tavern two boys were tussling on the ground in a semicircle of onlookers who egged them on.

"Marley, what are you doing up?" Luke strode into the cabin, his eyes widening when he saw me on my feet.

"I just wanted a glimpse of land, but something must have happened to my knees these past several days while I've been sick," I said. "They don't want to hold me up."

Swaying, I grabbed a corner of the desk to keep from falling. Luke jumped forward and scooped me into his arms, carrying me to the bed and easing me against the pillows. Dizziness blurred my vision and I closed my eyes until the sensation passed, opening them again to see a troubled expression on his face.

"There's not one speck of color in your skin," he said worriedly. "You were on the verge of fainting and I don't want you up unless I'm here with you, Marley. That's an order. You understand?"

"I'm much better," I murmured weakly.

"But not fully well by a long shot!"

I didn't have the strength to argue with him. Besides, he was right.

"If you aren't able to walk across the room, you certainly couldn't take a carriage ride out to the Richards' house tonight," he went on. "You don't have any business trying to traipse around Charles Town, either. I reckon you're disappointed not to get a change from the sea, but we'll be heading for the Bahamas soon. What can I buy for you on shore here?"

"Some fresh bread would taste good. And some milk. Beef jerky and ships' biscuits have begun to stick in my throat."

"Mine, too. I'm heading for Welbourne's business as soon as I change clothes. I'll ask him to have Nicolette fetch you something nourishing. A pot of soup or some custard—maybe both. She probably won't get here to the ship until tomorrow, but in the meantime, I promise you'll have food tonight which isn't jerky or ships' biscuits. Or pease porridge." .

"Luke, if Welbourne invites you to have dinner at his house tonight and sends his carriage or provides you with a horse, please go. I'll be all right here."

I didn't want to be left behind, but knew I didn't have the stamina to ride three blocks, much less out to the Richards' house. Luke made no reply and he began to dress, putting on clothes which Herr Gundst had finished just before we left Philadelphia. He had new tan leather boots, highly polished, black trousers tucked into the boot tops and a fawn-colored brocade coat. His white silk shirt was cut very full with the long sleeves gathered into wide cuffs at his wrists. I thought he looked rather dashing in the outfit and told him so.

Acknowledging the compliment with a bow from his waist, he said, "Thanks, Marley. But could you be just a little biased in your opinion?" His grin was broad, his eyes merry.

"Perhaps. But I expect all the women you pass on the streets of Charles Town will agree. How long will we stay in this port?"

"Only a few days. Welbourne always wants what he buys unloaded and put into his warehouse the moment the *Roxanne* docks. In the past he's had goods he contracted for sold to another merchant who offered a higher price. My crew will begin work on the cargo this afternoon and they should be finished by tomorrow. They're due a night or two on shore, but they're so eager to get to the islands for a spree that they don't much hanker to spend a long time here." He was serious again, his eyes searching my face. "Are you trying to tell me you'd like to linger here in Charles Town, Marley?"

"No, I was merely asking," I told him truthfully.

Luke was gone from the ship for several hours. Exhausted by the short walk across the cabin to look out from the porthole, I obeyed his order about not getting up, relieved to be able to remain in bed and do nothing. But while my body was too weak to function properly, my mind was whirling. I knew how I could find out about Bates!

When Nicolette arrived the next day with soup and custard, I'd ask her to make inquiries. She wouldn't have to go to the taverns personally, but could send one of her servants. She'd be more likely to get information than I would. Leaning back against the pillows, I was too excited at the prospect to sleep, marveling that such a plan hadn't occurred to me before.

The sun moved to the western sky on the opposite side of the ship from our quarters and the cabin was filled with muted blue shadows when I heard Luke's footsteps in the passageway. He came in with a basket in one hand and a jug in the other—and a dreadful scowl on his face.

"Food and fresh milk," he muttered as he set the basket and jug on the floor by the bed.

"Luke, what's wrong?"

"Wrong?" His voice was a bark, as dreadful as the frown creasing his forehead. "Nothing's wrong. Aren't you going to eat?"

His inner fury seemed greater than ever. His words were grunts and his eyes flashed fire. If he wasn't going to tell me what had changed his mood so abruptly since he left the *Roxanne,* I decided to try to force his good humor to come back.

"Am I getting another plate from Miss Amy's?" I teased.

"Good lord, Marley! What a thing for you to say!"

I giggled, which definitely was a mistake. "You're cute when you're embarrassed, Luke. You—"

"What sort of fool chatter is this?" he interrupted me savagely. "That food did *not* come from a brothel. *Not*—you hear me? If you think I've whiled the afternoon away at Miss Amy's, you're out of your senses!"

I sat up in bed and reached for his hands, holding both of them in mine. "I wasn't accusing you of anything," I said gently. "I don't care where the food was cooked. If it tastes as good as it smells I'm going to devour every crumb and that should help me get my strength again. Please stop growling and frowning, though."

"Sorry," he came back, still not himself but a little less gruff than he'd been before. "Open the basket."

Removing the napkin, I found thick slices of bacon with a dish of warm cornmeal mush, corn bread, a square of cake dark with molasses and cinnamon and a cup of pale yellow chunks which I didn't recognize.

"What is it?" I asked.

"Pineapple. I hope you'll like it. You'll find it growing in abundance in the Bahamas."

I tasted a small piece of the fruit and thought it was delicious, both sweet and tart at the same time, with a rough texture. Luke beamed when I reached for a second piece of pineapple. He poured milk from the jug into a cup for me. To my surprise, I was actually hungry. I hadn't felt that sensation in more than a week.

"How was Welbourne?" I asked as I ate a spoonful of mush.

"A few minutes ago I was taking my frustrations out on you, Marley," he sighed. "I had no reason to add to your suffering."

"It's all right. Was Welbourne well?"

"I didn't see him. In fact, the entire experience on shore today was unpleasant. I suppose that's why I blew off when I reached the ship. Welbourne and Nicolette left for England three weeks ago and won't be back until the middle of the summer."

My throat muscles tightened and I rested the spoon in the bowl of mush. It was impossible to swallow for a moment. Without Nicolette, I had no hope of finding out anything about Bates.

"So, I had to do my business with Welbourne's oldest son, Jason, who is a damn cocky lad with a big tongue in his mouth," Luke went on. "He always has been obnoxious to my way of thinking. Welbourne should know it by now except that he has a blind spot where his children are concerned, especially with Jason."

Luke began to prowl around the cabin, too restless to stay in one spot. I remained silent, eating slowly, my thoughts more on Nicolette than on what Luke was telling me. Once he began to talk the words tumbled from him as if they had to be spoken.

"Jason refused to take all the cargo I brought in. Just wanted half of it even though his father had ordered the entire load." Luke's lips hardened into a narrow line, his eyebrows drawing together in a frown. "Jason's excuse was that he couldn't locate a written contract and he knows damn well that Welbourne and I never needed pages of invoices or written orders. We shook hands and knew we could trust one another. Welbourne would tell me what he needed and I'd get it for him if possible and add whatever else looked salable for Charles Town. But that know-it-all son of his treated me like I was dirt under his feet!"

I hated for Luke's temper to flare in such a hot fashion. I tried to think of a soothing remark, knowing full well he had to work the anger out of his system in his own time.

"Can't you sell whatever Jason doesn't buy?" I asked. "Sell to another merchant in Charles Town, I mean? I think under the circumstances Welbourne wouldn't object. Surely someone here will be interested in your cargo. It would be a shame for you to lose money on this voyage."

"I won't lose money! You can bet on that! As to disposing of the cargo, I'll carry what Jason won't buy to another port and sell it there. It won't be a problem. Maybe I'll take it on to New Providence and see if a ship's captain wants it. But getting rid of it to somebody here in Charles Town—" he shook his head vigorously. "I won't. Why should I sell to Welbourne's competitors just because his back is turned and because he's sired a stupid oaf for a son? Welbourne and I have been friends too long for me to turn against him."

Pausing briefly, Luke added, "After Jason acted so uppity I didn't bother to tell him I had several crates of pistols aboard the *Roxanne*. They'll go in a hurry in the Bahama Islands. For a fat price, too."

"You'd sell firearms to pirates? Oh, Luke—"

"I'll sell to whoever gives me the most money. I don't deliberately choose to do business with pirates, so quit your worrying on that." Walking across the room to the porthole, he stared out at the darkening sky. "There's no point in my hanging around Charles Town. I just might hoist anchor tomorrow night or the next morning, Marley. I think I will for sure."

Apparently talking was helping Luke to unwind. His shoulders were no longer hunched up and the harried coldness had gone out of his eyes, his jaw muscles slackening and his body less rigid. Once he made up his mind to sail quickly, his normal good humor was coming back and I was thankful to see it happening.

Murmuring that it was too dark in the cabin to see, he went out and returned with a lantern. He hung it on a wall peg near the bed, the fragile golden light falling in a circle on me and my supper.

"You're actually eating, Marley," he exclaimed. "I'm relieved to see it."

"I told you I was getting well. The first of the week I couldn't tolerate the thought of food, much less have swallowed any."

"I hope these victuals are tasty to you."

"They are. Really, they are."

"They didn't come from Miss Amy's, Marley. It—"

"You don't owe me an account of how you passed the afternoon," I cut in. "I shouldn't have said what I did, making a reference to Miss Amy's because the food

from her place was just as good as this is. I didn't mean
to irk you. Besides," I ran my fingers over the blanket
on the bed, looking at the pale gray wool to avoid his
eyes, "I've been sick long enough for you to—to want a
woman, I'm sure."

"Making up your mind about everything, are you?"
he said gruffly. "Well, you're going to hear me out
about what I did on shore today after I left Welbourne's
business."

"Luke, you don't have to explain! You—"

"Yes, I do have to tell you," he insisted. "And you
have to listen. Is that clear to you?"

He was issuing another order, treating me as though
I was part of his crew. I said nothing and because he
was waiting for my reply, I nodded. That seemed to
satisfy him. I suppose he took it as a signal that I was
listening.

"After I finished talking to Jason, I went to a
boardinghouse about a stone's throw from the Powder
Magazine. I've eaten there before, several times when
my father was living. He knew the woman who ran the
place, but she's dead and some relatives of hers are
maintaining the house. They don't rent rooms, just
serve meals, and I asked if something could be fixed for
me to bring to my wife who'd been ill. I haven't been
near Miss Amy's nor have I wanted to go there."

I lifted my head, my cheeks feeling as flushed as if
the fever was returning.

"But I'm sick now, Luke," I told him. "I—I can
understand if you want—need—somebody else."

A misty look came into his eyes and he leaned across
the bed to smooth my hair away from my forehead, his
hand rough to my skin although his touch was unusually
gentle.

"Even if you're sick and we can't have any loving, my
feelings about you are the same," he said softly.

Chapter 33

THE SEA WAS sapphire blue and so clear I could look down from the deck of the *Roxanne* to watch brilliantly colored fish darting just beneath the surface of the water. New Providence Island was in plain view a short distance ahead. Luke was giving explicit instructions to the helmsman to keep us from getting stuck on a sandbar or snagging the hull on a coral reef.

Despite the fact that it was only mid-April, the warm weather made a wrap unnecessary on that sparkling morning. I was dressed for going ashore in a dark green linen dress with pale green embroidery around the square neckline and at the wrists of the long bell sleeves. I was over the fever and the weakness it left in my body. With the sweet tang of the balmy air and beauty on every side, I couldn't wait to be off the ship and to put my feet on solid ground. It seemed ages since we left Philadelphia and another eternity since we sailed out of Charles Town.

As the *Roxanne* neared New Providence I saw white sand glistening at the shoreline and behind it a lush growth of trees and bushes. Flowers with vivid red and lavender blossoms were in evidence everywhere. This island looked surprisingly hilly in contrast to the flat islands we'd already passed, some of them no more than tiny specks of green vegetation and sand pink from the coral, all of it appearing to float on the surface of the water. To the left—portside, Luke called it—the gently rolling waves foamed and lapped against two large sloops anchored away from shore. Several smaller vessels were tied to the docks which jutted out from land into the blue ocean.

Standing at the ship's rail with the breeze twirling my skirts around my ankles, I was conscious of an inner excitement, the same exhilaration and expectation which was affecting the crew. Sailors yelled to one another from their perches high in the *Roxanne*'s rigging, making comments about soon being with the "daughters of Africa" on New Providence Island and how before nightfall they'd be full of exotic tropical punch with flower petals in the rum mixture. They laughed and joked, some of their remarks suggestive and at times positively lewd, but all of it good-natured.

When we were a few hundred feet from the dock Luke joined me at the rail, shading his eyes with his hand.

"Gorgeous sight, isn't it?" he said, eagerness putting a musical quality into his voice. He seemed as excited as the rest of the men on the ship.

"I've never seen anything like it," I replied. "Luke, can we live on land while we're here as we did in Philadelphia?"

"I don't know. It'll depend on what kind of accommodations are available."

"It doesn't have to be a fancy place. Not as big as the room we had at Mrs. Hawthorne's or as expensive," I went on, pleading. "I can be satisfied anywhere. Besides, it's doubtful I'll want to spend much time indoors while we're here, not as lovely as this island seems. The colors of the flowers almost hurt my eyes with their brightness."

"I don't know, Marley." The musical quality gave way to a hint of exasperation. "This place is a paradise for seamen because of the bars and the wenches. Most of the men really go for the half-breeds. Claim they're out of the ordinary in bed and I'll have to admit some of them are rather easy on the eyes. But for a ladylike woman—especially for one with your beauty and your body, Marley—there could be trouble if you're in the wrong spot by yourself. I don't want you going ashore here until I have a chance to look around the island."

It was my turn to be exasperated and I made no attempt to hide my disappointment.

"You mean I have to stay on the *Roxanne* while you and everybody else have a great time on land, Luke? That I'm stuck here until it suits your convenience?"

He gave me a hard stare. "Do you think you could protect yourself if two or three drunk sailors with lust on their minds came at you?"

I had to admit that I couldn't, adding the silent reminder to myself that I wasn't able to protect myself against McGregor in the tunnel or Teach's men on the *Solace* or against Josh Harding in Bath Town. The memories made me quiver.

"Thanks for—for watching out for me," I murmured with a stifled sigh.

"Regardless of whether we find living quarters on shore or not, you'll get off the ship before dark," he said in a reassuring tone. "I swear to that, although you won't go the instant we drop anchor."

Obviously, the subject was closed. I knew Luke well enough not to continue talking about it or begging him when his mind was made up.

Most of the crew went ashore when Luke did, although he assigned half a dozen men to remain and guard the ship. Garlow was put in charge. My mind was whirling. I wanted so much to live on land that I convinced myself Luke could find us a roominghouse or an inn. I went to the cabin to pack my satchel with clothing for a day or two. My other lightweight garments could be taken to land at the same time Luke's belongings were transported, with winter dresses and heavy cloaks remaining on the ship.

Going to the deck once more after packing, I took a seat on one of the wooden chests and braced myself for a long wait, the satchel at my feet. Flowers growing on land gave off a delightful perfume and the sun was warm on my shoulders. I could hear voices coming from ships anchored nearby, not understanding what was being said, but recognizing all the voices as belonging to men. I would have enjoyed chatting with a woman.

The *Sweet Glory* wasn't docked at New Providence, at least not in my range of vision. I'd checked the names of all the ships I could see. Of course, Bates might not be on that vessel now if what Nicolette told me was true about the conversation she'd overheard in London. I didn't intend to run the risk of missing him, though, and I planned to make some discreet inquiries if the chance arose. If I'd spotted the *Glory*, I'd have questioned her captain regardless of the fact that I knew the ship was manned by pirates at the time Hannah Martin bought silk from her crew—and notwithstanding Luke's order about my staying on the *Roxanne*.

Luke returned to the ship in about three hours. The wait seemed endless before I saw him emerging from the green woods and coming across the beach toward the pier, his coat slung over his arm. I ran to the top of the gangplank to meet him.

"Ready and waiting, are you?" he said and grinned. "Come along, then."

When I picked up my satchel, he shook his head. "You won't need that, Marley. I couldn't find any decent place for us on the island. We'll have to continue sleeping in our quarters on the *Roxanne*."

"But there must be some place—"

"There isn't. Nothing where I'd be satisfied to leave you alone a second. You can go ashore each day while we're here, though, and you're in for a treat tonight. How would you enjoy having a meal with the Governor of the Bahama Islands?"

This was such a startling question that I temporarily forgot my consternation at not living on land.

"Do you know the Governor?" I asked.

"Woodes Rogers. I've known him for years."

I must have appeared blank because Luke gave me a quizzical glance.

"Marley, I'm amazed you haven't heard of Woodes Rogers since you grew up in a seaport town," he said. "The man sailed his ship around the world some ten years ago. It took him several years to complete the voyage and—" a crooked smile twisted Luke's mouth, "he did his share of plundering as he went and made no bones about it, but that gave him knowledge of the ways of piracy and helped him to clean up these islands after he became Governor. In fact, that's one reason he was given the Governorship. When the Lords Proprietors turned the Bahamas back to the Crown, Rogers and his company leased the royalties and quitrents and—aw, Marley—" he broke the sentence off, annoyance showing in his tone. "Don't get mad because you heard the term 'piracy.' I was only trying to tell you about Woodes Rogers before you meet him—*if* you want to come with me. And if you go to his house, I hope you'll have the decency not to get on a high horse if he says anything about sea plunder."

I hadn't been aware that my facial expression was giving my thoughts away. I wanted to go with Luke, and the one thing I desperately did not want was for Luke to lose his good humor so our afternoon would be spoiled.

"What's a quitrent?" I asked and tried to keep my voice light.

"A fixed rent for the use of land. If you're ready, let's be off."

"Shouldn't I change to a better dress? If we're going to see the Governor—"

"You look fine, Marley. Woodes is a plain fellow and doesn't demand a lot of ceremony just because he holds a high office. That linen ought to be cool and we have a climb ahead of us."

We went down the gangplank and crossed the pier and the beach, moving onto a sandy trail which took us to the woods. After we'd gone a hundred or so yards into the forest, the trail narrowed to a foot path, vegetation on either side of us so thick it was a tangle. There were strange trees whose twigs resembled feathers.

"Casuarina trees," Luke said in answer to my question. "On your right are some coconut palms and cedars, and further along you'll see pines. The cedar trees growing on this island are fabulous in size. Everything smells good, doesn't it?"

The heady scent of the cedars mingled with the flowers. Luke pointed out some of the blooms he recognized, yellow and pink hibiscus, masses of pink, red and white oleander, bougainvillea in rich crimsons and lavenders and the royal purple passion flower. A flock of green parrots chattered from the tree branches as we passed.

I stooped to pick up a rosy shell which lay on the path, commenting that I'd never seen a shell that red-orange color.

"It's probably been near enough coral to change from white to that red," Luke answered. "The sand on some of these islands is as pink as a sunset and the color comes from the coral reefs."

It was cool and dim under the trees with the sky visible in tiny bits and pieces. We walked a short distance further before hearing human sounds, a woman singing in a language I didn't recognize, her haunting voice blending with the lazy laughter of men. Luke touched one finger to his lips as a signal for me to be quiet and led me off the path through a thicket of green bushes taller than he was. The lush growth shielded us from view, but we could peep into a clearing and the scene in front of us was unbelievable.

Several men who appeared to be sailors of many nationalities sat on the ground and others lay on grass mats under the trees, most with rum mugs beside them and their eyes glazed from strong drink. Dusky-skinned women massaged their backs or fed them fruit or merely smiled. The women's sultry expressions never changed, and from their dark coloring I realized they must be the "daughters of Africa" I'd heard mentioned by the sailors of the *Roxanne*.

The woman who sang was crouched against a tree with her bare feet tucked under her. She was very dark and slim with her black hair parted into squares all over her head and plaited into pigtails, her smooth mahogany skin shining as though it had been oiled and her ebony nipples thrusting forward. The other women were half-breeds with flesh tones ranging from deep golden bronze to creamy brown, all of them wearing bright calico skirts tied about their waists, their breasts bare.

A hut of rough wooden planks apparently housed a bar. The other buildings—if they could be called "buildings"—were shanties, some merely shelters with thatched roofs of palm frond supported by poles and others were tents made from old sails. While we watched, one of the men got to his feet and put an arm around the shoulders of a girl who didn't look more than twelve or thirteen, playfully tweaking her budding breasts as he pulled her from the ground to a standing position. She put both of her hands over the bulging front of his britches and giggled.

Luke tugged at my arm, motioning me to the path once more. Neither of us spoke until we were far enough away not to be overheard.

"You didn't want to wait and see them fornicate, did you?" he asked.

"Not really."

"Now you know why I felt you'd be better off staying on the ship at night than sleeping here," he said. "There are any number of gathering spots on the island similar to what you've just witnessed. If there aren't enough native women available, some sailor might make a grab for you."

"But what about the towns?" I persisted, determined to live on land if it was at all possible. "Surely the towns have inns."

"You've just seen a local 'inn'," he chuckled.

"Luke, stop teasing me. Where do the people go to shop?"

"I'm being very truthful. They buy what they need at the dock straight from the ships. Everything else is growing here. Those half-breeds haven't had to make a purchase in years as they're paid for their services with whatever the sailors can scrounge up. I was hoping Woodes might suggest our staying at his house and that's the reason I sought him out first thing, but he's sailing for Bristol in the morning so we're lucky to have one visit with him. His wife has already left, he told me. She went two weeks ago. She's been ill and wants to see a doctor in England."

I stumbled over a tree root, the mention of Bristol bringing thoughts of Bates to my mind, and Luke put out his hand to catch my arm so I wouldn't fall.

"If Mrs. Rogers is sick, how did she ever get down this path to the ship?" I asked thickly.

Luke laughed again. "Take heart, Marley. It's not much further. There's a road to the Governor's residence, but I thought after being cooped up on the *Roxanne* for so long that you'd probably enjoy walking this way. We'll no doubt use the road going back. Besides, it's shadier on the path and that means cooler."

We came to an area where the forest was so dense the tree branches locked over our heads, shutting out the sky as well as the blazing sun and leaving us in muted green shadows with the sand path a pale ribbon before us. I was aware that we were climbing although the trail wasn't steep enough to make either of us pant. At last the trees thinned and ahead of us was a gray stone house built on a rocky ledge overlooking the ocean.

"That's it," Luke said.

He put on his coat. I brushed sand from the hem of my skirt and patted my hair, wishing we'd passed a spring or a stream so I could bathe my face and hands. As we stepped out of the forest and approached the house I realized how deliciously comfortable the tree-banked path had been in contrast to the late afternoon sunshine. The sudden heat was scorching.

"That gray limestone in the house is native to the

island," Luke commented. "It's so soft you can cut it like wood with a saw and don't need a mason's chisel."

The house was a square which would have seemed boxy if it hadn't been for the graceful second-story porch made of cedar which overhung a small courtyard paved with the same gray limestone. Red and white oleanders bordered the yard and grew in profusion beside the rock steps carved into the side of the cliff to the blue ocean some two hundred feet below.

As we walked across the open courtyard a man came from the house. He was tall and heavily built with dark eyes and a mouth too small for his other features until he smiled. I guessed correctly that he was the Governor as there was an air of authority about him. He was dressed completely in white with white knee trousers and white stockings, a white shirt and a thin sleeveless white silk jerkin which reached his thighs.

The men greeted each other enthusiastically as if they hadn't talked a few hours earlier. Luke drew me forward. "Woodes," he said, "I want to present my wife."

The introduction didn't surprise me nor did it cause me concern. After the stay in Philadelphia I'd grown accustomed to being thought of as Mrs. Nance. The Governor took my hand, bending low from his waist to brush his lips over my fingers, and I was enchanted at the gesture. My hand had never been kissed like that before, although I knew the custom was common in Europe. I could feel a tingling of excitement until I caught the merry reaction in Luke's eyes. He seemed to be saying silently to me, "So you like ceremony, do you, Marley?" and I knew he'd tease me about it once he and I were by ourselves.

Governor Rogers ushered us into a wide central hall running all the way through the house with red oleanders growing in the backyard visible from the entrance. The corridor was surprisingly cool. From it we went into a parlor with louvered shutters covering the broad windows so that no direct sunlight came in. The furniture was massive, made of wood so dark it was almost black and heavily carved, but with the chalky white walls and the bare floors the room seemed spacious and airy. A low table by the settee held a glass vase of purple flowers and a basket of round pinkish yellow fruit I'd never seen before.

The men talked about ships and the Governor seemed eager for firsthand knowledge of events in Charles Town. I tried to make occasional comments because I recalled all too well how angry Luke was at my silence the night he took me to visit Welbourne and Nicolette, and I didn't want a repeat of that situation. Of course, this time I hadn't been subjected to a shock. But even when I wasn't speaking I paid close attention to what Luke and Governor Rogers were saying.

A black manservant in loose white britches and a blue shirt brought us cups of pineapple juice laced with a sweet wine. The meal was served in the dining room where more servants stood on opposite sides of the long table, fanning the air with palm fronds to keep the insects away and to create a faint breeze. I ate barbecued pork drenched with a fiery pepper sauce and nibbled conch which I'd never had and didn't especially like. There was a platter of vegetables and a dish called cassava pie, which the Governor said was an island delicacy made from eggs, meat, spices and the starchy cassava root which grew wild in the area. The fruits which were our dessert were equally unfamiliar to me. I wouldn't have known what I was consuming nor how to handle the bananas and mangoes if Luke hadn't shown me.

By the time we finished eating the sun was going down and Governor Rogers suggested sitting on the second story porch which he called "the veranda." It was much cooler outside, and the air was sweet with the perfume of flower blossoms. Below us the surf splashed against coral rocks, the sound mingling with the cries of some birds with long, showy plumes who watched us from the trees growing at the edge of the courtyard.

I became silent, relaxing, enjoying the tranquility. It was heavenly to be on land again, to have had a delicious dinner and to see something other than water and sky. The men's conversation had to do with sea trade and Admiralty laws, and I caught the names of various ships, only half listening until the word *pirate* reached my ears. Stiffening involuntarily, I sat up straighter in my chair. Governor Rogers was speaking, mentioning "Acts of Grace," whatever that was.

"I'll tell you, Luke, I had an eerie experience when I came here to take charge of the Bahamas," he said. "I knew there were plenty of pirates here and somehow they'd got word that I was coming with the intention of making the islands safe again. So they had a welcoming party waiting for me. Benjamin Hornigold was their leader with a considerable number of other pirate captains who'd been ruling New Providence. Between them they had nigh to a thousand men."

He placed his hands behind his head, the fingers entwined, and he stretched his legs out, crossing them at the ankles.

"They took three hundred of the brawniest scoundrels and drew up two parallel lines from the water's edge," he went on. "I was certainly thankful I'd made my wife stay in England. I'd told her she could join me here as soon as there was a place for her to live. And I was mighty glad Teach was at sea instead of here, although Ben Hornigold could be almost as dastardly as Teach when he chose. For me it was either walk between those two lines or return to my ship and be branded a coward and have my usefulness over."

"What did you do?" I gasped.

"The only thing I could do, Mrs. Nance. I took the plunge and went down the lines." He slapped one of his hands hard on the wooden arm of his chair; the noise, a *thwack,* startled the birds into flying out of the trees.

"Those damn pirates fired volleys over my head but I wasn't touched so I assume they didn't plan to hit me, and neither were any of those with me hurt. As soon as I made it past the last man, I turned and announced then and there that I'd been given power by the Crown to extend the Acts of Grace and issue pardons to any pirates who would pledge themselves to behave."

"Did any men come forward?" Luke asked.

"I'm right proud of the results. My facing up to them must have convinced them I was serious about making these islands safe. Yes, Luke, a horde wanted quick pardons on the spot—among them, Hornigold himself."

The Governor paused, shrugging. "Some that I've pardoned have strayed and forgotten their promises," he said. "But plenty have abandoned piracy and settled down to be decent citizens. Incidentally, Ben Hornigold has stuck to his vow and I didn't believe that he would. That's how Teach got his start in plundering. Sailing under Hornigold, and it was on Hornigold's ship that Teach picked up the nickname of Blackbeard."

I shivered again despite the warm air, my feeling of peace gone. Each time the words *pirate* or *piracy* were uttered I felt the muscles in my body pulled taut with tension. The memories returned . . . those final nightmare hours aboard the *Solace* when the two pirates raped me . . . the laughter from Blackbeard and the pirate crew as Bates and I were ordered to get into the dinghy . . .

Suddenly it dawned on me that Governor Rogers might know where Bates was!

And I dared not inquire. Not in front of Luke. Not even if Luke left us briefly. The Governor would want to know why I was asking about a sea captain and I couldn't admit Bates was my husband, not without revealing Luke's lie that I was his wife. I swallowed around the sudden lump in my throat, thankful for the approaching twilight which I hoped would veil any emotion in my face.

"Woodes, did you know Teach was dead?" Luke asked.

Oh, God, Luke, don't tell that awful story again, I wanted to scream at him. *I'll lose my senses—and my supper—if I have to listen to every gory detail!*

I was spared. The Governor already knew.

"Yes, I heard about it," Governor Rogers said. "Teach came to a right brutal end, but it's probably no more than he deserved. I understand his head was carried to Virginia."

Luke glanced at me as though he realized the turn the talk was taking. I was still trembling inside, but with great effort I forced a wan smile. A few minutes later Luke said it was time for us to return to the *Roxanne* if we wanted to reach the ship before dark. I didn't object. The evening had been enjoyable until the last hour, but if we lingered the talk of pirates would persist.

"You must have matters needing your attention before you sail tomorrow," Luke said to the Governor. "And it's been a full day for Marley and me."

"I hope you'll dock here again soon, especially when my wife is on the island. She's always hungry to see a woman other than the natives." Governor Rogers turned to me. "Mrs. Nance, we don't have any wheeled transportation on New Providence except carts for hauling so I can't send you back to Luke's ship in a carriage. But my wife has a sedan chair which she finds comfortable and if you want to use it tonight, I'll have two of the servants carry you."

Thanking him, I declined. He went with us across the courtyard past the rear of the house to the road which was wider than the forest trail and paved with finely crushed shells. It wound down the hill to the pier between trees, flowering bushes and the ever-present undergrowth. Our good-byes were brief, the men shaking hands and slapping each other on the back, and the Governor giving me a stately bow as he kissed my hand again.

A milky rose-colored glow permeated the semidarkness as Luke and I set off down the road. Insects hummed in the tall grass. Night birds gave low, silvery cries. A sprinkling of early stars shone directly over us and on either side of the road the dense growth was now green-black. I tucked my arm through Luke's and we walked a short distance without speaking. Not another human being was in sight.

"Marley, you're more silent than usual," he said finally.

"Can you believe that for once I simply don't have anything to say?"

"Now that's a change from your usual behavior," he chuckled. "I was beginning to think Woodes had hypnotized you when he kissed your hand. No doubt he liked the feel and taste of your flesh because he kissed it twice."

"I liked his doing it," I admitted, adding in a saucy tone, "Why don't you greet me like that?"

"Because I'd rather kiss you on the mouth."

Both of us laughed. I felt happy and relaxed once more, the thoughts about pirates pushed to the very back of my mind.

"Well, you're giving me an explanation I can't quibble about," I murmured. "If you—"

Our conversation was interrupted by noisy squawking which came from a tree bordering the road, the raucous sound making me hush whatever I was about to say. Two large white birds flew out of the forest, still screeching shrilly as they passed over us and soared into the sky before disappearing.

"What in the world is wrong with them?" I asked. "They're too beautiful to make such an ungodly racket."

"Some animal may have climbed their tree and surprised them by their nest. Or that scream could have been their mating call. Hey, Marley—want to hear my mating call?"

There was a teasing note in his voice. I gave him an impish smile which he may not have seen in the dim light.

"Not really," I came back.

"You sure you don't want to hear it?"

"Positive."

"Aw, hell—and I was set to give it, too." He pretended to be distraught.

"But when we reach our bed I wouldn't object if you demonstrated your mating technique," I said. "Minus the yell those birds gave, of course."

He stopped walking and gathered me into his arms, kissing me in a passionate way which left me breathless. I responded to the fire in him, my lips parting so my tongue could meet his, my breasts flattening against his firm chest.

We hurried the rest of the way to the ship.

Chapter 34

I STOOD ON the deck of the *Roxanne* waiting for Luke and gazing at a three-masted ship coming over the horizon under full sail, her black prow dipping in and out of the blue waves. As I watched, she appeared to be changing course, heading for New Providence Island. Vaguely I wondered what cargo she carried or if by chance the family of the captain was aboard.

Governor Rogers had commented that his wife was hungry to talk to another woman. I knew the feeling since I was surrounded by men. My last real conversation with a woman had been in Philadelphia when I told Mrs. Hawthorne good-bye. The native women on New Providence island knew just a few words of English and I didn't speak their language at all, so we didn't actually communicate though we smiled at one another when we met.

It was a sparkling noon, the beginning of our third week in the Bahamas. I'd drifted into a delightfully simple routine of strolling on the beach or in the woods near the spot the *Roxanne* was anchored. Each day there was at least one trip to the short pier where residents of nearby islands came in open boats called shallops laden with fresh produce to sell. The mangoes were plump and juicy. I doted on the yellow bananas and the tart oranges as well as the vegetables. A variety of fish were available from the island waters, all of it having to be eaten quickly before it spoiled in the heat. Luke and I often cooked our supper on the beach, making a wood fire on the sand. We'd learned to wrap the fish in leaves and season it with lemon, roasting it in hot ashes as the natives did.

Part of the pleasant routine included a daily trip to the hidden cove where I bathed myself and washed Luke's and my clothing. It was a place he had discovered, a shallow pool only a ten-minute walk from the dock. On his orders I never went there alone. For once I didn't object. Luke and I had peeked into the clearing at the sailors and their women on our first afternoon in the islands. I didn't relish the idea of being naked alone in the transparent water if somebody happened along.

As I watched the horizon that noon the three-masted sloop was coming nearer the dock, the men in her rigging now in sight but no bigger than birds on a tree limb. She was, I reflected, a beautiful vessel. It was nice to have something new to contemplate. At the moment I was killing time waiting for Luke to finish talking to Hindermann, the *Roxanne*'s carpenter. As soon as that was done we were going to the cove. The basket on my arm contained the usual soap and towels plus some ripe bananas in case we lingered and were hungry.

My clothing from Philadelphia and even the lighter homespun dresses from Bath Town proved too heavy for the tropical climate. That morning I was wearing a native skirt of yellow-flowered calico, only instead of being bare-breasted as the island women were, I had on a white cotton blouse simply made with a round neck and very short sleeves. Luke had gotten the cloth for these clothes for me and I'd sewed them myself. He'd also bought the wide-brimmed white hat I was wearing. It was woven of sisal straw by the natives and offered some protection from the sun, although my skin had already lost its normal ivory tone and now was a golden tan.

"Sorry to force you to wait so long a time, Marley," Luke said as he came across the deck. "I wanted to see if Hindermann could rig some sort of shelter for you on land."

"You mean we're moving ashore at last?" I couldn't keep the excitement out of my voice.

"Not on shore here at New Providence. Tomorrow I'm going to take the ship to one of the uninhabited islands. We'll careen her to scrape off the barnacles."

In contrast to the limited knowledge of ships I'd had when the *Roxanne* was put into dry dock in Philadelphia, now I'd learned enough not to assume anyone would remain on board while the work was being done. The *Roxanne* would be lifted out of the water and turned slightly by ropes attached to tall trees.

"Where will the crew sleep while you're scraping?" I asked.

"Probably on the sand or they can string their hammocks between trees if they choose. But I thought you'd want more privacy than that, Marley."

"Won't you be with me?"

"Sure, I will. I certainly don't intend to leave you on land by yourself. Hindermann ought to be able to make a quick shelter out of planks and sail cloth large enough for the both of us."

Another fact I'd learned was that scraping barnacles was an indication we were preparing for a voyage. "Have you set a date for leaving these islands?" I asked, a wistfulness in my voice.

"Afraid so." Luke put his arm lightly around my waist as we walked down the ship's gangplank. "This lounging is a great existence, but I don't earn a living unless I'm transporting cargo. We'll be in these waters another week, more or less, and that will allow ample time to clean the ship and come back by New Providence to load up. I'm taking sugar and rum aboard, and also some spices."

"You'll sell these items in Charles Town?"

"I guess we'll stop briefly in Charles Town to replenish the water supply, but I'll get a better price for the goods in one of the northern colonies or in England. I'm considering Liverpool although right now I'm not sure which destination I'll choose, but my mind will be made up before we sail out of this harbor the final time."

"Luke, I dread leaving here. Of course, I know you have to go where you do business, but . . . well . . . it's so lovely in these islands . . ."

He squeezed my fingers gently and smiled without replying. I knew he'd enjoyed our stay in the Bahamas, but I could sense the restlessness in him, the same feeling he'd had those final days in Philadelphia. It was as though the sea was calling to him. Sailing was his life just as it had been Bates Hagen's.

The sun-baked sand felt warm to my feet. I smiled at the thought of how shocked I'd have been a year or even a month earlier at the idea of walking barefoot in a public place like the dock. The native women did it all the time and so did the seamen. Even Luke had put his shoes into a chest in the cabin after the night we visited Governor Rogers and hadn't had them on since. Now he wore calico britches and no shirt, the muscles in his chest and shoulders rippling under his sunburned skin.

I was thankful for the sisal hat which shaded my face

from the blazing sunshine. Our walk took us down the beach a short distance before we turned into the forest past a mass of pink hibiscus as tall as young trees. The tiny pool was a quarter of a mile further, a miniature lake surrounded by trees whose branches drooped low. The place had no real beach, only a narrow curving strip of sand less than four feet wide which bordered the pool, the water waist deep at the shore line.

When we reached the spot it was pleasantly shady. I undressed and spread my clothing over some bushes, slipping into the blue depths which were so clear I could see my toes wiggling on the sandy bottom. I ducked under the surface, my hair spreading behind me like a black lace veil. As I came up for air and shook droplets from my eyes, Luke was looking down at me from the bank, grinning, his feet set wide apart and his hands on his hips.

"How is it?" he asked. "Cold?"

That was a silly question and he knew it. The water was always warm.

I splattered his feet. "It's scrumptious," I said and laughed from sheer joy. "Aren't you coming in to see for yourself?"

He began to unbutton his trousers. "You should have been born a fish, Marley. I've never known anybody to enjoy getting soaked the way you do."

Ducking under the surface again, I reached to the bottom for a handful of sand, letting it slide through my open fingers. Luke, naked now, the flesh above his waist gleaming like burnished copper in contrast to the paler skin below his beltline, jumped in beside me, sending water in every direction. We began a familiar game, darting this way and that, playing tag, splashing each other until finally he caught my wrist and pulled me against him, our bodies touching as our mouths met in a damp, tantalizing kiss.

One of his arms circled my waist and as the kiss ended his other hand caressed my breasts, gently fondling the nipples until they were as rosy as ripe plums and fully erect. Spasms of fire shot through me.

"Want to?" he whispered. Desire glowed in his eyes.

He'd kindled a matching desire in me. "You mean here—in the water, Luke? How can we without drowning?"

"I wouldn't make you lie on your back under the surface," he said and laughed softly, continuing those enticing caresses. His mouth looked moist and red. Very, very red. "Just you stand still where you are and spread your legs a little."

My body throbbed. I did as he asked, gripping his back with my fingers, pressing myself on him, moving as he moved in a pulsating rhythm.

But it wasn't right. I couldn't give myself up completely to the loving, not while we stood hip-deep in the water. Nothing felt as good as it should have despite the burning need inside me.

"Luke, let's lie on the ground," I gasped.

Wordlessly he scooped me up in his arms and laid me down by the edge of the pool, then flung himself on top of me, both of us so filled with passion that there was no time for stroking or kissing. I clawed at him as though I could never hold him close enough, straining against him, my legs locked around his thighs, and when he entered me the instant explosions in our bodies left us reeling.

As the ecstasy ended neither of us moved for two or three minutes. We couldn't. He was a dead weight on me and I was too weak from the passion to tell him, powerless to think. At last Luke rolled his body off of mine and lay beside me, his eyes closed, his muscles relaxed, his chest rising slowly and falling just as slowly.

I was glad he didn't want to talk. I was too drained for conversation.

He was almost asleep. A faint wind shook the tree branches over us, dappling the ground with sunlight. I looked up at the dots of blue sky showing behind the quivering green leaves. My ragged breathing had become normal, the tempo easing, but my mind was awhirl with memories.

Maybe lying on the sand had something to do with the thoughts racing through my head. It wasn't Luke Nance I was daydreaming about, but Bates. Bates with his tawny hair and enchanting smile. I remembered the first time Bates made love to me when we lay beside the dinghy on the sand of the Carolina coast . . . his gentleness that night . . . the sweet-salt taste of his mouth on mine . . . the way his eyes glowed in the starlit darkness and how safe I felt in his arms afterward. . . . My body had been taken before, taken ruthlessly, but until that night I'd never known a man's love, never realized that fires could blaze in me.

Oh, Bates, I thought desperately and squeezed my eyelids shut, willing myself not to cry. I dared not allow myself the luxury of continuing to think about him when I lay naked beside another man. Because the memories of my husband caused such agonizing pain in my heart, I went into the water once more as if washing the sand off my back would make me forget.

It was a pleasantly lazy afternoon and we lingered at the cove a long time, Luke coming into the water with me after he waked from his nap. I washed my hair and let it dry in the breeze and the sun, not pinning it up but permitting it to fall loosely below my shoulders. Luke loved to see it that way and he fingered the long black tresses.

"Know something, Marley?" he said. "You sure look

different since we came to the Bahamas. In those garments and with your hair down and your skin growing browner by the day, I swear you could almost pass for one of the natives."

"A half-breed?" I came back and smiled. "Didn't you tell me once that they're supposed to be fantastic in bed? Are you paying me a compliment now—or complaining?"

"I sure as hell can't make any complaints," he grinned. "You're not bad in bed. Or on the ground, either."

"Not bad? Don't say it in such a negative way, Luke Nance." I was teasing, pretending to fuss with him although my voice was laced with merriment. "I don't want to be 'not bad.' That sounds as dull as eating cold pease porridge without any salt."

He gave me a quick hard kiss. "All right, forget the 'not bad,' you saucy minx. What about 'pretty damn good'? Does that suit your ladyship's fancy? You're pretty damn easy on the eyes and pretty damn good in bed or out of it, day and night, in sunshine and rain—hey, what have I forgotten?"

"You're forgetting supper," I said and laughed. "If you don't stop paying me compliments and we don't get back to the *Roxanne,* you're going to find yourself hungry for something other than me. I'm talking about food."

He agreed and took my hand, leading me away from the pool. When we came out of the woods the sun was a fiery circle half over the western horizon, its rays flecking the sea with scarlet. Ahead of us down the beach the ships tied to the dock were silhouetted against the sunset sky, the row of vessels appearing black in contrast to the shimmering colors behind them.

The glare was blinding. Nonetheless I stared at the ships. "Luke, I believe that three-masted sloop coming in as we were starting for the cove has anchored right next to the *Roxanne*," I commented. "She—"

He made an odd strangled sound. It wasn't actually a word and yet there was an ominous tinge to it. I turned to look at him, my eyes widening in horror. His skin was ashy under his tan, his forehead a mass of frown lines; huge drops of perspiration stood out on his upper lip and his temples.

"Luke, what's the matter?" I was hoarse with apprehension.

"Nothing," he growled.

"But—"

"I said nothing's the matter, Marley!" he interrupted me. "Come on. Let's get aboard the *Roxanne*."

He began to walk at such a fast pace that I had to run to keep up with him. Racking my brain to know what I'd said or done to put him in such an angry mood when he'd been laughing moments before, I couldn't think of anything.

"Luke, wait—" I panted.

He didn't wait.

"Luke, are you ill?"

"No, I am not ill!"

He continued his long strides but I slowed to a walk, letting my breathing return to normal. We were nearing the ships and I gazed at the new one, able to read her name for the first time. My heart jumped into my throat. The word painted on the prow of the sloop was *Marley*.

At first I couldn't take it in. That one word hypnotized me. My eyes were glued to it.

"Luke, do you see that?" I called out to him. "I've never met another person with my name, much less seen a ship with it! I wonder—"

My voice died. Luke paid no attention to me. He

continued to take long steps in front of me with his shoulders hunched forward, his head held at an odd angle as if his neck was stiff.

And then I knew!

It had to be! I realized Luke must have known the entire time and I dashed past him, running so fast my sides ached and my feet kicked up a fine spray of sand. My hat blew off my head, but I didn't stop to pick it up. Somehow I must have dropped the basket which held Luke's and my towels, because it was gone from my arm. I was aware of both my hands being fists as I sped past the *Roxanne* to the *Marley* and started up her gangplank.

A swarthy, muscular sailor stopped me halfway to the deck. He planted his feet wide apart to block my path.

"Wench, what's your business here?" he asked. "You can't come aboard. No wenches are allowed on the *Marley* but—" his voice became low and provocative, "I'll meet you on land tonight and—"

"Your captain!" The words burst out between my ragged gasps. "Where is your captain?"

"He can't make you as happy as I can. You—"

"Take me to your captain!"

At the sound of my voice which was almost a scream, a tall man emerged from the deckhouse, the setting sun turning his light hair into tawny gold. He looked older than when I last saw him, leaner, but his eyes were as gray as I remembered them and now they were filled with disbelief just as mine must have been. We stared at each other, my breasts rising under the cotton blouse as I gulped a deep breath of air which seared my lungs. I could not stop gazing at him. The pulses in his brow quickened. His mouth opened, then closed and opened again, the tip of his tongue moistening his lips.

"Marley," he managed in a strained voice.

I think I uttered his name. My heart was pounding so hard against my ribs I thought it would explode from my body and inside I was saying, "Bates! Bates!" but there was no way of knowing whether I spoke aloud. He came across the deck and started down the gangplank, brushing aside the sailor blocking my way. With a hoarse cry I stumbled forward and felt my husband's arms go around me.

Chapter 35

FOR A LONG minute Bates and I held each other, not talking or kissing, just clinging together with his arms circling me and my hands clasped behind his neck, our bodies molded against each other. I could not think or speak. I only knew I was soaring in the heavens, unaware of anything or anybody except the nearness of him and the familiar, wonderful strength of his arms.

It was Luke who broke the spell.

"Marley!" Luke's voice rang out from the pier between the two ships, his tone so rough it jarred me.

Spinning out of Bates' embrace, I came back to reality. Luke glowered up from the end of the *Marley's* gangplank, his mouth set in a grim line, his eyes flashing fire. Beside me, Bates had a puzzled expression on his face. The sailors of both ships watched and listened with open curiosity.

Under the seamen's ogling stares I was conscious of my low-cut blouse and the native calico skirt, of my hair hanging loosely about my shoulders and my bare feet. Earlier it had seemed a joke when I asked Luke if he thought I looked like a half-breed. Now I knew the

Marley's men must have assumed I was an island whore coming to every ship that anchored to try to sell my body to the highest officers. God alone knew what the *Roxanne*'s crew was thinking. They considered me Luke's wife, taking for granted we were married, and now they'd seen me in another man's arms.

It didn't concern me. Nothing mattered at the moment except knowing Bates and I were together at last.

"Marley, I'm waiting!" Luke called in the same bristling tone. "Come here at once!"

"What does Nance mean, Marley?" Bates' eyes were on me as he jerked his head toward Luke. "Are you with him?"

"C-Can we t-talk in—in p-private?" I stammered shakily.

"Yes. Come to my quarters."

"Marley! This instant! I'm waiting for you!" Luke boomed at me.

I turned toward him without taking a step, the lump in my throat so large it choked me. When I didn't speak because I couldn't, Luke put one foot on the bottom of the *Marley*'s gangplank and focused his scorching gaze on Bates.

"Request permission to come aboard," Luke muttered in the same forbidding voice.

"Do you want him here, Marley?" Bates asked.

"I—I—N-Not yet."

"Permission denied," Bates came back at Luke. "This way, Marley," he said to me, putting one hand under my elbow to guide me.

"Marley, you come here this minute!" Luke's voice crackled again.

I froze in my tracks, unable to move. Blood thundered in my ears and I looked first at my husband, then at the man waiting for me on the pier. "Luke, I—I have to talk to Bates," I managed and allowed myself to be led to the deck house.

For all the note I took of the surroundings on the ship we could have been in a dark attic. We went down a passageway and into a cabin, but I paid no attention to the furnishings. Bates closed the door and drew me into his arms, holding me so tightly I could feel his heart beating. Lowering his mouth to mine, he bruised my lips with his and I lost my senses in that kiss. My head spun and my knees trembled. I might have fallen if he had not held me with arms like iron bands, and yet his embrace was tender.

Finally we pulled apart just a little, still holding one another. Tears blurred my vision, but they were happy tears and I knew I must be smiling.

"Don't cry, Marley," he whispered. "Please don't cry."

"I'm not . . ."

Bates took both my hands in his, leading me across the cabin to a bench and sitting beside me, our thighs touching. "Are you with Nance?" he asked.

It seemed impossible for me to answer a question about Luke without stuttering. "I—He—Luke brought me here," I mumbled.

"Why didn't you wait for me in Bath Town, Marley?"

"I did wait!"

"But I went back and you'd gone."

"I stayed there over a year after you left."

"I told you I'd be back for you. Didn't you believe me? I've been half out of my head with worrying about you ever since I discovered you'd vanished."

"Bates, I couldn't remain in Bath Town any longer. There were—were circumstances." Because I was distraught, I began to accuse him. "You never wrote or sent me a message. I didn't know if you were alive or dead or hurt or where you'd gone or what you were doing! The reason I sailed with Luke was to search for you! That's God's truth!"

His mouth twisted as he clenched his jaws, the gentle expression leaving his face. As I looked at him the smokiness in his gray eyes turned to granite.

"While you and Nance were engaged in this 'search' for me, what was between you and him, Marley? You lived with him—in his quarters on the ship? Were you—are you his mistress? Did you forget you were married to me? Or did you overlook that fact and marry him or was there some other relationship between you two? He bellowed at you with orders as if he damn well owns you body and soul."

Bates' sarcasm hurt. We'd been together less than an hour and we were quarreling, something we'd seldom done in the past. All those months during his absence I'd planned for our reunion to be a glorious time. Now the cabin seethed with anger. Instead of wearing a handsome gown, I was dressed like a slut. Luke's jealous actions were causing one crisis to mar Bates' and my meeting, and Bates was causing another one with his ugly insinuations.

He was right about my being Luke's mistress, of course. But he hadn't given me a chance to explain. He was eager to think terrible thoughts about me. I lifted my chin, loving him so much I thought my heart might shatter from the stormy emotions surging within me. At that moment I also hated him.

"I've slept with Luke," I admitted. "I had to do it to get free passage on the *Roxanne*. I didn't have any money to pay for the voyage. But I never forgot I was your wife."

His eyes bore into me, silently accusing eyes, the lids hooded. There was no way of telling if he believed what I'd just said and that was too much.

"What right do you have to act as though I've

committed a crime, Bates Hagen?" I burst out defiantly. "It's been almost two years since you left our house in Bath Town and I was faithful to you the entire time I stayed in Carolina, although I had chances to do otherwise. I daresay you haven't lived the life of a monk all these months! Haven't there been some women in your bed since then?"

Tiny dots of red color appeared high on his cheekbones. All of the sudden I was conscious of how hateful I must have sounded. The realization was chilling even in the warm cabin. I seemed to be taking a delight in making him miserable.

Love must be a stronger emotion than hate. The fury went out of me. I met his eyes, aching to make him understand. "Bates, I'm not blaming you for anything you did with women while we were apart," I said, "but I don't think you should blame me, either. What I can't fathom is why you didn't let me know where you were or what you were doing. I'd have stayed on in Bath Town the rest of my life no matter how awful it was without you if I'd just thought you really were coming back there for me."

"I did go back, Marley."

"When?"

"A short time ago. I stopped in Bath Town on my way here to the Bahamas and didn't find any trace of you. Amos showed me the note you put under his door and said not one soul in the community had heard from you since you disappeared."

He was correct. I'd done the very thing I lashed out at him about, keeping my location a secret.

"Please let's not fuss," I said. "It's been so long . . . and I love you so much."

His face softened. I could feel some of the tension leaving him. He was no longer rigid. Sliding one arm around my waist, he pulled me against his chest and tilted my face up, kissing me on the lips. The kiss was light at first, becoming deeply passionate with his tongue plunging into my mouth and I melted against him, forgetting my anger, forgetting everything except the sheer joy of being with him.

"Marley, I reckon I don't have much cause to chastize you for whatever happened after I left Bath Town," he said when he could speak. "That night I told you good-bye—I've never done anything so painful. I knew I'd hurt you and that didn't help."

"Did you go to Massachusetts?"

"Yes. I went to see Seneca Irving and he couldn't put me into debtors' prison fast enough."

"Oh, Bates—"

"I let him know I had every intention of paying him for the *Solace* but had to work to raise the money. The old buzzard refused to listen. He already knew about the *Solace*'s fate. McGregor had told him."

"McGregor—Ugh!" I shuddered.

"Well, you don't have to worry about him. He's dead, killed in a knife fight in Charles Town last winter, I heard. God knows what lies he told Irving about me. One of them was that I was in league with Teach and gave up my ship willingly so I could share in the sale of the gunpowder." His lips thinned out, his face flinty at the memory. "That's over and done with now. I've managed to put it out of my mind most of the time. I'm just damn thankful someone else has already killed McGregor so I wouldn't be tempted to do away with him myself if our paths ever crossed again."

"How long were you in prison?"

"Four months and I'd be in that black hellhole of a jail today if some friends hadn't helped me escape. They got me out in the middle of the night and put me on a brigantine bound for England. Believe me, Marley, there wasn't a second for me to get a message to you. The brig was ready to sail when I boarded her. Besides, I couldn't have run up and down the dock searching for a ship heading for Carolina. Irving would have had me arrested again and put back in jail if he'd known my whereabouts."

I shivered, realizing I wasn't the only person who'd suffered. At least I'd been free.

"Once I was on the other side of the Atlantic my luck changed," Bates went on. "I sought out my oldest brother. We hadn't seen each other in years and I don't mind admitting I'd prepared myself for an icy greeting from him, but it wasn't that way."

"What about your parents? Did you see them?"

"Both of them have passed on, which makes my brother head of the family. Being the oldest he inherited all my father's property and he told me he was one of a group of men with money who had formed a company to outfit a ship. They had the vessel but needed a captain. After I met with them, the group asked if I'd take over the command. You can jolly well bet I jumped at the chance."

Pausing, he picked up my hand and brushed his lips across my fingers. "Marley, isn't the fact that I named the ship after you proof that I've never forgotten you? That I never meant to abandon you?"

A tremendous weight seemed to lift off of me at the realization of what he was saying.

"Yes, I'm convinced," I murmured. For some unknown reason I couldn't keep from adding, "But surely while you were in England you knew of some ship coming to Bath Town. If you'd only sent me a letter . . ."

"I inquired. That's a fact, but ships don't aim for Bath Town as a port. They go into that harbor when they're in the area and need supplies or want a hidden spot to repair the ship or scrape barnacles. I've been to a lot of places since leaving Europe. All the way to South America and—"

"And Charles Town!" I interrupted him.

"Yes, a storm blew us off course and damaged the ship so I was forced to put in there for repairs. How did you know?"

"Luke saw you there. Not on land, but you were sailing into the harbor when he was going out!"

A memory flowed to the surface of my mind—Luke's strange behavior the day I told him my first name soon after I boarded the *Roxanne*. He'd stopped talking abruptly, his face knotting into an immediate frown. My name had struck something familiar in his thoughts and at the moment I'd been unable to imagine what it was. But now I knew! He truly had recognized Bates aboard a ship near Charles Town after a storm and he must have read the word *Marley* painted on the hull of Bates' ship, although he denied recalling the name. Luke could guess I wasn't lying when I said Bates was my husband, only he'd never admitted that to me.

"Marley," Bates' voice brought me back from my recollections, "what happened to force you to leave Bath Town?"

I told him all of it. About how lonely I'd been after he went away and how I tried to run the school as best I could. About my rejecting townsmen who came to court me under the assumption that I was a widow, especially about my rebuking Calvin Martin and that it turned the Martin family against me. About Blackbeard building a home at Plum Point so he could move to land. About my final bitter conversation with Amos.

"There was one more reason, the reason I left when I did," I barely spoke above a whisper. "Josh Harding."

"What about Josh?"

"I—I thought he was a friend but—but he forced his way into the house and raped me."

Bates' face turned chalky. "Good God!" he gasped. "Josh—I'd never have thought he'd stoop that low. At least, not to attack you. Were you hurt badly?"

"I was hurt some. He was half drunk at the time and he swore he'd come back to have me again and I knew he would." Cringing as I relived that terrible night, I sucked my breath in. "The *Roxanne* was docked in Bath Town and leaving the next day. I'd already spoken to Luke, inquiring about you. I asked the same questions of all the captains who brought their ships there. After what Josh did to me, sailing on the *Roxanne* to search for you seemed to be the wisest action."

My voice began to quiver and I bit down hard on my lower lip to steady myself. "Bates, I never forgot you and I were married. Luke knew it from the start because I told him before I boarded his ship. He's been good to me and since then he's asked me to marry him many times, but I wouldn't. Even though I've slept with him, I always knew I was your wife."

Leaning toward me, he cupped his hands around my face, his fingers warm to my cheeks, his eyes looking deeply into mine.

"I want us to be together like we used to be," he said softly.

"Yes . . . oh, yes . . ."

I melted against him, savoring his kisses, my breasts tingling. His mouth touched my forehead, my hair, sliding to my lips and then my throat, his tongue caressing the little hollow between my breasts before he returned his mouth to my lips again.

"At first I didn't recognize you in that outfit," he smiled. "But when I heard your voice I knew it had to be you."

"Luke bought me these clothes after we reached the islands because my other garments were so warm."

Luke. His name rolled off my tongue. I half expected Bates to mention that, but he didn't. I would have to see Luke, to thank him and say good-bye. It would be an ordeal. Thinking about it filled me with dread, but I had no choice.

"Marley," Bates' voice took me away from thoughts of Luke Nance, "naming my ship for you isn't the only proof that I love you and was coming back for you. I've acquired some—uh—things and put them aside to give you. That chest on your left—" he gestured toward a large wooden box placed against the far wall, "has an 'M' made out of brass nailheads on its top and the initial means everything in it is yours."

Going to his desk, he removed an iron key from one of the drawers, crossing the cabin to the chest. The hinges gave a soft creak as he lifted the lid and he motioned for me to come to his side and inspect the contents. The room was dim, the last rosy rays of the sunset long gone. The shadows were misty, but enough twilight remained for me to see Bates' features when I stood next to him. My gaze followed his and I gasped at what I saw, swallowing hard.

The mass of glowing jewels was so dazzling I was speechless. Diamonds twinkled. The rubies and emeralds gleamed with rich brilliance. A long rope of pearls, each one perfectly matched with the others, was entangled with a gold chain from which dangled a sapphire pendant in the shape of a cross. Below the surface layer, other jewels were just as sparkly. Bates, smiling a broad smile, pulled some of the bracelets and necklaces aside to reveal silver plate. When I gasped once more, he moved the silver to expose gold bars on the bottom of the chest, the burnished metal glistening.

"It's yours, Marley," he said in a triumphant tone. "All of it, and there'll be more for you in the future."

"It's gorgeous, but—" I tore my eyes from the gleaming jewels to look at him. "I don't understand. Why is it mine?"

"Because I'm giving these articles to you."

That wasn't a sufficient explanation. I wanted to know more. "But where did you get these things?" I persisted. "They must have cost a fortune."

"I came by them legally. I know how much you've always longed for money and pretty clothes. Now you can buy whatever you fancy. Anyone as beautiful as you are deserves jewels. You—"

"Bates, answer my questions!" I stormed out. "Eighteen months ago you didn't have a pound to your name! You had to go to debtors' prison! Did your brother in England give you these riches? I can understand how you got this ship, but the items in that chest are another matter! How could you acquire diamonds and gold and silver unless—unless—"

My voice broke. The sentence hung there between us, the unspoken words scalding my tongue. I couldn't bring myself to add *unless you stole them,* but I was thinking that and maybe Bates read my mind.

"All right, it's sea plunder," he said coldly. "But taking it was legal and I have written proof. I have a Letter of Marque from the Crown giving me the power to take whatever booty I come across at sea, take it in the name of the company which owns this vessel. I get a share of the booty, too. Each time I've chosen some of the handsomest items to go into that chest for you."

The thunder in my ears was the crushing din of my own heartbeats. All of a sudden my mouth was so dry my tongue felt gritty. I continued to stare at my husband as if he was a stranger.

"That's piracy!" I rasped hoarsely. "You—of all men! How could you turn into a pirate, Bates? I'd never have believed this if I hadn't heard you admit it with my own ears and if I hadn't seen what you've stolen."

"Listen to me!" His voice was as ragged as mine. "I just told you about the Letter of Marque. I'm a privateer—not a pirate—and privateering is legal with the Crown's permission. The Letter of Marque gives me the right to seize goods."

"It's piracy by another term. You stole every item in that chest and stealing is a sin. Have you forgotten how you felt when Blackbeard stole the *Solace* and all your belongings? Have you? No matter what pretty term you want to call it, stealing is what pirates do—stealing and killing! Do you drop your victims into the sea after you rob them or cut off their ears and noses like Teach does or turn the women over to your crew so they can—"

He grabbed my shoulders, shaking me. "Hush and listen, Marley! I don't do any of those unspeakable deeds and you should know it! I told you I'm a privateer, not a pirate!"

I jerked away from him, sobbing, tears streaming from my eyes. "And all this time I've loved you and wanted you so much," I moaned. "Not a single day has passed that I haven't wished I was with you. But you've changed. Now you're not the man I fell in love with on the *Solace*. Or the man I married in the moonlight because I adored him. Or the one I lived with in Bath Town. I just don't know who you are now. How could you do this, Bates? How could you change so much? How could you?"

With a wrenching cry I ran across the cabin and out into the dark corridor, not waiting for whatever answer he might have made. Somebody must have lit a lantern for there was a faint light at the end of the passageway. I stumbled toward it, hearing Bates call my name, hearing his frenzied footsteps, his boots clattering on the floorboards.

I didn't stop, but he did. I reached the deck and when I went down the gangplank, there were no longer any footsteps trailing me.

Night had fallen. The sky was blue-black and the breeze had died. The air was so damp and heavy with the scent of decaying flower blossoms that it was sickeningly sweet. I clutched at the rope handrail on the *Marley*'s gangplank to keep from falling, then crossed the rough, splintery pier without turning my head to look behind and see if Bates was watching me or if he was following me once more.

Sobs choked me, rising into my throat, stinging my mouth. There were people nearby in the darkness. I could sense their presence, but my eyes were too full of tears to see anyone. At last I reached the *Roxanne*, feeling my way along to the deck.

"Miss, are you all right?" Garlow's voice came out of the blackness.

"I—I—" I couldn't speak coherently. My knees buckled and I clawed at the air for support.

"Here, Miss. I'll help you," he said and clamped an iron fist around my arm. "Captain Nance is in his quarters and he's half out of his mind worrying."

Everything aboard the *Roxanne* was so familiar I could have found my way blindfolded under other circumstances, but that night I'd never have made it to the cabin without Garlow. He guided me to the door and vanished without making a sound.

I felt for the knob and turned it silently. A lantern hung on the wall peg, its light a pale yellow circle. Luke sat at his desk, his two elbows propped on the open logbook and his face buried in his hands. He didn't see me at first. I tried to speak and I couldn't. I stood there numbly until finally he raised his eyes to give me a long, searching look.

"You came back," he mumbled. "Thank God for that."

Neither of us moved. I clung desperately to the door as if I needed it to keep myself upright. Luke looked as if he'd been ill, his skin gray and his lips colorless. At last he pushed his chair from the desk and got to his feet.

"Why, Marley? Why did you come back here?" he demanded gruffly. "When I saw you with Hagen I wanted to take a knife and carve his heart out on the spot. You've never gazed at me the way you were looking at him, all soft and dewy-eyed and wanting. I'd thought that occasionally I'd seen tenderness in your eyes for me, but not the way you were with him. Now you're back on my ship as pale as a ghost. Did you return to taunt me?"

I shook my head, still unable to speak.

"Marley, for God's sake, answer me! Are you here because I mean something to you in spite of him? What happened to bring you back here?"

"H-He's a p-p-pirate." My voice was a stark whisper.

Luke burst into hard, ugly laughter. There was no mirth in it, just a grating, humorless noise.

"A pirate?" he repeated when the guffaws stopped enough for him to speak. "That's a shocker. And all the time you thought Hagen was a saint, didn't you? He—"

Noise from the deck made Luke pause. Scuffling sounds and angry voices echoed down the passageway. Luke dashed to the door, flinging it open to be met by Bates with a pistol in his hand and Garlow pulling at him.

"I'll handle this, Garlow!" Luke barked.

"Captain, he didn't ask if he could come aboard!" Garlow seemed frantic. "He just stalked up the plank when my back was turned and he'd already made his path to the deckhouse before I saw him! I—"

"I said I'll handle it, Garlow!"

The faint amber light from the wall lantern illuminated the men's faces. I could feel the fury enveloping them. Bates still held the pistol, but it was pointed down at the floor instead of at Luke or at me. Luke faced him, hands on hips, his legs spread.

"This is my ship, Hagen." Luke's voice was deadly cold. "I suggest you get off at once."

"I came here to see Marley—not you."

"Damn it, Hagen! I told you to leave or I'll have you put off!"

Ignoring Luke, Bates turned to me. "Marley, I'd like to talk to you without an audience. If he won't leave us so we can be alone, will you come with me to my ship?"

"You had your chance to talk to her, Hagen," Luke said curtly. "I doubt if she wants to listen to whatever you have to tell. She doesn't hold with piracy."

Luke couldn't speak for me. I found my voice. "What else is there to say, Bates? I—I—" I couldn't go on. The unfinished sentence hung in midair.

The silence between the three of us was eerie. I felt as if I was drowning, my lungs about to burst, my body being pulled down to the bottom of the sea.

"All right, I'll speak my piece in front of him if I have to," Bates muttered. "Marley, if my Letter of Marque upsets you so much and that's what's keeping you and me apart, I'll surrender it and return to hauling cargo. I'll sail for London tomorrow to do it. I won't earn as much money and I may not even be able to keep command of my ship because the company outfitted her for the purpose of privateering. But it'll be worth whatever it costs if my action will bring you back to me."

"Can you put any faith in a pirate's promise,

Marley?". Luke sneered. "I sure as hell can't. Pirates talk out of both sides of their mouths, uttering whatever words they think will please their audiences. They—"

Bates raised the pistol, fury etched in his face.

"Put that gun down!" I gasped. "Please! Please!"

Bates did not move a muscle. His eyes were glued to Luke's face, his forefinger curved around the trigger. Springing forward, Luke pushed past me and went to his desk, opening a drawer and taking out his shoulder sling which held four pistols.

That was when I screamed with terror, a thin wail which came from the pit of my stomach and poured through my body into my throat. It was low, stark, horror-filled, a cry which frightened me with its piercing intensity. It must have amazed the two men just as much. Luke's black eyes were on me, his eyebrows lifted and I could feel Bates' burning stare.

"Stop it! Stop it right now! Both of you!" I stormed at them. "If it's me you're fighting over, I don't want either of you when you're like this!"

I whirled around, putting my back toward them, my fingers pressed to my trembling lips, my stomach lurching. The cabin was as still as Death. There was not even the sound of waves lapping at the ship.

Slowly, deliberately, I made myself turn again, not wanting to do it but knowing I must.

"Please put the guns away," I said desperately.

I was pleading. Bates moved first, lowering his pistol, the metal of the gun glimmering briefly as his hand passed through the lantern glow. He stuck the weapon into the top of his belt.

Luke removed the sling from his shoulder, extracted one pistol which he laid on the corner of the desk, and put the sling with its other three weapons into the drawer. My pulses slowed ever so slightly as a wave of relief washed over me. For the first time since the nightmare scene began, I drew an almost normal breath.

"Marley, you're going to have a make a choice," Luke said in a grim tone, addressing me while he kept his eyes focused on Bates as though he didn't trust the other man.

I managed to nod without speaking.

"I love you and want you," Luke went on. "You're bound to know it because I've told you often enough. I've wanted you since our first conversation in the publick house in Bath Town. We've had a good life together. It can be even better in the future, but I'm not going to share you with any man, least of all with *him*." He jerked his head at Bates, his mouth twisting in a sardonic way. "I can promise you one thing for sure, though. What I provide for you is honestly come by. It's not stolen."

"Marley, please . . ." Bates begged. "I'll do anything to make you happy. Anything! I swear it."

I swayed, my head spinning. Deep in my heart I knew what my choice had to be. I liked Luke and respected him and maybe I even loved him after a fashion, but I wasn't in love with him the way I felt about Bates. It was Bates Hagen I wanted forever. Bates was the man I cherished.

Tears came into my eyes and I blinked, but they didn't vanish completely. "Luke, I—I'm sorry," I murmured.

His body stiffened and a strangled sound came from his throat. "You can't mean you're going to Hagen, Marley?"

"I love Bates. I love you, too, but not in the same—"

Luke picked up the loaded pistol from the corner of his desk. The words I'd been about to utter froze on my lips. Panic engulfed me, panic which dwarfed any emotion I'd ever felt. I couldn't watch him kill my husband before my very eyes! With a flying leap I got to Luke and grabbed his hand holding the gun and a shot roared through the cabin.

The force of the explosion knocked me down. The noise was deafening, the sound going on and on, echoing until I thought my eardrums would burst. The ship rocked and I felt nausea rise into my mouth.

"Marley!"

I heard my name but didn't know which man had spoken it. One of them might be dead. Oh, God—I tried to make my eyes focus, afraid to find out if either of them had been hit or even if I was wounded because there was an aching pain in me. My legs were crumpled under my body and my head throbbed.

The mist in my vision cleared gradually. Bates was on his knees beside me and Luke was on the opposite side of the cabin, his back propped against the wall and the pistol still in his hand, the color drained from his face. The putrid odor of gunpowder was everywhere.

"She's not hurt," Bates gasped in a strangely remote voice.

"The shot went through the ceiling," Luke answered. He glared at me, his mouth twitching. "Marley, you ought not to have come at me like that! You made me fire the weapon when you hit my hand! What were you trying to do? You might have been killed!"

Or Bates could have been killed, I thought without saying it aloud. Or the shot could have struck Luke. I didn't want him maimed any more than I wanted Bates harmed.

Bates helped me to my feet. Trembling, I leaned against him, shrinking from the smoking pistol. I raised my tear-marked face to Luke.

"I—I'm sorry," I told him, my voice breaking. "I

have to go with my husband, but I didn't want it to end this way between you and me, Luke. No man could have been kinder or more thoughtful of a woman than you've been, but—but—"

I couldn't say more. The agony in his eyes cut into me like a knife, but I was hurt, too. All the good memories of my days with Luke, the happy times we shared in Philadelphia, aboard the *Roxanne,* the long, lazy hours in the islands, the warm loving and the laughter and the tenderness—every speck of it had been wiped out by that pistol shot.

The *Roxanne*'s crew was clustered in the passageway. They'd heard the shot, of course, and now they were listening.

"The weapon was discharged accidentally," Luke announced to them. "No major damage resulted and the hole in the ceiling will be repaired tomorrow. All of you return to your watches or your quarters."

They trooped out, silent at first, but the mutter of their voices reached us when they were away from the cabin. I shuddered to think what the crew would have done if Luke had been injured. Bates would be no match for them if they ganged up on him.

I suppose Luke realized there was no point in his pleading with me to change my mind. "I'll send your belongings to the *Marley,*" he said in the same toneless voice he'd used in speaking to the sailors.

"I can't take those things, Luke. They cost you too much. You paid for them so they're yours."

"What use would I have for your clothes unless I wanted to break my heart every time I—" He broke the sentence off, clamping his mouth shut, his features settling into a mask.

I ached for him, knowing how he was suffering, remembering my desperation the night Bates left me to go aboard the *Sweet Glory.* Only then I'd had hope that my husband would come home eventually. Now Luke knew I was gone from his life forever. I didn't doubt the depth of his love for me. It had showed in a hundred different ways every single day and night I was with him. But I couldn't change my heart any more than I could will myself to alter the color of my eyes.

"Ready, Marley?" Bates asked.

I nodded. With my hand in my husband's, I left the *Roxanne* for the final time. Luke did not speak as we moved past him. Bates guided me along the dim passageway to the deck. A light was suspended from a pole near the gangplank, its flame very small in the blackness. Some of the crew stood by the rail. I wanted to say good-bye to Garlow and a few others I'd come to know well, but I dared not trust myself to speak.

Bates kept his head erect, glancing neither to the left nor the right. Still clutching him tightly, we went down the plank and across the pier to the *Marley*. Some of the crew were waiting. My eyes were gradually becoming adjusted to the dark, but the sailors' features were hidden by the night. I was grateful for it. If I couldn't see them clearly, maybe they couldn't see me, couldn't stare at the myriad of emotions I must be showing in my face.

They cheered as we approached. A merry voice yelled, "So you got her for yourself, did you, Captain Hagen? Good for you!" Quick as a flash another voice called, "How many scars did you put on Nance, Captain?"

A low moan came from me as the men laughed. The sound was a reflex, out before I knew I'd uttered it. Bates tensed and I was conscious of his sudden intake of breath. He stopped walking so abruptly I'd have fallen if I hadn't had such a tight grip on him. He glared at his crew.

"Anything that happened on this ship tonight is my

personal business and of no concern to you," he said in a fierce tone. "Any man aboard who ever refers to the events of tonight here or on the *Roxanne* will be flogged until his backbone shows through his bloody flesh and then he'll be put off the ship whether we're in port or at sea. The subject is closed. Closed permanently. Do you understand?"

A chorus of ayes came from the shadows. I shivered despite the balmy tropical air. "Are you all right, Marley?" Bates asked softly and I nodded.

He took a lantern from one of the men, the same burly fellow who'd blocked me when I tried to board the ship in the late afternoon. All of that seemed a lifetime ago instead of merely a few hours. We started down the passageway, the shallow arc of light from the lantern marking a path for us through the darkness. It was an omen, I thought silently. An omen for the future. God willing, our dark times were ending.

Bates and I were scarcely in the cabin when he said, "We'll sail for London tomorrow, Marley. Originally I'd planned to stay in these waters a week or more and then go to England to turn over the company's share of plunder, but as soon as we take on fresh water and some food supplies, we'll be at sea before this time tomorrow. The crew will do some jawing about being denied a frolic on land in the islands, but I'll give them a bonus to make up for it." Glancing sideways at me, he added, "Leaving immediately will be best. I don't suppose you want to linger here and have to face Nance again."

There was a veiled question in his final sentence and I ignored it. "I hope you'll give the men who own this ship everything in that chest with the nailhead 'M' on it," I said.

"You've changed, Marley. You used to say, 'If I just had money. . . .' When we lived in Bath Town I felt I hadn't provided any security for you. We lived in a borrowed house and even slept in a borrowed bed. We had to accept whatever the townspeople chose to give us rather than being paid for our teaching services with a set sum."

"All of that is in the past now."

"I was right proud of myself for being able to pay off the price of the *Solace* in so short a time so I don't have to worry about being arrested if I put into a Massachusetts port."

"Will you detest hauling cargo?" I asked, afraid to hear his reply but knowing the question should be voiced.

"No, of course I won't detest it. I've done that before and done it successfully, but I can't store up much money doing it." He looked past me at the open porthole, although I had the feeling he wasn't actually seeing anything. "Having those valuables to hand to you gave me real pleasure, Marley."

"I can't accept those jewels! Not when I know how you got them! I simply can't!"

"Well, if it's what you want me to do, I'll surrender them along with my Letter of Marque. Eventually you might wish you had kept the gold. It would serve as security and we don't know what the future holds."

"Being with you is my security, Bates. Being in your arms makes me richer than possessing all the gems in that ch—"

A loud knock on the cabin door interrupted me and a voice from the passageway yelled, "Captain Hagen, the *Roxanne*'s first mate is on the pier with some baggage he claims belongs to the lady. He says the *Roxanne* will hoist anchor within the hour and he wants permission to fetch the stuff aboard the *Marley*."

Bates looked toward me and I mouthed the words, "All right," not speaking them aloud. How could I ever put on the blue velvet cloak trimmed with gray fur or wear the heather-colored cape without thinking of Luke? Would I be able to read the books he'd purchased for me or sew with the thimble carved from a whale's tooth? I choked down a burning breath. That time with Luke was as much a part of my past as my life in New Bedford had been or the months in Bath Town. I'd have to will myself to live with the memories.

Luke was sailing, also. Apparently he didn't relish seeing me again any more than I could put myself through the awkwardness of facing him.

"Aye, let the mate come aboard, Cooper," Bates told the seaman. "Keep the luggage on deck tonight and put a guard by it. You can bring it to the cabin in the morning."

The room was very still. The ship rolled gently in the long swells and the lantern flame flickered. Bates was watching me, his eyes veiled, misty.

"I suppose Luke couldn't wait to be rid of everything of mine, everything reminding him of me on the *Roxanne*," I sighed, speaking as much to myself as to my husband. "I'm so sorry about all of it, sorry for the heartache and the way things happened tonight. I thought Luke realized I'd come to you if I ever found you—I told him over and over—and I wanted him to understand. I didn't want to hurt him. I'd never deliberately cause him pain, but . . . but . . ."

The sentence died. Tears clung to my lashes and my lower lip was on the verge of trembling. *But somebody had to be hurt,* I thought. I just hadn't realized how deeply the agony would cut.

Bates came to me and cupped his hands about my face. "Nance is a good man. I might not hate his guts if I wasn't damn jealous of his having had you, Marley."

"You don't need to be jealous. You have me now—now and forever." I slid my arms to the back of his neck and pressed my body against his, feeling the warmth of his breath on my cheeks. "Luke only had part of me, Bates, but you possess all of me. I've come home now."

"Home? Why, you've never seen this ship before today! How can it seem like home to you?"

I laughed, exploding with joy, drawing his mouth to mine and kissing him hungrily. "Home for me is in your arms, my darling," I whispered. "Didn't you know?"

After that there was no need for words.